Praise for WATER OF DEATH

'An acclaimed crime series . . . Johnston brings an intelligent perspective to the dark excitement of the thriller'

Nicholas Blincoe, *Observer*

'Both prescient and illuminating'

Ian Rankin, *Daily Telegraph*

'Johnston's vision is shot through with the bleakest of black humour, never losing sight of the humanity of his characters. This series is getting better all the time'

Val McDermid, *Manchester Evening News*

'A thoroughly enjoyable tale'

Sunday Telegraph

'Trendily dystopian'

The Herald

'Not only a cracking thriller (with a hugely shocking climax), but a timely one. Johnston's vision of the future is highly entertaining'

Ham & High

'Sardonic wit, brilliant concept and a strong plot'

Birmingham Post

Praise for BODY POLITIC

'A hugely entertaining fantasy . . . engagingly imagined'
The Times

'Think of Plato's Republic with a body count'
The Sunday Times

'An intricate web . . . Johnston is a Fawkes among plotters . . . Quint's career looks set to blossom'
Observer

'Fascinating and thought-provoking'
Val McDermid, *Manchester Evening News*

'A thrilling hunt-the-psycho novel with countless twists . . . accomplished . . . offers real proof of the vigour and class of current Scottish crimewriting'
Ian Rankin, *Scotland on Sunday*

'Imaginative . . . remarkable . . . shows that crime fiction can be not only thrilling but intellectually exciting as well'
The Economist

About the author

Paul Johnston was born in 1957 in Edinburgh, where he grew up. He now divides his time between the UK and a small Greek island. He is the author of three previous novels, *Body Politic*, winner of the CWA John Creasey Memorial Dagger for best first crime novel, *The Bone Yard* and *Water of Death*. He is currently working on *The House of Dust*, his fifth crime novel featuring Quintilian Dalrymple.

The Blood Tree

Paul Johnston

NEW ENGLISH LIBRARY
Hodder & Stoughton

First published in Great Britain in 2000
by Hodder and Stoughton
First published in paperback in 2000
by Hodder and Stoughton
A division of Hodder Headline

A NEL Paperback

10 9 8 7 6 5 4 3 2 1

ISBN 0 340 71706 8

Typeset by Hewer Text Ltd, Edinburgh
Printed and bound in Great Britain by
Mackays of Chatham plc, Chatham, Kent

Hodder and Stoughton
A division of Hodder Headline
338 Euston Road
London NW1 3BH

THE BLOOD TREE

D ouble toil and double trouble in the independent city-state of Edinburgh.

Here, summer's been known as the Big Heat since global warming got into its stride. Temperatures in 2026 had been the highest yet. We were still undergoing trial by sunstroke in early October, when autumn crept in like an assassin one night and amputated most of the leaves from the city's trees. They fell to the pavements in their millions and were doused in a heavy dew. The infirmary quickly filled up with people who'd broken their legs. It definitely wasn't the best of times.

Our leaders in the Council of City Guardians tried to cope. Citizens were drafted into squads to clear the leaves and to distribute Supply Directorate provisions to the housebound. But, like everything else the guardians have been doing recently, those were only holding operations. The tourist income from the year-round festival has taken a major hit, so the Council doesn't have the resources to keep Edinburgh's problems at bay like it used to.

In the last few months it's become clear what the root of those problems is: the city's disaffected youth. In the early years of the Enlightenment, the Council had things easy. People were so sick of anarchy and crime that they

1

were prepared to accept the regime's tight grip. Not any more. These days, gangs of kids – some of them as young as seven – rampage through the suburbs; they've even been known to infiltrate the central tourist zone and terrorise the city's honoured guests. Most young people don't buy the Council's Platonic ideals and rigid regulations. They just want to be free.

I know how they feel – I've never been too keen on authority myself. But things are beginning to get beyond a joke. In late September some kids took on a City Guard unit and sent them back to barracks to think again. The Council, always quick to locate responsibility elsewhere, put the upsurge in civil disobedience down to the influence of democrats from Glasgow – there's been a big increase in breaches of the land and sea borders. The guardians may be right, but I'd be more inclined to blame the disciplinarian culture that they've instilled. Eventually people aren't going to take it any more.

That's not all the Council's been up against. The birthrate has dropped like a cannonball in the last couple of years. Ordinary citizens are justifiably concerned about bringing kids into a city that's no longer safe. Rumours started circulating that people were being bribed to reproduce. I wasn't convinced. I mean, in this city of rationing and restrictions, there's nothing much to bribe people with. What kind of offer are you going to make them? Get pregnant and get two eggs a week instead of one?

All of which was making me pretty jumpy as I stood on the castle walls and looked out over the darkening city. Soon it would be Hallowe'en, not that the Council allowed any celebration of the old feastday. A crow was perched in the branches of a tall tree in the gardens

2

below, its harsh cry suggesting it had eaten something seriously stomach-churning. Away to the west the clouds were massing and there was a crash of thunder that rose in volume as it headed our way. Then, as the sun died, a gash of red split the sky above the hills. The rain came down and I asked myself the big question – what if the Council lost its grip?

The answers I came up with made me feel worse than the carrion bird. There was an old bluesman called Willie Brown who used to sing about the "Future Blues". Recently I hadn't been able to get that lyric out of my mind.

CHAPTER ONE

"It's going to be a rough night, Quint."

"Some like it rough, Davie." I turned to the bulky figure by my side. He was pulling a waterproof cape over his grey City Guard uniform. My black donkey jacket was already sodden and my close-clipped hair wasn't exactly giving my head a lot of protection. I took a last look at the apocalyptic western sky. "Let's get off the ramparts."

"Good idea." He headed away, his heavy boots ringing on the flagstones. "What are you up to now?"

"Going to see my old man."

"Aw, come on, it's Tuesday. I thought we could down a few pints."

I normally visit my father on Sundays but I'd been tying up a grass-smuggling case last weekend. "Down a few pints? That's not how senior auxiliaries are meant to spend their evenings." Davie had been promoted to chief watch commander a couple of months back.

He glanced back at me, his bearded face set hard. "Up yours, pal. Senior auxiliaries can do what they like when they're off duty." He grinned. "And I'm off duty till tomorrow night. So how about that bevy?"

We walked out on to the esplanade and made a dash for the nearest guard vehicle.

"Fair enough," I said, pulling open the battered door of the pre-Enlightenment Land-Rover. "You drive me down to Trinity and we'll get them in afterwards."

Davie was nodding in resignation. "I might be a hot article in the guard, but as far as you're concerned I'm still your bloody chauffeur, eh, Quint?" He turned the key and listened to the grinding noise that came from the starter motor.

"So what are you waiting for, guardsman?" I said. "Drive."

He drove.

The rain squall had let off a bit by the time we turned down Ramsay Lane. A few bedraggled tourists were wandering around in the middle of the road, peering up at the castle through the murk. Davie made no effort to slow down and reduce the spray from the tyres.

"Stupid buggers," he grunted. "They should be in their hotel bars, buying the city's whisky."

"I thought auxiliaries were being told to make a special effort to impress the tourists." The big foreign companies have given up waiting for the Council to upgrade facilities. They say that other cities in what used to be Scotland, Glasgow in particular, have become more stable and more attractive to tourists.

Davie braked as we approached the smoke-blackened Gothic façade of the Assembly Hall – it was the home of the ill-fated Scottish Parliament around the millennium, as well as the original Council chamber. "Christ," he said, "the dead have risen."

I looked to the right and felt a frisson of shock. For a moment I thought a trio of skeletons had gathered at the building's entrance – the ghosts of political corruption past, perhaps. Then I realised they were workers in jackets with luminous lines across them that were glinting under the street-lights. Their faces were covered by protective masks, giving them snouts that made them look like pigs standing to attention.

"At least they're wearing all the right gear." Davie cut his speed right back and hung his head out the window. "Working overtime, lads?" he called.

"That's right," the nearest labourer said, raising his forearm to shield his eyes from our lights. His voice was muffled by the dust-mask. "Problem wi' the mains electric cable." He moved back towards a red pick-up with an open cargo space.

Davie nodded and drove on to the Mound.

"They're in luck, aren't they?" I said. In a classic piece of Council lunacy, the guardians introduced overtime payments for the evening and night shifts last spring in order to keep citizens happy – then banned all overtime a few weeks later to cut costs. Only emergency work is exempted from that ban.

"They'll just spend their extra vouchers on booze," Davie said.

"And you wouldn't, my friend?"

"Auxiliaries are different," he said piously. "We receive no payment whatsoever for our work."

"Apart from free barracks beer and whisky."

Davie flashed me a sour smile. "Which you, before you were demoted from auxiliary rank, never used to touch, of course. Anyway, we need something to look forward to at the end of a long day putting the boot into the city's lowlife. We've a lot more of that to do these days."

I nodded, watching the crowds as we cut across Princes Street. Some of the tourists were taking refuge

7

from the rain under the maroon and white striped awnings outside the cafés and shops, while others were queuing for the early shows at the sex clubs. The marijuana club on Hanover Street that the Tourism Directorate in its wisdom named The Grass Kilt was doing good business. Tourists are welcome to buy soft drugs in Enlightenment Edinburgh, but the locals aren't even allowed tobacco products – which makes for a thriving black market and plenty of smuggling.

There was a blinding flash of lightning and the statue ahead of us in the middle of George Street seemed to come to life. When I was a kid it had been a sleepy-looking prince, but he was torn down during the riots before the last election in 2003. The Council replaced it with a likeness of a female auxiliary with knees half-bent and arms raised in the officially approved stance for unarmed combat. Fortunately she didn't come through the windscreen to get us.

We passed through the guard checkpoint in Dundas Street, the auxiliaries on duty straightening rapidly to attention when they saw Davie, and entered the citizen area. The few people braving the rain were dressed in ill-fitting, not very waterproof clothes, their backs bent against the wind and their heads bowed to ensure they didn't trip over the uneven paving-stones in the poorly lit streets. This was the reality of Enlightenment Edinburgh for its inhabitants – the tourist zone was only where they worked as waiters and cleaners. They'd got so used to the untouchables wearing expensive jewellery and well-cut clothes that even envy had been completely burned away, leaving nothing but empty looks and dead souls.

Davie drove down towards the junction with Inver-leith Row. In pre-Enlightenment times there had been an insurance company's huge state-of-the-art computer centre on the bank of the Water of Leith. The Council, violently opposed to data processing equipment for security reasons, especially any that ordinary citizens could get their hands on, has turned it into an indoor running track and gymnasium – for auxiliary use only.

Suddenly the sound of sirens came up behind us and flashing red lights filled the rear windscreen.

"Shit!" Davie said, swerving towards the kerb to let a pair of guard vehicles past.

"What do you reckon they're up to?" I asked. "A spot of gang-busting?"

"Let's find out." He grabbed the phone from the left of the dashboard and called the command centre in the castle. "Hume 253 here. Location Brandon Street. Where are the two Land-Rovers headed?" He listened for a few seconds. "Right. They should be able to handle that. Let me know if there's any problem. Out."

"What is it?"

"Some kids broke into a Supply Directorate store in Granton. The guys that passed us are giving back-up to the Scott Barracks patrol that called the incident in. There are only eight of the little shitebags, apparently."

"I hope they're not carrying pick-axe handles with six-inch nails through them like the headbangers you caught in Leith last week."

"They'd better not be," Davie said grimly. "My people will give as good as they get."

"I won't tell the Council."

Davie laughed. "You think they don't know?" He moved off. "Isn't Katharine expecting you tonight?" he asked as we passed the old rugby stadium in Goldenacre that obscures the breeze-block mass of Scott Barracks.

I shrugged and tried to look indifferent. "Who knows?"

Davie glanced at me. "Has she been sticking her claws into you again, Quint?" He'd never been a fan of my on-off lover Katharine Kirkwood.

"We did have a slight contretemps a couple of days ago," I said, turning my eyes away from him. I was pretty sure he'd be delighted by that piece of news. "She's been working nights for the last month." Although she'd helped out in several of my biggest cases and could have worked full-time with me if she'd wanted, Katharine took a job in the Welfare Directorate six months ago. She had her own ideas about how she wanted to spend her time and recently they didn't seem to include me. I wasn't sure how to handle that so I buried myself in work, whisky and the blues. That hadn't gone down too well with her.

Davie sensed my mood. He kept quiet until we pulled up outside the former merchant's villa in Trinity that housed my father's retirement home. "I'll wait for you in the vehicle," he said.

"No, come up. It's freezing out here." I nudged him in the ribs. "Anyway, you know Hector. He'll want the latest gossip from the Public Order Directorate."

"Silly old sod," Davie said with a smile. "Do you think being terminally curious is a consequence of old age?"

"Not in the old man's case," I replied, shoving the Land-Rover door open. "We Dalrymples are genetically pre-conditioned to be curious."

"True enough," Davie said, joining me on the slippery pavement. "You're certainly the nosiest guy I've ever known."

"What are you after?" I asked. "You know I can resist anything except flattery."

"And barracks malt."

We entered the retirement home.

Simpson 46, the resident nursing auxiliary – a thin-faced woman of indeterminate but substantial vintage – was half-way across the hall. She turned and gave me a disapproving look. "I presume you're visiting your father, Citizen Dalrymple." Her voice was reedy and hesitant, as if she was still working on suppressing one of the local accents that the Council proscribed years ago. "Kindly don't stay long. He's been short of energy recently."

I stepped up to her. "Is there anything wrong?"

She shook her head dismissively. "Your father is over eighty, citizen. Spells of listlessness are to be expected."

I headed up the stairs at speed. There were a lot of adjectives that could be attached to my old man but listless wasn't one of them. By the time I reached the third floor, the breath was catching in my throat. I pushed open the door to my father's room without knocking.

There was a shape wrapped in a blanket sitting motionless in the chair by the window.

"Hector?" My father had insisted that I address him by his first name for as long as I could remember. "Are you okay, Hector?"

A cough came from the shrouded figure. "Is that you, failure? I thought I saw you come out of that Land-Rover." The voice may have been wheezy but the tone was firm enough. "Where the hell did you get to on Sunday?"

I smiled. "Did you miss me, old man? How touching."

My father coughed again, this time more deeply. "No, I didn't miss you, Quintilian." He was the only person who

11

called me by my full name, thank God. "I was hard at work translating a particularly scabrous piece by Catullus." He sniffed. "You could have left a message."

It was unlike him to feel sorry for himself. I went closer and looked down at him. The skin on his face was wan and there was a sheen of sweat on his forehead. "Are you sure you're all right?" I asked.

"Of course I'm sure," he said. "That idiotic woman says I need to get out of the house more. She thinks I'm—"

"Listless. So I heard. Too many dirty Latin poems, that's your trouble." Since he resigned from the Council in 2013, the old man had returned to his first love, the classics. He spent most of his time buried in old tomes.

"Don't be flippant, laddie. There are plenty of parallels between late Republican Rome and this city in 2026." He gave a long sigh. "More's the pity." He looked past me. "Is that you, Davie?"

"It is," the big man said. "How are you doing, Hector?"

"Never mind me. What has that old tightarse in charge of your directorate been up to?"

Davie grinned at that description of his boss, then frowned when he saw how happy it had made me. The public order guardian, Lewis Hamilton, was a founder member of the Enlightenment Party and had been on the original Council with my father.

"I haven't seen much of him," Davie replied. "He's serving his month as senior guardian." The Council instigated a rotating system for the top job a couple of years back because of abuses when the position was permanent. My mother had been one of the holders of the city's senior office, much to Hector's disgust. They hadn't been getting on for years and had taken advantage of the celibate state that used to be required of guardians to ignore each other completely.

"May the Lord protect us," the old man said, taking refuge in divine power like all the best atheists. "Lewis must be almost as doddery as I am."

Davie laughed. "Not quite."

Hector looked up, gave a stern stare then laughed weakly. "Very good, lad. Very good." He started to cough again.

Davie and I exchanged glances. The old man didn't sound too healthy, but he was still quick enough to latch on to our concern.

"What's the matter with you two?" he complained. "Have you never seen someone who's reached the end of the line before?"

"What are you talking about?" I demanded. "I'm worried I'll be spending the rest of my life coming down to Trinity every weekend."

The old man broke into a high-pitched laugh. "I know how much you look forward to these visits, Quintilian." He turned his hooded eyes back to Davie. "You didn't answer my question, Hume 253. What's been going on in the Public Order Directorate?"

I must have needled Hector. He'd normally have asked for my sarcastic take on the Council's crime prevention activities first.

Davie glanced at me uneasily, picking up the edge in the old man's voice. "Well," he said, "do you want the good news or the bad news?"

"Give me the bad first, laddie," Hector said, struggling to pull himself upright in the chair and glaring at me to discourage any offer of assistance. "That's what we've got used to in this benighted city."

13

"Em, right." Davie ran his fingers through the matted hairs of his beard. "Thirty-seven arrests for disorderly conduct in the suburbs in the last week – thirty-one of them involving minors."

"Disorderly conduct?" the old man asked. "What does that cover?"

Davie raised his shoulders. "Anything from stoning guard patrols to nicking old ladies' food vouchers. There's a mandatory six-month spell in a Youth Development Department facility for anyone under twenty who gets taken in."

"Except those places are all full now," I pointed out.

"So we send them down the mines instead," Davie said with a broad grin.

"What else?" Hector asked, the question ending in a long wheeze.

"Five holes cut in the fences on the city line, no smugglers or dissidents apprehended yet." Davie shook his head. "And at least three illicit landings on the shoreline, judging by the tracks and footprints the patrols have found on the beaches. Ever since the Fisheries Guard all but fell apart last year, the coast has been impossible to secure."

"The dreaded democrats from Glasgow," Hector said, his lips cracking into a bitter smile. "How will the Council manage to restrict the dangerous ideas they'll spread?" Although he'd been as hardline as any guardian in his time, my father had eventually become disillusioned with his colleagues' drive for total control over what Edinburgh citizens think and do. He reckoned that power had corrupted them. I reckoned he was right.

Davie wasn't buying it. "Democrats? Those people are

just after a cut of the tourist income. How democratic is it to peddle dope and burn people's lungs out with cigarettes?"

"I suppose a compulsory lottery like the one the Council runs is all right in your book, is it, Davie?" Hector asked sharply.

"Edlott's all right," Davie replied. "It doesn't do any harm."

"Not now it doesn't," I said. "Now that it's been cleaned up." In 2025 I'd opened and closed a very nasty can of worms in the lottery.

The old man started muttering about the iniquity of forcing citizens to accept fewer food and drink vouchers in exchange for the minuscule chance of winning a not very exciting prize. Then, suddenly, his legs shot out straight. His mouth fell open and his lips turned an unnatural shade of blue. The rattle that came from his throat made the hairs on my neck rise.

"Get the nurse, Davie!" I yelled.

I bent over my father and pulled the rug away from his chest. The citizen-issue grey pyjamas he was wearing were drenched in sweat. The noise in his throat had subsided. I put my head to his bony chest and listened for a heartbeat. For what seemed like an eternity I didn't pick anything up. Then a faint, irregular thump came through.

"Out of the way, citizen!" Simpson 46 pushed past me and leaned over the old man. "Stand back," she said as she took Hector's wrist and checked her watch.

"What is it?" I asked, feeling Davie's hands on my arms. He pulled me back gently. "What's happening to him?"

"Heart attack," the nursing auxiliary said in a clipped

voice. "Call the infirmary and get an ambulance down here right away."

Davie let go of me and pulled out his mobile. I was only vaguely aware of him talking as I watched Simpson 46 running through procedure that was clearly second nature to her. I stood there helplessly, fighting the impulse to shove the nurse out of the way and grab the old man's hand. I glanced round the dimly lit room. Hector's desk was covered with piles of books, the slips of yellow paper that he used to mark passages and make notes hanging limply like streamers the day after a parade. In the corner his bed was as neat as ever. He still made it himself every morning, as well as brushing the faded leather brogues – the sole mark of guardian rank he retained – that stood on the floor beneath.

Davie came up to me. "The ambulance is on its way. I told them to give it top priority."

I nodded and watched as Simpson 46 folded the blanket carefully over Hector's chest. Then a blast of anger hit me.

"Pity you weren't so meticulous in your care of my father earlier," I said in a low voice, shaking off Davie's hand. "He wasn't listless. He was building up to this."

The nursing auxiliary looked at me impassively then shook her head. For her I was just the latest in a long line of relatives who'd lost their grip.

"Leave it, Quint," Davie said. "At least Hector's still alive."

Simpson 46 nodded. "Quite so, Hume 253. Patients who survive the initial onslaught frequently recover."

I lunged forward. "And that makes your negligence acceptable, does it, you—"

I broke off as a faint sound came from the old man. His

eyes were half open and it seemed that he gave a shake of his head.

There was the sound of a siren in the street below, quickly followed by the pounding of auxiliary-issue boots on the stairs. Hector was placed on a stretcher and moved out of his room with consummate skill.

I stood there for a couple of seconds and looked at the books on the desk, wondering if my father would ever open them again.

Then I turned and followed the stretcher out of the retirement home.

There wasn't room for me in the clapped-out ambulance so Davie took me in the Land-Rover. We didn't talk as we drove towards the central zone then up the Mound to the infirmary. It was only as we pulled up outside the city's main hospital with its château-like towers and dark grey stonework that Davie broke the silence.

"He'll get the very best treatment, Quint. I told them to inform the medical guardian."

"Thanks, my friend," I said. I've never been one for queue-jumping but I wouldn't have had any compunction in doing all I could for Hector. I was glad that Davie felt the same way.

We got out and headed for the main entrance. There was a light drizzle falling, just enough to blur the lights of the infirmary and give the nineteenth-century pile the look of a fairy-tale castle. That impression lasted as long as it took me to push open the door and walk into the chilly reception hall. It wasn't drizzling inside, but the breath of citizens waiting for treatment even though it was after nine o'clock had made the place steam up like a surrealist's version of a sauna – one from which the heat-source had been omitted.

I accompanied the auxiliaries with the stretcher down the wide passageway that led to the intensive care unit. At one junction I forgot what I was doing and turned towards the morgue. I'd attended more post-mortems than I cared to remember in the infirmary. The way that I headed automatically for the autopsy room didn't make me feel any better.

A figure of medium height with white-blonde hair was standing at the door of the ICU. Despite the loose surgical robes she was wearing, the bulge in the medical guardian's midriff was clearly visible.

"Quint," she said, smiling faintly. "I'm very sorry. I've asked the chief cardiologist to attend."

"Thanks, Sophia." I went into the unit after her. Through a glass partition I could see a group of green-clad medics working on the old man.

"According to the ambulance-men your father's in a stable condition." The medical guardian was at my side, a file in her hands. "The next few hours will be critical."

I nodded, glancing at her. Her expression was cold, as befitted someone whose nickname throughout the city was the Ice Queen, but her voice conveyed some emotion. Which had nothing to do with the fact that we'd had a relationship back in 2025, I was sure. All that survived of that was her letting me address her by her first name, a privilege she allowed no one else.

"How have you been?" I asked, trying unsuccessfully to keep my eyes away from the bump in her otherwise slim figure.

Sophia looked at me blankly then caught the direction

of my gaze. "I'm not ill, Quint," she snapped. "Pregnancy's a perfectly normal state for a woman."

"Not for guardians, it isn't," I replied. Until a couple of years back, guardians were still expected to be strictly celibate. That was changed at the same time that their names were first published in the *Edinburgh Guardian* – in a belated attempt to make the city's leaders more human. The idea of a guardian getting pregnant was still pretty hard to cope with. Sophia was the first and I suppose I was suffering twinges of jealousy. She'd declined to tell anyone who the father was, prompting rumours in senior auxiliary circles that she was carrying out a eugenics experiment on herself. You never know with guardians.

"When's it due?" I asked.

"*It?*" she said, looking up from a clipboard. "The child is expected in mid-February."

"So you've got another four months of inflation to go." I tried a winning smile on her and got frozen out for my pains.

The city's leading heart specialist came out of the treatment area and pulled his mask down. "All is well, guardian," he said, nodding at his superior then turning to me. He was an elderly specimen, one who would have spent the last five years on the golf-course in a more frivolous and less hard-pressed society than Enlightenment Edinburgh.

"You must be Hector's son," he said, stripping off a surgical glove and offering his hand. "The famous Quintilian." He gave me a warm smile that took me by surprise. "I follow your cases avidly in the newspaper."

I eyed him dubiously. Groupies are all very well but I draw the line at superannuated males. "How's your patient, Simpson 13?" I asked, reading the barracks number on his tunic.

"Hector will pull through, I think." The cardiologist broke off when he saw that I was puzzled by his use of the old man's first name. "I knew him years ago." He glanced at Sophia. "Back in the Enlightenment's glory days."

"Complete your report, please," Sophia said, unimpressed by the implied criticism of the present Council.

"Yes, well, as I say, Hector will probably make a good recovery." The aged surgeon nodded at me. "He's a tough old bird. I suspect there's some narrowing of the arteries but we should be able to control that with drugs." He looked down at the tiled floor. "If the directorate can afford them."

"Thank you, Simpson 13," the medical guardian said tersely. "I'm sure you have other work to engage you."

The cardiologist gave me an encouraging nod and went back into the unit.

"As have I," Sophia said, turning away. "Don't worry, Quint. We'll take good care of your father."

"Hang on a minute," I called after her. "I want to make a complaint about one of your staff."

She stopped and looked back at me wearily. "Oh, for goodness' sake. Who?"

"Simpson 46, the nursing auxiliary at the retirement home." I went over to Sophia and put a hand on her arm to make her face me. "She knew there was something wrong with Hector before tonight, but she didn't do anything to prevent this."

The medical guardian glanced down at my hand and waited for me to remove it. "Prevent the heart attack? You must be joking. You know how stretched the city's resources are. We're lucky if we manage to treat every-one who's actually in need. Preventive medicine's largely beyond our capabilities."

I squeezed my fingertips into the palms of my hands and swallowed what I'd been about to say. There was no point in giving her the third degree. She was managing as well as she could with the dwindling funds the Council allotted her directorate and, anyway, she'd have had no hesitation in tossing me into the dungeons for insolence – no matter what we used to do together in my bed.

"Brilliant," I said under my breath. "Welcome to the third decade of the Edinburgh Enlightenment."

"Pardon?" the Ice Queen said.

"Nothing," I said, looking back at the old man through the glass screen. "Don't let me keep you from your duties, guardian."

I heard an impatient sigh, then departing footsteps. It struck me that maybe I'd been a bit hard on her. Too late.

I found a seat in the corridor next to a father-to-be who was waiting for the arrival of his first-born with extreme agitation. His nerves didn't surprise me. Apart from the natural insecurity of a man in his position, he was also under a lot of pressure. Since the birth-rate in Edinburgh began to slump every healthy baby attracts what pass here for generous allowances, but they're also monitored on a more or less daily basis. The Council claims that global warming and the pollution from poorly regulated factories in continental Europe have had deleterious effects on conception; most people believe the decrease in successful births is a direct result of the original Council's attempts to do away with the family. I mean, if you attend a weekly sex session with a different partner each time, what incentive is there to commit yourself to child care for years of your life? Sex sessions aren't compulsory any more, but plenty of people still attend them out of choice. I thought of Sophia and the lump under her surgical gown. I reckoned the stories about eugenics were off the mark – no doubt she was just doing her duty as a female and contributing to the city's future generations.

A fresh-faced nurse arrived to shepherd the nervous male citizen to the delivery room. I wished him luck and sank back in the uncomfortable plastic seat, waiting for an update on Hector's condition. I'd been trying not to think about him too much because the impulse to go and strangle Simpson 46 was still strong. But something the old man said to Davie and me just before he had his attack kept coming back to me – "Have you never seen someone who's reached the end of the line before?" The end of the line. Was that really where the old man saw himself? Then the realisation knifed into me. It wasn't just Hector who was at the end of the line. I was too – stuck in this isolated city that was falling back into the violence that destroyed the United Kingdom after the millennium. More than that, I myself was literally the end of the line; the last branch of the Dalrymple family tree. I'd never had kids, had no prospect of having any now, would be dubious about bringing any into this unstable place. Jesus. Now I had a better idea of what Jim Morrison meant when he sang "The End".

A heavy elbow jabbed into my ribs.

"Bloody hell, Quint, what is it?" Davie's voice was full of concern. "Is Hector okay?"

"Aye, don't panic. He's stable."

"Thank Christ for that. You look like death warmed up."

I nodded. "I was having some morbid thoughts, right enough."

"Well, snap out of it, pal. Tomorrow's another—" Davie broke off as his mobile went off. "Commander. I'm off duty, you know." He listened for a while. "Are you sure?" he asked, his brow furrowed. "All right, I'll get over there. Out."

"What is it?" I said.

He was shaking his head. "Now I've heard it all. Remember those skeletons we saw outside the Assembly Hall?"

"The lucky workers getting overtime?"

"Yeah." He stared at me in disbelief. "It seems they were fakes. But their labouring skills were up to scratch. They dug all the way down to the old Scottish Parliament archive in the basement."

"What?"

Davie nodded emphatically, his eyes wide open. "And now the bastards have disappeared."

CHAPTER TWO

D avie was heading for the exit at speed.

"Hang on," I said. "I'm coming with you."

He looked back over his shoulder. "Don't be an idiot. You're waiting to hear about Hector."

I caught up with him. "A case will take my mind off the old man. Christ, this could be an interesting one, Davie. The Parliament archive's been off limits since the Council came to power. Why's someone suddenly breaking into it now?" I put my hand on his arm. "Give me a minute to check with the nurses."

He stood in the corridor with his hands on his hips and shook his head slowly. "Bloody typical," he said. "Nothing gets in the way of the Quintilian Dalrymple detection addiction."

I ran back to the ICU and was advised that the old man was weak but still stable. I gave the auxiliaries the number of my Public Order Directorate mobile and told them to call me immediately if there was any change.

"Come on then," Davie said, looking at his watch as I got back to him. "There's a hole in the ground waiting for us."

"A pit, an underworld cavern, the infernal abyss," I said as we walked out into the clammy mist that had thickened while we were inside. "Some juicy symbolism there in this less than perfect city, eh?"

Davie opened the Land-Rover door. "You need a good lie-down, pal."

I nodded and climbed into the ancient guard vehicle. The adrenalin-inspired bravado that the start of a case always brought about was already beginning to fade. Even a cynic like me needs some motivation to keep on doing his job. Enlightenment Edinburgh didn't provide much in the way of that any more.

Mound Place. The lights of the guard Land-Rovers shone blearily out of the murk like the wreckers' torches that lure unsuspecting ships on to the coasts of the badlands in Fife and Berwickshire these days.

"Nice night for it," Davie said.

"Uh-huh." I peered ahead. "Oh shit. Who told *him*? You'd have thought he had enough to keep him busy."

"Ah." Davie didn't look overjoyed to see his boss either. "The command centre, I suppose."

Lewis Hamilton, public order guardian and currently acting senior guardian, came out of the mist. He was dressed in the tweed jacket and corduroy trousers that make up the standard garb of Council members and, despite the chill air, he wore no coat. He was probably making a point to his subordinates; something along the lines of "Look how hard I am – over seventy-five and never a day off work." No doubt the auxiliaries were very impressed.

"Hume 253." The guardian acknowledged his senior guard commander with the usual formality. Then he looked past Davie. "Is that you, Dalrymple?" The rheumy eyes above his white beard registered surprise. "I didn't expect to see you here. Then again, I can never find you when I want you so I suppose the reverse applies." His voice softened. "I heard about your father. Very sorry. Keeping his head above water, I was told."

I nodded. Lewis Hamilton had fallen out with Hector in a big way when they were on the Council. Still, at least he was making an effort to show sympathy. I got out of the Land-Rover and went round to join him on the slippery cobblestones.

"You don't have to involve yourself in this," the guardian said. "You've got other things to worry about."

"I've had enough of worrying," I said, remembering the dismal thoughts that had afflicted me in the infirmary. "Anyway," I added, going on the offensive, "my contract with the Public Order Directorate allows me to intervene in any investigation." I gave him a firm look. "And guarantees no interference from any quarter."

Lewis had taken a step back. "All right, man. I was only trying to help." He turned back towards the lights outside the Assembly Hall.

"Arsehole," Davie said in a low voice. "Can you never manage to talk to the guardian without biting him in the throat?"

"Sorry. Force of habit." Lewis Hamilton had been my boss when I was in the directorate – before my lover Caro was killed in an operation planned and led by me in 2015, and I ended up being demoted because I didn't care any more.

We walked up to the collegiate building with the high twin towers that stands in front of the Assembly Hall. Both the buildings had connections with organised religion, but those counted for nothing when the atheist Enlightenment came to power. The college was turned into an auxiliary training block, and the hall to the rear became the Council chamber for the first twenty years of the regime. Then, in what I took to be a mark of the guardians' burgeoning lust for the trappings of power, they moved the chamber to what used to be the Scottish Parliament building in Holyrood – a collection of up-turned boats that was raked with machine-gun fire during the riots leading up to the last election. Of course, the Assembly Hall itself served as the Scottish Parliament for a couple of years before the boats were launched, so the Council's love affair with the architecture of power had actually been going on from day one.

"What have we got?" Davie asked the guard commander at the entrance.

"Some pretty handy excavation works, Hume 253." The balding auxiliary nodded at the deep hole inside the gateway. "As you can see, they had all the necessary equipment. Compressor, drills, mini-digger, pick-axes—"

"Where did the gear come from?" I interrupted.

"Ah, citizen Dalrymple. Good evening." The commander gave me a brief smile. I'd had dealings with him from time to time in the command centre. He was one of a select group of senior auxiliaries who didn't have a problem with a demoted citizen like me being employed by the directorate.

I returned his smile. "How are you, Knox 111?"

"Fine, thank you. It's Labour Directorate equipment. We've just checked. It was taken from the Canonmills depot last night, along with a pick-up truck that's still unaccounted for. I've authorised an all-barracks search for it."

"How the bloody hell did they get away with it?"

Hamilton demanded, coming out of the mist like an irate werewolf. "What happened to the watchmen?"

The commander twitched his head nervously. "I've asked the local barracks for an explanation."

Lewis kept up his rant as I moved to the hole and looked down. Lights had been strung into it and there was a ladder leaning against one side. It was at least fifteen feet deep and at the bottom I could see a paved floor strewn with earth and lumps of stone.

"What do you reckon?" Davie said, squatting down beside me.

"I reckon these guys knew what they were doing." I looked round at Hamilton. "There were three of them. We saw them."

"What?" the guardian said with a gasp of surprise.

"When we were driving to Hector's. The commander here even spoke to one of them."

"Is this true, Hume 253?" Hamilton demanded.

Davie nodded sheepishly. "I didn't see much of him, though. He was wearing full work gear. I assumed they really were citizens on overtime."

"Good God, man," the guardian said. He started winding himself up for another harangue.

"I made the same assumption, Lewis," I said, taking the wind from his sails. I turned to Knox 111. "Who raised the alarm?"

"The sentry," he replied. "Eventually."

I glanced at my watch. Being poor-quality, ordinary citizen-issue, the glass was partially clouded by condensation, but I could see that it was after eleven. "It took him his whole shift to work out there was something dodgy about the workmen?" The second guard shift

28

starts at two p.m. and ends at ten. "What finally got to him?"

"The sentry's a guardswoman," Knox 111 said, stepping aside. "Ask her yourself."

I was confronted by a heavily built middle-aged woman in a tight guard uniform. Her face was ruddy and her mousy hair was tied back in a loose grip. The public order guardian's presence didn't seem to bother her. One of the old guard, literally.

"So what happened . . ." I leaned forward to read the barracks badge on her mountainous chest ". . . Moray 58?"

"The squad of labourers arrived when I was coming on duty." The guardswoman was standing to attention, her eyes fixed on a point above my left shoulder. I got the feeling that she wasn't enjoying making her report to an ordinary citizen. "I asked for their job authorisation form. It looked to be in order."

"Did you check it with the Labour Directorate as regulations require?" Hamilton demanded.

Moray 58 stiffened even more. "I was about to," she said. "Then a truck arrived with a delivery of supplies to the auxiliary training centre. I was busy clearing it through and the leader of the labour squad told me not to waste my time checking his papers."

The public order guardian snorted in disgust. "And you went along with that?"

"I presumed," the guardswoman said with less assurance, "that maintenance of the electricity cable was bound to be above board."

There was a frosty silence that made it clear to the guardswoman how limited her career prospects were.

"Can you describe the squad leader?" I asked.

Moray 58 nodded. "Certainly. He was approximately six feet two in height, fifteen stone in weight and wearing standard-issue labourer's overalls, boots and jacket with luminous stripes." She stopped abruptly.

"Is that it?" I said when the silence began to drag. "What about hair colour, facial characteristics, accent?"

The sentry was still looking above my shoulder. "I can't say," she answered after a long delay. "He was wearing a miner's helmet and a protective mask."

"What, even when he first arrived?"

She nodded.

"So he could have looked like Boris Karloff and sounded like Bela Lugosi and you wouldn't have noticed?"

"I am not familiar with those individuals, citizen," Moray 58 said stolidly. "I cannot describe the workman's face or voice, if that's what you mean."

I swore under my breath, loud enough for the guardswoman to hear and be appropriately scandalised by language citizens are not supposed to use.

"I suppose the same goes for all the others?"

The sentry nodded again.

"How many of them were there?" I demanded. "Assuming you can count."

Moray 58 ignored the jibe. "Three including the squad leader."

The public order guardian stepped forward. His cheeks were red, and not just from the cold. He couldn't cope with incompetence from his staff. "What finally raised your suspicions, guardswoman?" he shouted. "What finally woke you up?"

The sentry jerked back, somehow managing to remain at attention. "It . . . it was the way they were working, guardian. For all the rain and cold they were so . . . so diligent. I've never seen Edinburgh labourers go through a shift with such commitment. They didn't even stop for the tea-break."

I stifled a laugh as the guardian took in what the woman was saying. It's been the case for years that ordinary citizens, whose faith in the Council has been gradually eroded to the lowest level, have developed shirking into an art form – not that Lewis and his colleagues on the Council could let themselves believe that.

"So you began to realise that they were maybe up to no good?" I said.

Moray 58 opened her eyes wide and nodded slowly. She pulled out her guard notebook and flicked it open. "At eight-oh-five I came out here and asked for the job authorisation form again. I intended to get confirmation from the Labour Directorate." She broke off.

"And . . . ?" I said impatiently.

"And then the phone rang in the sentry box." She gave a shrug. "By the time I was finished there the workmen had gone."

"What?" Hamilton said. "In the space of a few seconds?"

The guardswoman bit her lip. "Well, it was longer than that, guardian. The command centre had a list of things for me to check."

I might have known. The City Guard is notorious for inventing activities to keep its people on their toes.

"All right, Moray 58," I said. "Give a full statement to Knox 111." I watched as she moved swiftly away without waiting for Hamilton to dismiss her. She had some sense.

Davie came over and we stood looking down the hole.

"We'd better find out what they were after," I said. "Where's the scene-of-crime squad?"

The public order guardian was shaking his head. "Oh no. That's a restricted area down there. We'll have to do the preliminary check ourselves."

"Really?" I said, my curiosity beginning to get out of hand. "Can we get in through the basement?"

Hamilton shook his head even more firmly. "The old Parliament records were sealed by Council decree in 2005. It'll need another Council order to get that seal broken. I want to know what's been going on down there before I ask the Council for such an order."

This was getting seriously interesting. I'd known for years that the pre-Enlightenment Scottish Parliament's archive existed, but I'd never allowed myself to get too excited by it since the Council, in its high-minded disapproval of what it regarded as a corrupt system of government, had put the records out of reach even of its own researchers.

I pulled on the protective white overalls and rubber gloves that Davie handed me. When he and Hamilton had done the same, I dangled my legs down the hole and felt for the top rung of the ladder.

"You don't mind me going first, do you, Lewis?" I asked.

"I'll be right behind you, Dalrymple," he replied grimly. "And don't open any files unless I'm present."

"I'd never do a thing like that," I said as I climbed into the surprisingly well-lit subterranean cavern.

The guardian snorted. "And the Tourism Directorate will be closing down its knocking shops tomorrow."

The electricity cable certainly hadn't been in need of maintenance. The vast basement was lit up like a shopping centre in pre-Enlightenment times – before looters nicked everything in sight, including the light fittings and bulbs. Roof-high shelves crammed with dark blue cardboard files stretched away in orderly lines. Dust that hadn't been disturbed since I was in my early twenties hung in the air like plankton in the southern oceans.

I moved forward carefully to give the others room then bent my knees and examined the floor. The flagstones in the vicinity of the hole were covered in rubble and earth, and there were plenty of footprints for the scene-of-crime people to take casts of later on. They looked like your standard work-boot to me.

"The size of this place," Davie said in astonishment.

Hamilton nodded. "It was enlarged in the early years of the century. The Scottish Parliament was a great producer of paper."

"And the Council isn't?" I said under my breath. "Have you been down here before, Lewis?"

"Em . . . a few times. When we were preparing to close it up."

"Great," I said. "You'll know your way around then."

The guardian shook his head. "Hardly. It's a long time ago." He frowned at me. "Anyway, you're the archive lover."

I glared at him. "If the Council used computers properly, I wouldn't have to spend most of my waking hours in the city's waste paper collections."

Davie stepped between us. "Shall we get on, gentlemen? Are we going to be able to tell what they were after?"

I gazed down the long passage in front of me. It was one of many. "Only if we're clever. Their boots would have been dirty so we may be able to trace the footprints they've left. We'd better split up."

So we did. But it wasn't long before we joined up again.

"There are blurred footprints in the dust all over the place, Dalrymple," Hamilton said, his brow lined. "They aren't going to tell us anything."

Davie nodded in agreement. "They seem to have been down all the stacks. Maybe they didn't know what they were looking for."

"Maybe not." I rubbed my hand across my face, forgetting that the protective gloves were now covered in dust. That gave me an idea. "Or maybe they had something specific in mind and walked up and down the passageways to throw us off their trail."

Hamilton looked at me sceptically. "What makes you think that?"

"Listen, they were organised enough to steal Labour Directorate equipment. They were daring enough to set up a fake dig a few hundred yards from the castle." I watched as the guardian's jaw jutted out in anger. "And they worked out an effective place to break into the archive. What does all that tell you?"

"That they were working to a plan," Davie said.

"Exactly. They wouldn't be running the risk of spending the rest of their lives down the mines just because they fancied a nose round the old Parliament records. They were after something particular. And I reckon they knew where to look for it."

Hamilton was staring at me. "You're saying that they didn't want us to know what they were interested in?" he asked dubiously. "That's pure guesswork, Dalrymple. The guardswoman told us that they cleared off when she was about to check their papers. Maybe they didn't find what they wanted." He looked at the stacks of paper.

"Anyway, everything in here is rubbish. I don't know why we don't burn the lot of it."

I wasn't keen on the way he'd defined my investigative technique. "Guesswork? That's what you think, Lewis. What if I can show you the documents they wanted?"

The guardian laughed softly. "Then I'll give you an auxiliary knife engraved with the word 'genius'. But it's not going to happen, man."

"Isn't it?" I bent over and looked at the flagstones again. I had a hunch I was right, but Hamilton had never been a fan of my hunches. There was only one way to find out.

Before I started going over the place with my magnifying glass, I called the infirmary and checked on the old man. He was asleep and as comfortable as could be expected. So I got down to work.

I had the feeling it was going to be a long night.

Fortunately, that feeling turned out to be a loser. Not long after half-past midnight I spotted the spots.

I had just reached the end of a stack and caught a glimpse of Lewis Hamilton. The city's law and order supremo and acting chief executive was bent over in the passageway like a cleaner chasing the piece of fluff that had got away. I was about to ask him if he was having a good time when I saw a six-inch line of dull red drops. The dust had been disturbed all around the stack-end. I'd come across several such places but this was the only one with traces of what looked very like blood. Well, well.

"Lewis! Davie! We're in business."

The sound of City Guard-issue nailed boots came at

35

me from different directions. I took up a position at the stack-end to protect the scene.

"What have you found?" Hamilton asked, wiping a cobweb from his beard.

Davie arrived and looked past me. "No dead bodies then," he said, a hint of regret in his voice.

"Only a small amount of corporeal matter," I said, turning to the area of the floor with the blood line. "Someone cut their finger, I reckon." I put my hand on the guardian's arm as he craned forward. "Don't go any nearer. I haven't checked for other traces yet."

Davie had dropped to his knees. "One thing's for sure. There are no distinct footprints here."

I nodded. The dust was so thick that it had swirled up when disturbed and resettled over the prints. But I wondered if there was more to it than that. Had the intruders made efforts to obliterate the traces they'd left in particular places? If so, the line of blood spots might be the only clue we'd get.

"That minuscule quantity of blood isn't going to get us far," Hamilton said discouragingly. "Especially since we don't have the equipment to carry out DNA testing."

"Another brilliant decision by the Council," I said under my breath. After the Public Order Directorate had driven out the drugs gangs and reduced crime in the city to what it claimed was level zero, the guardians declined to fund anything more than the most basic forensic service. That had made my working life a lot more fun.

"I suppose those blood traces mean we'll have to get the scene-of-crime squad down here now," the guardian said, shaking his head. "I need Council approval first. This is a restricted area no matter what's been going on."

"You've already let me down here and I'm a DM," I said impatiently. "Tell the Council tomorrow, Lewis. After all, you are the boss this month."

"That's not the way the system works, Dalrymple. As you well know." The guardian pulled out his mobile. "All right, the scene-of-crime squad it is. I'll advise my colleagues in the morning."

I gave Davie a quick smile. He didn't return it. Winding up Hamilton is off limits for serving auxiliaries – which is one reason I was demoted from the rank years ago.

The scene-of-crime people arrived in their white plastic overalls and flitted about the stacks like nosy but extremely fastidious ghosts. I had to let them get on with it, even though I wanted to have a look at the files in the vicinity of the blood spots. Eventually the auxiliaries finished taking photos, samples and prints there and started checking other parts of the vast subterranean hall.

"Don't you want an operative present when we pull the files?" I asked the guardian.

"Certainly not," he replied. "Everything in here is classified 'Guardian Eyes Only'."

"Right then," I said, turning away. "Hume 253 and I'll be off."

"Quint," Davie growled. "Get a grip."

"Quite so, Dalrymple," Hamilton agreed. "You and the commander are part of the investigative team. You don't need further accreditation." He smiled humourlessly. "Until I decide otherwise."

"Very good of you," I said, pulling my rubber gloves back on. I started examining the stack above the floor where the blood had dripped. "Doesn't look like any complete folders have been removed." The shelves were jammed tight with dark blue cardboard binders. "Give me your torch, Davie."

He passed it over. The Council used to issue torches only to auxiliaries. A couple of years ago they made them available to ordinary citizens when the curfew was put back to midnight – the street-lights in the suburbs are so unreliable that you need a torch to get home in one piece. The only problem is that there's been a shortage of batteries ever since, which is why I don't carry my own torch. I could get Davie to arrange a supply but, like I say, I'm not keen on pulling strings – unless I have to.

"See anything interesting?" the guardian asked.

"Not even an archive-rat like me could find Scottish Parliament minutes interesting," I said. "Wait a second." I looked closer. Under the torch's beam I'd noticed the spine of a folder with smudges on the dust covering it. I took out my magnifying glass. There was a small, dust-adulterated bloodstain on the fold between spine and back cover. "Hello there," I said, looking round at Lewis. "You know the 'genius' auxiliary knife you promised me?"

The guardian was staring balefully at the scuffs he'd got on his brogues. "What about it, Dalrymple?" he demanded.

I pulled the file out from the shelf carefully, keeping my fingers away from the area potentially bearing traces of the bogus maintenance workers. "You'd better get the engravers working on the inscription."

We headed back to the hole in the roof. I wanted to open the file in surroundings that weren't contaminated by dust and Hamilton wanted to open it as far away from unauthorised eyes as possible. Davie was behind us, organising the collection of the files in the surrounding shelves. My experience of archives is that you always need to cross-reference.

"Guardian?" the scene-of-crime squad supervisor called as we approached the piles of rubble under the hole. "We've found a complete footprint." She beckoned us over to the end of a stack.

There was an area of minor subsidence where seven or eight flagstones had canted over and raised small heaps of earth. The print was in the middle of one of the heaps, a couple of feet in front of a dark patch on the flags.

"We're about to take a cast," the female auxiliary said. "The intruder took a leak," she said, inclining her head towards the stain and grinning.

I smiled. It's unusual to find evidence of a sense of humour in Public Order Directorate personnel.

Hamilton wasn't impressed. "Do you recognise the footwear?" he asked testily.

The auxiliary nodded her head, spots of red on her cheeks showing that she'd clocked her superior's dis-approval. "Yes, guardian. Standard Labour Directorate rubber work-boot, I'd say. I'll be checking that."

"Make sure you do," Hamilton said, moving away.

I gave the scene-of-crime supervisor a friendly shrug. She just stared at me dully. Yet another member of the DMs Can Kiss My Buttocks Society.

Hamilton drove me to the castle in the Jeep that was his pride and joy. It had been donated to the city by an American company that had wanted to butter up the Council; somehow it had found its way to the guardian's personal parking place on the esplanade.

"What do you think that's going to tell you, Dalrymple?" he asked, nodding at the object in the protective plastic bag on my knees.

"Who knows, Lewis? If we're lucky, the guy with the bleeding finger will have left a consultation note giving his name, address and sexual preferences."

"Stop messing about, man. Do you think something's been taken from the file? And if so, why?"

"Patience, Lewis, patience," I replied as he pulled up at the upper end of the esplanade. Although electricity was restricted in the suburbs, the castle was lit up like a stripper's dressing-room. It wouldn't do to keep the City Guard's headquarters in the dark, would it?

I followed the guardian up the narrow ramp to the gate then across the cobbled yards to his quarters in what was formerly the Governor's House. There was no trace of red in the sky to the west now. The wind was lively enough from that direction though, spatters of chill rain whipping in like grape-shot.

"Season of mists and mellow fruitfulness," I said, leaning into the blast.

"Close bosom-friend of the maturing sun," Hamilton completed, provoking an inquisitive look from a passing guardsman. "I never imagined you were a devotee of Keats, Dalrymple."

"Keats was the original blues poet, Lewis," I said as we entered the granite building. "If he'd grown up in the American South in the first half of the last century, he'd have taken Robert Johnson to the cleaners, believe me."

"Really?" the guardian said, his mind already elsewhere. He led me up to his rooms on the second floor and gave the grey-suited female auxiliary in the outer office strict instructions to allow no one in. In his sanctum, he stood beside the conference table with his hands on his hips. "Right, let's see what we've got."

"Hold on," I said, putting the folder down carefully and reaching into my pocket for my gloves. "We've got to check for any other traces." I looked at the guardian. He was strangely nervous, he had been ever since I found the file. Did he know something I didn't? I took the dark blue cardboard object out and ran my eyes over it again. Apart from the bloodstain I'd noticed in the archive, I couldn't see any other residual evidence on the outside. Then something else struck me. "What about Davie?" I asked. "You told your secretary not to let anyone in."

"Hume 253 does not need to be involved in this part of the investigation, Dalrymple," the guardian said in a leaden voice. "Proceed."

I thought about insisting on Davie's presence, but I knew that when Hamilton made his mind up only acts of god – or whatever the atheist Council describes them as – could deflect him. So I bent over the file and took a final look at the cover. It revealed nothing apart from the Scottish Parliament logo and crest, the "Guardian Eyes Only" stamp that had been applied later, and a laser-printed reference line – GEC/02/04/ATTS1–2.

"Do you know what that means?" Hamilton asked. Something about the tone of his voice gave me the impression that he did.

"I don't know what the 'G' and the 'E' stand for," I said, scratching the stubble on my chin. "But I'd guess the 'C' is committee."

The guardian nodded noncommittally.

I scrabbled around in the recesses of my memory. I hadn't seen any Scottish Parliament documents since the early years of the Enlightenment, before the Council

locked them all up. A few shards of archival data came
back to me.

"They used to record the year first then the month,
didn't they?" I said. "So this dates from April 2002." I
shook my head. "Bad time to be a member of the Scottish
Parliament." Rioting had begun to tear the country apart
by then.

"Bad time to be a Scottish citizen," Hamilton said
darkly. "Go on."

I looked back at the reference line. "The last bit is
presumably Attachments Numbers One and Two."

The guardian nodded. "That was how the abbreviations worked, yes." His eyes were fixed on the folder
now, his bottom lip caught between his teeth.

"Are you familiar with the contents of this file,
Lewis?" I asked, moving closer to him. "Because if
you are, you'd better tell me now."

He shook his head slowly. "No, I'm not. At least not in
detail." He glanced up and saw the suspicious look on
my face. "Any more ideas about the letters 'GE'?" he
asked.

"General Excuses?" I suggested. "Now there's an idea
for the Council."

"No," he said, his voice suddenly less assured. "GEC
was the parliamentary committee which regulated genetic engineering."

CHAPTER THREE

I poured the last of the coffee into my cup. Lewis had ordered it at three a.m. and gone to the door himself to take the tray – he wasn't letting anyone else even catch a glimpse of the files that were lying dismembered across the table.

"Right, let's recap," I said, stifling a yawn. "As far as we know, the intruders were only interested in this file . . ." I tapped the folder with the bloodstain ". . . and Attachment Number Two has been removed from it."

The public order guardian moved his head dispiritedly.

"We'll have to get some senior auxiliaries to go through the other files more thoroughly." I pointed at the heap of folders at the other end of the table. They were the neighbouring ones from the stack which Davie had delivered outside the door earlier. He'd sounded very unimpressed when the guardian wouldn't let him in. No doubt he was now tearing several strips off the poor sods working the night shift in the command centre.

"But so far there's no sign of anything having been taken from them."

"No." I looked over at the guardian. His bloodshot eyes stared out between the white of his hair and beard. "Of course, they could have taken papers from completely separate folders. You'll have to get the whole archive checked."

"I'll think about that tomorrow," Hamilton said, waving his hand weakly.

"It's already tomorrow, Lewis." I reined myself in a bit. My ex-boss looked like one of the city's ancient diesel-spewing buses had recently run into him. "Anyway, as I said, one of the attachments is missing. And we don't know what it contained."

The guardian nodded. He hadn't allowed me to read anything other than the cover sheet of the folder. All it told me was that the contents related to three meetings of the Genetic Engineering Committee in April 2002. It gave the names of the Members of the Scottish Parliament, bureaucrats and scientists present, none of which I recognised.

"What was so interesting about a parliamentary committee nearly twenty-five years ago?" I mused.

"You were still in short trousers then, weren't you?" Hamilton said, without much evidence of playfulness.

"I was eighteen," I said, giving him a sharp look. "And a fully paid-up member of the Enlightenment." I shook my head. "That may well have been a mistake."

"The Enlightenment Party was the forerunner of the Council," the guardian said. "How could it have been a mistake to join it?"

"Oh, forget it," I said under my breath. Suddenly I was bombarded by images and memories from that time. I'd just started at the university and for all the social unrest and drugs-gang-inspired chaos, I was full of the joys of life. Not for long. I wondered how many of my friends from that time were still alive, let alone in Edinburgh – plenty had deserted in the early years of the Council, seduced by the allure of supposedly democratic cities like Glasgow.

"We'll continue later. I need to get Council authorisation for you to read that file." Hamilton raised his shoulders. "Sorry, Dalrymple."

I shrugged back at him. "Your loss, not mine. I want to check on Hector then hit my bed."

Hamilton looked at me blankly then concentrated on the checklist he'd written in his notebook. "I'll get the forensics people to examine the folder for traces and compare the blood with the spots you found on the floor."

"I don't think they'll find much. I couldn't see any fingerprints with my lens. Whoever laid hands on this file was wearing gloves." I raised my right hand which was still sheathed in its protective glove; the rubber dangled loosely from the stump of the forefinger. "Not heavy labourer's ones but thin ones like these, which were cut by the edge of a sheet of paper. Whence the blood traces and not much else."

The guardian went on down his list. "The guard will also be checking the removal of the equipment from the Labour Directorate depot and getting statements from all personnel involved."

"I smell something rotten in that directorate," I said. "Someone supplied the bogus workmen with a job authorisation that convinced the sentry. Maybe that someone also let them into the depot."

Hamilton looked at me aggressively like he always did when I accused auxiliaries of corruption. Then he nodded. "You may be right. I'll have the senior auxiliaries from the relevant departments in."

I stood up unsteadily and stretched my heavy limbs.

"Right, Lewis. That only leaves one thing before I get my head down."

He finished writing another note and raised his eyes slowly. "And what's that, Dalrymple?"

"Genetic engineering's been banned in this city for over twenty years," I said, meeting his gaze. "It hasn't been going on. So why's this file making you jumpier than a filly before her first outing on the racetrack in Princes Street Gardens?"

Hamilton claimed he didn't know what I was talking about. That didn't surprise me much, so I left him to his scribbling and headed for the esplanade. Under low cloud, the elevated parking area seemed to float in the air above the dim lights of the central zone. I flashed my directorate authorisation at a guard driver and got him to take me to the infirmary. Like I say, I only pull strings when absolutely necessary – and when I'm shagged out.

I stood at the glass partition in the ICU and stared at the old man. He was still hooked up to all sorts of tubes and drips and it was difficult to make out his face. There seemed to be a placid expression on it. The senior nursing auxiliary was optimistic about his chances but couldn't give any firm prognosis. I told her I'd be back later and returned to the Land-Rover. By the time I was dropped off outside my flat in Gilmore Place the first tinges of watery light had appeared in the eastern sky. So much for the night.

The stairwell let out its familiar discharge of sewage gas and infrequently washed bodies. I fumbled my way up in the darkness – the electricity supply to citizen accommodation isn't turned back on until the end of the curfew at six-thirty – and eventually managed to get my key in the lock. Although my living-room was as black as the heart of a drugs gang boss, I was capable of navigating my way to the bedroom on the other side. It wasn't the first time I'd come home after Council-approved bedtime.

I dumped my bag on the hamstrung sofa and heard the springs complain metallically. Then I pushed the bedroom door open, pulled off my donkey jacket and sat down heavily on the bed.

"Ow." An arm was wrenched from underneath me. "Mind where you put your backside, Quint."

"Jesus," I gasped, my heart pounding from the shock of finding my bed occupied. "Thanks for letting me know you were coming, Katharine."

"Where have you been?" she asked sleepily. "What time is it?"

I found the matches on the rickety bedside table and lit what remained of my last candle; I'd been putting off queuing at the local Supply Directorate store.

"It's so early in the morning that you're better off not knowing," I said, peering at her in the candle's feeble light. Her light brown hair was tangled and she was having difficulty opening her eyes, but she still looked a million dollars – not that a million dollars is a big deal in the remaining United States these days, what with the volcanic inflation that resulted from religious fundamentalist-inspired civil war.

"Great." She slumped back on the pillow and pulled the blanket up to her neck.

"You want to complain? I didn't close my eyes once last night."

"So close them now," she sighed, turning over.

I finished undressing. The cold started nipping at the extremities of my body before I got under the covers.

"Are you going to tell me where you've been or not?" Katharine murmured. "Not that I'm particularly bothered." She put her foot on my shin and rubbed it a couple of times. She obviously hadn't forgotten the fight we'd had, but at least she was making some effort to move on from it.

I felt awkward about hitting her with my bad news. I forced myself. "Hector's had a heart attack."

"What?" Katharine turned to face me in an instant, her eyes wide. "Is he . . . ?"

"It's all right. He survived it, at least so far. He's under intensive care in the infirmary."

"Oh Quint, I'm so sorry." Katharine took my hand then leaned forward and pressed her face into my shoulder. "What happened?"

I told her about events in the retirement home and the aftermath in the infirmary. "Sophia made sure he got the best treatment," I concluded.

Katharine's green eyes flashed for a second then she nodded. She and the medical guardian had a relationship based on mutual loathing, but there was no getting away from Sophia's icy competence.

"God, Quint, how awful," she said with unusual tenderness. "You must have been at the hospital all night."

I nestled against her, too exhausted to say anything about the archive break-in.

"Don't worry," Katharine said a few moments later. "I'm here."

As I fell into what was more like paralysis than sleep, I found that very comforting.

*   *   *

Unfortunately the paralysis didn't extend to my mind. I drifted in and out of consciousness like a junkie or a post-prandial pre-Enlightenment politician. Images of the old man with his legs rigid and his lips blue faded and were cut with the skeletal figures of workmen in reflective jackets. Then the dark blue cover of a Scottish Parliament folder was suspended before me like a medieval vision of the Holy Writ leading an army into battle. I opened my eyes and took in the sparse furniture and dingy walls of my bedroom in the autumnal morning light. I could hear sounds from the corner of the living-room where the Housing Directorate locates what passes for a kitchen.

My body was still numb so I lay there like a corpse and thought about the Council's short, sharp treatment of genetic engineering. During the four-year existence of the Scottish Parliament, experiments involving genes and embryos got seriously out of hand. They were encouraged, both above and below board, by the Parliament because of the potentially vast financial benefits. By the year 2000 the research institute responsible for the famous cloned sheep Dolly had been joined by several other such facilities, not all of them interested solely in scientific profits. Rumours soon began to circulate in what was left of the free press that experiments in human cloning were under way – and that large sums of money were flowing in, especially from countries such as the United States where such work was illegal. There was a lot of secrecy surrounding the experiments, mainly because the foreign investors insisted on it, but it was common knowledge amongst people in the know – which included many of the founders of the Enlightenment Party – that cloned human offspring had been produced

49

by 2002. Then the riots got serious, the drugs gangs took control and the United Kingdom and its component parts were torn to shreds. By the time the Council came to power in Edinburgh and declared an independent state, the research centres had been destroyed and people were more interested in where their next meal was coming from than in genetic engineering. Members of the Enlightenment had always disapproved of cloning on ethical grounds, despite their mentor Plato's interest in eugenics, so it was easy for the guardians to ban all such experiments. End of story – until someone took great pains to break into the sealed archive and nick a Genetic Engineering Committee file attachment.

"Coffee?" Katharine was standing at the door with a mug of something that I had a feeling smelled a lot better than it tasted. I occasionally manage to lay my hands on coffee from the tourist hotels, but I have to cut it with citizen-issue ersatz to make it last.

I managed to make an affirmative noise. She handed me the mug and sat down beside me. She was wearing standard-issue white blouse and black trousers but, as usual, she looked much better than the average female citizen, her long legs striking even beneath the poor-quality material. She'd added a pink and black scarf to stick out from the crowd.

I glanced at my watch and saw it was nearly nine. "No work?" I asked after I'd cleared my mouth and throat with a couple of gulps of surprisingly good coffee – Katharine was less stingy with the real thing than I was.

She shook her head. "I've got today off. I thought I'd spend it with you."

"Ah. I have to go and see the old man."

"I know," she said. "I'll come too." Katharine and

Hector were fond of each other, probably because they recognised their shared ability to be self-sufficient and awkward in diamonds as well as spades.

"Okay," I said, trying to kick-start my legs.

It was only as I raised myself out of bed like a revivified mummy that it struck me: Katharine and I were bound to run into Sophia at the infirmary. Light blue touch-paper and retire.

The sun actually made an effort to break through the leaden clouds as we walked up Lauriston Place, then thought better of it and signed off for the day. Katharine surprised me by slipping her arm under mine and smiling at me encouragingly. Serious illness in my family was doing wonders for flagging relationships.

"He's a tough old soul," she said. "He's got years in him yet."

"Wait till we see what state he's in today." I moved inwards on the pavement as a tourist coach passed. It was only half full. In the past, even in autumn, it would have been crammed with foreigners attracted by the low prices. A boy with his hair in beads raised his fingers to his nose and mouthed abuse at us. I resisted the temptation to flash my mutilated finger at him, but it was a close thing.

We were dodging ambulances in the infirmary courtyard when my mobile rang.

"Yes, Lewis," I said before the caller spoke.

"Ah, Dalrymple." The public order guardian went quiet. "How did you know—"

"Investigator's intuition," I said.

He grunted. "Where are you? I was expecting you at the castle before now."

"Unlike guardians, ordinary citizens need a minimum of three hours' sleep a night. I'm going to visit Hector. I'll be with you afterwards. Out."

That made me feel better. There's no better start to the day than hanging up on a guardian.

"What did the old headbanger want?" Katharine asked as she pushed the main door open. She turned towards me. "Surely you weren't working on a case last night?"

I raised my shoulders. "You know how it is. Criminals never sleep."

"And self-centred investigators never give up," she said sharply. "Even when their fathers are at death's door." She bit her lip. "Sorry. I didn't mean that."

I led her down the corridor to the ICU, hoping that Sophia was elsewhere in the building. It seemed I was in luck.

"Your father's doing fine, citizen." A young female nursing auxiliary with a splash of freckles across her pale cheeks had joined us at the glass screen. "If you get robed up, you can go in and talk to him."

"He's awake?" I asked.

"Oh aye," the nurse said with a wry smile. "He's very much awake."

Katharine nodded at me. "You see? Hector will have been telling the nurse how much he likes the female sex."

"That wouldn't have taken him long," I muttered, accepting a green tunic from the cheerful auxiliary. The old man was a misogynist with knobs on, but she'd have seen it all before.

"Just don't tire him out," the nurse said as she opened the door for us.

Some of the wires and lines had been taken off Hector and he looked less like Frankenstein's creature on the table now. But the skin on his face was still waxy and pale, and his breath was catching in his throat. I touched his forearm lightly and watched as the hooded eyes opened slowly.

"Is that you, Quintilian?" he said faintly, after struggling to recognise me under the surgical mask. "What happened?"

"Nothing serious," I said, glancing at Katharine across the bed. "They've got you in for your annual service."

He mumbled something that I didn't catch.

"What's that?" I asked, leaning closer.

"I'm glad you brought her," he whispered, jerking his arm in Katharine's direction. "She's one of the few good ones in the monstrous regiment." He had to pause frequently for breath.

"Katharine?" I said, looking up as she came closer. "Yes, she is."

Hector frowned at me. "Ka . . . ?" He broke off and gulped air. "Ka . . . ?"

"Katharine," I completed, nodding at her.

The old man twitched his head. "Ka . . ."

I moved my head nearer.

His eyes bulged with the effort to enunciate. "Caro," he gasped. "Caro."

I froze as the name of my first love struck me like a blow from a claymore.

"It seems like a long time since I've seen her," Hector continued, his voice firmer now he thought he'd recognised his other visitor. He looked past me and smiled loosely at Katharine. "Caro," he repeated. "How are you, my dear? Quintilian's been waiting for you."

"Bloody hell," I said under my breath. I turned my hands up helplessly at Katharine.

"It's all right, Quint," she said through her mask. "He's wandering." She looked at the old man. I thought she was smiling because the skin at the corners of her green eyes creased. "Take your time, Hector," she said in a louder voice. "You're in the lap of luxury here."

The old man moved his head weakly. His eyelids flickered and he drifted off. I squeezed his arm again and moved to the door.

"Sorry about that," I said to Katharine on the other side of the partition. "It must be the drugs. He's never confused you with Caro before."

"I don't usually wear a mask," she said, taking off her gown. "It doesn't matter," she added, turning away.

Obviously it did, despite the fact that Caro had been gone for eleven years. That didn't mean anything to Hector, though. Caro and I were together from my first term at the university; we joined the Enlightenment on the same day; we both ended up in senior positions in the Public Order Directorate. The old man had always contemplated our relationship with a benign air – even though he was a guardian and Caro and I, as auxiliaries, shouldn't have had close ties.

Katharine waited for me at the door of the ICU while I went over Hector's file with the nurse. The cardiologist had examined him again and his report was due soon, but the signs were good. I thanked her and headed for the exit.

Where I nearly collided with Sophia's protuberant midriff. She managed to fend me off with a clipboard. I heard Katharine's rapid intake of breath when she saw the medical guardian.

"Hello, Quint," Sophia said, giving me an unrestrained smile. That was before she saw who was with me. Suddenly everything got a lot chillier.

"Morning, Sophia," I said. "Hector seems to be on the mend."

She nodded, her eyes on her papers and nowhere in the vicinity of Katharine. "I've just received the cardiologist's report. It's still early but he's very optimistic that your father's condition can be controlled. He should be able to live a relatively normal life."

"In as much as anyone can do that in the so-called perfect city," Katharine said, giving the guardian a belligerent smile.

Sophia pretended she hadn't heard and ran through the report quickly. "The prognosis I can give you at the moment is that Hector will remain in the ICU for at least another day. After that he'll be moved to a geriatric ward until he's stronger."

"And then he can go back to the retirement home?" I asked.

The guardian nodded. "I think so." She handed the clipboard to the nursing auxiliary. "I've got to get on. Goodbye, Quint." She turned away without acknowledging Katharine.

That wasn't such a good idea.

"Guardian?" Katharine called. Her face was set firm and her eyes wavered as little as those of a sentry on the city line with a smuggler in her sights. "You don't seriously intend to bring a child into this crazy city, do you?"

Sophia gave Katharine a glacial glare. "Not all women in Edinburgh have the same attitude towards procreation as ex-prostitutes like you, Citizen Kirkwood." She moved away with her head held high.

I'd had my hand over my eyes while they were talking, but I managed to grab Katharine's arm before she launched herself at the guardian. Katharine had been forced to work in the Prostitution Services Department after she served time for dissident activities years ago.

"Come on," I said. "Let's get some fresh air."

I led her outside. The clouds were even lower than they had been. They were holding the fumes from the brewery in Fountainbridge over the city like a chloroform pad.

"Fresh air?" Katharine scoffed. "We'd have to leave this necropolis to find that."

"Necropolis," I repeated. "Neat word. City of the dead. Let's hope that's not where Hector's going."

She gave me a look which combined embarrassment with irritation. "He'll be all right, Quint." Her face hardened again. "And no doubt that deep-frozen cow will produce an immaculate child as well."

I glanced at her and decided against calling for a guard vehicle to take me to the castle. Katharine needed a walk to work off her indignation. We turned right on to Lauriston Place and headed for George IV Bridge. Hamilton could wait a few more minutes.

"What does she think she's doing?" Katharine raged as she strode over the cracked paving-stones. "Guardians can't bring children up."

"They don't have to," I said, struggling to keep up with her. "The Welfare Directorate's children's homes do that, remember?" The original guardians had tried to do away with the family, offering state care from birth – mainly because able-bodied adults were needed to work full-time. A surprisingly large proportion of parents went along with that, though the new-look, user-friendly Council has allowed more freedom of choice since 2025.

"Why does she want to have a kid anyway?" Katharine demanded. "It made more sense when the guardians shut themselves off from procreation, as the stupid bitch called it. They say she doesn't even know who the father is." She jabbed her elbow into my ribs. "You haven't been at her again, have you?"

"Get a grip, Katharine," I said with a glare. "You know I haven't. Everything finished between Sophia and me when you came back to the city." We passed a pair of stern-looking guardsmen. "Calm down," I said, worried that she was about to come out with an even coarser description of the medical guardian. "I don't know. She probably feels she has to make her contribution to the city's birth-rate." I shrugged. "She's in her late thirties. Maybe her body's putting pressure on her to reproduce."

Katharine flashed an angry look at me. "So women like me who choose not to reproduce – delicate turn of phrase, Quint – are failing in our duty to the city and the species, are we?"

We had to separate as a scruffily dressed elderly citizen on a ramshackle bicycle clattered down the road which used to be overlooked by Greyfriars Bobby. The statue of the wee Victorian dog was blown to pieces by a grenade during the drugs wars – now the plinth bears one of the city's many memorials to auxiliaries and citizens who didn't make it through the Council's early years.

By the time we joined up again Katharine's expression had changed.

"Sorry," she said quietly. "It's not been a very good morning so far."

"No," I agreed. I made a decision. "Do you want to give me a hand with the case I'm working on? Just for today."

Katharine looked at me suspiciously then nodded. "Why not? It won't be the first time."

That was true. She'd been deeply involved in some of my biggest investigations. She was also about as far as you could get from being Lewis Hamilton's cup of auxiliary-issue tea. I told her about the break-in as we walked towards the checkpoint below the Royal Mile. She asked so many penetrating questions that, by the time we got to the castle, I already had second thoughts about my invitation.

The cloud around the castle was even thicker now, shutting out the sights and sounds from the tourist shops and bars on Princes Street.

The guardswoman on duty in the gatehouse told us that the public order guardian was in the command centre. She gave Katharine a dubious stare but she couldn't argue with my Council authorisation – it entitles me to full co-operation from all citizens, auxiliaries and guardians. The Council's occasionally tried to have the wording changed, but I've managed to keep it intact. There's no point in being the city's chief special investigator if guardians can mess you around.

We walked up to the square formed by what used to be the palace and museums. Apart from the Scottish National War Memorial, left unchanged in a rare display of respect for the past by the Council, the buildings are all used by the City Guard now. The command centre is in what was the Great Hall, a tacky late-nineteenth-century restoration of the banqueting hall. The hammer-beam roof has been left but the rest of the decor is grade one barracks drab, the brightly coloured tapestries that used to adorn the walls removed to provide space for city maps, barracks reports and guard rosters. The hall's vast open space gives guard personnel the opportunity to impersonate ants in perpetual motion. They do that very well.

Hamilton met us at the entrance. "What's she doing here, Dalrymple?" he demanded, glaring at Katharine.

That only made me more determined. "She's helping me out, Lewis. If you don't like it, find another investigator."

"Oh, for God's sake, man." He turned away and went to the large central table which was his base camp. "Very well," he said unwillingly. "I suppose we need all the help we can get." He pointed up at the daily situation report board. "Look at that. Two sightings of unauthorised vessels off the coast, three gaping holes cut in the wire on the city line, four youth gangs rampaging in the suburbs—"

"And a partridge in a pear tree," I put in. "Any sign of the bogus workmen or the vehicle they used?"

The guardian shook his head. "All barracks and guard patrols have drawn a blank."

Davie came up. "And no sign of any discarded workmen's gear or clothes," he said. "Morning, Quint." He didn't offer the same courtesy to my companion.

"Katharine's working with us on this today," I said.

"Great," he mumbled.

"What about the scene-of-crime squad and forensics?" I asked, raising my voice above the ringing of numerous phones and the clatter of typewriters – even in the command centre there aren't many computers. "Have they found anything hot?"

"Not really." Davie ran his eye down a clipboard. "The traces of blood you found on the floor and the file are both group O. They haven't found any fingerprints on the file covers or in the archive generally."

"All our burglars were wearing gloves," I said. "Anything on the footprints?"

Davie shrugged. "Three different sets under the rubble from the roof. All standard-issue work-boots, sizes seven, ten and eleven." He looked up. "Only prints from the size eleven boots were found in the stack where the file was taken, and not many clear ones there."

"He was trying to cover his tracks," I said. "Lucky we found the blood spots." I rubbed the stubble on my jaw. "And maybe he was the only one who knew what they were after."

"You keep saying 'he'." Katharine's voice was sharp. "How do you know it wasn't a woman?"

"With size eleven feet?" Hamilton scoffed.

"It wouldn't be the first time a woman's disguised herself by wearing over-size footwear," Katharine replied. She was right. That reference to one of the city's worst murder cases back in 2020 didn't exactly lighten the atmosphere.

"How about the files?" I asked. "Any others missing?"

"We've only just started checking that," Hamilton said. "I had to ring round my colleagues in advance of the Council meeting to obtain authorisation for these restricted files to be seen by people beneath the rank of guardian. A team of senior guard personnel is going through them now. When they've finished checking the files we took from the shelves close to the one that was tampered with, they'll go down to the archive and start on the other stacks."

"Hell of a job," I said.

"It's a sealed archive," the guardian said. "We have to

know if anything else has been taken." He glanced at me. "Speaking of authorisation, you've been given permission to examine the file with the attachment missing." He looked at Katharine and Davie. "You and no one else."

I nodded, feeling Katharine stiffen beside me. Davie didn't look too impressed either.

"How about the job authorisation?" I asked.

"Fake," Davie put in. "There's no duplicate copy in the Labour Directorate."

"Aren't those forms numbered?"

"They are, Quint," Davie replied. "Unfortunately the sentry didn't note the number."

"No, but the likelihood is that someone took a form from a block."

Davie nodded. "I've got the Labour Directorate checking their unused blocks. They're also compiling a list of everyone who had access to their stationery stores."

"Good enough." I turned to the guardian. "Any sightings of the pick-up and the equipment taken from the depot?"

His lower jaw jutted forward. That was never a good sign. "I've dragged the auxiliaries in charge over the coals. I don't think any of them were involved." He glowered at me. "I think I've motivated them sufficiently to ensure they squeeze their subordinates hard." No doubt he'd reminded them of the joys of picking potatoes at this time of year.

"Right," I said. "Where's that file?"

"In my quarters," the guardian said. "It's not to be moved from there."

"What do you want me to do, Quint?" Katharine asked.

"Well," I replied, smiling thinly at Lewis and Davie.

"You can either stay here with these gentlemen . . ." I broke off as their eyes opened wide in horror at the idea of a DM like Katharine remaining in the command centre ". . . or you can come with me and check the whereabouts of various individuals we want to talk to."

"She's not to see the contents of that folder, Dalrymple," the guardian warned.

"Don't worry, Lewis," I said over my shoulder. "You can trust me."

As we walked out into heavier drizzle, I remembered Hamilton's unease about the subject of genetic engineering. And wondered exactly how much I could trust him.

CHAPTER FOUR

There was another of the public order guardian's thin-faced, middle-aged secretaries in his outer office. She took one look at my authorisation, one look at Katharine and got on the phone to her boss. While she was doing that, I relieved her of the key to his main office and let us in. Then I locked the door on her – well, Hamilton was very uptight about security.

Katharine raised an eyebrow. "Why did you do that, Quint?"

"Because I want to ravish you on Lewis's conference table." I pulled her towards the glistening mahogany surface and got a slap that made my ear ring. "Shit, I was only joking."

Katharine's eyes flashed. "Ha-ha. I am definitely not in the mood, Quint."

"I noticed." I went over to Hamilton's desk. It was in its usual pristine condition, the pens and pencils neatly lined up and the furniture polish glinting under the bright fluorescent light the guardian favoured. No grey areas in his office – or in his life. The dark blue folder, sheathed in a clear plastic bag, was sitting in the in-tray. I took it out. "Right, this is for you, Katharine," I said, extracting the cover sheet.

She looked at it. "What do you want me to do?"

"See the list of committee members? I need to know which of them are still in the city. They might be able to tell us why the file attachment was stolen."

Katharine frowned. "Is this another joke? The list's twenty-five years old. Most of the people on it are probably dead." She ran her finger down the page, counting under her breath. "Fifteen names. Only two women, of course." She gave me an acid smile. "Can I use the guardian's computer?"

I looked at the pre-Enlightenment machine in the corner. "Of course. Why do you think I locked the door?" The guardians have always restricted access to the Council's limited databanks – supposedly because computers are too expensive for the city to afford, but in reality so that they can control the flow of information. Lewis Hamilton detested the machines and he'd let me use his in the past. I'd omitted to ask him this time, though.

Katharine went over and switched the computer on. "Do you know the passwords?"

I nodded. "He never changes them like he's supposed to. Try 'colonel' every time you're asked." I looked up from the file. "You do know how to work one of those, don't you?"

Katharine let out a sigh. "What do you think I do most days?"

"Interview male young offenders?"

"That – and then write up their profiles."

"The Welfare Directorate has computers for that?" I asked in surprise. Most of the city's bureaucracy is driven by pencil power.

Katharine looked over her shoulder. "There's been such an increase in youth crime that the welfare guardian forced his colleagues to approve computerisation of the records. I thought you'd have known that."

I shook my head. "I just catch the little bastards."

"About one in fifty of them," Katharine said. "In a good month."

I couldn't think of a reply to that so I got down to reading the file.

After a couple of hours I'd had enough. The jackass who'd written up the minutes was fluent in the kind of civil service jargon that had a lot to do with the break-up of the old United Kingdom – if government documents had been comprehensible to the man and woman in the street, maybe people wouldn't have taken so much pleasure in torching ministries and hanging bureaucrats from the lamp-posts.

The gist of it was that the committee had been badly split over the granting of licences and partial funding for two new lines of research. One, which the members had decided by a narrow majority to approve, concerned the use of fetal material for transplant into adults. That was referred to in committee as "Fet-mat" and a full specification of the proposed research was contained in the first attachment. I had a go at reading that and soon gave up. Scientific English is even more tortuous than bureaucrat-speak and, anyway, there seemed no point in trying to understand it – the burglars apparently weren't interested in it.

Which left the research outlined in the missing second attachment. The committee members had been even more split over it, several of them arguing in an uncharacteristically resolute fashion that the procedures and ends were unethical. But that was about as much as I got from the minutes. The committee ranted on about "ethically monstrous" and "grossly immoral" but nothing was said, or at least recorded, in sufficient detail for me even to hazard a guess at what the research involved. Maybe the writer was incapable of producing transparent prose; or maybe he'd been told to make his text opaque to ensure that no hint of the research's nature remained. My suspicious mind automatically leaned towards the latter.

That wasn't all. While the Fet-mat research proposal had an abbreviation drawn from the relevant terms, the work specified in the missing attachment was referred to only by the numbers "4.1.116". That was about as much help as a citizen-issue sou'wester in a rainstorm.

I picked up Lewis's phone and called Davie. "You know those senior auxiliaries who're combing the files from the archive?"

"What about them?"

"I need them to check something else."

"I'm sure they'll be delighted to help." His tone was unusually sharp.

"Hey, lay off, big man. It's not my fault that the guardian doesn't want you reading this file. You're not missing much, I can tell you."

He was quiet for a while. "Okay. Sorry. I am a chief commander, for Christ's sake. You'd think he could trust me."

"I would. Anyway, look, I need them to see if they can locate a copy of the missing attachment. It's ATT2 from GEC/02/04. Maybe we'll be lucky and it'll turn up as a cross-reference somewhere."

"Are you relying on luck already, Quint?"

"Are you in need of a pencil up your—"

"No." There was a buzzing in my ear.

Katharine turned round in the swivel-chair at the computer. "Boys being boys as usual?"

"Pathetic, isn't it?" I said. I stood up and went over to the leaded windows. There wasn't much to see under the dull sky – just grey-black buildings and bare trees in the gardens below.

I found myself thinking about Caro. Hector's faux pas had brought her back to me strongly despite the passage of time. It sometimes happened that way. She'd be absent from my thoughts for months and, suddenly, something unexpected would remind me of my first lover. Her dark hair and brown eyes, her glowing face and her beautiful smile would return vividly for a short time, then disappear back into the void. The break-in and the file had already conspired to resurrect her, prompting memories of the time when we were first together in 2002.

I wondered how Edinburgh would strike her now. She'd been a fervent supporter of the Enlightenment – Christ, we all were in the old days – but I was pretty sure she wouldn't approve of the way things were coming apart. The problems with the city's young people would have depressed her. She always loved kids, although we never considered having any of our own. We'd already broken the regulations by committing ourselves to each other in secret. Like ordinary citizens, auxiliaries at that time were supposed to take a different partner at the weekly sex session and pregnancy was controlled by the Medical Directorate's worryingly named and now disbanded Auxiliary Reproduction Department.

"Quint?" Katharine's voice brought me back to the present.

I went over to her. "What have you found?"

She held up several pages of print-out with a lot of red

ink on them. "Not very much. There were fifteen names on the list, right? Eight were full committee members with voting rights – that is, Members of the Scottish Parliament. In addition to them, there were five scientific advisers, a senior official from the English and Welsh Ministry of Health and a civil servant who took the minutes."

"Okay." I pulled a chair over from the conference table and sat down beside Katharine in front of the screen. "Have you managed to track any of them down?"

She nodded. "It's not good news though. None of the eight MSPs is in Edinburgh now. Six of them had constituencies elsewhere—"

"Where exactly?" I interrupted.

Katharine looked at her list. "Three in Glasgow, one in the Borders, one in Fife and one in Shetland."

"We can write all of them off," I said. "The democrats in Glasgow would have strung up anyone tainted by membership of the Scottish Parliament. The others will either be long dead or standing guard over their crofts." Over the years we occasionally got reports of traditional farming methods being used in the outlying areas where the marauding gangs couldn't be bothered to swing their battle-axes on a daily basis.

"The two from Edinburgh are no use either. One was killed in a drugs gang attack on the Parliament buildings in 2003—"

"There were plenty MSPs who went that way," I interjected.

"And the other died of food poisoning in 2012."

"Another victory for the Medical Directorate."

Katharine nodded. "That leaves the scientists and the bureaucrats."

"We can forget the guy from the Sassenach ministry. He'd have gone scuttling back to London as soon as the riots started. Not that he'd have been any better off there."

"I got excited when I checked the minute-taker's records," Katharine said.

"Did you now?"

She gave me a cool look. "Not that excited. George Darling was his name. He joined the Enlightenment Party a month before the last election."

"No doubt he saw which way the wind was blowing."

"No doubt. Later he was an auxiliary in the Science and Energy Directorate."

I sat up straight. "Oh aye. What was he involved in there?" I'd come across some nasty secrets in that directorate in the past.

Katharine was aware of that. "Calm down. He was nailed for possession of cigarettes in 2006. They sent him down the mines for a month, but he collapsed and died after two weeks." She shook her head. "Bastard Council."

I touched her arm. She'd been on the receiving end of the guardians' hard-line corrective policies herself and it didn't take much to bring back the three years she'd spent on Cramond Island, Edinburgh's version of Alcatraz.

"That leaves the five scientists," she said after a few moments. "They aren't much use to you either."

I groaned.

"Two were from the University of St Andrews and one from the University of Glasgow." Katharine pointed to three large red crosses she'd put on her print-out. "There's no record of any of them being present in Edinburgh after the Council came to power."

"What about the other two?"

"Professor Dorothy Taylor from the University of Edinburgh and Doctor Gavin Godwin from Heriot-Watt."

"Ah-ha." I looked at her expectantly. "And?"

"Well, you're half in luck. One of them's still in the city." She glanced at her list and the notes she'd added in the margin. "Doctor Godwin. He's in a retirement home in Royal Terrace. He was an auxiliary after independence – he was granted exemption from the training programme because of his age. He worked in the Animal Resources Centre at King's Buildings until 2020."

"What age is he?" I asked.

"Eighty-five."

"Christ. I hope his memory's still in action." I looked at the print-out. "And the professor?"

Katharine twitched her head. "Nope. Deserted in 2009. Never been seen or heard of since."

"What was she doing until then?"

She gave a brief laugh. "Making meat pies."

"Making meat pies," I repeated. "You don't need to be a professor to do that."

"Anything goes in this city," Katharine said sarcastically. "The professor refused to acknowledge the Council or co-operate with the Science and Energy Directorate. So she stayed an ordinary citizen and was assigned work in the Food Production Department. Her last place of work was a factory in Saughton."

"Conveniently located near the city line," I said. "Back then the wire fences weren't the height they are now."

Katharine pushed back her chair and stood up. "That's it, I'm afraid." She bent over me. "Are you going to tell me what's in that file now?" she asked in a low voice.

"No."

She put her hand on my shoulder. "I feel a bit more in the mood now."

I looked round and caught her sizing up the guardian's conference table. "You don't catch me with that old—"

Her mouth came over mine and her hand moved down my chest.

Then the key rattled in the lock and there was a thumping on the door.

"Dalrymple?" Hamilton shouted. "Open this bloody door!" The pounding started again.

"Saved by the bang," Katharine said, giving me a wistful smile.

We managed to turn off the computer and move Katharine's papers on to the conference table before the guardian broke the door down.

"What took you so long, man?" Hamilton demanded, eyeing us suspiciously.

I shrugged. "We were busy. How about you?"

"I haven't exactly been having a rest-day," the guardian said, moving towards his desk then stopping when he saw the mess I'd made of it. "I've just finished chairing the Council meeting." He gave me a sharp look. "My colleagues expect you to clear up the break-in without delay."

"Do they really?" I glared at him. "Don't they expect your directorate to come up with any sightings of the burglars, Lewis?" It's always a good idea to remind guardians of their own shortcomings.

Hamilton twitched his head but didn't respond.

"Uh-huh." I beckoned to Katharine. "We're going to interview a scientist who was on the committee."

Lewis's eyes sprang open. "Who's that?" he asked

71

quickly, then tried to mask his interest by looking at the carpet.

"Gavin Godwin," Katharine said.

The guardian turned away and hung his tweed jacket up on a hook inside his spartan washroom.

"Lewis?" I said, going over to him. "Do you know him?"

He glanced at Katharine but kept his eyes off mine. "Em, no. Not personally. I . . . I just had the idea that all the members died or left the city years ago."

I stared at him. "Apparently not."

He looked at me then pushed past.

"Let me know what you find out," he said, starting to collate the pages I'd left strewn across his desk. "By the way, my people in the archive have found no copies of the missing attachment. There aren't even any references to it in the files they've checked so far."

"Brilliant," I muttered as I headed for the door.

"They'll keep looking," Lewis called after me.

"A needle and a haystack spring to mind," I said over my shoulder. "Or maybe just a haystack."

We picked up a couple of dodgy-looking sandwiches from the castle mess and ate them on the way to the esplanade. The cheese was hard, the butter was bogus and the pickle made my lips smart, but at least the bread was fresh – if a bit gritty. On the way down the drawbridge I pulled out my mobile and rang the infirmary.

"No change with the old man," I said after I'd finished the call.

Katharine felt for my hand and touched it briefly. "That's good."

The first vehicle in the line was a Land-Rover that

looked like it had spent several years at the bottom of a loch. Who knows? Maybe it had. The guard would be lost without its squad of specialist mechanics. They work continuous shifts to keep the fleet of pre-Enlightenment wrecks on the road.

A barrel-chested driver who'd had me in the front of his Land-Rover a few times in the past stepped forward enthusiastically.

"Afternoon, Citizen Dalrymple. Where can I take you?"

I'd already decided he was surplus to requirements. "Not today, Scott 139," I said, extending my hand for the keys. "Go and get yourself a cup of tea."

He raised his eyes to the leaden sky. "Tea?" he grumbled. "Nettles stewed in sheep's piss, you mean." He gave me a fierce look. "Make sure you take care of the roller."

"Yeah, yeah," I said. Guard Land-Rovers picked up that designation fifteen years back, when their suspensions began to suffer from the lack of genuine replacement parts. Their drivers have become over-attached to them.

When we were shaking and rattling towards Castlehill, Katharine leaned across and put her hand on my arm. Then she started to dig the points of her fingers in hard.

"Ow! What are you doing?" I gasped, braking to let a Supply Directorate truck stacked with grey bog-rolls negotiate the checkpoint.

"Tell me what that file's about," she said insistently.

"Shit! Let go, Katharine. Why do you think I sent the driver away?"

The pressure disappeared.

"Ah," she said, smiling. "Sorry. I should have known you would do the opposite of what the old tyrant in the castle told you."

I drove slowly through a group of tourists outside the Camera Obscura, getting a filthy look from their guide as his charges were forced to press themselves against the walls of the narrow street.

"It's nothing to do with Hamilton's orders," I said. "There's no point in you working with me if you don't know the whole story. Anyway, I know I can trust you." I glanced at her. "Can't I?"

Katharine caught my mocking tone but didn't respond to it. There had been times when I'd had what turned out to be misplaced suspicions about her and her bitterness towards the regime, but I reckoned I'd got beyond that now. So I told her about the minutes of the Genetic Engineering Committee and the missing attachment.

"And you've got no idea what this mysterious research was into?"

I shook my head. "Something sensitive enough to outrage most of the members of the committee."

"It must have been bad then," Katharine said ironically. "MSPs would go with anything as long as the backhanders were big enough."

I felt the Land-Rover's ancient steering jerk as the wheels slid over the soaking cobbles. "If what Hamilton said about there being no other copies of the attachment in the archive is right, we'd better hope that Doctor Gavin Godwin opens up to us."

The drizzle suddenly turned to rain and I switched the windscreen wipers on. They squeaked like demented lemmings in search of a cliff. For some reason that immediately brought the Council of City Guardians to mind.

Royal Terrace is one of the few streets in Edinburgh that were allowed by the rabidly republican Enlightenment to retain their names. Even in the early years of the Council tourism was king, so to speak, and it was recognised that many visitors wanted to commune with what remained of the city's regal past. So, although the city's children are taught that disillusion with the monarchy had been a major cause of social unrest at the beginning of the millennium, the central tourist zone retains an element of majesty — alongside the racetrack, souvenir shops and stripjoints.

I drove along the elegant Georgian terrace on the north of the Calton Hill, its upper slopes with the soot-encrusted monuments swathed in fog, and pulled up outside the retirement home. I wondered if this lead was what we needed to make sense of the break-in and felt my heart begin to beat faster.

"This is a bit flashy for a bunch of old people," Katharine said, gazing up at the high façade.

She was right. Although my father's home had once been a grand mansion, it was a long way out of the centre and it didn't have window-boxes filled with multi-coloured blooms.

"This is a place for former auxiliaries that the Council approves of," I said, pushing open my door. "Trouble-makers like Hector got stuck in with ordinary citizens — not that he cares. The arselickers are trusted not to disturb the tourists in the hotels down the street so they're put up in style."

"Very egalitarian," Katharine said as she joined me on the pavement.

"Who said anything about the Council being interested in equal rights for all?" I asked. "Apart from for all Council members and auxiliaries, of course."

We went up the steps and entered the building. My boots sank into a carpet that a pasha would happily have rolled around on with his harem.

A male nursing auxiliary in a tight, well-pressed white tunic came out of a side-office like one of the heat-seeking missiles the Iraqis used on Airforce One in 2001.

"Identification?" he said, running an eye down my less-than-pristine black sweatshirt and trousers.

"Please," I said before flashing my Council authorisation. I reckoned that would take the breeze from his spinnaker.

"Citizen Dalrymple," he read. His face was impassive as he wrote my name on his clipboard. "Purpose of visit?"

"None of your business, Simpson 357. Where can I find Napier 77?" That was Dr Godwin's barracks number.

He ignored me. "Identification," he said, sticking his hand out at Katharine.

"She's with me," I said, taking her arm.

"Identification," he repeated, keeping his eyes off me. "Please," he added in a low voice.

Katharine took a plastic-covered card from her pocket and held it up to the auxiliary.

That really did becalm him. It was an undercover operative's pass, known to all as an "ask no questions". I'd got one for Katharine on a case years ago and she'd held on to it.

"Can we see Napier 77 now?" I asked with a cold smile.

Simpson 357 nodded. "Second floor, room number 23."
We walked past him.

"Em, citizen," he called after me. "Don't expect to get too much sense out of him. He sometimes rambles."

"Wonderful," I said as we reached the stairs.

"Look on the bright side," Katharine said. "He could have had a stroke or a heart attack." She raised her hand to her mouth. "Shit. Sorry."

I started climbing. "Like I said. Wonderful."

The door to room 23 was ajar. I craned my head round and was rewarded with the sight of a small man standing in the middle of another top-quality carpet. He was urinating into a bedpan.

"What do you want?" he demanded. "Can't I even piss in peace?" He gave a breathless laugh. "Piss in peace? That's not bad." He had a heavy West Coast accent. The first Council banned all dialects and accents in an attempt to do away with socially divisive factors, but this guy had probably been too useful to be strongarmed.

"Right, I'm done," he said, holding the bedpan out to me. "Go on, take it. It won't bite." Napier 77 sat down in an armchair and wrapped a tartan rug round himself. He was a scrawny figure with thin, grey hair and large ears. I wondered if he was a man or a mouse.

"Who are you then?" He looked past me. "And who's your much better-looking friend?"

"Dalrymple's the name," I said, showing him my authorisation. "Call me Quint. And this is Katharine."

"Are you a special investigator too, dear?" the old man asked, giving her a smile that deepened the fault-lines on his face.

"Something like that," Katharine replied with barely concealed distaste.

I deposited the pisspot under the bed and moved between them before more than sparks started to fly. "Nice place you've got here, Napier 77."

"You think so?" he said, looking at me like I was a congenital idiot. "A mincing wanker in charge, a gang of dribbling yes-men for company and one copy of the *Edinburgh Guardian* for the lot of us? Aye, it's very fucking nice." He glanced at Katharine to see if his swearing had any effect. He was disappointed. "And stop calling me by that bloody number. Your lords and masters have turned the city into a colony of automata."

"I quite agree, Doctor Godwin," I said. That seemed to mollify him a bit.

"Gavin will do, Quint." He laughed again, the breath hissing faintly in his throat. "Quint. What kind of a name is that? You sound like a pirate out of *Treasure Island*."

That got a smile out of Katharine.

"Now we're on first-name terms," the old man continued, "tell me what you're doing here. Don't tell me the Council's finally decided to run me in for discourtesy to my fellow auxiliaries?"

I shook my head. "How's your memory, Gavin?"

"In perfect working order," the old man replied. "Quint? Is that short for something, son?"

I wasn't going to enlighten him. "The year 2002," I said.

"Oh aye?" He seemed to be watching me more carefully now. "What about it?"

Before I could answer a series of noises that made the hairs on my neck rise came from the bed. They were high-pitched and rapidly repeated, a cross between a wail and howl.

"What the hell's that?" I said, looking round.

"Uch, don't worry about him," Godwin said. "Come out of there, Cerberus."

Katharine and I exchanged glances as a black form manoeuvred itself from beneath the pillow. It stood peering at us, then jumped down and ran over to the old man.

"You call your cat Cerberus?" I asked, trying to work out what it was about the animal's appearance that didn't make sense. It was larger than your average domesticated feline and the short fur was thick and curly. Then it started washing itself and I felt my stomach flip. "Jesus."

Gavin Godwin laughed. "I did think of calling him that, but I reckoned the science and energy guardian would have taken it as an attack on the Council's atheist principles."

"What happened to its mouth?" I asked, staring at the heavy jaws and fearsome teeth.

"*His* mouth," Godwin said. "Cerberus is definitely male. Just look at his reproductive organs."

I bent down and clocked what looked very like a dog's dick and bollocks.

"He's a hybrid," Katharine said, her voice faint. "You crossed a cat with a dog."

The old man nodded. "Crossed hardly does justice to the complexity of the process, but yes, in layman's terms that's what I did. The Supply Directorate was having terrible problems with rats – big, ferocious bastards that nested in the old railway tunnels beneath the main depot in Waverley. So I came up with this little laddie and his pals. The cunning and ruthlessness of a Siamese combined with the speed and bite of a terrier."

"Didn't Cerberus have three heads?" I asked.

Gavin Godwin stretched a hand down – something I definitely wouldn't have risked – and scratched the creature's chin. It looked up at him, slanting its green eyes and making a strangulated purring noise that did nothing to reduce the impression of otherworldly viciousness.

"I put forward a research proposal along those lines," the old man said, leaning forward excitedly. "Think of the carnage three-headed rat-catchers could have generated." Then he twitched his head. "My idiotic superiors thought it would cause unrest in the depot. They used it as an excuse to retire me. That and the fact that being over eighty apparently means you're ga-ga." He stuck his finger into his pet's mouth and ran the nail along the line of solid teeth. The animal stopped purring and gave a cautionary growl. "No, the point of the name is that the first two embryos didn't come to fruition. Cerberus was the third so I gave him that name to preserve the memory of his brothers."

"Unusually sentimental for a scientist," I said.

The old man gave me a blank look. "Cerberus was also the guardian of the ancient underworld, you know."

"Which must make you Pluto," I said under my breath. "Getting back to 2002, Gavin."

He nodded slowly. "Aye. What are you after?"

"You were an adviser to the Scottish Parliament's Genetic Engineering Committee."

"I was," the old scientist agreed. "Along with several colleagues. Are you talking to them too?"

"None of the others is in Edinburgh," I said. "Unless you know different."

"No, no. I haven't seen any of them since independence."

"In April of 2002 there was a meeting that dealt with two research proposals."

Gavin Godwin was staring at me but he wasn't giving me any help.

"The first was called Fet-mat. It was approved."

He moved his head so slightly that I wasn't sure if he'd nodded.

"And the second was referred to as 4.1.116." I was watching him closely. His eyes, pale brown and narrowed, didn't give anything away. "Do you remember that proposal?"

Godwin shook his head slowly, squeezing his pet's ear.

"No?" I asked. "Are you sure? It caused a lot of argument on ethical grounds."

"Careful, Cerberus," the old man said quietly. "You don't want to hurt your creator, do you?" The animal was growling in what sounded like an affirmative way to me. "Do you know how many of those committee meetings I had to attend?" Godwin demanded. "The university started docking my salary eventually. Not that it mattered. It wasn't long till the drugs gangs ransacked Heriot-Watt and burned it to the ground."

"Proposal 4.1.116," I repeated. "Think about it. The research was outlined in an attachment."

"That was standard procedure," Godwin snapped. It looked like I was getting to him.

Katharine went up to him and knelt down by Cerberus. She even had the nerve to stroke the creature's furry back. He seemed to like it. His master was impressed too. He smiled slackly.

"Did you get a personal copy of the minutes and the attachments, Gavin?" Katharine asked in a low voice.

The old man's cheeks began to redden. I had the feeling the only women who'd been near him recently smelled of rubbing alcohol and haemorrhoid cream.

"Did you?" Katharine pressed.

Godwin looked away and shook his head. "No. We were given copies of the attachments to read before the meetings and we got the minutes to approve afterwards. In both cases the committee secretary's office retrieved all documentation." He shrugged his shoulders underneath the rug. "It was all top secret, of course."

"Of course," I muttered. "So we'll have to rely on your memory, Gavin." I smiled encouragingly. "Which you said is in perfect working order."

He looked at me shakily. "Well, almost perfect—"

"Rubbish!" I yelled, trying to shock him into talking.

Bad idea. Cerberus leaped to his hairy feet and came scrabbling towards me like a mouth on legs.

"Shit," I gasped, aiming a kick at him. It missed but that only made him more ferocious. I felt the points of his teeth through the leather of my boot.

Godwin fumbled in his pocket, pulled out a small metallic object and put it to his lips. His cheeks inflated, making him look more like a chipmunk than a mouse. I couldn't hear anything but the animal crashed to the floor and wrapped his front paws over his ears. I'd have burst out laughing if I hadn't been so worried about my foot.

"Don't worry," the old man said. "You won't need an anti-tetanus. Cerberus is clean of all infection. I built that into his system."

I wiped the creature's saliva off my boot on the curtain and turned back to the scientist. "Are you sure you can't help us on that research? What was it about?"

Gavin Godwin turned up his hands. "I can't recall. I'm pretty sure it didn't have anything to do with animals. That would have stuck."

Before I could make my mind up whether I believed him or not, my mobile rang.

"Quint? Where are you?"

"Retirement home number 20 in Royal Terrace, Davie."

"Get out of there fast. I'll meet you at the entrance to the Botanic Gardens in Arboretum Road." His voice was unusually tense.

"What is it?"

"Dead male auxiliary. Circumstances extremely suspicious."

"Bloody hell." I beckoned to Katharine. "We're on our way. Out."

I exited Godwin's room so quickly that even Cerberus was left for dead.

CHAPTER FIVE

I drove across Leith Walk, heading north-west through what used to be Edinburgh's gay quarter, the so-called Broughton Triangle. It still has that orientation, but the bars and clubs are for tourists only. The Council has no problem with homosexuality – given that the regime was founded on the doctrines of Plato, that would be one display of hypocrisy too many – but citizen liaisons are handled in leisure centres outside the tourist zone.

"Did you believe that old crazy?" Katharine asked, bracing herself as I swerved round a corner.

"About not remembering the research project? I'm not sure. He didn't strike me as being particularly senile."

"What about that pet of his? Poor thing. It must be suffering from a major identity crisis."

"Poor thing?" I braked as a football bounced across the road in front of me. A small girl stood with her mouth open at the sight of the guard vehicle. She was probably even more shocked when I didn't stop and take her name. "Cerberus is without question the most loathsome creature I've ever come across." I glanced at her and grinned. "And that includes senior auxiliaries."

Katharine ignored that observation. "It's not the animal's fault," she said. "I thought genetic engineering wasn't allowed in this city."

We crossed the bridge over the Water of Leith beyond Canonmills and approached the Botanics.

"Maybe its genes weren't engineered or modified," I said. "Maybe Gavin Godwin wasn't being straight with us. He might just have found a way to make dogs fancy cats."

"Come on," Katharine scoffed. "He was on the Genetic Engineering Committee. He obviously knew how to fiddle around with genes and embryos."

I nodded. "Don't worry. I'll be raising that point with Hamilton. He's been seriously twitchy ever since he saw which file had been tampered with."

Katharine shook her head as I turned into Inverleith Terrace, the branches of the trees in the Botanics hanging over the road. "You'll be far too busy with this suspicious death now to worry about the break-in."

Christ. The dead male auxiliary. I'd forgotten about him. I felt the extra rush that I always get at the beginning of cases involving suspicious death. The increase of youth gang activity has meant that homicide is more common than it used to be under the Council, but there still aren't many murders. Especially not of auxiliaries.

That may have explained why what looked like every guard vehicle in the city had pulled up in Arboretum Road.

"Bloody hell, Davie," I said as he came out of the mêlée of guard personnel. "Haven't these people got anything else to do?"

"This is a bad one, Quint," he said in a low voice. His

face was solemn. "You know what it's like when an auxiliary goes down." He glanced around. "Everyone wants to get involved."

"Where's the body?" I asked.

"I'll take you straight there," Davie replied. His eyes rested on Katharine. "What about . . . ?"

"I'm coming too," she said firmly.

I looked at her. "Are you sure? You've got to go back to work tomorrow, haven't you? There's no point in—"

"Sod the Welfare Directorate," she said. "I'm due some days in lieu anyway. This sounds much more diverting."

"It's definitely that," Davie said, biting his lip. "If you're sure, Quint . . ."

I shrugged helplessly. Arguing with Katharine was never a good idea. Besides, it's useful to have back-up you can rely on.

"This way then." Davie set off towards the gate. Guardsmen and women got out of his way, more because of the thunderous look on his face than his commander's insignia.

We went through the gate into the gardens' seventy acres. A temporary checkpoint had been set up and we had to flash ID. Fortunately the gardens are only open to tourists at weekends as they're outside the central zone. Special buses are organised and guard patrols are increased to ensure the locals don't do anything embarrassing in front of the paying guests – like gawp at their expensive clothes and cameras. At least we wouldn't be bothered today.

Davie bore to the left. "The body's in the copse," he said.

That area of the Botanics is less cultivated than the rest, the woodland and hedges sheltering foreign species of plants. Even in autumn there were patches of colour in the herbaceous border. Birds were hopping busily about the place uncovering worms beneath the carpet of leaves.

"It's over by that big copper beech," Davie said.

"Very appropriate," I said under my breath. The leaves of the great tree, most of them still attached, were a deep burned-red colour which reminded me of the blood-stained scenes of crime I'd experienced too often in my life.

There was a crowd of auxiliaries ahead of us. I made out the scene-of-crime squad and the Medical Directorate examiners pulling on their protective suits. A six-foot-high maroon tent had been erected beside the beech to keep the rain off the corpse and to shroud the scene. A Welfare Directorate child care facility had been built in the northern reaches of the gardens and this obviously wasn't a sight for kiddies. Hamilton and Sophia were standing beside the tent. They were always attracted to suspicious deaths on the grounds of scarcity – like me.

"Guardian alert," Katharine said. "This'll be fun."

I wiped the sheen of drizzle from my face and strode up to them.

"Before we start, let's get this clear," I said. "I want Katharine on the case with me. No arguments, no further discussion."

Lewis and Sophia looked at me blankly for a few seconds then nodded their heads reluctantly.

"We don't have time for this, Quint," Sophia said in a long-suffering voice. "Just make sure she doesn't get in the way."

I nodded and accepted a pair of rubber gloves from one of Hamilton's team.

"My hero," Katharine whispered as she pulled on hers.

"My arse in the fire if you screw up," I hissed.

"Go on, man," Hamilton said brusquely. "Get inside. My people are waiting."

"Not coming, Lewis?" I asked.

The guardian shook his head. "I've seen quite enough." He'd never been good at dealing with corpses. You'd have thought the drugs wars would have acclimatised him.

I opened the flap in the canvas and dropped to my knees to examine the ground inside the tent. A large battery-powered light had been hung from the apex. The grass was sparse around the trunk of the copper beech and there were some scuffed prints. I avoided the clearest ones and moved further in.

The auxiliary was dressed in a standard-issue grey suit and black shoes. He was lying on his left side, knees and arms bent uniformly. It looked like the body had been left in a carefully arranged pose, an impression strengthened by what was in the right hand. A branch had been cut from the beech and the fingers folded round it. The purple-red foliage was covering the dead man's arm and face. There was a lot of blood on the leaves.

"I told you it was bad," Davie called.

I turned round and saw Hamilton shaking his head.

"Can I come in?" Sophia asked.

"How about me?" Katharine added.

"Hold on a minute," I said. "I haven't even seen the face yet."

I edged forward till I was kneeling by the upper abdomen. I didn't want to move anything before photographs were taken so I bent down and peered through the leaves. What I saw made me jerk back uncontrollably.

"God almighty," I gasped.

"What is it, Quint?" Davie asked.

I looked again to make sure. No, I wasn't imagining it.

"Quint?" Sophia said.

"Someone thought this guy didn't see well enough," I said, rocking back on my heels. "So they gave him a third eye."

I finished my preliminary examination and let the scene-of-crime squad get on with photos, sketches, prints and so on. We watched as the branch was removed from the corpse's grip – it was loose, suggesting the branch had been put there after death. Then Sophia and I went back inside the tent.

"What do you reckon?" I asked after she'd inspected the dead man's face.

She sat back, her midriff bulging under the protective tunic. "Very curious. I won't be able to tell for sure until the post-mortem—"

"Of course."

She gave me a disparaging look. "But it would appear that what you described as a third eye is in fact the dead man's own left eye. There's a lot of blood about but if you look carefully you can see that the left eye's been torn out and forced into the cavity that was opened in the frontal bone."

I felt my stomach churn. "You're kidding. Why would anyone want to do that?"

"I'm a doctor, not a psychologist," Sophia said distractedly. "At first I wondered if the wound came from a bullet."

"Not many of those in Enlightenment Edinburgh," I said. "Only the city line and border guards have guns."

She glanced up at me. "Always quick to assume that auxiliaries are the criminals, aren't you, Quint?" She shook her head. "This is no bullet wound. Look at the ragged edges. This was done by a sharp instrument." She pursed her lips. "Wielded by someone with considerable strength. The bone is thick there."

"Jesus," I gasped, "this gets worse by the minute. What kind of sharp instrument? Don't tell me – wait for the p-m."

She nodded. "Exactly. But it would have been something at least six inches long to allow for the leverage required to gouge out the hole. The rough edges suggest it didn't have honed edges and I don't think it would have been pointed – the leading edge would have been at least half-an-inch wide to make that hole."

"A chisel?"

"Mm, possible."

I looked at her. "Not much doubt that this was murder."

"None at all, Quint. He could hardly have committed suicide like this. Or got that hole in his forehead and had his eye moved by accident."

"What about the time of death?"

Sophia put her hands on the head and neck, then ran them down the arms and legs. "Rigor's almost complete. That and the temperature reading makes me say around twelve hours ago. To be confirmed."

"So an hour or two after midnight?" I asked.

Sophia stood up. "Something like that." She stepped over the markers to the tent flap. "I'll be waiting for the body," she said over her shoulder. "The Council will want the p-m to be done as soon as possible."

"I know." I moved over to the body and tried to make

out the barracks number on the left side of the suit jacket. It was pressing into the ground. "Davie! I need a hand."

He appeared, Katharine not far behind him.

"Lift him up from the other side."

Davie did so.

"That's interesting," I said, touching a tear in the jacket fabric. "The barracks number's been torn off."

"Why would the killer do that?" Davie asked.

"Maybe he wanted to keep a trophy," Katharine said, her eyes locked on the mutilated face.

"Or maybe it just got lost in the struggle," I said. "There are some ritualistic elements here – the branch over the face, the third eye. Jesus, look at the side of his head."

I leaned forward again. There was a mass of pulped bone and blood above the ear he'd been lying on.

"Looks like someone smashed his head in," Davie said. "Before or after the eye was taken out?"

I shrugged, briefly wondering about Sophia's failure to spot that injury.

"Meanwhile we have the problem of identifying this guy. I don't fancy getting everyone of auxiliary rank to look at these features and see if they recognise him." I slid my hand into the inside jacket pocket. "Hang on." I pulled out a black leather wallet. "This might help." I opened it and took out a Knox Barracks ID card.

Davie let the body back down on to the ground and leaned across. "It's not a very recent photo but it looks pretty like him."

"Knox 43," Katharine read.

"Date of birth 10.10.75," I continued, "height five feet ten, weight ten stone three—"

"Seems about right," Davie said.

"Hair grey—"

"Check," Katharine said.

"Eyes brown."

Neither of them volunteered to confirm that. The right eyelids were gummed together with dried blood. I had to force myself to look at the eyeball that had been moved from its socket and stuffed into the hole in the forehead. Lidless and not exactly free of blood, it stared out like one of the large, sticky sweets that kids used to suck before the Council banned confectionery on health grounds.

"That one's brown," I said. "Who knows about the other?"

"It must be the same," Katharine said, looking away.

"I'm not sure if we can be sure of anything in this case yet," I said. "But, yeah, the likelihood is that this is Knox 43."

Davie got up. "I'll go and find out about him."

I nodded and ran my fingers into the other pockets. A pristine handkerchief, an auxiliary-issue condom (unused), a pencil and a notebook were my haul. I put them into separate clear plastic bags.

"What do you think, Quint?" Katharine asked. Her face was pale and her hands were quivering. She'd seen plenty of dead bodies in her time, but this one wasn't easy to live with.

I got to my feet and was immediately attacked by pins and needles. Heavy rain began to drum on the canvas above. "What I think is that our friend here needs to be taken to the morgue sharpish. Then we'll have to look for witnesses – not that there would have been too many of them after curfew. Check the guard patrols, check—"

"I don't mean all that procedural stuff," Katharine

interrupted. "I mean what do you think about this killing? It's giving me a really bad feeling." She twitched her head. "Reminds me of the scumbags in the drugs gangs who used to mutilate people for fun." Her eyes flashed at me. "I thought you'd got rid of all those animals."

I took her arm and led her to the tent flap. "So did I, Katharine. So did I."

The rain was coming down in torrents so we ran to the gatehouse where a temporary operations room had been set up. I hoped the forensics people had got all the traces and prints they needed from the vicinity of the body because the Botanics were about to be turned into a titanic sunken garden.

A pimply trainee auxiliary who looked well out of his depth handed us mugs of oily tea. As usual there was no milk. Outside, the pile-up of guard vehicles had dissipated. Hamilton had no doubt told them to get about their business in words of one syllable. An ambulance moved slowly past the checkpoint – Knox 43's last ride.

"Does this place have a sentry overnight?" I asked Davie.

He nodded. "Because of the child care facility at the Botanics." He looked at his notebook. "Raeburn 266 was the sentry on the nightshift. I've already questioned her. She's an experienced guardswoman." He shrugged. "She saw nothing out of the ordinary all night. There was a mist and visibility was poor."

"Also," I said, "the railings were removed for resmelting during the drugs wars so getting in and out of here anywhere along the boundary isn't too difficult."

Hamilton glared at me. "We needed all the iron we could get at that time, Dalrymple. You know that."

"Uh-huh." I turned to Davie. "Any other witnesses?"

"None has come forward yet. I've got auxiliaries from Scott Barracks knocking on all the doors in the area."

"How about the child care facility?" I asked.

"Ah." Davie's cheeks coloured. "I haven't got round to that yet."

It was unlike Davie to overlook a place in close proximity to the scene. That showed how much the body had affected him.

"Don't worry," I said. "We've got the perfect person to handle this. Katharine works in the Welfare Directorate." I looked at her. "Can you go and check the facility out?"

She nodded. "Anyone got an umbrella?"

Hamilton reluctantly handed over his. "Make sure you bring it back," he said.

Katharine peered at it. The words "Public Order Guardian" had been stencilled over the maroon and white fabric. "What possible reason would I have for keeping it?" she asked, then left.

"Don't say a word, Lewis," I warned.

There was a buzz from Davie's mobile. He answered and listened intently, making notes before he rang off.

"That was the command centre. They've pulled the dead man's file." He was suddenly breathless. "Listen to this."

Hamilton and I stepped closer.

"As Knox 43's low barracks number suggests, he was a fairly senior auxiliary," Davie said. The twenty auxiliary barracks were originally set up with fifty members each – they have five hundred-plus now.

The guardian nodded impatiently. "We know that, commander. Continue."

Davie nodded, a faint smile on his lips. "He was also a civil engineer – in charge of the Roads and Power Maintenance Department."

I had a flash of the skeletal figures in workmen's protective overalls outside the Assembly Hall. "Shit. That department's in the Labour Directorate, isn't it?"

"It is," Davie confirmed. "Interesting, eh?"

Hamilton was following the exchange, his head moving from side to side. "Wait a minute, you two. What are you getting so excited about?"

"The break-in at the Scottish Parliament archive, Lewis," I said. "Remember the job authorisation form that your sentry omitted to check up on?"

The guardian's face went as white as his beard. "It came from the Labour Directorate."

"Correct," I said.

"And the pick-up and equipment were taken from a Labour Directorate depot," Davie added.

Hamilton looked at us dubiously. "Aren't you jumping to conclusions? It could just be a coincidence."

"It could be," I admitted. "We'll need to question his colleagues in the directorate and in Knox Barracks – see if there's any evidence that he was unreliable."

"Or that he had any very nasty friends," Davie said, pulling out his mobile. "I'll start lining up people who knew him."

I nodded and looked at the plastic bags I'd spread out on the table earlier. The forensics team would be taking them off to check for fingerprints soon. There wasn't much to go on – apart from the dead man's notebook. I picked it up and slipped it out of the bag.

"Looking for the killer's name and address?" the guardian asked.

I flicked through the pages. The poor-quality recycled Supply Directorate paper was grey, the lines on it almost invisible. Knox 43's handwriting wasn't exactly the copperplate taught in the city's schools but he'd grown up in pre-Enlightenment times. I managed to decipher most of what he'd written – locations he'd been working on (nothing about the Assembly Hall), reports to be completed, that kind of thing. I'd get Hamilton's people to follow up the notes but none of them looked too hot. For one thing, the notebook was new and he'd only written on five pages.

My mobile rang.

"Are you coming to the post-mortem or not, Quint?" Sophia asked. "The body's arrived."

"Right, I'll be up as quickly as I can. Sophia? Anything more on my father?

"He's still stable." She paused. "Don't worry. I think he's past the worst."

"Thanks. I don't think we are though."

"What do you mean?"

"This killing, Sophia," I said. "There are some very worrying aspects to it."

"For instance?"

"I'll tell you later." I wasn't going to talk about a potential link with the break-in on the phone. "Out."

I headed for the door, taking the Land-Rover keys from my pocket. Then my mobile buzzed again.

"Quint?"

"Yes, Katharine."

"You'd better get over here," she said, rushing her words. "I've got a witness."

"To the murder?"

"Looks like it."

"Jesus. I'm on my way. Out."

The p-m would have to wait.

The rain had turned back into drizzle. As I walked across the waterlogged ground all I could hear were myriad drops falling from the trees to the puddles below. Blind Lemon Jefferson was singing the "Risin' High Water Blues" somewhere in the back of my mind.

Katharine was standing at the door of the child care facility underneath Hamilton's umbrella. The single-storey wooden building had been erected inside the Botanics' northern wall, its walls painted in pastel shades. It was one of the Welfare Directorate's better efforts, a bucolic environment for some of the city's most troubled kids. I'd tracked down a singularly persistent pickpocket here a year ago. He was a smiling, freckled boy of ten who'd been separated from his mother when he was a baby. The city had done its best, but I didn't go away with the impression that growing up in close proximity to flowers and trees had been an adequate substitute for parental care.

"What have you got, Katharine?"

"Facility supervisor," she said. "Scott 124. She's in her office."

"Let's go then." I didn't ask her any more questions because I wanted to hear it from the auxiliary's own mouth.

The corridor was festooned with chains of coloured paper and the walls were covered in paintings and drawings. Kids' voices were audible behind every door we passed. They actually sounded happy, which isn't always the case in Welfare Directorate centres – a lot of the supervisors are members of the Mr Squeers Admiration Society.

This one certainly didn't seem to be. Scott 124 was rosy-cheeked and unusually rotund for an auxiliary. Her barracks number and greying hair suggested she was in her late forties, but the quick movements she made as she came to meet us cast doubt on that.

"Citizen Dalrymple," she said, smiling. "I've read about you in the *Guardian*. Have a seat. Some tea? It's a fresh pot."

I'd already had enough of the supervisor's good cheer. I didn't bother resisting the temptation to rattle her.

"Scott 124, I'm told you saw what went on in the gardens last night."

She caught my sharp tone. "Well, I saw something, citizen. I . . ." Her voice trailed away and the smile left her lips.

"Why didn't you call the sentry in the gatehouse?"

The auxiliary bit her lip and glanced at Katharine. No support was forthcoming. "Well, as I told your colleague, there was a thick mist and I couldn't see very well. And . . ." She looked down. "And I didn't want to have the children disturbed at night."

I raised my eyes to the ceiling. A brown and orange papier-mâché spider was dangling above my head. "Tell me exactly what you saw, please."

The supervisor nodded. "As I say, the visibility wasn't good. I was just finishing some reports—"

"The time?" I asked.

"A little after midnight," Scott 124 replied. "I know that because I heard the chimes." She nodded towards a grandfather clock in the corner that had been decorated with streamers and balloons.

"Go on."

She started fidgeting, her thick fingers tapping on the

desktop. "It's . . . it's a bit embarrassing really," she stammered. "At first I thought I was dreaming." She looked at me uncertainly. "You see, I read a lot of fairy stories to the children. And . . . and suddenly I see a bogeyman in the Botanics."

I opened my eyes wide at her. "A bogeyman? What are you talking about?"

"A bogeyman," the supervisor repeated, her voice fading again. Then she shivered and sat up straight. "He was very tall, well over six feet, and wearing what looked like a cloak, you see. I couldn't make out anything else. Then . . . then a light shone and I got a glimpse of his face." Her voice was trembling now. "It . . . it was scarcely human."

I looked at Katharine. She shrugged at me and went over to the woman.

"Try to describe it," Katharine said softly.

Scott 124 licked her lips. "That face . . . the colour was all wrong for a start. It was grey and there were lines across it. Like it had been stitched back together after some terrible injury. And the eyes . . . they stared out of ragged holes."

I glared at Katharine but she shook her head insistently to let me know she hadn't told the supervisor anything about the state of the dead man's face.

The auxiliary looked away. "That was all I saw. Except he had a beard too." She quivered. "That didn't look natural either. It was long and wispy. A funny reddish-brown colour."

"You didn't see anyone else?" I asked.

"No."

"And was your bogeyman carrying anything? Dragging anything?"

"No, citizen. He was bending over but there was mist at ground level and I couldn't make out much. Apart from the light – a torch, I suppose." Scott 124 started chewing her lip again. There was a spot of blood on it now. "I only saw him for a few seconds. Then he was gone."

"I still don't understand," I said angrily. "If the guy looked so horrifying, why didn't you call the guard?"

The supervisor put a podgy hand to her eye. "I was frightened, citizen. Don't you understand? I was frightened when I saw him, frightened for the children." She looked down. "Then when all the fuss started in the Botanics today, I was worried that I'd be blamed for not raising the alarm."

Katharine squeezed her arm. I was pretty sure that the auxiliary wouldn't have opened up to anyone except her.

I got up and put my notebook into my pocket. The idea that the murder might have been carried out by an inhuman monster wasn't exactly making me shake my tailfeather.

I left Katharine to take a detailed statement from the supervisor and went back to the gatehouse. Hamilton was on the phone tearing a strip off some unfortunate subordinate.

"Anything?" Davie asked, looking up from a sheaf of papers.

I filled him in about the bogeyman.

"Sounds to me like that auxiliary's got a problem with the booze," he said.

"Maybe. Have your people check her file, will you?"

Davie nodded then looked at me more closely. "Don't tell me you believe her?"

I shrugged. "Someone deposited Knox 43 here with a copper beech branch in his hand, a dent in his head and a transplanted eye. That's exactly the kind of thing mothers used to scare their kids with in the old days, isn't it?"

"Aye, but a tall guy in a cloak with a face a Prussian duellist would have been proud of? Give me a break." He paused. "He took a hell of chance though, didn't he, Quint? The so-called bogeyman and his mates. What if they'd been seen? This is hardly the most deserted area of the city, even though it's mostly parkland."

"That's what's bothering me, Davie. Why risk being caught? What was so important about leaving the body here? Unless . . ."

"Unless what?"

"Unless these guys are so crazy they don't care who runs into them. They didn't send Knox 43 off into the endless night with much sensitivity, did they?"

"Christ," Davie said with a groan. "What have we got on our hands?"

"Big trouble," I said, turning towards the door. "I'm off to the infirmary."

"Aren't you going to ask if I found out anything?"

I stopped. "Have you found out anything, Davie?" I asked mechanically, still facing the way out.

"Yeah, as a matter of fact I have. The scene-of-crime squad have confirmed that the footprints are from three different pairs of boots. And get this — they reckon they're work-boots like the ones in the archive. They're going to compare the casts when they're dry."

I looked round. "Nice one, big man. What are you doing now?"

"I'm finished here. I thought I'd get up to the Labour Directorate and talk to the dead man's colleagues."

"Okay. I'll see you there later on."

Hamilton broke off from his rant on the phone and eyed me suspiciously. I still wanted a word with him about the Council's attitude towards genetic engineering but that could wait. There was a body to be dissected.

I'd rung Sophia to tell her I'd been delayed, but she still looked unimpressed when I hit the morgue. Or rather, when the morgue's cloying reek of chemicals and decaying bodies hit me.

"I should have started without you," the medical guardian said, pulling up her surgical mask. "I'm sick of waiting for Public Order Directorate representatives to attend post-mortems." Then she looked across at me. "Have you obtained any new information pertaining to the deceased?"

I smiled at that turgid Council turn of phrase as I pulled on a green gown. "Nothing that'll make your job any easier." I didn't think Sophia would be greatly taken by the intrusion of fairy-tale elements into the case.

Knox 43 had been formally identified by a barracks colleague. His body had already been stripped, photographed and washed. The morgue assistants circled the slab busily, plucking hairs, scraping behind fingernails and sticking swabs into orifices. Apart from the facial mutilation and cranial damage, the dead man looked strangely at ease, his knees and arms still bent. He could have been asleep. In Raymond Chandler's terms I suppose he was, but I didn't like the way he'd got into that state.

Sophia was standing by the head. She broke off from

102

the speech she was making into the microphone that hung from the ceiling. "Ready, Quint? I'm going to examine the frontal bone."

I moved up the slab and watched as she carefully removed the displaced eyeball from the jagged hole. She began to clean the cavity of blood and debris. The left socket had been washed out and was sunken, the lids collapsing into it. Sophia called the photographer over and got him to take several shots of the now gaping wound. Then she shone a light into it and probed the depths.

"Quite remarkable," she said. "The instrument – chisel or whatever – penetrated over an inch and a half. It went through the bone and into the frontal lobe of the brain. That would have required massive force."

"Maybe a hammer was used to drive the weapon in," I said, feeling a shiver of apprehension run down my spine. I'd seen the worst the drugs gangs could offer and none of them had ever dealt with anyone that way.

"Possible," Sophia said. She didn't show any sign of being disturbed by the method. She wasn't called the Ice Queen for nothing. "Or a mallet. The damage to the left side of the skull was caused by a blunt instrument. At least three heavy blows, I'd say."

I glanced back down at the body. "Did those blows kill him?"

"They would certainly have rendered him unconscious immediately. Injury caused by splinters of the skull in both areas would subsequently have led to the arrest of brain functions with some rapidity."

I nodded. "So he was killed where we found him?"

"I would say so, yes." Sophia drew her sleeve across her forehead. "There were no scrapes on the ground to suggest he was dragged, were there?"

"No. His shoes weren't abnormally scuffed either. So he was either coerced into going with his killer or killers, or he went along willingly." I pulled out my notebook. "Anything more on the time of death?"

"Not yet. As I told you, the rectal temperature suggested at least twelve hours have elapsed. I'll be testing the potassium level in the eye fluid." She twitched her head. "At least from the eye that's still in situ. I expect that to confirm my earlier estimate of between midnight and one a.m."

I took a last look at Knox 43's forehead. "I don't suppose you've formed any theories to explain why his eye was moved? Or the branch put in his hand?"

Sophia's mask bulged as she exhaled hard. "That's hardly my territory, Quint."

I was afraid she'd say that.

CHAPTER SIX

T he Labour Directorate is a grimy concrete mass at the top of Leith Walk. In pre-Enlightenment times it was the St James Centre, a vast complex of shops and offices so ugly and out of synch with the rest of central Edinburgh that the architects must have been taking the piss. No one takes the piss out of the Labour Directorate though. It determines who gets sent to the mines and the city farms, and it controls citizen work details with a lack of feeling that reflects the original Council's severity – which has made it one of the most hated places in the city as far as the locals are concerned. The tourists are much better off. There are enough shops for them on Princes Street and the Royal Mile, so they don't have to go anywhere near the former shopping centre's dreary portals.

I ran up the steps and flashed my authorisation at a dozy-looking guardsman. He suddenly jerked into activity and lifted his clipboard.

"Hume 253 left a message for you, citizen. He's on the third floor. Room 39b."

Typical Davie, I thought. Guard commander efficiency oozing from every pore. I sometimes wondered why he took time away from his normal duties to work with me. It was because, deep down inside, there was an insubordinate free-thinker struggling to get out. I've always done my best to encourage that alter ego.

Except the bugger wasn't where he was supposed to be. I pushed open the door to room 39b, an archive of work rosters all over the walls, and found a pair of very young trainee auxiliaries trying to swallow each other's tongues.

"Take your time," I said when they eventually noticed me. "Have you seen Hume 253?"

"No," the male said gruffly, his eyes running over my citizen-issue clothes.

I flashed my authorisation. That shook them into line.

"Yes," the female said, contradicting her pal. "He took some records and went that way." She pointed to the left.

"I won't interrupt your work any longer," I said, turning on my heel. In the corridor I pulled out my mobile and called Davie. "Where the hell are you, big man? I could spend years looking for you in this rabbit warren."

"Staff supervisor's office," he said. "First floor. Hurry."

"Stay there till I show up," I said, registering the tension in his voice.

Grey-suited auxiliaries stared at me as I ran down the long corridor and took the stairs in bounds. They might have been in charge of the city's workforce, but none of them looked like they were busting a gut – the dead hand of bureaucracy strikes again.

The male clerk in the supervisor's outer office was polishing the leaves of a large rubber plant. Despite the near tropical temperatures during the Big Heat there weren't many of those around. The first Council regarded indoor plants as a distraction and tried to ban them, but people persisted in bringing them into their homes and workplaces so more recently the ban's been relaxed. Every little helps.

"Go ahead, citizen," the clerk said. "You're expected."

I opened the door and found Davie bending over a desk and an unusually attractive female auxiliary. I smiled at him and he straightened up, looking sheepish. Evidently there was something in the air.

"Bell 18, this is Citizen Dalrymple," Davie said.

"Bell 18." I nodded at the statuesque woman at the desk. She was wearing a tight white blouse that emphasised the heavy curves of her breasts and her black hair was pulled tightly back in a chignon – unusually stylish for a senior auxiliary.

"Citizen." She held her gaze on me for what seemed like a long time and I felt my hands quiver. She was one of those women who do catastrophic things to your self-assurance. "I understand Knox 43 has met with a grisly end."

"That's one way of putting it," I said. "The death is classified information, not to be shared with anyone in the directorate or in your barracks."

She greeted my attempt at laying down the law with an amused twitch of her lips. There was more lipstick on them than you'd expect with someone in her position. The Council lets its servants get away with a lot these days.

"What do you want from me, citizen?" Bell 18 asked, managing to make the question operate on more than one semantic level. She turned and looked up at Davie. "I know what Hume 253 wants."

Davie glanced at her uncomfortably then consulted his notebook. "Lists of Knox 43's work colleagues and current projects; his personal file; directorate facilities he was entitled to enter."

The female auxiliary nodded. "My people are in the process of gathering all that together." She looked across at me expectantly. "What's your pleasure, citizen?"

I wasn't aware that the Council had been recruiting Sirens — I suppose they cost less to feed than your average auxiliary. "I'll settle for your own thoughts on the dead man," I said. "I presume you knew him personally."

Bell 18 got to her feet and went over to the window. Through the mist the Calton Hill and its monuments were just visible, but I didn't waste time trying to make them out. The supervisor's rump and legs, sheathed in tightly cut grey trousers, were almost as spectacular as her upper body.

"Oh yes," she said, "I knew him all right. It's my job to know all the senior staff personally." She glanced over her shoulder at me, her expression suddenly more serious. "But Knox 43 was a difficult man to get to know well."

"In what way?" I asked.

Bell 18 came back to her desk and took out a thick file from the drawer. "These are my private notes on my department heads," she said. "I wouldn't normally show them to anyone." She flashed me a smile. "But in your case I'll make an exception." She shook her head. "Or rather, in Knox 43's case I'll make an exception. Because he was definitely beginning to lose his grip."

That sounded interesting. I watched as the supervisor's carefully manicured fingers detached pages from her file. Then she handed them over and I settled down to read. While I did, a series of auxiliaries came in and laid files and reports on the desk. Davie started leafing through them, but he didn't seem to get as many surprises as I did.

"Jesus," I said, putting Bell 18's pages down after five minutes, "shouldn't you have got help for the poor sod?"

The supervisor's face flushed. "I suppose I should have, yes. But he'd been in the directorate for years. No one wanted him to be reported."

Davie looked up from his papers. "Why? What was he up to?"

"You want a list?" I asked. "Arriving late on shift, leaving early, taking extended meal-breaks, feigning illness—"

"That was only suspected," Bell 18 put in.

"None of that's very serious," Davie said. He was laying on the hypocrisy with a roadworker's shovel. If any of his staff behaved like that, he'd hang them upside down from the castle flag-pole.

"Wait till you hear the rest," I said. "What do you think about purloining directorate material and supplying it to tourists?"

"You make that sound worse than it was," the supervisor said. "It was mainly just pencils and screwdrivers with 'Labour Directorate' stamped on them."

I gave her a dubious look. "How about removing female auxiliaries' underwear from changing-room lockers?"

Davie liked that more than Bell 18 did.

"As I suggested, Knox 43 was going off the rails," Bell 18 said, wringing her hands.

"But you didn't put any of this in his official report?"

The supervisor shook her head. "He was harmless, really he was."

I glanced at Davie. "Did he have access to the directorate depot in Canonmills?"

Bell 18 nodded. "Of course. There's a store of surveying equipment kept there. Knox 43 would have gone down often."

I was thinking about the pick-up and the gear taken by the archive burglars. Had the dead man got them into the depot? And if so, why would he have helped them?

I stood up. "Right, let's talk to his work colleagues now." I looked at the supervisor. "They're not to know about his death, remember. The Council hasn't ruled on publicity yet."

The auxiliary nodded feebly. She wasn't giving off too many Siren vibes now. When the guardians found out she'd been protecting one of her staff, even on humanitarian grounds, her career would hit the wall with a loud crash.

What a waste.

Davie and I left the Labour Directorate a couple of hours later. The light was beginning to fade and the streets had filled with tired citizens making their way home. We stopped on the steps outside the depressing block and watched the mass of humanity flow by.

"What do you think, Quint?" Davie asked. "Was Knox 43 bent or was he just losing his grip?"

"His workmates seemed to think he was pretty harmless, didn't they?" I pointed at the heap of files he had under his arm. "And there's nothing in there to suggest he was on the take – apart from a few souvenirs flogged to tourists."

Davie shook his head. "Why would a tourist want a Labour Directorate screwdriver?"

"To jemmy open the minibar in his hotel room?"

"Maybe," he replied doubtfully. "Do you think Knox 43 could have copied the depot keys and given them to the archive burglars?"

"It's possible. The people you've sent round the Supply Directorate locksmiths might find one who recognises Knox 43's photo," I said. "We've also established that he could easily have slipped into the directorate stationery store and taken a job authorisation form."

The rain started to come down again.

"I'm bloody starving," Davie said. "Let's get over to Knox Barracks. At least they've got a half-decent canteen."

My phone rang before I could pass comment on Davie's appetite.

"Is that you, Katharine? You're very faint."

"Useless machines," she shouted. "I've finished in the child care facility, Quint."

"Took you long enough."

"You know what kids are like. I had to read them stories and play with them before I could get them to talk."

"And did any of them see a bogeyman last night?"

"No, not one. I'm pretty sure they were all fast asleep like they claimed. No sign of concealed fear."

"There wouldn't be if it was concealed."

"You know what I mean, smartarse. By the way, I found out from the staff here that the supervisor is teetotal. So if she imagined the guy under the copper beech, drink probably wasn't responsible. What next?"

"We're going to Knox. Join us there if you want."

"Good," Katharine said. "I could do with a hot meal."

"You're not the only one. Out."

As we walked towards the Land-Rover, I suddenly remembered something. "When I called you in the Labour Directorate, you told me to hurry, Davie. Why?"

He grunted. "You saw the way the supervisor was putting herself about. I was in fear of my life."

"You?" I said with a laugh. "You're a professional skirtchaser."

"Exactly," he said ruefully. "I want to be the one who makes the running."

"Jesus, Davie. It's 2026, not 1926."

He looked around at the clapped-out buses and the poorly dressed citizens, some of them with ragamuffin kids in tow, and asked, "How can you be so sure, Quint?"

There was no reply to that.

Knox Barracks is in Charlotte Square at the west end of Princes Sreet. It's one of the more spectacular auxiliary barracks in the city, located in what was originally a church and subsequently a record office. Its great green dome had disappeared into the early evening murk and the recessed portico gave it the look of an ancient temple, although the insertion of numerous windows into the nineteenth-century façade was a good example of Council-inspired architectural vandalism. Knox Barracks is responsible for providing security for the guardians' residences in Moray Place, though these days its auxiliaries spend as much time overseeing the tourist gambling facilities like the one in the middle of Charlotte Square.

"Right then," Davie said, getting out of the vehicle and moving quickly towards the main entrance. "Refuelling stop."

"Give me a call when you've finished stuffing yourself," I called after him. "I'm going to talk to the commander."

He raised his arm and disappeared inside.

The sentry checked my authorisation and let me pass. I knew where his chief's lair was and headed straight for it, breathing in a mixture of acrid floor polish and damp uniforms.

Knox 01 was having a meeting with some of his subordinates. He dismissed them as soon as he read the note I sent in. "I was expecting you, citizen," he said. "The public order guardian advised me of Knox 43's death and told me to keep it quiet." He nodded at me punctiliously and a drop of sweat fell from his bald head on to a file on his desk. It wasn't hot in the office.

I took out my notebook, keeping my eyes on the commander. He was about fifty, thin and careworn like most senior auxiliaries. He was wearing a guard uniform. Not all barracks chiefs have done time in the City Guard, but Knox commanders are always guardsmen or women because they have to look after the guardians. That wasn't good news for me. Senior guard personnel are harder to put the squeeze on than ordinary auxiliaries.

"So," Knox 01 said uncertainly when I kept quiet. "What do you need to know, citizen?"

"Is that the dead man's file?" I asked.

He glanced down at the maroon cardboard folder in front of him and more drops of sweat landed on it. "It is, citizen." He didn't volunteer to hand it over.

"Anything in it that you're worried about, Knox 01?"

"Certainly not."

"Uh-huh. Did the public order guardian tell you what was done to Knox 43?"

The commander shook his head. "He said that was restricted."

I nodded. "I think I can trust a senior auxiliary like you." I was patronising him because I wanted to see how he would react. I ran through the injuries sustained by his barracks member.

"Appalling," Knox 01 said when I finished, though he didn't look exactly heartbroken. "That kind of attack can't be allowed to happen to auxiliaries."

"Would it matter less if an ordinary citizen suffered such an attack?"

"Em . . . of course not." The commander got to his feet and picked up the file. "Read this. I'll answer any questions you have on it."

That was evenhanded enough, but I was still curious. There was only one way to find out if Knox 01 really was nervous. I ploughed into the file. He got on with his work, only looking up from his papers occasionally.

On the surface everything seemed in order. Knox 43 was in his early fifties. He'd been in the Labour Directorate since 2007 and it had taken him ten years to get beyond the lowest level of surveying staff. His barracks reports confirmed that he wasn't much of a star. His superiors weren't impressed by what was referred to as his "indecisive nature" and his lack of overt commitment to the Council; Knox 43 himself was pretty lukewarm about his achievements and aspirations in the Personal Evaluations that auxiliaries have to write each year.

"Not one of your favourite people, was he?" I said, holding up the Barracks Commander's Notes sheet at the front of the file. Auxiliaries have no chance of promotion without a positive endorsement from their commander.

Knox 01 looked across the desk. " 'More enthusiasm

required,'" he read. "'Insufficient zeal displayed.'" He sat back, shaking his head. "To be honest, citizen, I'd have recommended demotion for him. But you know how it is. We need every serving auxiliary we've got. Every year it's harder to fill the auxiliary training programme." His face set in a bitter expression. "Edinburgh's young people don't seem to care any more."

Whose fault was that, I wondered. If the Council could make up its collective mind whether to set the guard on to kids or let the Welfare Directorate pamper them – or even find a third way between the two extremes – then maybe there would be more co-operation. I kept those thoughts to myself. I had something else to needle the commander about.

"From what I've seen, there wasn't any suspicion that Knox 43 was dirty." I made the comment as innocently as I could. Staying cool tends to make senior auxiliaries lose their rag even more comprehensively.

"Dirty?" Knox 01 looked at me like a virgin who'd spotted the vampire's dental horrors too late. "You mean corrupt?" He stood up and pushed his chair back so hard that it toppled over with a crash. "How dare you, Dalrymple? How dare you suggest that I allowed a rotten apple to remain in my barracks?"

I shrugged. "If you did, I'll find out about it, commander," I said, gathering up the dead man's file. "You can be sure of that." I didn't think that an ultra-conscientious specimen like him would have connived at anything criminal that Knox 43 had been up to, but there was no harm in making him squirm.

"What are you doing with that?" Knox 01 asked, the outrage suddenly absent from his voice. "That's barracks property."

PAUL JOHNSTON

"Don't worry," I said, "you'll get it back." I gave him a cold smile. "When I've finished with it."

I met Katharine as I was crossing the main hall. She'd just flashed her "ask no questions" at a sentry who wasn't concealing his interest in her anatomy very well.

"There you are," I said. "Come down to the canteen. Davie's down there."

"I hope he's left something for us," she said.

"There's always enough food and drink in an auxiliaries' mess hall."

"Unlike in the ordinary citizens' stores."

We went into the basement and entered the cavernous refectory. Heads turned immediately and auxiliaries started examining our citizen-issue clothes dubiously, but no one tried to throw us out. They knew that we must have had authorisations to get past the sentry. That didn't make us look any better in their eyes. If they didn't recognise me, they would assume we were undercover operatives – auxiliaries are almost as suspicious of them as citizens are.

Katharine took a plate of vegetable stew. Before Sophia became medical guardian the only kind of stew you could get contained lumps of bony meat, but she programmed healthier options. That didn't stop your average guardsman stuffing his face with all the meat he could get. I stuck to what the menu board called "Edinburgh Broth" and piled up barracks bread, which is a sight better than what you get in citizen bakeries.

We went to join Davie. He'd covered most of a corner table with empty plates and bowls. The Knox personnel on the neighbouring tables began to move away as soon

116

as we approached. That suited me – I didn't want anyone to hear us talking about their dead colleague.

"Had enough, big man?" I asked.

Davie was clearing away the remains of his banquet. "It'll do me for a while, Quint." He turned to Katharine. "Slumming, are you?"

She had her mouth full so all he got was a glare.

As I spooned soup into my mouth, I looked around the mess hall and tried vainly to get a feel for the dead man. He'd have eaten thousands of meals in the basement, drunk buckets of barracks tea. But already he had disappeared, his involvement with the place gone and nothing left to suggest he'd ever passed through it.

When we'd finished eating, I opened Knox 43's file. "Right, let's split this up." I undid the binding and extracted sections. "Katharine, I'll give you the pages on the dead man's social and sexual activities. I see he was registered as hetero."

"Women's business then," Davie said ironically.

"Shut up, guardsman." I turned back to Katharine. "See if any of the people he was close to are in barracks at the moment and talk to them."

She nodded.

"What about me?" Davie asked.

"You can have the sections on his auxiliary training and his barracks duty rosters. Talk to his contemporaries and try to trace any pattern of abnormal behaviour."

Katharine laughed. "You're an expert on abnormal behaviour, aren't you, Davie?"

"Grow up, you two," I said. "We're investigating a murder, remember."

Davie's face took on a more sombre expression. "What about you, Quint?"

"Knox 43 was nearly thirty when the Enlightenment won the last election. I'm going to concentrate on his life before he was an auxiliary." I looked at my watch. "We'll meet back here in two hours, okay?"

They both nodded.

"And children?" I said.

They froze.

"Try not to get in each other's way."

Katharine left via one exit and Davie via another. It's always good to have a team that gets on.

My mobile rang a few minutes before the two hours were up.

"Quint? Sophia."

I'd forgotten about my old man. "Is Hector all right?" I asked in alarm.

"Calm down," she said, her voice warmer than usual. "That's why I'm calling. I've had the cardiologist's latest report. Your father's doing well. Barring unforeseen circumstances, he'll be moved from the ICU tomorrow morning."

I took a couple of deep breaths. "Brilliant. Is he conscious?"

"He has been, but he's sleeping now."

"Okay. I'll be round later." I looked down at the papers on the table. "Have you got anything more on Knox 43?"

"We're still waiting for the full test results. I don't expect anything radically different to what we know already."

I failed to suppress a laugh.

"What's so funny, Quint?"

"I'm just trying to remember when I last heard a member of the Council use the word 'radically' about anything."

"Oh for goodness' sake," Sophia said, sighing. "What about you? Are you any further on?"

"A bit."

"Well? What have you found out?"

"You'll have to wait for the next Council meeting to find that out. Out."

Katharine sat down opposite me. "Who was that?"

"No one you're interested in." I picked up my notebook and looked at what I'd scrawled on the top page.

"It was her, wasn't it?" Katharine said, keeping her eyes off Davie as he sat down next to her. "The frigid one in the infirmary."

I gave her a cautionary look. "She told me that Hector's condition is improving. That's all that matters to me at the moment, okay?"

Her face slackened. "Sorry."

"Forget it." I took out the dead man's file photo. It wasn't a recent one. A younger Knox 43 stared out at us, his expression a combination of exhaustion and resentment. "What have you got on the deceased, guardsman?"

Davie was shaking his head. "Nothing much. He seems to have been seriously lacking in any kind of drive from the day he applied to become an auxiliary. One of the guys who went through the training programme with him told me he reckoned Knox 43 joined because he didn't fancy life as an ordinary citizen."

"He wasn't the only person who did that," Katharine said.

"No, but the selection panels usually spotted that type from several miles' distance," I said. "What else, Davie?"

Before he could answer, my mobile went off again.

"Dalrymple? Public order guardian." Hamilton still

hadn't got used to the Council's ruling that guardians can use their names instead of their titles.

"Yes, Lewis."

"Get yourself over to the Council building. I've decided to call an emergency meeting."

"What brought this on?" I asked suspiciously. Council meetings take place every day at twelve noon but Hamilton, in his capacity as acting senior guardian, had the power to call additional gatherings.

"Well, some of my colleagues are disturbed by the murder of an auxiliary . . ." His voice trailed away.

I wasn't buying it. "Since when did you care what your colleagues think, Lewis? Have you got something up your guardian-issue shirtsleeve?"

"Just get over there, man. At the double."

"All right." I glanced at my companions. "But Davie and Katharine will have to attend. They haven't had time to brief me yet."

"Very well," Hamilton conceded after a pause. "Out."

The rain was coming down in sheets when we emerged from Knox Barracks. By the time we got to the Land-Rover our clothes were soaked through.

"Bloody hell," Davie said, starting the engine and turning on the lights. "I can hardly see the road."

"Didn't you want me to drive?" I asked.

"No way," Davie said, shaking his head.

"Why not?" I asked innocently. The Council's ban on private cars meant that I hadn't had much opportunity to drive over the last twenty years. Davie had experienced my skills in the past, though I was on my own the time a barracks vehicle I was driving ended up in Leith docks. Nothing to do with me – the brakes were faulty.

Davie pulled away from Knox.

"Don't you want me to tell you what I found out about the dead man?" Katharine asked.

"Aye. You didn't hear everything I got either," Davie said, manoeuvring expertly between a tourist bus and a maroon bollard.

"No point," I said, shrugging. "You'll have to repeat it all for the guardians."

Katharine glanced at me. "Have you discovered something juicy, Quint?"

"Wait and see," I said, trying to draw my thoughts together. Council meetings are tricky – some things you can tell them, others you definitely want to keep to yourself.

"It's years since I've been to a meeting," Katharine mused. "The last one was when they offered me a job."

"Which you, being a totally loyal citizen, turned down," Davie said, peering through the curtain of water that was cascading past the ineffective windscreen wipers.

"That didn't get me off working with you though, did it, Hume 253?" Katharine said bitterly.

"I can drop you at the next corner, Citizen Kirkwood," he replied.

I grinned. Their double act would liven up the Council meeting, as well as give me the chance to concentrate on how the guardians reacted to the murder. Some of my biggest cases turned out to have links with the city's rulers.

The Council meets in an upturned boat. Given the amount of water that was falling from the heavens, I could hardly make out the home of the former Scottish

Parliament, but the architectural metaphor was obvious enough – what we had here was the Edinburgh version of Noah's Ark, housing the survivors of the pre-Enlightenment political system. I hoped it wasn't about to be turned upright by another massive crime wave.

The courtyard was jammed with guardian vehicles. They weren't in much better nick than the City Guard's contraptions, and certainly in much worse nick than the taxis provided for the tourists. Davie got as close to the entrance as he could and we made a dash for it. Another cold shower.

"Go straight into the chamber," a helpful male auxiliary said. "The guardians are all present."

I led the others through the ornate doorway. The Council meeting place was still decked out in its original munificent trappings. The Parliament buildings had been funded by a Westminster government desperate to give the impression that it was handing over the reins of power. Then the riots came. Only this building of the cluster making up the seat of government was left in reasonable shape. The original fittings were beginning to suffer from a serious lack of maintenance.

Three chairs had been put out in the middle of the wooden floor. As we occupied them, the fifteen guardians looked down on us from their seats in the large chamber. Hamilton was in the centre of a daïs in what had originally been the presiding officer's throne. The computers and sophisticated communications systems that each member of the Parliament had been provided with had been removed long ago. But they weren't all that was missing. Now I realised at least one reason for Hamilton's sudden desire for an emergency meeting. The ordinary citizens who, in the drive for openness a few years ago were allowed to act as observers and even provide a daily honorary guardian, were nowhere to be seen. The old bugger was using the provision in the City Regulations which denies citizens access to unscheduled gatherings.

The public order guardian frowned at me and my companions then got the proceedings under way. "You will be aware of the reason for this emergency meeting, colleagues. Citizen Dalrymple and his fellow investigators—" He broke off and gave Katharine a sceptical look after he'd spoken the last word. "Citizen Dalrymple's team are investigating the murder of an auxiliary in the Botanic Gardens last night."

The guardians' faces bore the horrified expressions they reserved for violent attacks on the city's servants. As far as they were concerned, people who lay a finger on auxiliaries should be put up against a wall, as many were during the drugs wars. Things had been a lot quieter on that front; until recently, when the youth gangs started to carry knives and clubs.

Hamilton glanced around his colleagues. "This was a particularly brutal killing, as the medical guardian will shortly describe."

Sophia was sitting with her hands supporting her back, which made her midriff protrude even more than usual. Her face pale, she nodded impassively.

"We will then hear from Citizen Dalrymple and his team," the public order guardian continued.

I sat up with a start. What was the guardian playing at? Something was going to happen before Sophia and the rest of us were allowed to speak. I didn't have to wait long to find out what that something was.

"First I have to tell you about a piece of evidence that

is potentially of great significance." Hamilton paused to make sure that all eyes were on him. "Scene-of-crime personnel from my directorate scoured the area where the body was found with their usual diligence."

Trust Lewis to get in a plug for his people and, by extension, for himself. I looked to my left and caught Katharine's brief sardonic smile.

The public order guardian held up a clear plastic bag with a couple of small, light brown objects at the bottom. "These are cigarette butts." He smiled triumphantly. Smoking had been banned for all Edinburgh inhabitants by the original Council so cigarettes inevitably suggested external involvement in the murder.

"What is the place of origin?" the tourism guardian asked nervously. He was a skinny specimen well known for his single-minded devotion to the interests of the city's visitors.

"Don't worry," Hamilton replied, "your precious tourists aren't implicated." He gave his colleague a look that made clear his dislike of the year-round festival and the people it attracted.

I was wondering what he meant. I got it just before he explained. Shit. Now I knew why the extra meeting had been called. This case was beginning to get out of hand.

"My people found a match to the tobacco and filters very quickly in their files," the public order guardian said, gazing straight at me. "These cigarettes came from the source of most of Edinburgh's present troubles." He paused to increase the tension. "These cigarettes were made in Glasgow."

CHAPTER SEVEN

There was a brief lull, then the Council chamber turned into pandemonium. Eventually Hamilton restored order by pulling out his City Guard whistle and blowing a long, uninterrupted blast. Not bad given the age of his lungs – and of his whistle.

"That will do, colleagues," he declared. "We need to consider all aspects of the case calmly and analytically." He looked round the guardians and brought them into line with the power of his gaze. They were all considerably younger than he was and I'm pretty sure he compared them unfavourably with the members of the original Council – the first guardians had a lot more to worry about than a couple of Glaswegian coffin nails.

Those of us involved in the case were called upon to report. Sophia ran through what she'd already told me, passing round photos of the dead man which made some of her colleagues blanch. The time of death was still estimated at between twelve and one a.m. Knox 43 had no other injuries or illnesses, though his general physical condition prior to death was described as "average to poor". He apparently had some signs of malnutrition – he hadn't been visiting the Knox mess hall as often as regulations prescribe.

"Citizen Dalrymple?" Hamilton said, nodding at me to proceed.

"Citizen Kirkwood and Hume 253 will bring you up to date with their lines of enquiry first," I said, playing for time. I wanted to hear what the others had discovered so I could get my own story straight.

"Thanks a lot," Katharine said under her breath. "Guardians." She pronounced the word like it was a witch's curse. "I can advise that Knox 43 – whose name, by the way, was Donald McBain . . ." She broke off and looked round at the Council members' faces. Although guardians' names had been made public, auxiliaries were still supposed to be known only by barracks numbers – something about them being anonymous servants of the city.

"Get on with it," Hamilton barked.

Katharine smiled. She'd made her point. "Right. Knox 43 was a bit of a loner. The Close Colleagues List in his file has only two names on it. I've spoken to the two auxiliaries concerned and neither of them was actually very close to him at all." She looked at her notes. "Knox 73 played chess with him once a week but never talked to him about anything in depth – he identified the body. And Knox 100 said she'd tried to get him to open up about himself after a sex session and failed completely. She couldn't understand why Knox 43 had put her on his list."

The welfare guardian, an earnest-looking young man with glasses who'd only recently been appointed to the Council, leaned forward. "You mentioned sex sessions, citizen," he said in a reedy voice. "I gather the dead auxiliary was hetero?"

"Correct," Katharine replied.

"And did he fulfil his sexual obligations?" The welfare guardian's voice had a prurient tone which I didn't like much.

Neither did Katharine. "If by that you mean, did he attend the weekly session as required, the answer is yes." She gave him a steely look that made it clear she thought auxiliaries shouldn't have their sex lives controlled, especially now that ordinary citizens have been let off sex sessions. "If you mean, did he show much enthusiasm for copulation with a different partner every week, the answer's no. Surprise, surprise."

The welfare guardian looked at her curiously. I wondered if he knew that Katharine worked in his directorate – and that she was once in the Prostitution Services Department.

"That'll do, citizen," Hamilton said. "We don't need criticism of Council policy from the likes of you." If Katharine was bothered by that turn of phrase, she didn't show it. "Kindly sum up your findings."

She shrugged. "From what I can gather, Knox 43 was a profoundly withdrawn and unhappy man, particularly over the last year. But I've found nothing to explain why he ended up dead in the Botanics."

Davie got to his feet. "I've come across some irregularities that might help, guardians," he said.

That made me sit up straighter. I turned to a blank page in my notebook.

Davie went on. "Knox 43's reports from the time of his auxiliary training to last autumn were never better than satisfactory. But this year they've shown a marked decline from that less than impressive level. He picked up several minor non-compliance charges for turning up late for appraisals, refusing to attend physical exercise classes and the like." He looked up to make sure everyone was paying attention. "But there's more. In the last month he was reported three times for unauthorised absence from barracks."

The guardians exchanged confused glances. As far as they were concerned, it wasn't in auxiliaries' natures to break regulations – certainly not to go missing from base.

"Any idea where he went during those absences?" I asked.

Davie nodded. "I checked the guard command centre log. There's no cross-reference to the first date he disappeared, but I've turned up references to the second and third." He paused, foolishly expecting a pat on the back.

"And?" Hamilton demanded. "Come on, commander, get a move on."

"Yes, guardian." Davie's cheeks above his beard reddened. "On 7 October he was apprehended in a field on City Farm Number 7. And on 11 October a guard vehicle picked him up in Davidson's Mains."

"City Farm Number 7?" Hamilton asked. "That's in Barnton, isn't it?"

Davie nodded. "Yes, guardian. It used to be the Bruntsfield Links golf-course."

"The second time he was caught, he could have been on his way back from the farm," I put in. I was trying to visualise the farm's location. It was in the city's northwestern corner, about a mile from the fortified line and not much more than half a mile from the Firth of Forth.

"Exactly," Davie said. "I've spoken to the farm manager. He didn't know anything about Knox 43 or what he might have been doing out there. It's all arable land and they've been busy with the ploughing and sowing. There hasn't been any surveying or maintenance work done there for a couple of years so the dead man had no professional reason to be on site. He's checking with his staff but he's not optimistic any of them will have a clue either."

"What about the farm workers?" The labour guardian had finally summoned up the nerve to involve himself in the discussion of his former staff member. His bald head was glistening with sweat and his bulky body was slumped over his desk.

"You won't get anything out of them except a pair of fingers," I said. Citizens are drafted on to the farms for a month at a time and they don't like it. They'd rather choke than open up to an investigator. "You didn't know Knox 43 personally, did you?"

The labour guardian shook his head and looked downwards. The dead man had been in the directorate for years and its chief hadn't even noticed him. I wasn't sure whether that said more about Knox 43's invisibility or the guardian's management skills.

Sophia raised her hand. "Aren't we in danger of making too much of this?" she asked. "Perhaps the dead man was just going for walks. Perhaps he just needed to get away from the barracks." She might have been right but I wasn't convinced.

"Anything else, commander?" Hamilton asked Davie.

"No, guardian," he replied, sitting down. He looked unimpressed that his discovery of Knox 43's absences was being sidelined.

My turn. I filled the guardians in about the scene of the crime and the few traces we'd found there. I also told them about the witness and her report of the supposed bogeyman. That didn't go down well.

"What's the child care supervisor talking about?" the welfare guardian demanded. "She's been reading too many fairy-tales to the inmates." Auxiliaries are trained to be rationalists, their imaginations kept strictly under control.

I raised my shoulders in a shrug. "She saw someone, that's the main point."

Katharine's directorate chief let out a high-pitched laugh. "So is the whole of the City Guard looking for a tall, ghostly figure in a cloak wearing a monster mask?"

Out of the mouths of babes and guardians. Of course. The bastard was in a mask. That explained the unnatural pallor and the stitching. I wasn't going to give him the pleasure of knowing he'd beaten me to that.

"That's exactly what the guard will be doing," I said, looking at Hamilton. Time to move on. "As regards the cigarette butts the public order guardian mentioned, they might be significant but then again they might not. Cigarettes from Glasgow and other city-states are not that uncommon – smugglers get through the line more often than you'd like to think. On their own they hardly constitute evidence of dissident or politically inspired activity."

I paused. The guardians looked down at me stonily. They might not believe in fairy monsters but they were still haunted by ogres – and democratic ones from Glasgow intent on overthrowing the Enlightenment were their worst nightmare.

"On the other hand," I continued, "Knox 43 – or Donald McBain, if you prefer – was actually born and brought up in Glasgow."

The intake of breath was sharp and extended.

"He moved to Edinburgh in 1994 to attend Heriot-Watt

University," I added. "He joined the Enlightenment before the last election and stayed on to become an auxiliary."

"I presume the appropriate checks into his background were made," the science and energy guardian said. She was a brilliant biologist in her thirties whose black hair was curly and untidy. She had a reputation for being bitter because she hardly ever won any battles for financing her directorate's research programmes. She didn't sound particularly bitter to me — more like extremely interested.

I nodded. "In as much as the checks in 2005 were worth much. The riots and the drugs wars were in full swing and anyone who was devoted enough or crazy enough to stay was very welcome. As long as you were a member of the Enlightenment, you were in."

"But there's no suggestion that the dead man was secretly working for some outside interest?" the biologist asked. "I don't suppose we're the only regime to run undercover operatives."

"There's nothing in his file that even hints at that," I said. "It's hard to believe he was spying for another city-state, at least from the beginning. Edinburgh might have had a hard time after independence was declared, but Glasgow and the other cities had troubles on the scale of Stalingrad in 1943. No one would have bothered about setting up a long-term agent."

The science and energy guardian looked at me doubtfully. She probably had no idea what Stalingrad was — most senior auxiliaries have purged their minds of everything except Edinburgh-oriented material. She wasn't giving up though. "Does the murder have any connection with the break-in at the old Parliament archive?"

I'd been hoping no one would ask that question. By the look on Hamilton's face, so had he. Then again, the Council had discussed the break-in at a previous meeting and the science and energy guardian was entitled to be concerned about the missing genetic engineering attachment.

"Em, possibly," I said, going into prevarication mode. "It's too early to say." It was also too sensitive, even for guardians. I didn't intend saying anything that might incite Hamilton to emasculate me.

"Thank you, Citizen Dalrymple," the public order guardian said, putting a stop to that strand of the discussion. "If you have nothing else, my colleagues and I will move on to matters of policy. You and your team may leave now." This time he didn't even give Katharine a suspicious look when he included her. He must have been rattled.

"Report to my quarters at ten p.m. for further debriefing," Hamilton added.

Shit. So much for early to bed.

I stood up quickly and led the others to the door before the guardians tried to get any more out of us. Rule one in sensitive cases: never tell Council members anything more than you have to. Rule two: confuse them by mentioning Second World War battles.

I stopped outside the Council chamber and looked at the others.

"Right, you two," I said. "Bugger off."

"Charming," Davie said. "Where shall we bugger off to?"

"Wherever you like," I replied. "I'm going to visit my old man." I wasn't surprised when neither of them volunteered to come with me. Katharine was probably still smarting from Hector's confusion of her with Caro; Davie no doubt wanted to hit the castle mess hall.

"All right," Katharine said. "I'll meet you at Hamilton's office at ten."

I shook my head. "I need to talk to him on my own."

"What?" they said in unison.

"The guardian ordered us to report," Davie said. "I heard him with my own ears."

"So did I," Katharine said. The pair of them agreeing was a collector's item.

"What? You heard Hamilton with Davie's ears too?" I asked Katharine.

"Up yours," she replied. "He's expecting all three of us at ten, Quint."

"I don't care what he's expecting. I've got to talk to him about the connections between the break-in and the murder. You saw how twitchy he was when the science and energy guardian started probing." I looked at them individually. "You both know he won't discuss the genetic engineering attachment in front of you. Well, don't you?"

They nodded reluctantly.

"Exactly. So let me find out if he knows what the hell's going on. Then I'll tell you."

Katharine didn't look convinced. "Will you really? What if he swears you to secrecy?"

I headed for a guard vehicle with a driver at the wheel. "Citizen Kirkwood," I said over my shoulder, "you know it's against my religion to swear."

Davie laughed while Katharine shook her head hopelessly.

"You're an atheist," she called after me. "You haven't got a religion. And as for swearing, you can—"

"Wait for me at my place if you like," I interjected rapidly.

She didn't bother to respond to that invitation.

My father was asleep, his condition stable. I watched him through the glass screen for a while then left him to it. Then I drank some dire coffee in the infirmary canteen and tried to get my plan of attack organised. After I'd done that I walked out into the night and stuck out my hand. To my surprise the skin on my palm remained dry. As the temperature wasn't particularly low I decided to walk up to the castle.

Although the citizen curfew wouldn't come into effect for over two hours, the streets were empty of Edinburgh locals. Those who weren't already at home were hard at work in the tourist bars and clubs. A group of half-cut Japanese was weaving its way up George IV Bridge like an incompetent siege party. The guards on the checkpoint were paying as little attention to them as possible. No sign of any murderers in cloaks or Glaswegian infiltrators with cigarettes hanging from their lips. I wondered if I was allowing my imagination to run away with me. Then I remembered the lengths taken by the bogus workmen to get into the Parliament archive; and the hole in Knox 43's forehead with its gruesome implant. There were people in the city who were definitely not playing games. If Hamilton was keeping the slightest piece of information from me, I was going to squeeze it out of him. Even if it took all night and a lot of eyeballing. Shit. Wrong word.

The lights around the castle were glowing brightly through the misty gloom as I crossed the esplanade. At midnight the citizen suburbs would be plunged into darkness to conserve power, but the headquarters of the City Guard would remain lit up all night. It was supposed to be a beacon of hope. Yeah, yeah.

I crossed the courtyard to the east of the former Governor's House. Guardsmen and women were scurrying about despite the late hour. Castle staff work night shifts as a matter of course.

The public order guardian looked up from his desk wearily as I entered his quarters. He had the usual pile of papers in front of him. To my surprise I noticed that his pencils were strewn all over the surface rather than arrayed in the usual neat lines. Something had definitely got to him.

"Ah, Dalrymple," he said in a low voice. He glanced past me. "On your own?"

I nodded. "Yes, Lewis. I thought you'd prefer it that way." I sat down heavily, suddenly realising that my legs were protesting.

The guardian sat back and rubbed his eyes. "I suppose so." He pointed to a table by the wall. "There's coffee over there if you want it. Standard barracks stuff, I'm afraid." There was no way he would pull rank to get his hands on the high-quality brand used in the tourist hotels.

I wasn't complaining. I filled a mug and sat down again. "You owe me some straight answers, Lewis – if you want me to stay on this case. The archive break-in and the murder are both the same case, aren't they?"

"You're the investigator," the guardian replied distractedly.

I stared at him. "What is it that you're so worried about?" I demanded. "Ever since that attachment disappeared from the Genetic Engineering Committee file, you've been as nervous as a trainee auxiliary on his first housing scheme patrol." I didn't see the point in keeping my suspicions bottled up any longer. "The Council's gone back on its ban on genetic research, hasn't it?"

Hamilton's eyes registered only a brief flash of shock. "I didn't think it would be long before you worked that out, Dalrymple." He looked down. "But there are certain complications."

"Oh aye, Lewis? And they are?"

He sat up straight and gave me an imperious glare. "You are not to share this information with anyone, do you understand? Not even with Hume 253, and certainly not with your female companion."

I shrugged, making no commitment and expecting to be pressed again. But the guardian seemed to be in need of confession and I got away with it.

"You're right, Dalrymple. The ban on research into the potential applications of genetic engineering has been – how can I put it? – repealed. After a fashion."

"What the hell does that mean?"

Hamilton was looking shifty. "Em, it means that the measure hasn't been put to the full Council."

"What?" I don't shock easily but that admission made my jaw hang very loose. "Guardians aren't permitted to make unilateral decisions about policy issues," I said, dropping into Councilspeak – it's hard to avoid when you talk about the way Edinburgh is governed. "Under City Regulations the Council is required to take collective responsibility for all policies and their implementation." The point of that was to avoid precisely the situation we had here – cliques of guardians operating to their own agendas.

Hamilton kept his eyes off mine. "Yes, that's technically correct," he said haltingly. "But in this case the issue is so sensitive that the decision was taken a year ago by a small group of guardians. Those whose remits were directly affected."

I was still recovering from the breach of Council procedure that its longest-serving member had just come clean about. Then I began to wonder who might be in the small group Lewis had mentioned.

"Apart from you, the guardians involved presumably include your colleague in the Science and Energy Directorate." That explained the dark-haired biologist's question about whether the break-in and the killing could be linked.

Hamilton nodded.

"And obviously you had to be included because of the potentially damaging effects on public order if anyone found out that one of the Council's founding principles was being subverted." I shook my head, still in shock. Because of the public revulsion at some of the genetic engineering projects in the early years of the century, the Enlightenment was on to a guaranteed vote winner when it committed itself to a total ban on such research. I'd come across Council members who'd gone against the spirit of the Enlightenment in the past, but I never expected Hamilton to join that number. Then I considered who else would be in on the plot and got another jolt.

"The medical guardian's involved as well, isn't she?" I said, a vision of Sophia with her swollen midriff flashing up before me. Jesus. Hamilton said the research had restarted a year ago. Was there a connection with her pregnancy?

He nodded. "And the finance guardian. Obviously the work had to be funded one way or another."

"What's so important about this research, Lewis?"

This time he shook his head. "I've told you enough. Concentrate on the case and let me be the judge of the wider implications."

I almost laid hands on him but I managed to get a grip on myself instead. What I'd heard was disturbing. On the other hand, it didn't add anything material to my conviction that the archive break-in and Knox 43's murder were linked. I needed to work more on that.

"All right, don't tell me," I said. "But I take it that the missing file attachment pertains to the research that the science and energy guardian is doing."

Lewis stretched his arms out and gave a frustrated shrug. "There's no way of knowing. We haven't been able to find a copy of the attachment or any references in other files to clarify its contents."

"And there was no sign of it in Knox 43's dormitory or office," I said, looking at my notes. "None of the city locksmiths remembered him either but that doesn't prove anything. He may have used a directorate key."

"It must have been him who let the suspects into the depot though," the guardian said.

"I agree. I'll tell you something else, Lewis. I reckon his trips out to City Farm Number 7 were more than just walks in the country. I reckon he was making contact with people from outside the city."

Hamilton gave me a worried look. "Because of the proximity to the line?"

"And the coast. Maybe they're infiltrating by boat. They wouldn't be the first."

The guardian suddenly looked wide awake. "Christ," he said, his voice taut. "Dissidents. Glaswegians. Remember the cigarette butts."

"Yeah, well. They're circumstantial at best."

Hamilton started scrabbling through the papers on his desk. "Something else. The forensics people have reported that the three sets of footprints at the murder scene definitely match those we found in the archive."

"God, Lewis, thanks for confirming that as soon as you heard it. It's pretty significant."

"Sorry," he mumbled. "Too much going on."

He'd got that right. "You'd better increase the watch on the coast and on the city line. If these guys are from Glasgow or somewhere else outside the city, they're going to want to leave at some stage."

"I'll advise the command centre." He shook his head. "I know what the Fisheries Guard will say though – not enough boats."

I got up to go.

"How's your father?" the guardian asked, his voice softer. "They're terrible things, heart attacks."

"Getting better," I replied. "Thanks." His sympathy got to me. Apparently the old bugger still possessed a streak of pre-Council, pre-Public Order Directorate humanity.

"What do we do next in this bloody case, Dalrymple?" Hamilton demanded.

"Sleep, Lewis," I replied. "I'll think of something in the morning." I wasn't going to tell him what I had in mind – he'd been pretty lax about telling me what was going on and now it was my turn.

"Don't forget, Dalrymple," the guardian called after me. "Keep all of this to yourself. Don't talk to Kirkwood, don't talk to Hume 253 and especially don't talk to any of the guardians involved. They'll put the knife into me if they find out I've told you about this."

I gave him a wave to reassure him. The idea of anyone putting the knife into Lewis Hamilton struck me as pretty far-fetched. Then I remembered what had been done to Knox 43. Some crazy bastard had jammed a chisel or the like into him. That made me look over my shoulder more than once as I walked towards the esplanade.

It was a bit before midnight when I got to my flat and I could see from the street that there were no lights on. Katharine had either gone straight to her own place or given up waiting. My legs felt heavier than lead as I climbed to the third floor.

I intended to crash out straight away but I couldn't switch my mind off – like Hamilton said, there was too much going on. So I made use of the last few minutes of electricity to listen to some blues. By a trick of fate what came on when I stuck in a compilation cassette was J. B. Lenoir singing "People Are Meddlin' in Our Affairs". That made me laugh. Then the power shutdown cut the old bluesman off in his prime and I had to stumble to the bedroom in pitch darkness. I had no idea where I'd left a candle and matches.

Before I found them my mobile rang.

"It's me. Where are you?"

"At my place, Katharine. You obviously didn't fancy it."

"I wouldn't say that. I wanted to clean up and change." She paused. "Did you find out anything interesting from Hamilton?"

"Not really. Just routine."

"Is that right? How about coming round and telling me about it?" Her voice was husky and alluring.

"I'm a bit knackered," I said, trying my best to resist.

"Fair enough, I'll come round to you."

"No, wait—" I broke off when I realised she'd cut the connection.

It looked like debriefing was on the cards for the second time that evening.

"Why don't you get a flat in an auxiliary block with twenty-four-hour electricity, Quint?" Katharine asked as she came into the bedroom. In the candle's flickering glow her face shone like it was part of a disembodied head.

"What, and un-demote myself?" Auxiliary accommodation in the central zone is a sight better than my run-down citizen flat. It's also in dedicated blocks, so your comings and goings are known to all. That was too much of a sacrifice for me, though the idea of being able to listen to music any time of the day or night was very seductive.

Katharine sat on the bed and started taking off her clothes. Unfortunately the candle didn't reveal much. "You don't have to become an auxiliary again to get a flat in the tourist zone," she said. "I didn't."

That was true. When she came back to the city in 2025, Katharine moved in with me. It wasn't a success. My flat isn't big enough for two people, especially two people who need their own space. When she started working in the Welfare Directorate, she got a flat in a tenement in Grindlay Street. It was within walking distance of my place but far enough away to let us live our own lives. I wasn't sure what that showed about the nature of our relationship.

Naked, Katharine slid under the covers and crushed against me.

"Christ, you're freezing," I gasped.

"I'll soon warm up," she said, leaning over to blow out the candle. "So what did the old Tartar tell you?" she asked.

"Nothing much," I said, feeling her long fingers gliding up my stiffening cock.

"Nothing much?" She squeezed hard.

"Ow! Don't!"

"You want me to stop?" She removed her hand. "No problem." She turned away. "Good night."

I put out my hand and pulled her back. "No, I don't want you to stop, Katharine." I took a deep breath. If I couldn't trust her, who could I trust? I knew that Katharine was with me because she wanted to be, not because she was after something. After Caro's death it had taken a long time before I could accept anything as straightforward as that.

So I told her about the genetic research that the small group of guardians had sanctioned. She was surprised, though not as much as I'd been — she was even more cynical than I was about the probity of Council members.

"What exactly do you think this research is into?" she asked. Her hand hadn't taken hold of me again.

"God knows. Hamilton probably doesn't understand the science and he warned me off talking to any of the others."

"I know what it's into," Katharine said.

"What?" For a second I was taken in.

"I mean, I can guess." She nudged me in the ribs. "Come on, Quint, it's obvious. What's your ex-girlfriend carrying around in her belly?"

"You reckon they're working on embryos?" That thought had struck me when I was with Hamilton.

"To improve the quality and quantity of children born in the city?"

"Who's a clever boy?" she said sarcastically. "I might have known the Ice Queen would get her sperm from a refrigerator."

This time I nudged her. "Lay off Sophia. What's she done to you recently?"

"Didn't you see the way the arrogant cow was looking at me in the Council chamber? If she had her way, she'd have me under the knife in a flash."

I felt a wave of exhaustion break over me. It was now or never. I moved my hand up her back and cupped her breast.

"Oh, talk of Sophia's got you going, has it?" Katharine asked.

"No," I said simply. I was too tired for chat-up lines. "I want you."

She laughed. "Fair enough."

I heard her fingers move across the bedside table.

"Got a condom?" she asked.

"Oh shit." I remembered that we'd used the last one. I hadn't had time to queue up in the Supply Directorate store recently.

"Forget it then." Katharine sank back into the sagging mattress. "I'm not taking any chances. The last thing I want is a kid at my age."

"There are other ways of achieving satisfaction," I said, quoting the Medical Directorate's pamphlet on sexual relations.

"Be my guest," she murmured.

A few minutes later I could tell from her breathing that she was fast asleep.

I went the same way soon afterwards but I didn't pass

a restful night. I kept surfacing from clammy, fog-ridden dreams featuring a villain in a cloak with a chisel in one hand and a mallet in the other, a cigarette hanging from his swollen, unnatural lips. And all the time in the background was the schizophrenic howling of a genetically modified guardian of the underworld called Cerberus.

CHAPTER EIGHT

I woke up to the scent of half-decent tea.

"Come on, Quint," Katharine said, drawing the curtains. "You'd better make the most of that Welfare Directorate tea-bag. It's a foul day. The rain's coming down heavier than Davie's boots, there's a freezing mist off the sea and you're out of coal. Good morning, Enlightenment Edinburgh."

I accepted the mug from her, rubbing sleep from my eyes. "What are you looking so pleased about?" I mumbled.

She held up a small packet. Citizen-issue condoms — given the problems with the birth-rate these days, they probably came ready pinpricked.

"I got up early and went down to your local store."

I grabbed her arm. "Come on then."

Katharine pulled away, laughing. "Not now. We've got work to do." I must have looked very disappointed. "Don't worry, we'll have plenty of time later."

"You never know what might happen," I said. "Don't put off till this evening—"

"Shut up, idiot," she said, moving to the door. "I'm going to the Welfare Directorate to see if anything urgent's come up. I'll call you when I'm finished." She stopped and looked back at me. "What are you going to do?"

"I've got a rendezvous with Doctor Godwin's file."

"Lucky you. Don't forget to check out Cerberus as well." She produced what she thought was a cover version of the creature's cry.

Then she left me to the tea and a bad case of what Lightnin' Hopkins used to call the "Morning Blues".

I called the infirmary and found out that my old man was awake and in reasonable shape. They were planning to move him into a general ward at eleven a.m. I told the nursing auxiliary I'd be there, then got dressed and considered my options. Gavin Godwin – a.k.a. Napier 77 – would feature both in his barracks archive and in the Science and Energy Directorate's records. Since Hamilton had warned me off his colleagues' territories and since what I was really interested in was the old geneticist's Glaswegian background, I decided to check his general file in Napier first.

Davie came on the mobile as I was on my way down to the guard vehicle I'd called. "Morning, Quint. I'm in the command centre and I heard you ordered a vehicle. Where are you off to then?" He sounded pretty down in the mouth. "You said you were going to tell me what you and the guardian talked about last night."

"I will, guardsman, don't worry." I reverted to Katharine's strategy. "Later."

"I'll be waiting."

"Any news?"

"Nothing that pertains to the case. No sign of any bogeymen or of the pick-up they took."

"They'll be keeping that out of sight." A thought struck me. "Christ, if these guys are as smart as they seem to be, they'll probably have changed the number-plates. You'd better amend the all-barracks alert to include *all* red pick-ups."

"Right. Anything else?"

"Nope."

"Quint?" Davie said suspiciously. "You didn't answer my question. Where are you off to?"

I didn't want Davie to know where I was going in case Hamilton forced it out of him. I had the feeling that the public order guardian wouldn't like me digging around in the background of a former Genetic Engineering Committee member.

"You're breaking up," I lied. "Out."

I sent the guardswoman who arrived in a clapped-out pick-up back to the castle on foot – auxiliaries need all the exercise they can get – and headed south.

Napier Barracks is spread across a group of buildings at the crossroads which used to be called Holy Corner. The four churches that led to the name are now components of the barracks and the junction about a mile out of the city centre has been renamed Napier Cross. To me that has ironic undertones considering the Council's hardline atheist principles, but for most ordinary citizens it's become a gag about the irate nature of the auxiliaries in the barracks. From past experience I knew that the archive was in one of the former churches. I showed my authorisation and walked into a weird juxtaposition of stained-glass windows and shelves full of maroon and grey folders.

I pulled Napier 77's file and headed for a table in what was once the chancel. Before I got there, an officious-looking senior auxiliary stormed towards me. He'd obviously been informed by the sentry that there was an alien in his domain. I quickly obscured the barracks number on the file from him.

"What is the meaning of this?" he demanded, eyeing my donkey jacket and black trousers. "Procedure requires that all visitors report to my office before entering Napier facilities." That's commander-speak for "I'm the cock of the walk here – prepare to be fertilised." He must have been one of the few people of his rank who didn't know who I was.

I soon put that right. "Dalrymple," I said, showing him my authorisation. "Now fuck off, Napier 01."

His face went beetroot, then he complied. That made me feel great.

Unfortunately Gavin Godwin's file didn't. It confirmed what I already knew – that he was originally from Glasgow, that he was eighty-five years old and that he'd been a professor at Heriot-Watt before independence. But I ran into the same problem as I had with Knox 43. There was very little about the subject's life and activities before the last election. For all I knew, the pair of them could have been best boozing pals in the Glaswegian tradition, or they could have been members of a ring of deep-cover operatives. The reality might well have been that they didn't even know each other. The dead man was over thirty years younger than Godwin and he'd studied surveying at Heriot-Watt, not biology or anything even vaguely connected with genetic engineering. And there was no chance of me checking out the university's archive – the place was stomped to pieces years ago by the drugs gangs.

All in all, the file was remarkably uninformative about the old scientist. It hadn't been weeded – I checked the contents pages and the binding – but it was still much thinner than the average auxiliary's. Like many of his kind, Godwin had a dispensation from barracks duties and seemed to spend almost all his waking hours at the research centre in King's Buildings. His Personal Evaluations were sparse and nebulous, his Superior's Reports were single sentences and his Close Colleagues Lists had been left blank for the last ten years. It was obvious that Godwin had powerful patrons in the Science and Energy Directorate who kept the barracks off his back. Of course, there was nothing at all about his work – I'd have to ransack the directorate archive to get that.

Eventually I closed my notebook – not that there had been much point in opening it – and glanced at my watch. Ten to eleven. I'd have to hurry if I was to get to the infirmary in time for Hector's transfer.

I ran out to the pick-up. Before I got to it, my mobile went off.

"It's Katharine. I'm finished in the directorate. They've agreed to let me have a week off."

"I wish I could have a week off," I said, getting into the vehicle and turning the key. The starter-motor screeched like a banshee with a hangover.

"Not a week's holiday," she said. "I had to fill out a form seconding myself to you."

I pulled away from the kerb, making a guardswoman leap out of the way. "So that means I come first and you come second, does it?" I asked.

"Only in your dreams. Where do you want me to meet you?"

I accelerated past a citizen bus. "At the infirmary. They're moving my father."

There was a pause. "Okay," she said. "I hope he remembers who I am this time."

I signed off. I hoped he remembered who I was too.

I made it just in time. The nursing auxiliaries were in the process of removing the last of the tubes and lines from Hector in the ICU. I waved at him through the glass screen and received a scowl for my trouble. It looked like the old man was back to his normal state – cantankerous and proud of it.

"He seems to be doing all right," Katharine said from behind me.

"Mm. I get the feeling he's had enough of lying on his back without his precious books."

We were ushered away from the door as the mobile bed was wheeled out. Then we followed it down the corridor. I could hear the old man grumbling as he went.

Katharine laughed. "No sign of any major personality change."

I nodded. "If he's complaining now, wait till he gets into a ward full of other patients. He'll soon have them talking in whispers so he can read in peace."

It didn't take long for the formalities to be completed and for Hector to be set up in his next temporary home. All the infirmary's general wards are mixed sex to maximise the space. He found himself between an elderly man with yellowish skin and a young female citizen. Her broken leg was on a pulley and her looks were definitely above par.

"How are you feeling then, old man?" I enquired.

"How am I feeling *now*, you mean, failure," he replied impatiently. "You do have a command of English, don't you?"

"Apparently not," I said, leaning over and taking in his lined face and pallid skin. "Answer the question. How do you feel?"

"All right, I suppose." Hector looked away disconsolately, as if he'd suddenly realised that he wasn't going to be the centre of attention for much longer. Then he turned his head back towards me and beckoned to me to come close again. "Your woman friend," he said in a low voice. "I made a fool of myself, didn't I? She's Katharine, not Caro."

I nodded. "Don't worry. She's forgiven you."

The old man twitched his head in irritation. "Pathetic," he complained. "How could I make a mistake like that? I must be going senile."

"Don't be ridiculous. You had a serious heart attack. And now you're going to make a full recovery."

He wasn't listening. "I'm sorry, Quintilian. It was just that Caro seemed very real. Even though it's over ten years now . . ." He looked at me awkwardly, his eyes damp. "She and you were so close. I've never seen love like that. I'm sorry I never told you I was happy for you. I had to follow the Council's bloody guidelines and feign indifference to human feelings." He shook his head. "God, if the Enlightenment hadn't taken over Edinburgh, you two would have got married, you'd have had children—"

This was becoming hard to cope with. I squeezed my father's hand then pulled away, aware that my own eyes were wet too.

"You've nothing to blame yourself about, Hector," I said quietly. "I always knew how you felt about us. That's all that matters." I took a step back. "Now, you do what the nurses tell you. It won't be long before you're back with your dirty Latin books."

He nodded weakly, raising his hand at Katharine.

Before we reached the door I heard him asking the woman in the next bed what her name was. For a card-carrying member of the Misogynist International my father was remarkably good at charming members of the opposite sex when he could be bothered.

"So," Katharine said as we hit the corridor. "What next?"

I stopped. I was seriously thinking about disobeying Hamilton's instruction not to pester his colleagues and going down to Sophia's office. What she knew about the current genetic research might help me out in the investigation. Then I made myself reconsider. Sophia wasn't corrupt, nor was she stupid. If she knew about some link between the murder and the research, she'd have told Hamilton if not me. Before I could make a final decision, I got a surprise.

"Quint? I wondered if I'd find you here." The voice came from behind me, at the level of the small of my back.

I recognised it before I turned. "Billy?" I looked down at the crumpled figure in the wheelchair. "Christ, long time no see. How have you been?"

The guy who had once been my best friend was ignoring me now. He only had eyes for Katharine. "I remember you," he said to her. "January 2022, wasn't it?" Trust a financial wheeler-dealer to have perfect recall for numbers.

"Billy Geddes, Heriot 07 as was," Katharine said, showing that she had a good memory for figures too. "Demoted for corruption in 2021. You were sent to rehabilitation, weren't you?" She smiled humourlessly. "Have they let you out of the human zoo?" Demoted auxiliaries sent to rehab are given animal codenames, supposedly to emphasise the bestial natures that are to be programmed out of them. Billy had been known as the Jackal.

Billy cackled like a broody hen. "She's really something, this squeeze of yours, Quint."

He was taking his life in his hands, referring to Katharine in those terms. Even though his arms and legs had been shattered in an accident I was partially responsible for in 2020, I suspected she might still use force on him. I frowned to warn her off.

"You in here for a check-up, Billy?" I asked. "You look pretty well."

He ran his fingers over the thin hair that was plastered on to his scalp. "Pretty well?" he repeated ironically. "Oh aye, I'm fine. I'm brilliant. Thanks for asking, Quint." He gave me a harsh stare. "Course, if you ever bothered to visit me, you wouldn't need to ask."

I nodded, feeling my cheeks redden. Billy and I had once been very close but I never really came to terms with his self-interest and his greed. I still felt guilty about cutting him loose though.

"You got out of rehab in the spring, didn't you?" I said.

"I knew you'd have your spies keeping an eye on me," Billy said, froth dotting his lips. "No doubt you're aware that the Council's using me to check their biggest deals with the tourist companies and the like."

I shrugged. I'd actually suggested that to Sophia when she was acting senior guardian a year back. It seemed a waste of talent to ignore Billy, for all his past sins and his inherent untrustworthiness.

Suddenly Billy's expression softened. "I heard your father had a heart attack, Quint. How is he?" When we were kids before independence, Billy was a frequent visitor to our house in Newington. His own parents had divorced and he eventually got quite attached to mine – until they became Council members and cut themselves off from personal contact with everyone, including me.

I filled him in about Hector, touched by his concern. It didn't last long. He saluted me with a sardonic laugh, gave Katharine an attempt at a winning smile and propelled himself down the corridor at what I thought, given his shrunken frame and twisted arms, was impressive speed.

"He's crazy," Katharine said, shaking her head.

"No, he's not," I said, feeling the need to defend my former friend. "Despite the pounding he took, his mind's as sharp as ever."

It was only as we were walking out of the infirmary that a couple of things struck me about Billy's sudden appearance. The first was that he hadn't answered my question about what he was doing in the hospital. There hadn't been any nursing auxiliaries in attendance and he looked no worse than he had the last time I saw him. And the second was that he'd headed down the passageway that led to Sophia's quarters. Bloody hell. Surely he couldn't have something to do with the genetic engineering group. Hamilton had told me that the finance guardian was in charge of funding the research. But that didn't rule out the possibility that Billy's talents and his contacts outside the city were being used. It wouldn't be the first time I'd come across Billy's traces during an investigation.

Then my mobile buzzed and Davie gave me some news that blew all thoughts of Billy Geddes away faster than the first north-westerly of winter.

*   *   *

"So what?" Katharine said as we climbed into the guard vehicle. "Kids go missing from time to time in this city whatever the Council might like to pretend."

"Not from the Lauriston Facility, they don't." I ground the starter motor into action and pulled away. "It's got an eight-foot fence round it."

"There's something else, isn't there, Quint?" she said suspiciously. "Something connected with the murder."

I screwed my eyes up, trying to make out citizens on bicycles without rear lights in the mist. "You're right," I said, nodding. "There's a witness who saw someone familiar." I gave her a quick glance. "A tall, fearsome guy wearing a long cloak."

The Lauriston Adolescent Care Facility, to give it its full title, isn't your standard Welfare Directorate cross between a crèche and a prison, despite the fence. It's a home for the city's next generation of smartarses. They're the contemporary equivalent of the nobility who built the sixteenth-century Lauriston Castle – in twenty-first-century Edinburgh we have intellectual aristocrats rather than chinless gits with ridiculous accents. The facility stands in a large expanse of gardens overlooking the Firth of Forth to the far north-west of the central zone. Not that we could see the water. Visibility wasn't much more than twenty yards and the drizzle was in the process of becoming heavy rain. Perfect weather for a kidnap.

There was a guard presence in addition to the normal barracks sentry at the gate. We showed ID.

"Ah, Citizen Dalrymple," the grizzled guardsman said. "Hume 253 said you were on your way."

"Where is he?"

"He's waiting for you at the facility entrance." The guardsman drew himself up. "The public order guardian is here too."

"Great," I said under my breath as I engaged first gear. "It didn't take the old vulture long to get stuck in."

The driveway curved to the left through woods and cultivated ground. No doubt having stratospheric IQs didn't get the inmates off potato digging and kale gathering.

"Why's there so much security?" Katharine asked. "Not that it's done much good."

"You know how highly the Council rates intelligence. The city's young geniuses have to be nurtured and protected. We wouldn't want them squandering their abilities on dissident activity or crime, would we?"

"But I thought the Council set up an equitable system that took into account the talents and needs of all citizens," she said, quoting the Enlightenment's manifesto.

"It did. But the guardians need some citizens' talents more than others'."

Stationary guard vehicles, including Hamilton's Jeep, loomed out of the murk. Behind them rose the turreted tower of the castle, which put the nineteenth-century extensions and Council-inspired outhouses to shame. It looked like something out of a Gothic romance – one in which the villain flits in and out of sight like a hungry ghost. I could see pupils in classrooms turning their heads surreptitiously towards Katharine and me.

"Hello, Quint," Davie said from beneath the hood of his rain-jacket. He didn't favour Katharine with a greeting. "The guardian's in the supervisor's office. He wants a word before we check out the grounds."

I got out and ran to the ornate porch, splashing through pot-holes and soaking my trousers. A guardswoman pointed at a door to the right.

"Dalrymple," the guardian said curtly. He looked past me at Katharine. "Citizen Kirkwood."

Katharine was as surprised as I was that he'd greeted her.

"Lewis." I deliberately used his first name. That shocked the female supervisor at his side, who probably thought he answered to Jehovah. That was the effect I was after. It's always good to unsettle senior auxiliaries, especially those you're about to question. I craned forward and read the barracks number on her chest. "Adam 102."

Hamilton turned to the supervisor. She was tall and skinny, her severe face making her look older than I reckoned she was. "I wanted Adam 102 to make clear how disturbing the disappearance of these three adolescents is."

The auxiliary nodded. "Indeed, guardian. These three – one female and two males – are the outstanding intellects of their age group. It is essential that you find them, citizen."

"Pity your security procedures weren't up to keeping them on campus," I observed.

Adam 102 went on the defensive. "Security is the joint responsibility of the facility and the Cramond Barracks guard unit––" She broke off, remembering that the City Guard's commander-in-chief was standing next to her.

"Leave the security issue to me, supervisor," Hamilton said testily. "It's clearly beyond your capabilities."

I intervened. "So what you're saying, Adam 102, is that

if someone – for whatever reason – wanted to deprive the Council of the three best young brains in the city, these were the ones to pick?"

The auxiliary nodded. "Lesley is already at post-graduate level in applied maths. Michael and Dougal have attained a wide-ranging knowledge of science and medicine. They are all on the Council's fast-track auxiliary training scheme."

Lewis Hamilton caught my eye. "Dalrymple, I suggest your colleague talks to Adam 102 and her staff." He glanced at Katharine nervously. Now I understood why he'd acknowledged her existence. Amazing. He'd finally understood that handing over people – even auxiliaries – to guard interrogators isn't the most effective way to gather information.

"Okay?" I asked Katharine.

She nodded.

"Everything you can find out about the kids, their backgrounds and their recent behaviour."

"Right. What are you going to do, Quint?"

The guardian was anxious to reassert his authority. "We're going to find out how the inmates were spirited through the fence," he said, giving the supervisor an acid glare. "And why the staff in this facility left them unattended."

I had the feeling Adam 102 wasn't going to be in charge of the budding geniuses who were still in Edinburgh for long.

The rain had let off when we went outside, but the mist was still down. I sniffed the air. It was dank and redolent of dead leaves.

Davie pulled down his hood and pointed to the north.

"The wire was cut over there. The scene-of-crime team is looking at the area now." He moved off.

"Do we know what the missing kids were doing prior to their disappearance?" I asked, striding to catch up with him.

Hamilton supplied the answer. "Adam 102 told me that they went for the normal morning run with a physical training auxiliary at seven. They were supposed to be working on an unsupervised group project after that. They were seen walking in the grounds around ten o'clock, despite the weather. The alarm was raised when they didn't turn up for the daily Platonic philosophy lecture at ten-thirty."

"Who saw the bogeyman in the cloak?" I asked.

"A gardener," Davie replied. "He's down at the wire."

"Why on earth didn't he report it earlier?" the guardian demanded.

"He couldn't," Davie said. "He was bound and gagged. One of his mates found him at ten-forty, not long after the alarm was raised."

"What about the physical training guy?" I asked.

Davie shook his head slowly. "No sign of him yet. I've got search parties out in the area beyond the wire."

We reached the fence a couple of minutes later. Three guard vehicles had been parked in front of it. I made out white-overalled figures moving around, examining the ground and the wire.

The scene-of-crime squad leader came to meet us. "Guardian, commander, citizen," he said, choosing his word order carefully. It wouldn't do for an efficient young auxiliary to prioritise the likes of me, special investigator or not. "There are a lot of prints on the ground. Several auxiliary-issue training shoes – presumably the inmates'; we're checking their shoe sizes – and several other prints."

"Not by any chance workmen's boots like those you found beneath the Assembly Hall and in the Botanics?" I asked.

"Some of them are, I think," the auxiliary replied. "I'll confirm that as soon as the casts are compared."

"What about the wire?" Davie asked.

"Cut from four feet to ground level, pulled back and fastened to the ground with a couple of two-foot wooden stakes."

"Any equipment left behind?" I asked, thinking of the dead man's injuries and the idea that a mallet or the like might have caused them.

"No, citizen." The auxiliary led us past the marked footprints to the fence. The ends of the stakes had been knocked in with a heavy blunt instrument all right. Could it be the one that had smashed in the side of Knox 43's skull?

Davie was looking ahead into the mist. "The firth's less than a mile down there," he said.

I raised my left arm. "And City Farm Number 7 where Knox 43 was caught is just over there."

Hamilton frowned at me. "You think there's a connection?"

I shrugged, turning back to the scene-of-crime squad leader. "Any signs of a struggle? Heels dug in, that sort of thing?"

He shook his head. "Not really. One of the inmates slipped over here—" he pointed to a shallow furrow. "The ground's so damp that he or she could easily have done that accidentally."

"What are you getting at, Dalrymple?" the guardian asked. "You think they went willingly?"

"Could be. On the other hand, they might have been so terrified by the guy in the cloak that they did everything he said." I looked across to a slumped figure in the front of one of the Land-Rovers. "Time to talk to our witness." I turned to the others. "I'll do this. You know how most ordinary citizens react to guard uniforms."

Lewis and Davie weren't happy but I wasn't going to let them argue. I turfed the guard driver out and sat down on the warm seat. The crumpled figure next to me didn't bother to look up.

"I'm Dalrymple," I said. "Call me Quint."

He glanced round and took in my citizen-issue clothes. "You one of us?" he asked in a low voice.

"Aye. What's your name?"

The gardener still wasn't sure about me. "You're no' an undercover shite?"

"Naw, I'm a fully out-in-the-open shite, me."

He gave a laugh then choked it off abruptly and sat up straight. Now I could see that his cheeks were marked where a gag had been tied tightly around his head. His eyes were jerking about uncontrollably. I guessed he was around fifty but he could have been less – ordinary citizens age quickly in Enlightenment Edinburgh.

"What's your name?" I repeated.

"Didn't your friends outside tell you?" he responded, sullen again.

"I told you, I'm not one of them. I work with them, sure, but that doesn't mean I share their views about where ordinary citizens belong."

"In the mud with the worms and the dead leaves," he

said. Pretty poetic for a gardener, I thought. "Andy Skinner. What do you want to know?"

"What did you see, Andy?"

He grunted. "Fuck all. This bastard weather. You know what it's like being outside all day in this wet without a decent coat. Those fuckers in the guard have their special waterproofs, but what do we get?" He spread his arms in a sodden donkey jacket that matched my own. "These things keep you about as dry as a tart's mattress."

"True enough," I said. "So what did you see, Andy?"

"I wasn't joking, pal," he insisted. "I saw fuck all. The shites must have crept up on me. Before I knew it I was in the bushes with my mouth stopped up and my hands tied to my ankles."

"How about the three inmates? What were they up to?"

"I didnae see them." Then, having led me up his garden path, he gave me a weak smile. "But I heard them." He shook his head. "Bastard know-alls. They were on about how easy it was to con their tutors in some project."

That didn't sound like teenagers who were about to abscond. "You heard them before you were attacked?"

Andy Skinner nodded. "Aye, for a minute or so. I was over by that herbaceous border." He pointed to a strip of earth near the fence.

"Then you were grabbed. How many guys?"

"Three, I think. Two of them got hold of me. They didn't exactly attack me though. Just dragged me over to the bushes there."

"Did you see them?"

"No. They got something round my eyes pretty quickly. They stuffed it in my mouth afterwards and tied something thicker round my eyes."

I looked at him. "But you did see something before they blindfolded you, didn't you, Andy?"

His jaw was slack. "Aye . . ." He shook his head. "Some*thing* is right. Jesus Christ, I almost pissed my pants. This big fella's coming towards me like he really means business. He's wearing a fuckin' great cloak that's spread out around him like a pair of wings. And he's got a fuckin' great mallet in one hand."

"Anything in the other hand?"

The gardener looked at me curiously. "I don't think so. Why?"

I ignored his question. "What about his face, Andy? What did he look like?"

A tremor shook his body and he stared at me, his lower jaw hanging loose. "Christ, he was a right monster. He must have spent his life fighting, his face was that torn up." He straightened up again. "I'll tell you something though. His beard didnae look real."

His beard and what else, I wondered. "Did you hear him speak?"

Skinner shook his head. "Uh-uh. He came up after I'd been blindfolded and I heard him breathing." He shivered again. "Christ, it was weird, like a kind of gasping. Then I was dragged off and dumped in the bushes. They rammed the blindfold into my mouth and left me there. I couldn't see anything. I was behind a tree trunk and anyway, the mist was as thick as a guardsman."

I smiled. I reckoned he'd given me all he had.

There was a tap on the window. Davie.

"Quint, come over here," he said. There was tension in his voice.

I followed him to the fence.

"One of the search units has found the physical

training auxiliary who was with the kids earlier in the morning."

Hamilton appeared at Davie's shoulder. "What's going on, commander?" he asked.

"They've found the trainer," Davie said, his face pale. "Dead."

"Bugger," the guardian said, lapsing from normal standards of auxiliary language.

"That's not all," Davie added. "He's got a branch over his face like Knox 43."

CHAPTER NINE

A young guardswoman came out of the mist beyond the wire. "This way, guardian," she called nervously. I got the feeling this was a big day for her – first violent death and first encounter with Lewis Hamilton. I wasn't sure which was making her twitch more.

We followed her past auxiliaries who were crouching to examine footprints in the mud, and entered the woods. A maroon and white tape had been run along the ground to indicate more prints and traces. We kept to the left of it and tried to avoid the heavy drops of accumulated rainwater that were falling from the branches. As we got deeper into the trees, the birdsong faded away. The blackbirds and thrushes were keeping well clear of the body we had to confront.

"It's . . . I mean he's over the wall there," the guardswoman said, gulping hard.

"All right," Hamilton said gruffly. "Stand back if it's too much for you."

The female auxiliary swallowed again, caught between the desire to impress her superior and the urgent need to empty her stomach. The latter took priority.

We straddled the low dyke and approached the search squad members. They were standing in a huddle on the pot-holed asphalt of the Cramond Road but when they spotted us, they dispersed like a flock of frightened sheep.

"Bloody hell," Davie said under his breath. "The branch is from the same kind of tree."

I kneeled by the corpse after looking quickly at the road surface to check for prints. There was nothing obvious. The dead man was wearing an auxiliary-issue tracksuit and mud-encrusted running shoes. He was lying on his left side, his knees drawn up like Knox 43's had been in the Botanic Gardens. I pulled on protective gloves and picked up the right hand. The skin was clammy and the joint was still loose. He hadn't been dead for very long. The fingers were closed around a branch of blood-drenched copper beech that was covering his head and right shoulder. Some of the reddish-brown leaves had fallen away and a mutilated face was visible through the remaining foliage.

"See if you can find the tree this was taken from, Davie," I said over my shoulder. "There might be prints on or around it."

"Right." He moved away, to be replaced by the public order guardian.

Hamilton steeled himself to look at the mass of blood that had hardened around the hole in the forehead. An eyeball was protruding from the shattered bone, staring back at us at a crazy angle.

"Good God," the guardian exhaled.

"The Council says there isn't any god, good or otherwise," I reminded him.

"This body is evidence of that," Hamilton said with a shiver. He stood up and took a couple of paces back. "It's the same killer, isn't it?"

"Looks like it," I said. "Same modus operandi, same

body position, the branch is from a copper beech again."
I rocked back on my heels. "I wonder if they're devotees
of Sherlock Holmes. There's a story called 'The Copper
Beeches'."

"They?" the guardian asked, ignoring the literary
reference.

"The gardener reckons there were three of them,
which would square with the footprints around Knox
43's body," I said, standing up and shaking the pins and
needles from my legs.

The scene-of-crime squad leader climbed over the wall
and came up.

"Another customer," I said to him. "You'd better get
going with the photos and trace searches. I want the
body taken away for post-mortem as soon as possible."

The auxiliary nodded.

"What's the hurry?" Hamilton asked. "The cause of
death is pretty obvious."

"I want to get some idea of the time of death," I replied.
"The missing kids went for a run with the dead man at
seven o'clock, but they were seen outside again around
ten. If this guy was killed soon after he finished the run,
it would mean that the kidnappers were hanging around
for several hours. In that case they would have left traces
somewhere."

"Quint!" Davie called from beyond the wall. "We've
located the tree the branch came from." His face broke
into an unlikely smile. "And that's not all we found.
There's a cigarette butt on the ground by the trunk that
looks very like the ones found in the Botanics."

We split into pairs and searched the woods. A few
isolated footprints were found, but most were concen-

trated in a small clearing inside the tree line on the castle side and on a track leading to the hole in the wire. All of those were confirmed as matching the prints in the Botanics.

"What about the prints I found at the tree?" Davie asked when we broke off to compare notes. "They aren't from workmen's boots."

"No, they aren't, commander," the scene-of-crime squad leader said. "They run from the copper beech to the wall and then to the roadside ten yards from the body." He shook his head. "I can't identify them without recourse to the files in the castle but I don't think they're Supply Directorate issue."

"Maybe they're from Glasgow like the cigarette," Hamilton said, his jaw jutting. "Bloody democrat dissidents."

I ran my fingers over the stubble on my face, trying to fathom what had happened. Did the bogeyman and his friends change footwear? And if so, why? Reluctantly I let the line of thought go. "Anything on the dead man's background?"

"Cramond 333 was his barracks number. He was thirty-eight years old," the guardian said. He held up a file. "I had this sent over. He seems to have been a reliable auxiliary. A bit limited in ambition, perhaps."

"Which is presumably why he was a physical training instructor," I said.

Hamilton glared at me. "There's nothing wrong with physical exercise, Dalrymple. Plato saw it as one of the most important—"

"Let's leave Plato out of this, Lewis," I interrupted. "I'm more interested in the location of the body. Why was it left on a public road? There are no blood traces in the undergrowth so the auxiliary may have been killed on the road. Why take the chance of being caught in the open?"

Davie looked round. "The mist was even thicker earlier on today. And there isn't exactly a lot of traffic on this road."

I shrugged. "There's probably some farm vehicle activity though. How about guard patrols?"

The guardian suddenly looked unusually sheepish. "I asked the local commander about that. He told me that he only runs patrols during the night. There isn't much of a youth gang problem around here."

"What about smuggling?" I asked.

"That's the point, man," Hamilton said impatiently. "Cramond Barracks deploys most of its forces on the coastline."

I rubbed my hand across my chin. "Maybe the killers knew that," I said speculatively. "Maybe they had inside knowledge."

Davie raised his eyes to the sky, but I was lucky – the guardian didn't react to that attack on the integrity of the Council's servants.

An auxiliary came up to the scene-of-crime squad leader and spoke to him in a low voice. His boss listened then dismissed him.

"We've found some drops of engine oil on the asphalt," the squad leader reported. "About fifteen yards from where the body was lying."

"In what direction?" I asked.

"South, citizen," he replied.

Davie looked at me. "The stolen Labour Directorate pick-up?"

"Maybe. They could have sat in there before they took

the kids. I wonder if it headed towards the city or towards the coast afterwards."

Hamilton glanced through a sheaf of barracks reports. "No sightings of the missing vehicle. All red pick-ups on the roads have been checked. If the teenagers were moved in it, they would have been obvious enough."

I nodded. "They would. Three of them plus at least three kidnappers. There wouldn't be room for all of them in the cab. The rest would have been out in the open in the cargo space."

The public order guardian clapped his hands together to silence the auxiliaries around us. As if by magic, the rain came down like steel lances. Unfortunately we weren't wearing steel bonnets.

"Let's get indoors," I said, grabbing the dead auxiliary's file from Lewis and heading for the gap in the fence. The body had been removed by the ambulance team. All that was left of Cramond 333 was a puddle of blood on the asphalt. It wouldn't be long before every trace of that was washed away, but that wasn't what was bothering me most. I couldn't understand why the body had been left in such an obvious location. It was as if the killer and his associates wanted us to find it sooner rather than later. The question was, who were they? Not only that. What the hell was their agenda?

Back in the former Lauriston Castle, Hamilton commandeered the supervisor's office and hung his dripping jacket over her chair.

"Lunch!" he shouted. "Beer and sandwiches in here now!"

"Good idea," Davie said under his breath.

I shook my head at him and settled down to scan

Cramond 333's file. It didn't take me long to find what I wanted. "Well, well."

Katharine appeared at my side, a pile of folders under her arm. "What's so exciting?"

I filled her in about the dead man. I had reached the page outlining his life before the Enlightenment. There hadn't been much of it as he was only sixteen at the time of the last election. But there was still something that caught my eye.

"Listen to this. Both his parents came from—"

"Glasgow?" Davie interjected.

I glared at him. "How did you know that, guardsman?"

He grinned. "It was obvious, citizen. There's been a Glaswegian connection running through this case from the beginning like a tapeworm."

An elderly male servitor was laying out food and drink on the supervisor's conference table.

"That's enough of the zoological imagery, Hume 253," Hamilton ordered. He was looking queasy. I didn't realise that creepy-crawlies had the same effect on him as cadavers. "What are you suggesting, Dalrymple? That Cramond 333 was a secret admirer of those anarchists on the Clyde? That he spent over twenty years evading security checks and working for his parents' friends?" The scowl on his face became more pronounced as the tirade continued. "That he passed on information about Edinburgh's brightest adolescents and was then brutally murdered for his trouble?"

I leaned forward and picked up a sandwich. "Very good, Lewis," I said, giving him an icy smile Sophia would have been proud of. "I'm glad our minds are working along the same lines."

"It's pure supposition," the guardian said dismissively. "You're always far too quick to assume that auxiliaries are corrupt."

I bit into what was wholestone rather than wholemeal. "Shit." I felt around in my mouth and removed the offending object. Fortunately my teeth seemed to be intact. "The local barracks baker has obviously been supplementing the flour with grit." I smiled ironically at the guardian. "Nothing corrupt about that, of course."

It wasn't a relaxing meal-break.

Davie drove Katharine and me back up to the city centre. We took the files on the missing kids with us, a breach of procedure that the facility supervisor had objected to. Hamilton overruled her when I pointed out to him that an emergency Council meeting was in the offing – and that he'd be in the firing line if I wasn't allowed to prepare for it in my own way.

We ground along the Queensferry Road in the fog, passing defeated-looking citizens weighed down by bags of coal and potatoes.

"Find anything hot on the kids?" I asked Katharine.

She looked at her notes. "Depends what you mean by hot, Quint. They've certainly been glowing very brightly on the academic front." She turned to me. "I can't see what that could have to do with their abduction though. They're smart all right but they're not rocket scientists or prize-winning chemists – people who might have some value on the open market. Not yet, at least."

"Mm." I opened Michael MacGregor's file. "Born Edinburgh, 15/2/10. Parents Sheena and Finlay, born Edinburgh, auxiliaries in Simpson and Nasmyth Barracks respectively, both died in the flu epidemic of 2012." I shrugged. "Nothing too suspicious there."

Katharine nodded. "The same goes for the others. Both born in Edinburgh, both to parents who were auxiliaries."

I closed the maroon folder and glanced out of the window. A small boy was urinating into the gutter behind a Supply Directorate delivery van. He was taking more than his tiny dick into his hands by breaking the sanitation rules so openly. "What did you get from their friends?"

"They're fast-track auxiliary trainees, remember? They're not supposed to have friends." The tone of Katharine's voice showed what she thought of that requirement. "But their classmates seemed to like them – or rather, revere them. Apparently the three of them stuck together a lot."

"And their teachers?"

"Some of them – the males, mainly – had severe difficulty opening up to a DM like me. I managed to gain the women's confidence—"

"Congratulations," Davie muttered, swerving as a tourist bus on the way to the airport pulled into our lane.

"Up yours, guardsman," Katharine said.

"Give it a rest, will you?" I said. "What did the female teachers tell you?"

"Basically, the same as is in the kids' files. They were all star pupils, they were all major intellects and they were all very conscientious."

I glanced at her. "You presumably caught the odour of decaying rodent?"

She laughed. "Of course. So I wheeled and poked a bit—"

"Aye, you're good at that," Davie said.

"Shut it, big man," I said. "You can always go and play with yourself in the command centre if this case is boring you."

He grinned at me and floored the accelerator.

"God almighty," Katharine said, shaking her head. "As I was saying, I got beneath the surface and – lo and behold – the trio turned out to have an intriguing side after all."

We slowed at the checkpoint by Buckingham Terrace and flashed ID, Davie giving a smart-looking guardswoman an over-the-top salute. She was probably one of his legion of admirers.

"What was suspicious then?" I demanded as Katharine held out on us.

"Well, believe it or not, all three kids are extremely advanced sexually."

Davie looked at her with interest. "Oh aye?"

"Don't even think about making any smartarse comments, guardsman," I warned.

Katharine kept quiet, daring him to have a go, but he refrained. Apparently my threat about taking him off the case was having some effect.

"Extremely advanced sexually?" I asked. "What exactly does that mean?"

Katharine leafed through her notes. "It means that from the age of ten the boys and the girl were supplied with sexually explicit literature and photographs, and from the age of fourteen they were given sex sessions by experienced auxiliaries." She paused. "Of both sexes."

"Christ," Davie gasped. "I didn't realise that was part of the fast-track scheme."

"Neither did I," I said.

"I wonder how they chose the experienced auxiliaries," Davie mused. "I never saw a notice asking for volunteers anywhere."

Katharine turned to him. "I suppose you'd have applied like a shot."

"No chance," he replied. "Fourteen's too young for me."

"Fourteen's too young for anyone," Katharine said.

I nodded. "You're right. But the fact that they were sexually precocious doesn't get us any further on with their kidnapping, does it? Unless they were taken by a white slaver with a client demanding an unusually cerebral standard of post-coital conversation."

The fog was thicker over the Dean Bridge. We drove into the dense mass and the outside world completely disappeared from view. Just like the three kids and their kidnappers had done.

Katharine and I got out at the infirmary — Davie was going on to the castle to check on developments.

"You don't have to attend the post-mortem," I said to her.

Katharine looked at me coolly. "I've seen worse."

"I know you have. It's just that—"

"You don't want me to have another run-in with the Ice Queen." Her voice was sharp.

I didn't argue. The last thing I needed right now was the pair of them exchanging glares over the body of Cramond 333.

"Don't worry," Katharine said, relenting. "I'll go and visit Hector. I wonder who he'll think I am this time."

We separated in the entrance hall which, as usual, was crammed with ailing citizens. I watched as Katharine turned away towards the general wards. She walked with long strides, her head held high and her arms moving gracefully. It was hard to believe that she'd suffered prison and years of hard labour, and come through with her spirit unbroken. I knew I wouldn't have pulled that off.

I went into the mortuary and put on surgical robes in the outer room. I could see Sophia at the slab through the glass screen. She was standing at the head, directing an assistant who was wielding a dissecting knife. I pushed open the connecting door.

"Ah, there you are, Quint."

"Sophia. How are you getting on?"

"About half-way through." Her eyes above the mask opened wide. "I decided not to wait for you this time."

I followed her over to a table by the wall. "Same modus operandi?" I asked.

She nodded, pulling down her mask. "Heavy blows with a blunt instrument to the left side of the head, then a similar cavity opened in the forehead above the nose."

"And the left eye transplanted there."

"Correct." Sophia was looking at me intently. "Those missing teenagers. They must be in terrible danger." Suddenly she sounded very apprehensive. "You've got to catch this killer, Quint. He's a madman."

"You're assuming the killer's a man and that he's psychologically unstable?"

She twitched her head. "All right, I realise 'madman' isn't a term that either the medical texts or the Council would approve of. Too unspecific, too emotive. But, yes – I do think the killer is male. A fair amount of physical strength is required to break through thick bone such as that of the forehead. The blows to the side of the head also suggest a well-conditioned arm."

"There are plenty of guardswomen with well-conditioned arms," I said. "And as for psychological instability, it seems to me that the killer knew exactly what he – or she – wanted to do. The murders were carried out with precision. Think of the identical body positions, think of the mutilation, think of the branch in the right hand."

"It's like a ritual, isn't it?" Sophia said, biting her lip. "But in the Council's judgement ritual and religious rite are clear signs of mental instability, so my characterisation stands after all."

"Maybe," I conceded. I didn't want to get into a psycho-theological discussion. "I don't suppose you found any significant traces of the assailant, did you?"

"We took scrapings from the fingernails, but I think they'll turn out to be mud and the like from the locality. We found no blood or fibres from anyone else. The first blow the victim took to the head would have dropped him on the spot. There wouldn't have been a struggle."

"Anything out of the ordinary with the cadaver physiologically?"

She shook her head. "Cramond 333 was a healthy auxiliary – unusually fit even for that rank. There were no traces of alcohol or drugs and no medical irregularities."

"Time of death?"

"The organ temperatures suggest that he died between eight and nine this morning."

I looked up from my notes and nodded. "That early?"

"Does that surprise you?"

I shook my head. She'd confirmed what I'd been thinking earlier. But if the physical training instructor was killed between those hours, why had the murderer and his group waited so long before they kidnapped the nascent geniuses?

"Quint?" Sophia said, breaking into my reverie. "What is it?"

"Em, nothing." I ran my eye down her robed form, taking in the bulge in her abdomen. I wondered if daily exposure to diseased and dead bodies was good for a fetus. Then I remembered that two of the kidnapped adolescents were hotshot science and medicine students.

"Sophia, did you know . . ." I flicked the pages of my notebook ". . . did you ever meet Michael MacGregor and Dougal Strachan?"

Her eyes flicked open a touch too quickly and I remembered her apprehension about the missing kids.

"Michael . . . ?" She looked at me uncertainly. "Oh, Michael and Dougal. They're two of the kidnapped adolescents, aren't they? As a matter of fact, I did talk to them once. They were at a lecture I gave a few months back." She shook her head. "Brilliant boys," she said, her eyes locking on to mine. "You must find them, Quint. We . . . the city needs them badly."

I returned her stare, but she quickly broke away and pulled her mask back up. I wanted to ask her about the change of policy on genetic engineering that Hamilton had told me about, and I wanted to ask her why she was so concerned about the missing kids. But she'd already returned to the slab. She gave the instruction to her assistant to start sawing the skull apart.

I'd have to find a more appropriate setting for those questions later.

I met Katharine in the corridor.

"How's the old man?"

"All right, Quint. He's just dropped off to sleep. The nursing auxiliary told me he was making good progress." She laughed. "And I'm glad to say that he knew exactly who I was. No mention of Caro at all."

I was about to go to the ward to look in on Hector when my mobile rang.

"Public order guardian here."

"Yes, Lewis."

"Emergency Council meeting at four o'clock. Be there. Out."

I glared at the apparatus and then at my watch. "Bloody guardians. Why can't they give more advance warning of emergency meetings?"

"Because they're emergencies?" Katharine suggested.

"Ha. We'd better get over there. So much for going through the files on the missing kids in detail."

"I've already done that, Quint. You'll just have to trust me."

"I do, I do."

Now it was Katharine who was glaring.

The lower reaches of the Royal Mile were sunk in fog. The heavy drizzle almost defeated the windscreen wipers of the decrepit guard van that took us there. We could have hitched a lift in Sophia's vehicle, but the idea of the medical guardian and Katharine in the close confines of a Land-Rover wasn't a winner.

Inside the former Parliament building there was

plenty more gloom. The guardians were milling around the Council chamber like zombies with hangovers. Even Davie looked like he could do with a mugful of painkillers. Katharine and I took our seats next to him in the middle of the bullring.

Hamilton took the chair and got things going. "This emergency meeting is in session. As you've heard, we have a second murder on our hands."

The welfare guardian shot to his feet. "Even worse, acting senior guardian, we've lost three of the city's most promising young intellects. What do you propose to do?" His voice was even reedier than usual and his glasses had steamed up.

The public order guardian gave his colleague a crushing stare. "If your directorate's facility in Lauriston had been run more efficiently, perhaps the teenagers wouldn't have disappeared."

The welfare guardian blushed but he wasn't off the hook yet.

"And if you'd allowed me to finish," Hamilton continued, "I would have informed you of the current state of the investigation." He turned his eyes on me. "Or rather, Citizen Dalrymple and his team would have. Go ahead, citizen."

"Thanks a lot, Lewis," I muttered. I looked back at him then ran my eye round the semi-circle of Council members. They were all staring at me, Sophia and the science and energy guardian with particularly severe expressions. "Right, guardians. I believe that what we have here are the components of one case, not a string of disparate ones. The footprints and other evidence suggest that the same group of three individuals broke into the archive beneath the Assembly Hall, murdered Knox

43 in the Botanics, murdered Cramond 333 in the vicinity of Lauriston Castle and abducted the teenage prodigies. That raises several questions."

"Such as why," the raven-haired biologist said. "If, as you assert, this is one interconnected case, a single answer to that question must underpin everything. Why did the criminals break in and steal the GEC attachment? Why did they kill the two auxiliaries? And why did they kidnap the adolescents?" She gazed down at me. "Any ideas, citizen?"

I met her gaze. I had an idea all right but Hamilton wouldn't thank me for airing it – there had to be a link between the killings and the secret genetic research that she and the small group of her colleagues were involved in. If I couldn't talk about that openly, I needed another angle of attack. It didn't take long to zero in on one.

"Why is always a complex issue," I said. "Think of the philosophers who have tied themselves in knots over reasons and causes." If I thought that appealing to the guardians' predilection for analytical thought would soften them up, I was wrong. They went on gazing at me stonily. "How about approaching the case differently? How about concentrating on where?"

That got them.

"What are you talking about, Dalrymple?" Hamilton demanded. "We know where the criminal activities occurred."

"You're taking me too literally," I said. "I mean 'where' in conjunction with the science and energy guardian's insistence on 'why'."

Davie turned to me, a smile spreading across his face. I nudged him to shut him up. This was my game.

"The where I'm getting at is a city-state. It's the source of the cigarettes found at both murder scenes." I opened my arms wide. "It's your favourite place. The democratic paradise of Glasgow."

The predictable outbreak of outrage followed. I indulged them for a bit then struck back.

"On the other hand, guardians, all is not well in your own fair city." That pulled them up hard. "Both Knox 43 and Cramond 333 had Glaswegian antecedents. Given that the killer's group had access to the Labour Directorate depot and that someone told them who Edinburgh's three best young brains were, it's reasonable to assume that either or both of the auxiliaries provided inside information."

There was a long silence. Eventually the science and energy guardian rallied.

"Let's consider practicalities. How do you intend to find the missing teenagers, citizen?" she asked, her tone less assured now. "Do you think they're still in the city?"

I raised my shoulders. "I don't know, guardian." I looked at Davie. "Anything from the command centre?"

He stood up. "We've increased guard patrols all round the city line and on the coast. There have been no sightings of the stolen vehicle or of a group including three adolescents on foot."

"They may be hiding out somewhere, waiting for dark," I said, lifting my eyes to the windows in the roof. "Not long to go. There's enough fog to make spotting them a hell of a job even before nightfall."

Hamilton was sitting with his head on his left hand. With his white beard and furrowed brow, he looked like an elderly king whose forces had just been decimated on the battlefield.

"We still don't know why," he said in a low voice. "Why is all this happening?"

No one, myself included, was up to answering that.

Katharine and I went to the central archive on George IV Bridge and worked on correlating the files all evening, but we came across nothing that stood out. Davie and Hamilton supervised interrogations of everyone that knew Cramond 333 and the three nascent geniuses. There was no sign of the missing kids or their kidnappers. They were obviously getting somewhere, but the same couldn't be said for us.

At about eleven p.m. I went through Michael MacGregor's file for the third time. I studied a report he'd written about the lecture Sophia had given on "Medicine – the Social and Ethical Interface". The teenager seemed to have been very impressed by the medical guardian's ideas about how medical professionals could improve the lives of ordinary citizens. I got the impression that he was pretty keen on Sophia too, but maybe I was just imagining things.

I leaned back in my chair and watched Katharine rubbing her eyes. We'd gone as far as we could for the day and it was time to crash. But instead of packing up, I found myself thinking about eyes and the issue of sight. Why had the killers given the victims a third eye socket and transplanted their left eye there? If it was a ritual, did it have something to do with vision? Was the point that we see only what we want to see and close our eyes to the rest? After all, the third eye socket that had been chiselled out wasn't equipped with eyelids or lashes. It couldn't shut off unpleasant sights. I had a flash of the physical training supervisor's lifeless eye staring up at an unnatural angle through the blood-drenched leaves of the copper beech. And started to shiver.

"Come on, Quint," Katharine said, noticing my movement. "Let's go."

I stood up and started gathering the files together. "Where to?"

"The house of sleep," she said, yawning.

"Ah. You didn't fancy making use of those condoms you picked up this morning then?"

She stood up slowly. "God, was that this morning? It feels like a week ago."

"That was a no, I take it?"

"Give me a break, Quint. You're welcome to spend the night at my place if you want, but I'm too exhausted for sex."

"No, thanks," I said, shaking my head. "Too many nosy auxiliaries around there for me." I smiled at her. "Besides, you left the condoms at my place."

She headed for the exit. "Forget it. I'm not destroying my back on that mattress of yours for the second night running. Why don't you get a new one?"

"You don't like my flat, you don't like my mattress," I said, unable to resist the temptation to bait her. Frustrating cases often make you behave like a seven-year-old. "Next you'll be telling me you don't like me."

She turned and faced me. "Watch it, Quint."

I'd gone too far. I kept quiet and waited for her to start walking again.

A guard vehicle was lumbering up the street towards the Lawnmarket. I flagged it down and got the female driver to take us to Grindlay Street. I followed Katharine on to the pavement outside her flat and waved the Land-

Rover away. The lamp outside the auxiliary block was wreathed in mist, its light dim.

"Coming up?" Katharine asked. "Last chance."

"I don't think so."

"You don't think you'll come up or you don't think this is your last chance?" Her voice had an edge to it.

"Katharine?" I asked, taking her hand. "What is it?"

She shook me off gently but firmly. "I don't know, Quint. Sometimes it all gets too intense. The killings, the Council, your banter with Davie . . ."

I shrugged. "It's a way of surviving," I said lamely.

She turned and put her key in the lock, then twisted back and kissed me once on the lips. "Go and sleep it off. That's the best way of surviving. Night."

I watched the door close and walked slowly away. The broad thoroughfare of Lothian Road was almost invisible in the fog. I managed to find my way home by a form of ambulatory braille, narrowly escaping death from a guard Transit that came out of the murk as silently as a creature of the deep.

The lights were still on in Gilmore Place but the curfew would kick in soon. I pushed open the street door and ran up the stairs, promising myself a quick burst of the blues before turning in. Bumble Bee Slim singing "Cold-Blooded Murder" was what I had in mind.

As usual the stair light-timer gave out before I reached the third floor. While I was fumbling in my pocket for the key, I heard a quick movement behind me. I had a sudden vision of the cloaked figure with the criss-crossed face, then of the dead men with their mutilated foreheads.

"Dalrymple?" came a male voice in an unmistakable Glaswegian accent. "Quintilian Dalrymple?" He pronounced my name like it was bad joke.

185

"Yeah. Who the hell are—"

A gag was whipped round my mouth and I felt a sharp pain in my thigh. I tried to struggle but my limbs had already turned to lead.

Then I went on a trip to another galaxy.

CHAPTER TEN

They have their backs towards me, the three figures in black. They're wearing long cloaks and their hair is all over the place, bird's-nest style. I try to call out but I don't seem to be able to make any sound at all. Then I remember the guy seen by the witnesses, the guy with the stitched-up face who carries a mallet – the footprints showed that he had a couple of side-kicks. I decide against trying to make any more noise. It doesn't make any difference. The gang of three are turning to face me. Then I get a real fright.

At the left of the trio Katharine stares at me, her face blotchy and her green eyes glinting like pale fire. She doesn't speak, just looks at me accusingly then turns to the taller figure next to her. Christ. It's Hector. The old man's face is ashen, the skin taut over his cheeks and hooked nose. He stares too, his gaze cutting into my brain and forcing me to close my eyes. When I open them again, the third figure takes a single step towards me and extends a hand. It's Caro. My long-dead lover's perfect face has been ravaged by time, lines etched deep around dull brown eyes and slack lips. Caro. This time I manage to emit a cry. She frowns and steps forward again. Now the features I used to love, still love, could never stop loving, are those of a mouldering corpse.

I blink and choke as I realise that something even worse has happened to Caro's face. Now, above the line of her nose in the centre of her forehead, a third eye has blossomed. There's no mistaking the colour of the iris. This eye isn't brown like the other two. It's a piercing, visceral red.

I hear myself scream.

"Keep quiet." The voice was a harsh whisper. "Or do you want the gag tighter?" Spittle drizzled on to my cheeks.

I opened my eyes cautiously and was confronted by a face covered in heavy stubble. The head had a half-inch carpet of a similar material. I tried to move my limbs, without much success.

"Struggle all you like, pal. I tied the knots double." My captor let out a humourless laugh. "Just as well, the way you were jerking about. Nice dream, was it?" He grunted and moved away.

I recognised the voice. It belonged to the Glaswegian pillock who'd stuck the needle in me outside my flat. What the hell was going on? Above me was a low wooden ceiling and I made out a bunk to the right. The slight bobbing movement clinched it. I was on a bloody boat.

"Sleeping Beauty's woken up," I heard the bristle merchant say.

Light footsteps approached. I turned to the wall, feigning indifference.

"So he has." This time the voice was female. The West Coast accent wasn't as heavy but there was the same aggressive edge to it. "If you want something to drink you're going to have to keep the noise down." The woman leaned over me. "Or else."

I suddenly realised that my throat was drier than the

average Edinburgh stand-pipe during the Big Heat. I looked up at the face that was now above mine. If it hadn't been set in a hard expression, it would almost have been pretty. The grey eyes set above a button nose and full lips were surrounded by a mass of brown curls. But there was something worryingly forbidding about the way the woman was regarding me.

She took my lack of movement as acquiescence and loosened the gag. "Give us some water, Tam."

I drank deeply from the can that was put to my lips, the man called Tam having undone the rope that bound my upper body to the bunk. He lifted me up and stuffed a pillow under my shoulders, giving me a blast of sweaty armpits as he did so.

The woman noticed my grimace. "We've been on the road for a few days. No chance of a bath." She removed the can. "So you're the great Quintilian Dalrymple." She gave an ironic laugh. "What kind of pretentious Edinburgh name is that?"

"It's Roman, actually," I muttered, glancing at her companion. "And it's a bit classier than Tam."

"Is that right?" The bristles were up against my face again. "How would you like your Roman name stuffed up your Roman arse?"

The woman laughed again. "Now, now, Tam. Our leaders want this specimen brought back in full working order."

That sounded interesting but I didn't react. I was working on giving the impression that I was semi-comatose.

"We should be moving soon," she continued. "The skipper says the fog's thick enough to cover us."

"The sooner the better," Tam said. "This arsehole's mates will be looking for him."

I felt their eyes on me, then jerked as a shudder ran through the boat. It looked like Full Speed Ahead was on the cards. I needed to give myself a chance.

"I feel like shit," I mumbled. "I need some air."

They both laughed.

"Nice try, pal," Tam said. "Fancied a swim, did you?" He grabbed my throat. "Forget it."

The woman pulled him back. "That's all right," she said. "Quintilian can come up on deck." She pulled a large automatic pistol from her belt. "As long as he promises to behave."

"I promise," I said quickly. I meant it. You don't see many guns in Edinburgh. They scare the shit out of me.

"Let's go then." She signalled to Tam to loosen the rest of the ropes.

I stood up unsteadily and tried to shake the stiffness out of my legs.

"Here, lean on me," the woman said. She wasn't much more than five feet three but she was solid enough. She was wearing a high-quality green parka and well-oiled brown leather boots.

"Thanks," I said, staggering out of the cabin. "By the way, call me Quint. I only use my full name on special occasions."

"Like when your Council of City Guardians is crucifying Christians?" she asked

"That'll be right," I replied. "What's your name then?"

"Helen Hyslop," she said. "Chief Inspector, All-Glasgow Major Crime Squad." She gave a tight smile. "If you feel like taking a chance, you can call me Hel."

I kept my mouth shut.

*   *   *

On deck, the visibility was down to twenty yards. My watch told me it was eight-thirty in the morning. A watery light filtered through the mist, so faint that you'd hardly know the sun was up. I could just make out that the boat we were on was a medium-sized trawler with Edinburgh Fisheries Department insignia on the wheel-house.

"Don't worry," said Tam. "We didn't nick it. The *Argyll*'s one of ours. We just fitted it up to look like one of your rustbuckets." He grinned at me. Getting under way seemed to have brought about an improvement in his temper. "Sergeant Tam Haggs," he said, extending a thick-fingered hand. "All-Glasgow Major Crime . . ."

"Isn't kidnapping a major crime in your hell-hole?" I demanded, ignoring his hand.

The inspector turned round at the sound of her name. "Oh, we're not kidnapping you, Quint." She gave me a thin smile. "We've got a warrant to bring you in."

I was about to register a formal complaint when I remembered the teenagers who'd been kidnapped from the Lauriston facility. I wondered if this pair of Glaswegian cops had anything to do with the kids' disappearance. There wasn't much room to hide them on the boat, but I would need to keep my eyes and ears open. Then I remembered what the inspector had said about being on the road for a few days. What else might they have been up to in my home city?

"When you say you've got a warrant for me," I said, "what am I supposed to have done?"

"What's the matter?" Tam Haggs said with a derisive grin. "Have you got a guilty conscience about something?"

I definitely had one of those from my years in the Public Order Directorate, but not over anything to do with Glasgow. I shrugged and slowly moved my hands towards the pockets of my donkey jacket.

Hel Hyslop was on the ball. "Looking for this?" she asked, holding up my mobile. "We'll soon be out of range." She wiped moisture from her face. "If you behave, I might think about giving it back."

I looked out into the fog. It was insulating us very effectively from the outside world. All I could hear was the dull thud of the engine and splash of the waves against the hull. "Where are we?" I asked.

"Pretty near the old rail bridge," the inspector said. "We hid up in an inlet near Cramond overnight."

"Worried about the patrols?" I shook my head. "The Fisheries Guard only has a few boats these days."

She nodded. "We know that. But we had instructions to be very careful." She stared at me curiously. "You're important cargo."

That didn't make me feel any better.

"Look at the state of that," Haggs said, pointing out through the murk.

"God didn't save the king," I murmured, as we flitted past the wreck of *Britannia*. The former royal yacht had been moored in Leith and used as a tourist attraction at the end of the last century. When the crown prince got himself tied up with a Colombian drugs heiress, the man and woman in the street suddenly became rabidly republican. After ransacking Holyrood Palace, some of them cut *Britannia* loose and let her drift away – having first relieved her of every single movable object. The ship had been lying on her side on a mudbank for over twenty years, her funnel canted over her superstructure and her hull heavily pocked by machine-gun bullets from passing pirate and guard vessels. Some bright spark had picked out the words "Ship of Fools" under the name on the bow.

"Say goodbye to the perfect city, Quint," Hel Hyslop said as one of the supports of the Forth Rail Bridge loomed up on the starboard beam. The great stone pile shot up into the sky, but the tubular steel structures it bore for over a century had been in the water since the early years of the Enlightenment. In its wisdom the Council decided to destroy all road and rail connections with Edinburgh to safeguard our independence. So the furthest western boundary of the city's territory is marked by the battered remains of one of the greatest engineering feats in European history – one of many monuments to the guardians' enlightened approach.

The fog had lifted almost completely by the time we came alongside at an improvised jetty next to the remains of the Kincardine Bridge – it hadn't fared any better than its larger neighbours. I struggled with my memory to orientate myself and reckoned we were around thirteen miles upstream from the rail bridge. Given that I hadn't been outside Edinburgh territory for over twenty years, I was impressed I remembered that much.

I watched as the crew manhandled a gangway over the side. There was a flashy dark green off-road vehicle on the quay. I hadn't seen the make before. The logo told me it was a Llama. Presumably it was South American – that part of the world has been booming recently. I pretended to take an interest in the surroundings as I ran my eyes over the hold in front of the deckhouse. No sign of any other kidnapped individuals.

"Move, Quintilian," Haggs said, grabbing my arm. He led me down the gangway.

The inspector walked past us and got into the Llama's driving seat. Haggs shoved me in the other front door and crushed up against me.

"Tell me, do Glasgow police officers often go to Edinburgh, inspector?" I asked.

"MC squad operations are classified," Hyslop said, pulling away from the dock and on to a pock-marked asphalt road.

I looked back at the boat. The crewmen were still on deck but there was no one else around. There were no cloaks or mallets in the back of the vehicle either, let alone any Labour Directorate work-boots. It didn't look like Hyslop and Haggs had anything to do with the missing adolescents or the killings.

"So what do you think of the real world?" the inspector asked.

I glanced round and realised we were still very much on our own. "Where the hell is everyone, Hel?"

"Very funny," she said, giving her sergeant a look which wiped the smile off his face. "When you say everyone . . . ?"

"I mean, where's the native population? The place is completely desolate." I looked out across overgrown fields and derelict houses. Back towards Edinburgh the shattered ruins of the oil and chemical installations in Grangemouth glinted dully in the weak sunlight. They'd been casualties of the civil disorder in the early years of the century. So far I couldn't fault the Council's line that the terrain west of Edinburgh was a wasteland.

"We call these parts the desert," Haggs said. "Anyone

with any sense moved to Glasgow when the drugs wars started." He snorted. "The brainless ones went to be abused in totalitarian Edinburgh."

I let that pass. It wasn't a totally inaccurate description of the Council's regime, even though the original guardians did try to be benevolent dictators. Some of the later ones decided the adjective was unnecessary. Anyway, I was too busy looking at the road we were driving down. Burned-out lorries and overturned cars, most of them at least twenty years old, had been bulldozed out of the way. We were moving down the single passable lane at a speed I wasn't too happy about.

"What happens if we meet someone coming in the opposite direction?" I asked nervously.

Hel Hyslop laughed and hit the accelerator even harder. "What's the matter, Quint? Scared?"

"No," I lied. "I'd just like to survive this excursion if at all possible." I watched her as she concentrated on the road, her grey eyes fixed on the uneven asphalt and her expression impassive. Something about her made me uncomfortable, but I couldn't work out what it was.

She glanced at me. "Look at this." She tapped a small screen on the dashboard. I made out a maze of green lines and a few flashing red dots. "This tells me we're the only vehicle moving on the road within four miles."

I whistled. "Nice toy." I hadn't seen apparatus like that since pre-Enlightenment times. The Council purports to hate modern technology – in reality, it can't afford even bog-standard digital equipment. I was impressed that the Glasgow police had invested in it – not that I was going to tell Hyslop and Haggs. Christ, I didn't even know that a police force existed in the west. The stories we heard gave the impression that Glasgow was Anarchy City.

"Aye," Tam said, "you'll survive the drive all right, pal." He laughed emptily. "I wouldn't put money on you surviving Glasgow though."

Great. I stuck to looking out the window. Fields grown high with thistles and weeds were interspersed with devastated towns and empty villages. My first impression was that there was no one living in the roofless houses, many of which had walls holed by the anti-tank shells favoured by the drugs gangs. Then I realised that some of the windows had been covered by plastic sheeting and that patches of land had been dug out into vegetable gardens. But the inhabitants were keeping their heads down. What Haggs called the desert was no doubt scoured by raiders desperate for anything to eat.

I sat up with a start. "Jesus, what was that?" The sound I'd heard above the faint purr of the Llama's engine made my hair stand on end.

Hyslop was unperturbed. "Wolf."

"There are wolves out here?" I said incredulously.

"Oh aye," Tam Haggs put in. "They escaped from the zoos during the break-up of the UK." He grunted. "The fighting gave them plenty to eat. I suppose you don't have trouble with them in your perfect city."

I shrugged. "I've never heard of any, not even on the farms."

"Wolves know what's good for them," Hel Hyslop said. "They don't bother with underfed philosophers."

Haggs guffawed.

Then the sun burned off the last of the cloud and

everything changed. We stopped at a checkpoint. Lines of wire fencing stretched out on both sides and there was a fortified guardpost by the roadside. That wasn't what caught my eye though. Ahead of us a vast expanse of cultivated land stretched away. There were large modern tractors ploughing and sowing the fields all around. That was when I began to wonder how much the Council in Edinburgh really knew about the world beyond the city line. Maybe the guardians had even been spreading baseless rumours. For years we'd been told that Glasgow was falling apart, its citizens starving and all but the centre plagued by warring drugs gangs. With its supposedly reckless attempts at democracy, Glasgow was the guardians' number one hate object, responsible for all the dissidents and criminals who sneaked into Edinburgh. Suddenly I felt more gullible than a jackass in one of Aesop's fables.

While Hyslop was talking to the sentry, I read the sign on the guardpost wall. "Banknock Checkpoint", it proclaimed in green and yellow lettering. "Welcome to the Democratic Free State of Greater Glasgow – Let Glasgow Flourish!" Underneath there was a smaller sign directing prospective immigrants to a reception centre down the road. I looked ahead and saw a queue of ragged families. Apparently Glasgow was doing well enough to attract people from the outlying regions. Not many people had volunteered to enter Edinburgh in recent years.

"Right," said Hel. "The road's better now. We'll be able to go even faster."

"Brilliant," I said under my breath, clutching the seat as the Llama did a passable imitation of a missile being launched at Serbia before the millennium.

Haggs had been handed a bag at the checkpoint. "Here," he said. "Have a sandwich."

I opened the package he gave me and discovered a plaited roll that smelled better than any bread I'd ever had. There was a thick layer of smoked salmon and sour cream inside. "Christ, I haven't had salmon for a long time," I said, taking a large bite.

"Really?" said Hyslop. "There are fish farms in the Clyde. We can have it every day if we like."

I tried to hide my envy by asking about the surrounding countryside. "So how far does Glasgow territory extend?"

"Twenty miles to the south and over thirty to the west," she replied. "All the way to Dumbarton and Beith."

"We're looking to expand as well," Tam Haggs put in. "Except there are some serious headbangers on the coast who're giving us a hard—"

"That'll do, sergeant." The inspector gave him a look that made his ears burn. "Security information is not to be divulged to non-citizens."

Haggs bowed his head and bit his lip like a schoolboy who'd been caught with his hand down his shorts.

So I was a non-citizen, was I? That didn't make me feel optimistic about the treatment I could expect in Glasgow. Why was there a warrant out for me? It must have been something very hot for the city's leaders to authorise a snatch mission. What did they have on me? I almost asked the inspector but stopped myself in time. I had the feeling that she'd be enormously gratified if I showed any more nerves.

"How many people live inside the wire?" I asked. "If that information isn't classified."

Hel Hyslop glanced at me. "Why should it be? The population of greater Glasgow is nearly one-and-a-half million."

"Jesus," I said. Edinburgh's population had dropped by half since the turn of the century. "And you manage to feed them all?"

"Of course we do. Glasgow is a thriving modern state, not a decrepit tourist trap like Edinburgh."

I was about to argue with that description of my home town but, looking at the pristine machines in the fields and the well-maintained highway, I decided to hold my peace.

"That's right," Tam Haggs said. "And you haven't seen the half of it yet."

I had the feeling I was about to be even more surprised. Edinburgh already seemed to be on the other side of the world. As did my old man and Katharine. I wondered if Hector was all right. Then I remembered what Katharine had said about my last chance. I wanted to see her again very badly. But every mile that the Llama went was taking me further away.

"What the hell . . . I mean, what are those?" I said, peering through the windscreen.

"Thank you," Hyslop said primly. "They're the Glasgow balloons. Haven't you heard of them?"

"Obviously not." I peered at the large coloured shapes in the sky ahead. There must have been at least thirty of them, some round, some cigar-shaped, one even fashioned like a star. I could just make out cables tethering the balloons to the ground. They were floating above the tower blocks like thought bubbles above cartoon characters' heads.

"Each ward of the city has its own balloon in a colour they choose themselves," Haggs said. "In Govan it's blue." He nudged me in the ribs. "Remember Rangers? The football team?"

"Vaguely," I replied. I wasn't going to give him the pleasure of a positive answer. In fact I had very clear memories of Old Firm matches between Rangers and Celtic in the early years of the century. The riots had been so bad that the army had been sent in. The clubs claimed that drugs gangs infiltrated the grounds — maybe they did, but relations between the two sets of fans had never been what you'd call problem-free.

"Each ward is autonomous," the inspector said, stopping at a traffic light on the outskirts of the built-up area. "The idea came from the devolution movement at the end of the last century."

"I hope your system runs better than the Parliament Scotland got then," I said. "It caused a lot more problems than it ever solved." That reminded me of the break-in at the Parliament archive and the subsequent murders. Hamilton and Davie would have to cope with all that on their own now.

I looked out at the street. There were plenty of cars, most of them in brighter colours than the official green of the Llama. "Citizens are allowed their own transport, are they?" I asked.

They both looked at me as if I were crazy. "Course they are," Tam said contemptuously.

"And they can afford cars?"

"The city offers low-interest loans for car and house purchase," Hyslop said.

I tried to hide my amazement. On the streets, people were dressed in clothes that were brightly coloured and

– by Edinburgh standards – well-cut and stylish. Kids on expensive-looking bikes were riding on cycle tracks between the road and the pavement. Behind them the shops were crammed with merchandise and customers. Even the blocks of flats were in good nick, paint fresh and balconies overflowing with flowers and plants. It was hard to believe that the grimy, dilapidated citizen housing of Edinburgh was less than fifty miles away. And there weren't any obvious signs of the crime we'd been told bedevilled Glasgow. No steel shutters, no junkies, no vandalism – and only a few officious-looking sods in green outfits and peaked caps. Even the pubs looked salubrious.

"Now we're getting to the best part," Haggs said, leaning forward in his seat.

Hel Hyslop pointed to her left. "Just in case you were wondering, free-thinking is encouraged in this city."

I looked up the slope and made out the crosses and memorial stones of the necropolis, Glasgow's version of the Père Lachaise cemetery in Paris. It had been fully kitted out with neo-classical temples and catacombs in the 1800s, but now it made me think of a time several centuries before that. Draped across the incline was a huge white banner which proclaimed "Macbeth Has Returned! Share the Experience!" The letters were surrounded by lifesize colour paintings. There was a saturnine Macbeth wearing a crown, a supercilious queen and several trios of witches, all of whom were younger than my readings of the play at school suggested.

"What's all that about?" I asked. "Have the city fathers turned the graveyard into a theme park?"

The inspector slowed to let a group of Middle Eastern

tourists in full robes and head-dress cross – a year or two ago they'd have been staying in Edinburgh.

"That's the kind of shite your home town unloads on its visitors, isn't it?" Hyslop said. "We're not like that. We assume our tourists have minds as well as wallets."

"Is that right?" I asked sceptically. "So what's the game with Macbeth?"

"It's a cult," Haggs said.

"A cult?"

"Yes, a cult," the inspector said irritably. "Aren't you familiar with the word? I suppose it's been proscribed in your glorious city."

"True enough, the Council is pretty keen on atheism," I said, glancing up at the necropolis again. Figures in medieval costume were dancing around the gravestones. "They do tolerate people with genuine religious beliefs though. Believe it or not."

Haggs swallowed a laugh when he saw the inspector's expression.

"In this city," Hyslop said, "there are dozens of religious sects and cults. Some of them are versions of the organised religions of the late twentieth century and some of them are more recent. We allow people to believe what they want – no matter how off the wall it might be."

"And how off the wall is the Macbeth cult?" I asked.

Hel gave a humourless laugh. "As off the wall as a free-standing mirror."

Tam Haggs was shaking his head. "Aye, those lunatics actually believe that the guy in charge is a reincarnation of Macbeth. Apparently he's come back to make Scotland a nation again."

I could remember a lot of stuff in that vein at the turn

of the century. Most politicians who spouted about nationhood ended up dead in the riots. "Harmless, are they?" I asked.

Hel raised her shoulders. "Not my squad's brief." She sounded unhappy about that. "They put on productions of the play for the tourists as well as the locals."

"Fair enough," I said. "Culture on the streets."

The inspector nodded. "This city's always been good at that."

We drove past Queen Street railway station and I watched crowds of people passing in and out the doors. Obviously Glasgow's trains were still running – I hadn't seen one in operation since the early years of the Council. Then we moved into the commercial centre of the city and I rubbed my eyes in disbelief. The streets were packed with shoppers, some of them tourists but the majority Glasgow people – you could tell because they were wearing fist-size badges that said "I'm Glaswegian and I'm Proud". But that wasn't all. I assumed "the best part" that Tam Haggs had been on about was the city itself. It was a revelation. The buildings had been cleaned and the place was resplendent in rosy-hued sandstone and glinting, silvery granite. Anything concrete had been painted in pastel shades and flags and banners were strung across every available space. There was a band on every main junction, some playing traditional Scottish music, some blasting out jazz rhythms the like of which I'd never heard in Edinburgh. There was even a blues combo. They were having a go at David Alexander's "Standing By a Lamp-Post" – they weren't bad either.

"So what do you think?" Tam asked as we pulled up outside a towering Victorian block with grandiose columns and capitals carved all over its reddish-brown façade.

"Neat building," I said. "What is it? Your kennel?"

"What do you think of the city, arsehole?" he said, dragging me on to the pavement.

I shrugged. "It's not bad. Not a patch on—"

"Bollocks," he said. "Your place is a midden compared with this."

"All right, sergeant," Hel Hyslop said, joining us beside the Llama. "This is your hotel, Quint," she said, looking up at the magnificent edifice.

"Glad to see you're keeping me in the manner to which I'm accustomed." I wasn't going to tell them how much I was looking forward to checking in. Now I looked more closely, I could see the place's name. The sign was small, suggesting the owners didn't feel the need to boast. Then again, the hotel's name was the St Vincent Palace.

Hel gave me a frosty smile. "My superiors presumably want to soften you up." She ran an eye down my undernourished frame. "And fatten you up."

"Why?" I asked. "Is cannibalism how you keep this wonder city going?"

"You'll soon find that out for yourself, Quint." The inspector turned away.

Tam Haggs grinned and led me into the luxurious entrance. If eating people was what they were into, who was I to complain? As long as I had the free run of the hotel for a day or two.

The smiling goon in reception knew who we were. There was no messing about with filling in a registration card – that had already been taken care of. My room was on the seventh floor. Haggs took me up, told me I could order anything I wanted from room service – I got the impression he wasn't over the moon about that – and left, locking me in. Fair enough. If this was the Glasgow version of captivity, I could live with it.

The room, or rather the rooms were amazing. The top floor must have been the boardroom of the insurance company whose name still adorned the stonework on the façade. It had been split up into smaller rooms, but mine was still big enough to swing several lions. The main room was twice the size of my whole flat in Edinburgh, while the bathroom could have accommodated an extra-large harem. In fact, most of the harem could have got into the bath at one go. It stood on ornate dragon's-claw feet and was surrounded with enough marble to have reduced an Aegean island to sea level. I filled the ridiculous receptacle with more water than I'd seen in a year's worth of weekly showers in Edinburgh and wallowed, having ordered a luxury high tea complete with kippers and Dundee cake – neither of which I'd seen for a couple of decades.

After soaking and stuffing, I looked out over the city's rooftops. The skyline was still disfigured by tower blocks, but at least the multicoloured balloons and bright paintwork blunted the effect. I could see a couple of the river's bends. The Clyde actually looked inviting. The city must have invested a hell of a lot in pollution and flood control – or perhaps the Council back home had made up the story about the Clyde basin being flooded as a result of global warming a couple of years ago.

There was a knock on the door then the sound of a

key in the lock. A smiling specimen in a dress suit appeared.

"Good evening, sir," he said with what he thought was an appropriate mixture of charm and obsequiousness. "I wonder if you'd care to try these on." He produced several large paper bags from behind his back. "We estimated your various sizes when you arrived."

I pulled out a pair of sharply cut black trousers and a lime-green silk shirt. I didn't think much of the colour but it was the first silk that had been anywhere near my anatomy, so I didn't send the shirt away. There was also a selection of top-of-the-range underwear and a pair of loafers – I decided against wearing the latter, reckoning that my boots with their steel toe-caps might come in handy. And last but very definitely not least, there was a seriously cool black leather jacket. That did it – I was there for the duration. I was about to ask the hotel to get me the relevant immigration forms when the phone rang.

"Quintilian Dalrymple?" asked a smooth male voice.

"Call me Quint," I said, running my hand down the jacket.

"Right you are, Quint it is. My name's Andrew Duart, Quint. I'd like to invite you to dinner."

I waved the hotel employee away. "Do I have a choice?"

There was a dry laugh. "Realistically, no."

"Who are you, anyway?" I demanded.

"We don't usually bother with titles in Glasgow, Quint." The voice had suddenly acquired the superior tone that I'd been aware of in Hel Hyslop's. "When we do, mine is first secretary. I run the city. Is that any help?"

I wasn't going to show him any respect. "Help would be an explanation of why I'm here, pal."

"Which you'll get," Duart said. "At dinner. You'll be picked up shortly."

Maybe the luxury high tea hadn't been such a good idea after all.

CHAPTER ELEVEN

T am Haggs unlocked the door and ordered me to come with him. Under normal circumstances I would have told him to sit on the contents of his shiny holster, but I was too excited by the prospect of wearing the leather jacket. In Edinburgh vanity has been suppressed for over twenty years. I had a lot of lost time to make up.

"Where are we going?" I asked as I was led towards the lift.

"You've been told, haven't you? You're going out to dinner." It sounded like he hadn't been invited.

"Yeah, but where?"

"You'll see."

Extricating information from the sergeant was harder than getting a smile out of an auxiliary in Edinburgh. We exited the lift and skirted a group of animated Chinese tourists. Outside it was hard to tell that night had fallen. The streets were lit up brighter than Berlin in 2003 when a bunch of neo-Nazis firebombed the Reichstag. The shops were all still open and there was no shortage of customers. Glasgow seemed to be shoppers' paradise.

"Where's the inspector?" I asked as Haggs pushed me into the Llama.

"You'll see her soon enough."

"Shouldn't you be giving me the guided tour?" I demanded. "After all, your bosses seem to think I'm worth pampering."

"Shut your face, you Edinburgh poof!" the sergeant yelled. "If I had my way you'd never have got as far as the border." He slammed his foot on the brake.

I put my arms out to stop myself crashing into the windscreen. "Fuck you, Haggs!"

He grinned at me malevolently as he waved an old lady across the road. "Always fasten your seat-belt before commencing a journey." He gave me a derisive look. "Course, you don't have cars where you come from, do you?"

I ignored that. If Haggs started thinking he'd got the better of me, maybe his concentration would drop and I'd be able to give him the slip. I twitched my head. What the hell was I thinking? Even if I got loose, how would I get out of the city?

We turned east on to the road that ran alongside the Clyde. Pleasure boats festooned with lights were moving slowly up and down. There were plenty of people having a good time on board.

"Tourists?" I asked.

"Some of them," Haggs said. "Most will be Glasgow people. We all get a free evening's entertainment from the city once a month." He glanced at me. "I bet you wankers don't."

"No, we spend our spare time down the mines."

The sergeant laughed. "And sucking off the tourists, I heard."

"That'll be right, dickhead," I said under my breath.

"Watch it, son. I've got very good hearing."

So I watched the city and its lights. Soon we turned

away from the river and cut past an expanse of parkland.

"Isn't that Glasgow Green?" I asked, a distant memory stirring. I once ended up there with a girlfriend when I was a schoolboy daytripper. A park keeper caught me with my hand down her blouse and called his mates over to have a laugh. That was the last time I went out with the girl in question.

Haggs was nodding. "And this is where you get off." Ahead of us was a squat sandstone building. Bright lights shone off the high semi-circular glasshouse to the rear. "The People's Palace," he said, a note of pride in his voice. "This is where the elected representatives hold all their evening events."

They were certainly keen on stressing the informal nature of the city. The so-called palace looked more like an oversized café than a gathering place for the high and mighty. The car park to one side was full of Llamas. Someone in the administration must have done a major deal with the manufacturers. I wondered if there were any kickbacks involved – so far everything about Glasgow was too good to be true.

"Come on," the sergeant said. "They're waiting for you, Christ knows why."

I stepped out and checked my leather jacket was hanging right, which made my escort smirk. Then he saw his superior and got serious.

"Everything all right, Tam?" Hel Hyslop asked. She was wearing an elegant black trouser suit that managed to say "I am a responsible city servant" and "I'm pretty cool" at the same time.

"He's a real pussycat," Haggs replied. I got the impression he had a large collection of gangster movies.

"Uh-huh." Hyslop looked at me dubiously. "A pussy-cat in leather." She turned to her sergeant. "Stand by in the squadroom," she ordered. "I may need you later."

Haggs nodded and hit the road. I knew one thing about him for sure – he was bloody keen on his job. I wondered when he'd last slept.

"Right," the inspector said. "They're waiting for you."

"They?" I asked. "Who are they, exactly?"

"The ward representatives. All fifty of them are here."

I stared at her. "Fifty of them? What do they want from me?"

She met my gaze. "I imagine they want to examine a specimen from Edinburgh, Quint."

It was then that I remembered the crack I'd made about cannibalism. Being invited over for dinner suddenly lost some of its appeal.

The people in the long function room stopped talking as soon as I appeared. I noticed a couple of things immediately. One, they were all – both men and women – wearing clothes that by Edinburgh standards were very high-altitude fashion. And two, most of them had a heavy gold chain of office round their necks, each with a different design.

A tall guy with unnaturally black hair swept back from his face and a carefully trimmed goatee beard stepped forward.

"Good evening, Quint," he said, smiling broadly. "We spoke earlier. Andrew Duart." He nodded to the inspector. "Hel."

"Andrew," she riposted. First names were obviously de rigueur.

"So, Andrew," I said, accepting the glass of what

smelled like extremely rare malt that he handed me, "are you the one who signed the warrant for me?" There was still silence all around us. I went for broke. "Are you the one who authorised my kidnapping?"

The smile on Duart's face didn't fade and there were no sharp intakes of breath around the room. Maybe they were all in on it. Oh well, it was worth a try.

"Drink your whisky, Quint," he said. "There are no secrets here."

I drank my whisky and let him give me a refill, but I didn't buy his line. Long experience of the Council's love affair with information control made me suspicious of any power structure that flaunts its openness. Still, the whisky was excellent and I didn't have anything better to do that night.

People started coming up to me and shaking my hand. They were all cheery and welcoming — something I couldn't square with the way I'd been brought to Glasgow. The women were smart, like Hel Hyslop carrying their clothes with a lack of affectation, and the men had strong grips and jutting jaws. After a while I began to realise that none of them looked more than fifty — Duart probably wasn't even that old. So how come there weren't any more mature ward representatives? Did this supposedly free and equal state discriminate against its aged citizens?

Then, as if to deal conclusively with that line of thought, two older men confronted me. The first was of average height and his face was very gaunt. His chest was poking forward like a pigeon's, gold chain to the fore.

"From Edinburgh, are you?" he said, his bright blue eyes fixed on mine. "What are you doing over here,

Quintilian Dalrymple?" He suddenly seemed to remember his companion. "This is Mister Trent Crummett of Ohio. He's also a long way from home."

Before I could answer, Duart took my arm. He led me towards the centre of a long table. Hel Hyslop kept close behind.

"Who was that guy?" I asked, glancing back at the man with the piercing eyes.

"David Rennie," the first secretary replied, twitching his head. "One of our more . . . um . . . enterprising ward representatives. He's brought a lot of American business to the city."

I got the feeling that Duart wasn't a fan. Then I was distracted by the spread in front of me. "Jesus," I gasped. A cold collation that Mrs Beeton would have been impressed by was laid out on the pristine table linen – everything from lobster and crayfish to legs of lamb and mounds of rare roast beef. There was also a huge display of fresh vegetables and fruit, including many varieties that I hadn't seen since I was a kid.

"Better than you're used to in Edinburgh?" Duart asked, his lips twitching into another smile.

"Just a touch," I mumbled, but I wasn't going to let him have it all his own way. "This produce wasn't all grown in Glasgow and its environs."

"A large part of it was," he said, contradicting me smoothly. "Glasgow agriculture has been very successful in recent years. Of course, we do trade intensively with other parts of Britain and Europe, not to mention the rest of the world." He sat down and draped a spotless napkin over his lap. "Glasgow is totally committed to equality and the sharing of produce and profit. Free enterprise flourishes and all citizens are treated in the same way."

I glanced down the table at the ward representatives in their flash clothes. "If everyone's equal, how come this lot get designer suits? How come they wear gold chains to distinguish them from everyone else?"

Andrew Duart didn't show any sign of irritation. Instead he just gave me another of his annoying smiles. "I meant to ask you, Quint. How do you like the clothes we sent over?" He ran his eyes over me. "The jacket fits very well, doesn't it?"

I shrugged. "If you want to expand my wardrobe, why should I object? I haven't bought into your brand of democracy."

"No, you're the one who's spent the last twenty years working for a dictatorship." Even now Duart's tone was light and his eyes playful. "But leaving that aside, I'm happy to answer any questions you might have. As regards clothes, all Glasgow citizens receive an allowance for fashion items such as these you see around the table. We have some of the best designers in the world and the fashion industry here is very well developed." He gave a smile which, this time, was definitely self-satisfied. "We see no reason why the populace at large shouldn't gain some benefit from the industry's success."

Christ, Glasgow a centre of world fashion? Things had definitely changed since I was a teenager.

"As for the chains of office," Duart continued, leaning back to allow a waiter to fill his wine glass, "they were donated by one of the multinationals we work with. They're the property of the city, not the individuals who wear them."

"But the individuals who wear them stick out from the masses, don't they?" Suddenly I felt a hand on my left thigh. Hel Hyslop was holding a glass in her other hand but she was definitely the guilty party.

"It's a mark of office, not of material difference from the citizen body," Duart said, serving scallops on to his plate.

"But—" I broke off and winced. Strong fingers had just gripped my cock very hard.

Duart glanced at me. "Something wrong?"

"Em, no, nothing at all." I gave Hel Hyslop a loose smile then picked up my glass. "Pretty interesting wine, Andrew," I said, taking the inspector's hint. As soon as I changed the subject, the hand was withdrawn.

While Duart gave me a detailed description of Glasgow's trading links with the wine merchants in the parts of France that had shaken off fundamentalist Muslim rule, I looked at Hyslop. She was a lot less fierce in her evening outfit, her brown curls and small nose making me think of an innocent schoolgirl. Then I remembered where she'd had her hand.

The meal passed quickly. Despite having filled my belly earlier on, I found that the lobster tails and prime-quality beef were irresistible. As I ate, I kept encountering curious looks from the ward representatives. It seemed I was an object of fascination to them, an alien from a pariah state that didn't allow its citizens to vote. The man with the gaunt face who'd found out my name was at the far end, but he favoured me with several long stares – in between helping his heavy American friend to the best of the food.

After coffee – better than anything even the VIP tourists get in Edinburgh – and more top-quality malt, Duart got to his feet and led me away from the table. Hel Hyslop was close behind.

"Let's retire to the conservatory," the first secretary said. "We'll be able to talk more freely there."

We went into the great domed glasshouse. A semi-circle of wicker chairs had been set up at the far end, facing an open expanse of grass that was lit up brighter than a blaze in a distillery. I could make out men in green parkas patrolling, automatic pistols in holsters hanging from their belts.

"I see you need to protect yourselves from the ordinary citizens," I said after the waiter had brought a tray with a selection of whiskies.

Duart gave an unconcerned shrug. "Standard security procedures." He glanced at Hyslop. "Isn't that so, Hel?"

She nodded. "We have criminal elements like every other city."

"And you use guns to keep them at bay?" I said, shaking my head. "Welcome to the Wild West of Scotland."

Duart was smiling as usual. "The police are issued with firearms, yes. But citizens may also carry them if they so desire."

I looked at him in disbelief. "That's your idea of democracy, is it? Don't you remember the massacres that tore the US apart after the millennium?"

Duart didn't rise to that. "The Americans had severe problems with religious extremists and ethnic suprema-cists. We do not."

I was thinking about the Macbeth cult I'd seen earlier, one of the many apparently permitted to function in Glasgow. As I poured myself a slug of an island malt that I hadn't seen for decades, I wondered if Duart knew what he was talking about.

"And besides," the man with the goatee continued,

"this city observes the rule of law. Unlike Edinburgh, we have an independent judiciary."

I gave him a guffaw Tam Haggs would have been impressed by. "The rule of law? That includes kidnapping people from other states, does it?"

"A full and proper warrant was made out for your—" Duart broke off and cleared his throat. "For your admission to Glasgow."

"So I keep hearing. And who wrote the law empowering you to sanction abduction? Some minion in your so-called independent judiciary, no doubt." I glared at the pair of them. "Have you told the ward representatives how I came to be here?"

Duart laughed. "They know all they need to know."

The Council's top-heavy regime back home had made me extremely suspicious of anyone who wields power. "Who elected you anyway? How come you haven't got a golden necklace to wear?"

Hel Hyslop was giving me the eye but this time she couldn't reach my groin.

"I and all the members of my executive office were elected by the ward representatives," Duart said.

"Oh, very cosy," I said ironically. "So as long as you feed the representatives well, you've got a free hand."

"We don't have to listen to this," Hyslop said, sitting forward and taking a mobile phone from her pocket. "I'm taking this piece of Edinburgh crap to the squadroom."

Andrew Duart raised his hand. "Hold on, Hel. Quint is entitled to know why he's here."

I'd had enough of first names and of being given the run-around. "Look, Duart, I don't give a fuck why you kidnapped me. I'm needed in Edinburgh." Hector's wizened face had flashed in front of me, but I decided against telling them about the state of the old man's health. There was no point in giving them even more of a hold over me. "I've got pressing business."

"Pressing business?" Hel Hyslop asked intently. "What are you working on at the moment?"

"That's classified," I replied. "Just do what you have to do and let me get back home." I was flying a kite here. For all I knew my ticket to Glasgow was stamped "one way only".

Duart was studying me, one hand supporting his chin. "Listen to me carefully, Quint. Whatever you've heard in Edinburgh, Glasgow has been a major success story over the last five years. Our software industry is at the cutting edge, engineering is coming back on stream, our clothes designers and manufacturers have a worldwide reputation." He smiled encouragingly. "Remember what used to be referred to as the Asian tiger economies when we were young? We're the northern European equivalent."

"Didn't the tiger economies go down the toilet faster than a deep-fried haggis around the millennium?"

Duart's expression didn't change. "We're in much better shape than any of them ever was."

"Well, good for you, Andy. What's any of this got to do with me?"

"The name's Andrew," Duart said, his tone harsher. He leaned forward and poked a finger into my thigh. I wished Glaswegians would leave the lower half of my anatomy alone. "We've got a good thing going here, Quint," he said. "I'm not going to let anyone screw it up." He jabbed his forefinger in hard. "Especially not a sick, murdering bastard from your home town."

Now he had my full attention.

Hel Hyslop must have felt left out in the cold. She

leaned forward too, her eyes locking on to mine. "And that sick, murdering bastard will only talk to you, Quint," she said. "Meaning that, for the time being at least, you're very important to us." She glanced at her boss. "If you co-operate, you might see Arthur's Seat and the castle again. If you don't . . ."

She didn't finish that sentence, but I got her drift.

Shortly afterwards a soberly dressed young man came to attend Andrew Duart. The first secretary rose and offered me his hand.

"Inspector Hyslop will look after you, Quint," he said, nodding to her. "No doubt I'll see you tomorrow. Good luck with your investigation." He strode away.

"Investigation?" I said as Hel led me towards the exit. "What investigation?"

"Not now," she said, skirting the long dinner table. Many of the ward representatives were still there, their faces sweaty and their voices loud. A heavy cloud of cigarette and cigar smoke was hanging over them.

"I see people are encouraged to look after their lungs in Glasgow," I observed.

Hel Hyslop shot me an angry glance. "Unlike in Edinburgh, people are given the freedom to choose." Her voice was even more sarcastic than mine. "If they want to damage their health by smoking, that's their decision. Marijuana and hashish are freely available too, which removes the incentive for smuggling soft drugs."

"Very enlightened," I said under my breath.

In the entrance hall the inspector collected her pistol belt and strapped it round her waist. I could see plenty more firearms in the cloakroom.

"Does everyone in this city have a gun?" I asked.

She shrugged. "A lot of people do. Most citizens are trained how to use them. There are very few accidental deaths."

"How about incidents of people taking the law into their own hands?" I asked as we went out into the night air. The evening temperature in the west seemed to be a few degrees higher than in Edinburgh at this time of year.

"Stop finding fault, you tosser," Hyslop said acidly.

I grinned at her as we approached the Llama. "You're the ones who've got a sick, murdering bastard on your hands, not me." Then, as I got in, I remembered the mutilations I'd recently seen in Edinburgh and realised how inaccurate that statement was.

"Where exactly are we heading?" I asked as we drove back into the city centre. The streets were still busy, people going in and out of the numerous up-market bars and restaurants. There was no sign of any misbehaviour, even though I could see the tell-tale bump of firearms under some jackets. Maybe they were just fashion accessories.

Hel Hyslop's mouth was pursed. "Wait and see."

I was glad I'd wound her up, but it was about time she started filling me in. "Come on, Hel. If you want me in on a case, you'll need to trust me."

She ran her tongue along her lips then nodded reluctantly. "All right." She gave me a hostile glance. "But I want you to know that this was the committee's idea, not mine."

"The committee being Duart's baby?"

Hyslop shook her head. "The executive committee is nobody's baby. It has collective responsibility to run the city's centralised departments so, in effect, it runs the whole city – even though local power rests with the wards."

She pulled up in a restricted parking area in George Square.

"That used to be the City Chambers, didn't it?" I said, angling my head towards the vast Victorian pile that took up the whole of the wide square's eastern end. The domes on its corners and the tall central tower were brightly lit.

"Still is," the inspector said. "That's where the committee's offices are. And the Major Crime Squad's."

I followed her across the square. The tarmac on the roads around the paved area was green and yellow – the colours of the city. It was damp underfoot, a group of cleaners removing every speck of dirt. I wondered if the wards could afford to look after their neighbourhoods so fastidiously. I had the feeling that the wards weren't as much in control as their representatives might imagine. Duart's executive committee reminded me of what the Council had done in Edinburgh: get yourselves installed in power, find a striking building and concentrate all departments including the law enforcement agencies in it. Then do what you like.

Hyslop pushed open one of the high doors and flashed ID at a sentry who was clutching a machine-pistol. "He's with me," she said, glancing over her shoulder. "If you see him anywhere on his own, cuff him."

I gave the young heavy a provocative smile and walked into the main hall. There was marble all around, as well as granite, mosaic floors and enough pillars to equip a Hellenistic new town. It didn't look like the executive committee had done much to publicise its occupancy though – apart from a direction board covered in impenetrable abbreviations and numbers. A defining characteristic of bureaucratic structures is "Confuse The Public". Not that many ordinary Glaswegians would get past lover boy on the door, I reckoned.

Hel Hyslop led me to a lift and hit the button for the fourth floor.

"I fancied walking," I protested. "This place is spectacular." I also fancied having a nose round.

She gave me a brief smile. "If you think I'm letting you stroll about the committee's offices, forget it."

"You never know, I might pick up some good ideas to take back home."

The inspector shook her head slowly and stared at me with unwavering eyes. "A lot has to happen before you see Edinburgh again."

I felt my stomach somersault. It may have been the movement of the lift that got to me, but the smart money was on Hel Hyslop. When she wanted to, she could scare the shit out of me effortlessly.

Tam Haggs stood up like he was on parade as soon as we walked into the Major Crime squadroom. It was a large open-plan area with dozens of desks and dozens of state-of-the-art computers. Well, I guessed they were state of the art. Compared with them, the Public Order Directorate gear back home was neolithic.

"Hiya, Tam," the inspector said. The informality wasn't particularly convincing. "Anything new?"

He shook his head. "The prisoner's in your office." He grinned. "Shackled, of course."

"Right," Hel said. "Let's see how pleased he is to see his friend here."

Haggs went over to a door in the corner and unlocked it. I felt my heart begin to pound in my chest. "His friend"? Who the hell was insisting on my presence before he would talk? And who was so significant to the Glasgow authorities that they ran the risk of crossing the Edinburgh border to abduct me?

The sergeant stepped back and stood by the open door.

"Go on then," his superior said tersely, opening her eyes wide at me. I caught a curious glint in them. I reckoned she was a lot more interested in my reaction to the mysterious captive than she wanted to let on.

I stepped forward into the room. The only light was a shaded one over the desk so there wasn't much to see. A window at the far end looked out over the wide street to another office block. I could see some poor sod pounding away at his keyboard. I hoped they had overtime in Glasgow.

Then the overhead light flashed a couple of times and came on. I became aware of a figure slumped in a chair to my right. He was wearing a bright yellow boiler suit and his arms and legs were chained to rings set in the floor. I couldn't see his face but his skull was shaved. The skin was discoloured by bruises and there were spots of dried blood on it.

"Wake up, ya shite!" Haggs yelled, leaning over the prisoner and slapping his face. "Wake up!"

The form in the chair slowly came to life. He raised his head with difficulty and glared up at the sergeant.

"Suck . . . my cock . . . Weegie dogfucker," the prisoner said with a series of gasps.

I caught Tam's arm before he gave the helpless man another belt. "Do you want me to talk to him or not? He's no good to you unconscious, is he?"

223

"Unconscious? That bastard'll be praying for oblivion soon."

"All right, sergeant," Hyslop put in. "Let Quint talk to him."

At the mention of my name, the bound man twitched and slowly raised his head.

That's when I recognised him. The voice had already got me going and the ravaged face was the clincher.

"Jesus," I said, bending over the guy and lifting his chin higher. "Is that you, Leadbelly?"

He batted his eyelids a couple of times then opened his mouth in an attempt at a grin. There was only one tooth visible. "My saviour," he said with a hoarse laugh.

Then he passed out.

Hyslop sent Haggs to get water.

"What have you been doing to the poor bugger?" I demanded.

"So you do know him?" she said, ignoring my question.

"Yeah, I know him." Until I found out what was going on, I wasn't going to tell her that Leadbelly had been a member of one of the most savage drugs gangs that ever plagued Edinburgh. We caught him back in 2015 and I'd used him a couple of times in big cases. After the second one, I got him released from the prison on Cramond Island. It was about four years since I'd last seen him.

Hel Hyslop gave me an infuriated stare. "Well? Did he have a record? Was he a known killer?"

"Yes" was the answer to both those questions but, again, I kept that to myself.

"Inspector," I said, as Tam Haggs reappeared with a bucket, "you owe me information first."

Leadbelly shook and came round as the contents of the bucket landed on him, then on the tiled floor.

Hel bit her lip then nodded. "Very well. Sergeant, dry him down and give him something hot to drink. We'll begin the interrogation in five minutes." She moved away to the far side of the squadroom.

"What I'm about to tell you is completely confidential," she said when I caught up with her.

"Who am I going to spill my guts to, for Christ's sake? I don't know anyone in this bloody city."

"No one except Leadbelly," the inspector said with a tight smile.

"So what's he supposed to have done?" I asked impatiently.

Hel Hyslop moved up close to me and started speaking in a low voice. "Over the last two months there's been a string of horrific murders in the city. Eight people – four men and four women – were slaughtered in the same way. In the first seven cases their bodies were left at prominent road junctions in different wards."

"Anything to do with the firearms carried by every man, woman and dog around here?"

She shook her head emphatically. "Absolutely not."

"What was the modus operandi then?"

Hyslop stared at me, her mouth suddenly slack. "The victims were killed by heavy blows to the head with a blunt instrument."

I felt my own jaw begin to drop.

"That's not all," she said. "In each case a hole was smashed in the forehead. One of the eyes was then torn out and rammed into it."

I tried to disguise my amazement. Fortunately the inspector had lowered her eyes.

"Your friend Leadbelly was found unconscious at the scene of the eighth killing a week ago. There were the traces of a heavy heroin fix in his system." Hel raised her eyes to mine again. "The victim was a nineteen-year-old woman, Quint. She was six months pregnant. When we got there, the psycho shitebag had passed out. He had a blood-stained mallet in his right hand and a chisel bearing fragments of bone and brain in his left hand." She grabbed my wrist. "I'm going to see to it that the fucker's executed but I need a confession. If you don't get one from him, I'll make sure you go the same way."

Jesus, Leadbelly, I thought. Whose nightmare have you dragged me into?

CHAPTER TWELVE

T he atmosphere in the corner office was getting seriously sweaty.

"Come on then, you bastard," Tam Haggs, said, bending over Leadbelly. "Fucking talk."

The prisoner looked up at him and shook his head. Drops of water spattered on to Haggs's bristles. "No way, pig. I told you. I'm only talking to Quint."

I glanced at Hel Hyslop. "This guy was in solitary confinement for years. He's used to keeping his mouth shut."

Haggs pulled out a cosh and measured up a swing at Leadbelly's jaw. "Don't worry, I'll open it for him."

Hel put her hand on his arm. "Leave it, Tam. This is why Quint was brought in." She turned to me. "So he's got a record, has he? Right, I'm giving you half an hour." She moved to the door.

"Wait a minute, woman." Leadbelly's voice cracked when he raised it. "I'm not thick. You'll be recording everything we say."

The inspector looked back, her face blank – for me that was more worrying than a scowl.

"So I'll tell you what you're going to do," the prisoner continued. "Get us a disc with some music on it and stick it in the machine over there." Leadbelly grinned loosely. "And no lip-reading through the windows."

Hyslop's expression hadn't changed. "Any particular kind of music you'd like?" she asked.

"Aye." Leadbelly's grin widened. "The blues. Quint and me are big fans."

Hel Hyslop's eyes rested on me, long enough to imply that she wasn't much of a twelve-bar enthusiast. "See to it, sergeant," she said, stepping away briskly.

Leadbelly kept quiet until Haggs came back with a disc, a thunderous look on his craggy features.

"Later on I'm going to stick this up your arse, you shite," he hissed, brandishing the disc and lifting his heavy boot over Leadbelly's bare foot.

I pushed him off before he could do any more damage, feeling solid muscle in his arm when I made contact.

"Watch yourself, Quint," Big Tam said. "Nobody pushes me around." He moved towards the player.

"Nobody except Hel Hyslop," I said, giving him a mocking smile when he looked back.

Leadbelly laughed.

Haggs didn't say a word, he just turned on the music and left. It was Whistlin' Alex Moore singing the "Ice-Pick Blues". Brilliant choice.

"So what's the story, Leadbelly?" I asked after a short break to enjoy the track and to make sure that Hyslop and Haggs had moved away from the glass.

He lifted his battered head. "Give me some more of that coffee," he said. "Better than anything we ever got in Edinburgh, isn't it, man?"

I held the mug to his lips. They were scabbier than a

late-twentieth-century politician's reputation. "Is that why you came to Glasgow?"

"Shit, yeah," he said, sitting back and shaking his chains. "No rationing of booze, decent food, clubs with blues bands playing every night, plenty of grass—"

"And plenty of opportunities for the professional criminal?"

The former drugs gang member shook his head. "I wouldn't know about that. I've gone straight."

I sat on the desk opposite him and gave him the eye. "That's not what I'm hearing, Leadbelly. Christ, I never had you down as a serial killer. Hyper-violent, dope-trafficking scumbag, yes, but cold-blooded psycho, no. Or did your time on Cramond Island drive you right over the edge?"

"No, it fucking didn't," he said, staring up at me with rheumy eyes. "You've got to help me, man. I never murdered that woman. They're going to slaughter me for something I didn't do."

"Slaughter you?" It seemed to me he was in need of a tranquilliser dart. "I wouldn't pay too much attention to what Hyslop and Haggs say. They're just trying to put the shits up you. Successfully, it appears."

Leadbelly was shaking his head desperately. "No, Quint, that's not what I'm talking about." His hands were shaking too. "They've got capital punishment in this city. Each ward chooses its own method. In Kelvin-grove murderers get hanged, drawn and quartered."

"Jesus." I leaned back and thought of the carousing ward representatives I'd seen earlier. Duart and his hard-edged charm came to mind as well. "So much for the civilised state of Glasgow."

The prisoner stared at me. "It's not that much worse

than Edinburgh, pal. At least they don't treat you like a slave here."

"There's more than one way to achieve that end, my friend." I leaned forward again. "You'd better tell me what you've been up to, Leadbelly." I raised a finger. "And no bullshit. My return ticket depends on you. I'm meant to get a confession out of you."

He let out a scornful laugh. "You're in a dumper truck full of shit then."

I nodded. "I'm not the only one. They found you stoned and covered in blood at a murder scene. How are you going to talk your way out of that?"

"Simple," he said. "I was framed. I don't do the big H, I never did. You remember that, don't you?"

I cast my mind back to Leadbelly's record. He was right. I couldn't recall any mention of him being an addict. Drugs gang members in Edinburgh tended to smoke grass and avoid the real thing—they preferred to make as much profit as they could on heroin, cocaine and the new designer drugs rather than waste them on themselves.

"So what?" I said. "Maybe you started after you got here. Soft drugs might be legal but what kind of a hard drugs scene is there in Glasgow?"

He laughed darkly. "What kind do you think? This place has got a history. You can get anything you want. From what I've heard, the operators in each ward have got the representatives in their pockets."

I saw the city's top rank round the dinner table again, their flash clothes and jewellery glinting under the chandeliers. Wherever you go, excrement floats.

"Are you sure that isn't what you've been doing, Leadbelly? Working your old trade?"

He shook his head. "No way. I couldn't have muscled

in on the business even if I'd wanted to. Those guys are serious headbangers."

There was a gap between songs. During the silence I studied his wrecked features and decided he was probably telling the truth. He'd always been smarter than your average heavy.

"Have some more coffee." I held the mug to his mouth. "What have you been doing over here, Leadbelly? Why did you come to Glasgow?"

He cocked an ear. "Do you know this one, Quint?" he asked.

"Peetie Wheatstraw, 'Gangster's Blues'."

He nodded, grinning. "Are those cunts trying to tell us something?"

"Probably."

"Why did I come here?" Leadbelly pushed against his shackles. "I wish I hadn't. But I'd had enough of Edinburgh to last me a lifetime. After you got me off the island, I tried to buckle down." He laughed bitterly. "The Welfare Directorate wasn't much help. They recommended me for a job in the Sewage Department. I got the message."

"So you took your chances with the border guards?"

"That was no problem. I hadn't forgotten all my tricks. I met some Glaswegian smugglers on the other side of the line. They brought me back with them."

"Very decent of them. They didn't by any chance suggest a line of work for you over here, did they?"

Leadbelly looked at me thoughtfully. "I'm glad I asked for you, Quint. You're still sharp."

"Yeah, yeah, I'm still so sharp I got myself kidnapped." I bent over him. "And all because of you. Spill your guts or I'll let the executioner do it for you."

He jerked back. "All right, all right. Listen, man, there's something really big going down. Pretty soon you'll be kissing my dick for the in I gave you."

"At this rate it won't be long before your dick's being waved around by the man with the chopper. What's going down? And what were you doing at that murder scene?"

The prisoner stared at me then nodded slowly. "Okay, here's how it was. I'd had a few whiskies—"

"What a surprise."

"Aye, all right," he said, dropping his eyes. "I was pissed. But not so bad that I don't remember what happened, you fuck." He clammed up.

"Spare me the sensitive soul act, Leadbelly. I've been pissed myself occasionally. Like three times a week since I was seventeen."

He laughed. "Is that all? Okay, so I was in my local all night."

"Where is your local?" I asked.

"Parkgrove Terrace, next to Kelvingrove Park. The pub's called the Paddy Field. They grow rice in the flooded bits next to the river there."

I shook my head. Rice in central Glasgow? We had the Big Heat in Edinburgh too, but the city hadn't turned into Shanghai.

"Who were you with?" I asked.

Leadbelly raised his shoulders. "No one special. Just the regulars."

"You haven't got a circle of scummy friends who share your interest in the blues?"

He shook his head. "Naw. I keep myself to myself. Seven years in the slammer doesn't make you very sociable."

THE BLOOD TREE

"No, I don't suppose it does." I found myself thinking of Katharine. She'd done three years on Cramond Island and it had left its effect on her. I wondered where she thought I'd got to, then banished her from my mind and turned back to the prisoner. "What time did you leave the pub?"

"I'm not sure. Late. They stay open till three here."

"Very good of them. Then what happened?"

The former drugs gang member looked away. "Em . . ."

I grabbed his clammy chin. "What happened, Leadbelly?"

He shied away. "I . . . I don't know."

"That's convenient," I said, turning his face back towards mine. "If you're into personal disembowelment."

He shivered. "I'm no' bullshitting you, Quint." He shook his head hopelessly. "I don't know, honest. I stopped for a piss down the road and that's all I remember. I reckon some bastard took me from behind."

"Where do you live?" I asked.

"I've got a flat round the corner from the Paddy – in Royal Crescent."

"Sounds up-market."

He looked at me shiftily. "It's not bad."

"I'm not very hot on Glasgow geography, Leadbelly. Is Park Terrace Lane where you and the body were found on the way from the pub to your place?"

He shook his head. "Naw. Park Terrace Lane's about five minutes' walk to the north-east of the Paddy."

"And there's no way you could have wandered up there in a drunken stupor?"

Leadbelly took offence. "Listen, you. I can take my drink, okay?"

I leaned over him. "The victim was a young woman.

You sure you didn't fancy your chances with her?" I had a sudden flash of Caro lying on the barn floor in Soutra surrounded by members of the gang Leadbelly used to belong to, a rope round her neck.

He must have realised what I was thinking about. He twitched his head. "No, man. I'm not like that. I wasn't even like that when I was with Howlin' Wolf. The others thought I was bent."

I sat back, nodding. I believed him. He'd informed on his arsehole colleagues more than once. So what the hell was going on?

"If you can afford a flat, you must have a source of income, Leadbelly. What is it?"

He looked round, straining against the chains to check that no one else was in sight. "Turn that music up, Quint," he said.

I went over to the machine and increased the volume, not enough to attract attention.

"What's the big secret?" I asked when I got back to the chair. "And what's this big deal you mentioned?"

Leadbelly motioned his head to get me even closer. "I'm not telling you everything, Quint. I'm not that stupid. I need an insurance policy."

I glared at him. "When did I ever let you down? I sent you blues tapes when you were inside, I got you out when you helped me."

"Aye, I know that. But this is bigger than you. This is a fucking nightmare." He looked down. "Believe me, you don't want to know the whole of it, Quint."

"Oh, thanks a lot, Lead. You get me kidnapped, you pull my dick and then you go all coy." I stood up. "Time to call in Hyslop and Haggs."

"No, no." Leadbelly was looking round again, his

eyeballs popping. "I need you to get me out of here, Quint."

"So help me to help you, for Christ's sake."

He got his breathing under control. "All right." One last glance over his shoulder. The outer office was dimly lit and there didn't seem to be anyone near the glass door. "All right. When I got to Glasgow a couple of years back, I stuck with those smugglers I told you about for a bit. They weren't exactly professional criminals, more like traders trying to open up new areas of business. The wards here support budding entrepreneurs, especially when they're looking to sell Glasgow produce. My guys were mostly into cigarettes and grass."

"There's plenty of black market potential for those commodities in Edinburgh."

"True enough." Leadbelly scraped his chin on his shoulder to deal with an itch. "Anyway, it was all pretty minor action and the money was shite. So I headed into the centre and checked out the employment agencies." He gave a sad smile. "Reckoned it was time I cleaned up my act a bit. Then I got myself interviewed by this handy-looking bird in an office in Sauchiehall Street. She offered me a job before I even finished telling her the working history I'd made up. I thought I'd died and gone to heaven." He shook his head. "I should have known that the other place was the only destination for someone with my record." He looked over my shoulder to the desk. "Coffee."

I gave him another drink and watched him lick his chapped lips.

"Thanks, man. Well, this bird – Melanie was her name – turned out to have a major client on her books."

"Who was that?"

Leadbelly glanced round again. "I'm getting to that. She was a smart lassie, had a doctorate in psychology or something. After we went out for a drink, she came clean. She was looking for guys to work on a special project. Guys with dead eyes, she said."

I stared at him, only vaguely aware that the musical accompaniment was now Leroy Carr's "Six Cold Feet in the Ground". "Guys with dead eyes?" I repeated.

He nodded. "And I definitely fall into that category."

I couldn't argue with him there. "What was the special project for this major client?"

"Security work," Leadbelly said in a low voice.

"What kind of security work?"

He was shaking his head.

Through the glass I saw Hel Hyslop coming towards us at high speed. "Tell me, Leadbelly. Tell me before it's too late."

He saw where I was looking and jerked round. "Oh shit," he groaned.

"What kind of security work?" I insisted.

He slumped forward and mumbled something I didn't catch.

I took hold of his chin again and forced his head up. "Tell me, for Christ's sake."

He blinked a couple of times, his eyes damp but still vacant. "Security work at the Rennie Institute." He shook my hand away. "The people who work there call it the Baby Factory."

I stared at him. "The Rennie Institute? It's not something to do with David Rennie, is it?" I was remembering the ward representative with the piercing blue eyes from the banquet.

Leadbelly stared back. "He founded the place. He's some kind of professor. Do you know him?"

"Why's it called the Baby Factory?" I asked, disregarding his question.

For a moment it looked like he was going to tell me, then he shook his head and slumped in the chair.

Hyslop arrived a second or two later, closely followed by Tam Haggs. They both looked agitated.

"You've had your half-hour and more," she said. "And the shit has just got deeper. Come with me."

I shrugged at Leadbelly and followed her into the squadroom. She didn't show any sign of stopping.

"What's the rush?" I called after her.

"Another body's been found," she said over her shoulder. "There are signs of mutilation."

"Christ. Whereabouts?"

"You'll find out. Duart wants you in on it."

I could tell what she thought of that by her tone of voice.

"What about Leadbelly?"

She pushed open the door and held it for me. "Don't worry about him. Haggs will stay in charge here."

"Now I'm really worried."

She gave me a sharp look and headed for the lift.

Glasgow nightlife had a lot going for it.

We were hurtling down the road in Hel's Llama, the siren screaming like a soprano on a window-ledge.

"Where are we going?" I asked, my fingers clutching the bottom of the seat.

"Benalder Street," the inspector said, her eyes fixed on the road and her hands moving the wheel skilfully. "There's a bridge over the River Kelvin."

I found a map in the glove compartment. "Benalder Street," I repeated as I found the reference. Interesting. It was to the west of the Kelvingrove Park, less than half a mile from the pub where Leadbelly had been drinking. It was also between two large hospital complexes. The caption told me that the Rennie Institute was based in the southern complex, a few minutes' walking distance from Benalder Street. I thought about asking Hyslop about David Rennie then decided against it.

"He didn't do it, you know," I said, closing the map book.

"Who didn't do what?" she asked in clipped tones, swerving to avoid a group of drunken locals. I could hear the abuse they shouted after us. Glaswegians obviously didn't fear the police like Edinburgh folk fear the City Guard. Then again, Edinburgh folk can't lay their hands on firearms.

"Leadbelly. He didn't kill that woman."

We were out of the lattice of central streets now, the street-lamps to our right shining against the park's trees. The paddy fields must have been behind them.

"How can you be so sure?"

"Believe me, I'm sure. Leadbelly was once a piece of shit – he may still be for all I know – but he was never into mutilation. Or heroin, for that matter. You can't throw him to the executioner for something he didn't do." I gave her a disapproving look. "By the way, hanging, drawing and quartering went out in the Middle Ages."

Hyslop glanced at me. "I think you've got the wrong idea about your role in this, Quint. We've been after a multiple murderer for months. Now we've found him. Duart and his team want a copper-bottomed case to present to the Procurator Fiscal, whence our trip to Edinburgh to locate the only person our suspect will talk to. That's what you're here for. No social analysis required."

"If Leadbelly's your man, how come another victim's turned up while he's in custody? And how come I'm being taken to the scene if my role's so limited?"

Hel Hyslop bit her lip. "Maybe your friend had an assistant."

She pulled up behind another Llama. Lights were flashing and figures moving rapidly around. Some were wearing jackets with luminous stripes which made them look like mobile skeletons. I remembered the fake workmen we'd seen outside the Parliament archive in Edinburgh – where were they now?

I got out and followed the inspector into the blaze of light. A generator was running, its racket making everyone shout at each other. Or perhaps, as the revellers we'd passed suggested, shouting was par for the course in this city.

"He's over here," said a white-haired policeman in green fatigues. The sight of Hyslop made him stand to attention and drop the cigarette he was holding. "The crime-scene squad's been waiting for you, inspector."

We passed through a group of figures in white overalls, keeping to a pathway marked out with green and yellow tape. There was a small expanse of open ground, overgrown with willowherb and thistles, and a line of trees. To our right I could see another strip of flattened vegetation.

The body was lying on its side, legs together and knees bent. I felt my heartbeat race as I clocked the branch over his face. I could see blood on the leaves. Jesus, another one. The dead man was wearing blue jeans and a good-quality silk shirt, and on his feet was a pair of brand-new slip-on shoes – I'd only ever seen the richest tourists in Edinburgh with footwear of that quality.

Hyslop was talking to a crime-scene squad member, so I kneeled down and examined the trail leading away from the corpse's feet. I couldn't see any sign of another person, only spatters of blood forming an uneven line on the grass.

"It appears he crawled through the undergrowth," Hel said.

"So I see."

"Time to look at the body," she said, squatting down beside the head.

I joined her and pulled on the protective gloves she handed me. In the artificial light, the blood on the branch glowed bright crimson. This time, however, the branch wasn't from a copper beech. It was some kind of pine, a cypress perhaps. I looked around and saw a likely specimen a few yards away.

"The photographers have finished," Hyslop said. "Let's move the branch."

I knew what I was going to see before I saw it. A bloody pulp on the side of the head and a rough hole in the centre of the forehead. Hel leaned forward and shone her torch at the wound. An eye had been stuffed roughly into the cavity.

"Yes," the inspector said. "It's the same pattern as the other eight murders." She shook her head. "But it's the first time a branch has been put over the face. What's that all about?"

I looked at her, surprised that she sounded almost human. I watched as she took a series of deep breaths, then eased the torch from her hand and flashed it round the scene. It didn't take her long to find the tree that the branch had been taken from. There was blood on the trunk, suggesting that the mutilation had been carried out before the branch had been torn away.

I rocked back on my heels and tried to work out what was going on. I forced myself to examine the dead man's face again and realised that he wasn't a man. His face was soft and covered with wispy stubble. He was an adolescent. Then it hit me. I'd seen that face before. In a Welfare Directorate file. He was Dougal Strachan, one of the hyper-intelligent kids from the care facility in Edinburgh. How the hell had he ended up dead in Glasgow?

Before I could work out how much to keep to myself, Andrew Duart arrived. He spent five minutes in a huddle with Hyslop and the crime-scene supervisor then came over to the body.

"I'm glad you're in a position to give us the benefit of your expertise, Quint," he said suavely.

"I'm not exactly in a position to refuse," I said, trying to keep my interest hidden.

He gave me a tight smile. "I feel the Major Crime Squad needs all the help it can get with these killings. Provide that help and you will not find me ungrateful." He sounded just like an Edinburgh guardian.

"The inspector's not exactly overjoyed by my presence."

Duart glanced over at Hel Hyslop. "The inspector will do as she's told."

"Very democratic," I said.

He ignored the jibe. "And she's been told to work this case with you."

I turned away from the dead youth as the inspector and the crime-scene squad came back to it. "This case? I thought I was here to squeeze the suspect you have in custody."

Duart gave me a curious look. "Is this death not connected with the others?"

"Probably. We're not talking suicide, are we?"

"If thine eye offend thee, pluck it out . . ."

"For it is better for thee to enter into life with one eye, rather than having two eyes to be cast into hell fire," I completed.

"Matthew 18:9." Duart looked at me thoughtfully. "Not bad for an atheist. I didn't think the Bible was read in Edinburgh any more."

"Oh, we read it," I replied. "We just don't believe it."

He shook his head. "Unlike many of the cults we have in Glasgow. Crazy people, most of them, but they're harmless in the main."

Hel Hyslop came closer. "I'm not so sure of that. We've just found this in the dead boy's pocket."

Duart and I craned forward and clocked a lurid hand-bill. There was a picture of a kingly figure in robes and crown holding a sword that dripped blood. The lettering was in crimson ink and read "Macbeth – Die for the Experience, Live Forever!"

It seemed Dougal Strachan had only managed the first half of that exhortation.

Duart left soon afterwards. Hyslop and I watched the medical examiner and the crime-scene personnel work for a while. We were given cups of strong, sweet tea from time to time – unlike at Edinburgh scenes of crimes, there was plenty of milk available.

"Any identification?" I asked. I wasn't going to tell anyone who the dead adolescent was until I found out why he was in Glasgow.

The inspector shook her head. "Nothing. No wallet, no credit cards—"

"What are they?" I asked.

Hel looked at me like I was retarded. "Credit cards? You use them to buy . . ." She broke off when she saw my smile.

"I remember them from pre-Enlightenment times," I said. "At least with our voucher system you don't run up enormous bills and pay interest rates that a loanshark would think twice about demanding."

She frowned at me. "As I was saying, there's nothing to identify him at all. We're pretty sure the clothes and shoes are from Glasgow shops so the chances are he was a local."

In your dreams, I thought. The clothes were interesting though. How had the teenager got a hold of them so quickly?

"The doctor reckons he was dead before the eye mutilation," Hyslop added. "Subject to the post-mortem, of course."

"It looks like he took a blow to the side of the head then crawled through the grass until he died," I said. "How about time of death?"

"The temperature suggests around three hours ago. The police patrol found him at eleven thirty-seven." Hyslop looked at her watch. "An hour and a half ago, so he lay undiscovered for over an hour."

"No witnesses?"

"We're still canvassing the area. Nothing yet."

"Have the blood spots been traced back?"

She nodded. "The first ones we found are on the grass this side of the bridge."

"Suggesting he was first hit there. The killer may have left footprints."

Hylsop nodded. "We're looking for traces."

I thought about the other missing adolescents. If this had happened to Dougal, what was in store for them?

"Quint?" Hel's insistent tone brought me back to the scene. "What happened to you? You looked like you were on a trip."

I smiled at her coldly. "I am on a trip, inspector. The worst one of my life."

Hyslop drove me back to the hotel. As we went past the lights of the hospital, I remembered Hector. Christ, how was the old man? He was lying in a recovery ward while I was stuck in the middle of an investigation in the city Edinburgh had been demonising for decades. I hoped he was all right. And that he hadn't antagonised too many nurses.

"What about the Macbeth cult then?" I asked, remembering the handbill found in the dead boy's pocket.

"Don't worry. I've already upped the surveillance on it. Tomorrow we'll check the Macbeth out in depth. There's a squad in the department that keeps an eye on the cults."

"Keeps an eye on them?"

She shot me an angry glance. "That's not funny, Quint."

"Suit yourself. Can I see the files on the previous killings?"

She looked at me, her eyes open wide. "They're classified."

"Do you want me to ask Duart for them?"

She looked back at the road. Ahead of us the city centre glowed brightly. The balloons floating above each ward were lit by spotlights.

"No, I don't want you to ask Duart," she said leadenly. "I'm getting enough hassle from him already."

"How about sending them round to my room as soon as possible? I don't think I'll be sleeping much tonight."

"All right. Anything to keep you quiet."

It would take more than a heap of files to shut me up, but who was I to get in the way of the inspector's delusions?

Back on the seventh floor I called room service and ordered a bottle of top-notch Islay malt, a steak sandwich and all the local newspapers – well, I needed something to keep me going till the files arrived. I also experimented with the television. I hadn't seen one of those since I was in my first year of university, before the last election in Edinburgh. I was reassured to see that I hadn't missed much. All the channels had late night shows involving partial or total nudity – the newsreader's breasts were bare, the weather-forecaster had his foreskin on display, there was even a game of mixed football in which the participants were wearing only boots. I was thankful that most people were the right side of thirty. Then I found the over-sixties channel and hit the off-button pronto.

The newspapers were a bit more interesting. Not as regards content. That was as ephemeral as the papers before the break-up of the United Kingdom – fawning features on fashion icons (I remembered that Glasgow fancied itself as a design capital), interviews with people who reckoned they'd been shagged by extra-terrestrials, horoscopes, etc., etc. No, what was fascinating was the reporting of politics and current affairs. In the supposedly democratic city-state of Glasgow there was as much propaganda and opinion dressed as objective comment as there is in the guardians' Edinburgh. *Plus ça change.*

Then the murder files arrived and I got down to some serious reading.

CHAPTER THIRTEEN

I tried to keep at the files, but the malt whisky was as subtle as a top-rank pickpocket. It removed my insomnia without me noticing and left me flat out on the hotel room's wide and welcoming double bed. Not that I slept well or for long. The photos of the eight murder victims kept flashing in front of me and I was awake again by five in the morning. So I called room service for a bucket of coffee, failed to resist the jumbo croissant with heather honey that they specially recommended – after all, Glasgow was picking up my tab – and got back to work.

Eight victims before the Edinburgh teenager, the first nine weeks ago and the last ten days back. Alternately male, female. Murder scenes all over the city, from Milngavie and Chryston in the north to Nitshill and Pollokshields south of the Clyde. No obvious pattern as regards age, social background, work, sexuality, race, religious denomination, whatever. The only thing that linked the killings was the modus operandi – heavy blows to the side of the head with a blunt instrument and the same third-eye mutilation that I'd seen in Edinburgh. There was one difference though – only the last of the victims, Dougal Strachan, had a branch over his face. I wasn't sure what to make of that link to the murders back home.

The Major Crime Squad's files weren't exactly a picture of bureaucratic rectitude. That would have made Lewis Hamilton gloat. For a start, the Public Order Directorate back in Edinburgh was much more demanding when it came to victim profiling. Maybe people in Glasgow told the police where to stick their questions — that was hardly a realistic option in my home city. Or maybe Hel Hyslop's team was just massively overworked. Whatever the reason, they'd dug up only the scantiest details about the deceased. Only a couple of each victim's relatives and friends had been interviewed and their work histories only covered the last two jobs they'd had. There were plenty of other gaps too. If I hadn't seen the inspector in action, I'd have got the impression that she ran a ship manned by the crew of the *Marie Celeste*.

None of which speculation got me much further as regards the dead youth or Leadbelly. The latter knew more than he was telling, but I could see why he wanted an insurance policy. Hyslop and Haggs needed a killer and he fitted the bill for at least one of the murders. Too well, I reckoned. I could smell a set-up even more pungent than the reek from the former drugs gang member's armpits. But why him? And where had Dougal Strachan been since he arrived in Glasgow?

I went over to the window and drew the heavy velvet curtains. There was a mist over the city. It was keeping the dawn's light at bay, swaddling Glasgow and its river in an insulating blanket. I thought of the paddy fields at Kelvingrove and the ploughing I'd seen on the way in. Global warming had apparently made the west of Scotland more fertile than it had ever been. Then I thought about Leadbelly's Baby Factory. More fertility there, by the sounds of it. Was there some connection between it and the deaths, or had Dougal Strachan been in the vicinity by coincidence? I wondered how I could find out about the Rennie Institute and the hospitals near the latest crime scene without telling Hyslop what I knew. That was something I was definitely not keen on doing. Like Leadbelly, I wanted to use what I could for my own ends.

I went towards the centre of the luxurious room and looked at the giant television screen. That was it. When I was jumping from one shitty channel to another last night I'd come across a menu page. One of the options was called "Library and Information Services". Digital archivist dreamland. I grabbed the handset and called up the menu, then highlighted my selection. That gave me a surprise. A keyboard layout appeared on the screen and I was invited to type in what I wanted. There was a voice option as well but I didn't fancy having a conversation with a machine. Touch screens and voice interaction don't exist in Edinburgh as most of the computers hogged by the guardians and auxiliaries date from before the millennium.

I requested information about the Rennie Institute, not expecting to be told much apart from "Piss off, ya nosey Embra shite". But no, in democratic Glasgow it seemed that information was in the public domain. The institute had a mission statement that must have been written by a public relations expert who spent his spare time on the hot line to the almighty:

The Rennie Institute is dedicated to the sanctity of human life. Our research is intended to enable human beings to achieve their full potential, to live

*without fear of hereditary disease, to bring healthy
and highly intelligent children into the world. At
the Rennie, nothing is impossible – humanity can
reach the stars!*

There was plenty more of that; plenty more self-satisfied
bullshit that didn't mention the words "genetic engineering", but made it pretty clear that's what they were into
in a big way. I sat back on the bed and thought what that
might mean. The Rennie was a baby factory, the Rennie
carried out research into humans' "full potential", whatever that was; and the Rennie was located in the southern of the two hospitals in Kelvingrove, the one that was
a few minutes' walk from where Dougal Strachan was
found. I remembered the break-in at the Parliament
archive. Could there be some connection between the
Genetic Engineering Committee file attachment that had
gone missing and the murders in Glasgow, as well as
those in Edinburgh?

A key rattled in the lock. I leaped to the screen and
cleared it just before Hyslop and Haggs walked in. They
were both wearing casual clothes – all the better to
perform surveillance operations with, presumably.

"You're up early," Tam said. He sounded disappointed. No doubt he'd been looking forward to giving
me a wake-up kick. He looked at the files I'd strewn
across the floor. "Where did you get those?" he demanded.

"It's all right, sergeant," the inspector said. "Quint was
to be fully briefed – Duart's instructions."

"Great," Haggs muttered. He looked even less impressed when he saw the bottle of malt. Obviously he
couldn't afford stuff like that.

"Are you coming then?" Hel Hyslop asked.

I looked down at the towel I was wearing round my waist. "Not so's you'd notice."

They glowered at me like cows in a fly-blown mud-patch.

"Where are we going?" I asked, heading into the bathroom to dress.

"The Macbeth cult, remember?" Hyslop's tone was sharp.

"Verily I do. Haven't you got them all banged up by now?"

Hel appeared at the door and watched impassively as I pulled on my trousers. "Certainly not. Unlike the guardians in Edinburgh, we don't treat citizens like that in here. We're going to watch them, then we're going to talk to them—"

I grinned at her. "*Then* you're going to bang them up."

"You don't have to come," she said, turning away.

I followed her out. "Don't worry, I'm coming all right. *Macbeth* is one of my favourite plays." I got the impression from Big Tam's face that he probably preferred *Titus Andronicus* – all that mayhem and people having their tongues ripped out.

"Here, what about Leadbelly?" I asked as we walked towards the lift. "Shouldn't I be talking to him again?"

Hyslop glanced at me. "Don't worry about Leadbelly," she said in a low voice. "He's not going anywhere."

I was pretty sure I wouldn't be going anywhere either – certainly not back to Edinburgh – unless I played my cards very carefully indeed.

The mist had lifted but that didn't mean there was much light in the sky. The cloud was leaden and low. Suddenly everything seemed much more autumnal, in the sense of imminent winter rather than harvest-home. That wasn't stopping the locals flitting in and out of shops like demented chipmunks, their hands full of brightly coloured bags. I wondered where they got the money to shop so professionally, then I remembered what Duart had told me about the subsidies Glasgow citizens received. But how was the city able to afford those?

Haggs revved up the Llama's engine and pulled away like there was no tomorrow.

"Jesus," I muttered. "Has somebody died?"

"Too many people," he said bitterly. "And I don't trust those Macbeth bastards."

"Nothing like giving your fellow citizens the benefit of the doubt," I said.

Haggs grunted. "Fellow citizens? Half of those tossers are immigrants from the Highlands. There's a rumour that the arsehole who thinks he's Macbeth is English."

"Not called William, is he?" I asked.

Tam didn't get it. "What?"

"William Shakespeare?"

He narrowed his eyes at me. "Fuck off, you fucking smartarse."

Hel Hyslop was shaking her head. She put her hands out as Haggs braked hard behind a tourist bus full of wide-eyed Germans. "Watch it, Tam. Duart will have your balls if you damage any of our visitors."

That was one thing that Glasgow had in common with Edinburgh – an exaggerated respect for foreign revenue. But was that income enough to support the citizens in the way they'd become accustomed to? It even looked like the Celtic and Rangers shirts worn by a lot of the young people on the street were silk.

We drove eastwards past the City Chambers, its upper dome almost lost in the low cloud. Haggs ran the Llama on to the paved area outside the cathedral, showing what he thought of the No Parking signs, and killed the engine. Obviously Major Crime Squad surveillance activities didn't require operatives to leave the company car in a discreet location.

"Who are that lot?" I asked, pointing at a group of people in dark robes standing motionless outside the old church with its low steeple.

"People call them the Mungo Saints," Hyslop said. "They're members of what's officially called the One True Protestant Church of Glasgow. They're old-style religious lunatics, keen on hair shirts and wife-beating. Until the Macbeth cult got going, they were the most popular sect in the city."

I took my eyes off the grim-faced, bearded men. Oddly enough, none of the Mungo Saints seemed to be female. "Do they resent their rivals' success? They don't look very forgiving."

The inspector shrugged. "They're not violent, if that's what you mean. At least, not to other men."

We got out and walked over the bridge towards the gate of the necropolis. People of all ages were going in and out continuously, some of them in weird garb but the majority dressed normally.

"Pretty popular for a cemetery, isn't it?" I observed.

Hel nodded. "It's more than that. Since the wards opened up Glasgow's graveyards to the cults, they've become some of the liveliest places in the city. People pitch tents between the headstones and put on shows. The authorities are happy – it's good for the tourists and it keeps the locals busy as well."

I saw what she meant. The necropolis stretching up the hill ahead was covered in multicoloured fabric and plastic sheeting. There were flags and banners everywhere, all of them connected with *Macbeth* – some were advertising performances, some were selling books and associated merchandise sporting quotations from the play. They were dead giveaways if you were looking for evidence of murderous activities. "Blood Will Have Blood", one T-shirt read; another, "I Have Done the Deed".

"Bloody hell," I said under my breath.

"Precisely," Hyslop agreed. "They've no shame, have they? And don't take my name in vain."

I was amazed. Evidence of humour.

In the distance there was a deep rumble of thunder, then the steady tolling of a bell. That made some of the crazies in witches' costumes and the like look up in excitement. People started moving towards a makeshift stage near the top of the hill.

"What's going on?" I asked.

Hel glanced at her watch. "There's what they call the morning session at nine o'clock. We're going to take a look."

We were caught up in a crowd of spectators who'd suddenly piled into the necropolis. A few of them were tourists – earnest ones with copies of the play in their hands – but most were locals. Some even had their kids with them. The young ones didn't look anything like as enthusiastic as their parents.

Another peal of thunder, far off to the east. The rain was probably pissing down in Edinburgh already. The clouds above us were louring. If you listened hard, you'd no doubt hear a raven croaking himself hoarse. Al fresco *Macbeth* in

Glasgow didn't need much stage management. We joined the mass around the wooden stage. Beneath the stanchions I could see gravestones, some of them canted over at crazy angles. I wondered what the sleepers in the tombs thought of what was going on above them.

Hel nudged me. "Look."

I followed the direction of her gaze. Over the stage was a banner that matched the handbill she'd found in Dougal Strachan's pocket: "Macbeth – Die for the Experience, Live Forever!" I still didn't have a clue what that meant. Maybe I was about to be informed.

A band of musicians in tartan trews and sashes wandered into the cleared area in front of the stage. They were clutching instruments, several of which I realised to my horror were bagpipes. Apart from drums I had trouble identifying the others. I had a nasty feeling that the conductor was an expert in ancient music and the artefacts used to make it. That was confirmed when they struck up. What was it in the play? "Lamentings heard i' the air; strange screams of death"? Willie the Shake got that right.

Then the main man appeared and the cacophony wheezed to a halt. I recognised him immediately from the illustration on the hoardings – tall and saturnine, a crown on his long, dark locks and a scarlet robe to his feet. There was a lot of scarlet stuff on his broadsword too. At his side was Lady Macbeth, her face pale and her plaited hair a deep shade of auburn. I've always been a sucker for auburn hair but in this case I was prepared to make an exception. This queen had the air of a walking corpse, her eyes lifeless and her arms thin and bony. At least she wasn't washing her hands continuously. No doubt that was a delight to come.

"Friends," Macbeth bellowed. "Supporters of our noble movement. Countrymen."

He paused for effect. I was trying to work out which countrymen he was appealing to. The tourists were as well. Scotland had been more unified when his namesake was in charge a millennium ago than it was now.

"Welcome to our morning devotions." He corrected himself. "Our morning session." I got the impression that he was all too used to people being devoted to him. His voice was deep and ringing, in the style that actors imagine gives them gravitas – pomposity is the term in the real world. I watched him carefully. There was something familiar about his face.

"We in the Macbeth cult are dedicated to the story of Scotland's greatest king. The king who brought together the warring barons and governed the old country wisely until his unjust death." He looked around the audience, eyes burning, challenging us to give him credence. It was quite gripping, even for a sceptic like me. "But we aren't only dedicated to Macbeth as a historical memory." More eye contact with the plebs. "We intend to bring Scotland back into existence, using the example of Macbeth as a talisman, an inspiration, a destiny."

"What a load of shite," Tam Haggs said, not bothering to lower his voice too much. He glared back at the people who turned towards him with injured expressions. Then Hel Hyslop gave him the eye and he gave up.

The king was still declaiming. "In the evening we will perform our version of the play which made Macbeth famous around the world. For all his poetic ability, the English playwright made numerous egregious historical errors which we have corrected."

The English playwright? That struck me as a pretty

limited way to refer to the world's greatest writer, even if the speaker was English himself. Actually his accent sounded more like upper-crust, educated Scots – maybe the bugger was from Edinburgh.

As the rant continued, I let my eyes pan round the stage. Lady Macbeth still looked as if the pair of daggers had snagged in her underwear, while a man and boy I took to be Banquo and Fleance had clearly heard the speech several hundred times before. The same went for the old man in bloody robes – I got the impression King Duncan would much rather be in the hospitality tent.

"So join us, friends," Macbeth proclaimed. "Come to our play and lend your help to our cause. Democracy is a poisoned chalice, Glasgow is unsafe, our leaders have their own agenda. We must break down the barriers between the states of Scotland, we must re-create our nation." He looked round the crowd imperiously. "Our destiny has already been written." He held up a handsome leather-bound book with the play's title embossed on the cover in large gold letters. "Macbeth!" he cried. "Die for the experience, live forever!"

Haggs was shaking his head. "Christ, why do we let these mad tossers sound off? The only destiny Macbeth's got is at the end of my boot."

I watched as the royal couple graciously acknowledged the spectators' applause and swept to the wings. There was a sudden burst of thunder much nearer to us. Everyone started. It was then that I saw a shadowy figure at the edge of the stage. A tall man in a heavy cloak with a sword hanging from his belt. That wasn't all. His face was criss-crossed by ragged scars and the long brown hair that circled it was coarse and unnatural. Jesus. My mind immediately went back to Edinburgh and the dead auxiliaries in the Botanic Gardens and at the Lauriston care facility. The witnesses had described a fairy-tale monster very like this guy. Could it be him? If it was, what was he doing in Glasgow alongside a cult leader who thought he was a reincarnation of Macbeth?

"What's the matter?" Hel Hyslop asked. "You look like you've seen a ghost." She peered at the stage as heavy clouds blocked out the sun completely.

I watched as Macbeth's entourage, including the bogeyman, followed him off. The mutilated faces of the victims in the two cities came up before me. The third eye. Was this the killer I'd been chasing?

"Quint?" the inspector said, her voice insistent now. "What is it?"

I took a deep breath and tried to sound calm. "Nothing. I was just bowled over by the king's speech."

"Rubbish," she said, her eyes wide. "You're hiding—" She broke off as her mobile rang. "Hyslop." She listened for a few seconds. Now she was the one whose face registered surprise. "What? There were two men on him."

I felt my stomach flip. I had a bad feeling about the identity of "him".

"All right, we'll be there in ten minutes. Out."

"What's happened?" I asked.

She looked at me blankly then turned and moved away quickly. "Come on. We'll catch up with these lunatics later. Your friend Leadbelly tried to hang himself. He's alive but unconscious."

"What?" I strode after her. "Leadbelly wasn't suicidal."

Haggs crashed into me from behind. "You reckon the fucker was looking forward to seeing his guts being ripped out, do you?"

I looked round, catching a glimpse of the empty stage and the banners flapping in the wind. "No," I replied. "He was hoping I'd get you off his back."

The sergeant gave me a derisive grin then pushed past to catch up with his superior. I brought up the rear, feeling more isolated than ever in Glasgow's city of the dead.

We reached George Square in under five minutes, giving several tourists serious panic attacks on the way. By the time we got there, the clouds had finally opened. I got drenched as I ran into the City Chambers. The rain was unusually warm. Good for the rice, I suppose.

Hyslop led the way to the rear of the grandiose building. "There's a medical room down the corridor," she said over her shoulder. "He's been taken there."

"He should be in a bloody hospital," I said angrily.

Haggs glared at me. "Watch it, dickhead."

"Clear the way!" Hel shouted.

Police personnel in green uniforms let us pass. We entered a small room with a single bed. The motionless figure on it was being tended by a male doctor in a white coat. A saline drip had been fed into Leadbelly's right arm, which was cuffed to the bed frame.

I groaned. "How is he?" The prisoner didn't look good at all. What I could see of his face around the respirator was ashen. His neck was bisected horizontally by a deep furrow. The skin there wasn't broken but it was a dark red colour.

"Alive, just." The medic was young and reptilian, his round glasses magnifying cold blue eyes. "It's too early to say whether the brain's been irreversibly deprived of oxygen."

"Why isn't he in hospital?" I demanded.

The doctor glanced at Hyslop. "I was told to keep him here until you arrived, inspector."

She nodded. "Category Z prisoners cannot be transferred without approval from a senior officer." It sounded like she knew the regulations off by heart.

"So fucking approve the transfer!" I yelled.

The room went dead quiet, the only sound coming from Leadbelly's assisted breathing.

The inspector wasn't going to be rushed. "Would additional treatment be beneficial?" she asked the reptile.

The doctor raised his shoulders noncommittally. "Possibly. The patient's stable now."

I shook my head. "Anyone would think you're not interested in keeping him alive," I said to Hel Hyslop, moving closer to the bed and examining the impression in the skin. "What was round his neck?"

A policeman stepped forward and addressed Hyslop. "A boot-lace."

She nodded but didn't speak.

"He was barefoot last night," I said pointedly.

Another silence.

"Yes, well, we'll be looking into that," Hel said. Then she glanced at the door where there had just been another parting of the personnel.

Andrew Duart walked up and gave Leadbelly the once-over. "What's going on, chief inspector? I've just heard that your prime suspect tried to kill himself." He turned his gaze on Hyslop. It wasn't friendly. "Very careless of your department to allow that, wasn't it?"

Hel's cheeks reddened. "I haven't had the chance to find out what happened yet."

"Then I suggest you do so immediately." Duart looked at me. "I can assure you we'll take better care of the prisoner from now on, Quint."

"Before you execute him?" I said bitterly. "He should be in an emergency unit."

He nodded. "See to it, inspector." He turned to leave. "I want to see a full report on this unfortunate incident by the end of the day," he said over his shoulder. "As well as the one you owe me on the death in Kelvingrove last night." He stopped and shot Hel Hyslop a piercing glance. "Both are to include the input of our Edinburgh expert here, of course." He headed off.

I stood back to allow Leadbelly to be carried out. Hyslop and Haggs weren't looking at me. It was pretty obvious that I wasn't their favourite alien.

That feeling was now even more mutual than it had been.

We went up to the fourth floor and occupied the corner office. The chair that Leadbelly had been sitting on last night was still in the middle of the floor, the shackles lying beneath it. At least they weren't attached to me. But the sight of the chair made me wonder about the former drugs gang member again. He wasn't the suicidal type. Christ, he'd survived seven years' solitary on Cramond Island without any hope of release. Why would he give up now, the day after his demand that I be brought to him was met? No, I wasn't buying suicide. The question was, who wanted rid of him?

I took a look at Hyslop and Haggs. They were at her desk, opening files and making checklists. Neither of them was a fan of Leadbelly. On the other hand, he was their chief suspect for the murders. Why would they

want rid of him? Besides, they were with me when
Leadbelly's air supply was cut off – though I was sure
they had plenty of willing helpers in the building.

"What's your problem, pal?" Big Tam demanded,
glancing up. "See something you like?"

"No," I replied. "Nothing human, at least. What's in
those files?"

Haggs grinned. "Are you a man or a bureaucrat?"

"Shut up, sergeant." Hel Hyslop's face was drawn.
"You heard what Duart said. Quint's in on this with us."
She sounded as happy about that as an American pre-
sident who'd been caught in an intern.

"Brilliant," I said with heavy irony. "So I can expect
full co-operation, can I?"

"From me, you can expect a truncheon enema," Haggs
said, his stubbled jaw jutting forward.

"No, thanks," I replied. "I'd prefer a corned beef and
beetroot sandwich."

To my amazement, I got one. And a mug of decent
coffee. Then we got stuck into the files.

An hour later there was more bad news.

"You're kidding, aren't you?" I was staring at Hyslop
but she wouldn't look up.

"You heard my end of the conversation," she snapped,
her hand still on the desk phone. "The post-mortem on
the dead adolescent has already been carried out."

I leaned over her. "What kind of regulations have you
got in this poxy city? Surely at least one member of the
investigation team has to be present when it's a suspicious death."

She nodded. "Under normal circumstances the regulations do require that."

"What do you mean 'under normal circumstances'?"

Hyslop pushed her chair back and stood up. Haggs moved away, his eyes still on me and his face set hard.

"Exceptions can be made," the inspector said.

"Exceptions?" I was having difficulty restraining myself. "Exceptions on what grounds?"

Hel shrugged. "On medical safety grounds."

"What does that mean?" I demanded.

"If the cadaver is infectious, for example."

I straightened up. "Was there any indication of that with the adolescent?"

"I don't know, Quint. They're sending the p-m report over now."

"That's something," I said between my teeth.

Haggs stepped towards me. "You want to get a grip on your temper. We don't speak to senior officers like that around here."

"Maybe you don't," I said. "Junior officer."

He raised his fist and pulled it back.

"Forget it, Tam," Hyslop said. "I can look after myself."

Haggs nodded. "I know you can. I'm just not sure that this cunt does."

I didn't bother responding to that. Instead I picked up the notebook I'd been using and turned away. "We're going nowhere fast with this. No one saw D . . ." I broke off, coughing loudly. Using the Edinburgh youth's name would have been a major faux pas. ". . . no one saw the dead boy in the streets, no one's been able to identify him, and we don't know why he died. Bit of a result, eh?"

The others looked at their files leadenly.

"Still," I continued, "at least we've found out which arsehole was responsible for giving Leadbelly back his boot-laces." I was glaring at them but they still weren't

responding. Half an hour earlier a sheepish young policeman had been dragged in. His story was that Leadbelly
had complained of cold feet in the holding cell. Constable
Plod Minor claimed he didn't know prisoners weren't
allowed laced footwear. I wasn't convinced. He looked
thick enough, but I found it hard to believe that a high
priority suspect like Leadbelly would have been assigned such an inexperienced guard. The latest news
from the hospital was that Leadbelly was still unconscious. If someone had wanted to shut him up they may
well have achieved that end, even if he wasn't dead.

There was a rap on the glass door. "Special delivery,"
said a fresh-faced young policewoman. Apparently the
Major Crime Squad recruited straight from primary
school. She handed Hel a large envelope and departed
after giving Tam Haggs a frosty look. Perhaps he'd tried
it on with her in the past. If she'd told him where to go,
she wasn't as stupid as her male counterpart from the
cells.

"What have we got then?" I asked, moving to the desk.

"P-m report," Hyslop said, running her finger down
the typed front sheet. After a minute she sighed and
handed it over to me. "No great help."

I tried to make sense of the pathologist's tortured
syntax in the summary. It didn't help that the layout
of the report bore no resemblance to that of the forms I
was used to – trust Glasgow to do things as differently
as possible from Edinburgh.

"Time of death, between nine-thirty and ten p.m.," I
read. "Cause of death, massive brain injuries caused by a
single heavy blow to right side of cranium. Medical
history unknown but no debilitating or malignant conditions. No traces of any drugs or alcohol. Stomach

contents show ham and wholemeal bread and tea, consumed approximately three hours before death." I glanced over the back-up pages but failed to find anything else of significance.

Hel Hyslop was sitting back in her chair with her hands crossed, her eyes on me. "So, Mister Investigator, what next?"

"If there were no debilitating or malignant conditions, why was the p-m carried out in secret?" I asked.

"The pathologist isn't required to provide that information," she replied. "Perhaps he was given orders by a superior."

"Like who? Surely there would be a reference to that in the report?"

She raised her shoulders.

I sat on the other side of the desk. "Look, Hel, I was born with a suspicious mind. If I don't attend a p-m, I don't trust the report."

Her eyes flared. "Don't you dare question our procedures, Quint. You're a guest in this city and—"

"I'm an unwilling guest in this city," I interrupted. "And anyway, your procedures stink."

This time Haggs completed his punch.

I hit the floor.

CHAPTER FOURTEEN

We were in the Llama, Hel Hyslop at the wheel. Haggs had been banished to the back seat after his attempt to dislocate my jaw. Fortunately the evasive action I took meant that he only scuffed the end of my chin. Round one to Quintilian on points, but I knew I had to watch my back – and my front – even more carefully from now on.

"Don't we need tickets for the show?" I asked. "There were a lot of people in the necropolis this morning."

"I've arranged that with the Cult Squad," Hyslop said, stopping at a crossing to let a group of youths stream over the road. They must have been at the magic all afternoon. In Edinburgh going over the top like that would have got them a month down the mines. "As long as you give a big enough donation to Macbeth's cause, you're in." Her tone was heavily ironic.

I peered out into the street. Despite the bright lights of the shops and bars in the city centre, it was a gloomy evening. The idea of watching an open-air production wasn't at all enticing. "His cause? You think he's serious about reuniting Scotland? He's just a smalltime crazy, isn't he?"

Hel shook her head. "I'm not so sure. My opposite number in the Cult Squad reckons the so-called king's been getting much stronger in recent months. Unlike most of these madmen, he doesn't seem to be corrupt. Everything he takes is used to recruit new members and set up branches across the wards."

I looked at her face. It was glowing green in the light from the dashboard. "Yeah, but how can he seriously imagine that Scotland can be brought back into existence?" I asked. "Apart from a few city-states with varying degrees of civilisation, the land is wilder than it was in Viking times."

Haggs stirred in the back. "There's only one state with any degree of civilisation, pal, and it's not the one you come from."

I turned to him. "Glasgow, city of the right hook, you mean?"

"Stop it," Hel Hyslop ordered. "Otherwise I'll send the pair of you to Greenock, city of continuous shifts in the shipyards."

Round two to the inspector.

This time we left the Llama down a back-street and walked a couple of hundred yards to join the crowd that was streaming into the necropolis. The place was even weirder at night. Although the bright glare from the stage up the hill was obviously produced by electricity, the path that led through the ranks of funeral monuments and headstones was lit by wooden torches dipped in pitch – the return of the Dark Ages.

A tall guy in casual clothes appeared at Hyslop's elbow and handed her an envelope.

"Tickets," he said in a low voice. "My people are all in position. All you have to do is give the word."

Hel nodded and he disappeared. She'd spent the afternoon planning a heavy-duty raid on the cult. It wasn't just the handbill from the dead boy that had got her going – apparently there had been a couple of reports of people going missing after showing interest in Macbeth. The king had some awkward questions to answer. I had a few I wanted to ask his henchman with the messed-up face mask as well.

The area around the stage was packed. There was a ring of seats at the front and behind it a great throng of people had gathered. A lot of them were in medieval costume: leather jerkins and tights for the men, low-cut dresses and frilly blouses for the women. In Glasgow even the cult members were as chic as it comes.

We took our seats in the fourth row, Hyslop making sure she sat between Haggs and me. I wasn't complaining. She looked around surreptitiously, locating her colleagues. I stuck to examining the stage. Apart from the ubiquitous "Die for the Experience, Live Forever!" banner, there was a line of shields with what I recognised to be the coats of arms of Scottish cities. Glasgow's tree and fish were to the fore. Edinburgh's emblem was there too – not the Council's maroon heart but the original heraldic castle. I wondered what the guardians back home would think about Macbeth's ideas. Not much, I was sure. But ordinary Edinburgh citizens might be persuaded to give reunification a chance – many of them had forgotten the disasters brought about by the Scottish Parliament after the millennium.

Then, without any warning, the lights were killed. The audience shrieked for a few seconds but soon settled down to watch the spectacle. Except there wasn't one. Darkness and silence reigned. All you could hear was the steady tolling of a bell in the distance and the croak of the ubiquitous raven. Where the hell had the witches got to?

It turned out they weren't on yet. The first change the new Macbeth had made to the play was to start it with himself, not the three old bags. It was his cult so I suppose he could do what he wanted. There was a roll of thunder that sounded pretty fake, then a spotlight picked out the king standing centre-stage. He was in full regal garb from crown to calf boots, his legs apart and his claymore planted in front of them. His hands were resting on the haft, which almost reached to his neck.

"Friends, welcome!" he cried. "I pray your indulgence for a few short minutes."

We were in for a message from the management.

"I have looked into the seeds of time," the king continued. "I have seen which grain will grow and which will not. I shall give a happy prologue to the imperial theme."

It was a long time since I'd read the play, but I could tell that we were now in Glasgow, city of paraphrase. If he went on like this, he'd soon use up all the juicy bits.

"Our movement is under way," he went on, "our cult is growing. But we are more than that. We are Scotland's destiny made manifest. Politics are not enough for us, neither is religion. We are a historical imperative, an unstoppable force. Scotland will be one again!"

To my amazement, there was a huge burst of cheering and applause. Jesus, what were people playing at? Surely they didn't go along with this lunacy. As the rant continued, the ovations increased in magnitude. At least the king had given up mangling the play. Now he was on about how he would drive out the marauders from the glens and the inadequate rulers from the cities.

"Getting a bit close to the bone, isn't he?" I said to Hyslop. "Does Duart like this kind of thing?"

She had her eyes fixed on the king, her grey eyes glinting. "Duart doesn't like attacks on the system at all. That's one reason the Cult Squad's been on Macbeth's back recently."

"I'm sure Glasgow's democratic institutions are strong enough to take criticism," I said with an ironic smile.

She turned her steely eyes on me. "People are being murdered, Quint. People are going missing. The state's entitled to take action." She shook her head. "I suppose your dictators in Edinburgh would just sit back and let the killers get on with it?"

The king ended his address with a flourish and the crowd exploded again.

"Why are you so sure there's more than one murderer?" I asked as the lights were dimmed. "And why should there be a connection with this cult?"

She pursed her lips. "I was making a general point." She turned to the front again. "I don't know how many people are behind these killings, but I'm pretty sure that bastard in the crown knows something about them. Why was the handbill in that dead boy's pocket?"

"It isn't much to go on," I said, wondering if she was telling me the whole story.

There were more rolls of thunder and the raven was croaking like there was no tomorrow. Show time. The witches had finally made it. In the dull red glow from the fire under the cauldron they started capering and prancing, making the most of the bard's great first scene. I sat back in the back-wrenching chair to enjoy the production.

They hadn't changed the structure much – just the

whole point of the play. Macbeth was no longer a tragic figure racked by ambition, fate, the defects in his character and a manic spouse. Now he was made out to be a virtuous general with his country's rather than his personal destiny at heart. So out went the scenes leading up to the murder of Duncan and in came a fantasy about the old king's duplicitous nature. Out went everything about Banquo's suspicions and his family's eventual accession to the throne and in came a sub-plot showing him to be Duncan's assassin. And out went anything critical of Macbeth – now he was brave and generous throughout. It reminded me of a dire movie I saw when I was a kid, William Wallace played by a wanker spouting an American accent till he was blue in the face and making up history as he went along.

But there were two scenes that made me sit up. The first was in the fourth act, when the witches conjure up apparitions to show Macbeth what lies in the future for him and Scotland. They started with a paraphrase. In the text, before the king arrives one of the hags says "By the pricking of my thumbs, something wicked this way comes". Except this witch said "something wondrous". That was just the beginning.

This scene was always one of my favourites; anything to do with evil spirits and ghostly manifestations appealed to me when I was a kid and didn't know any better. The present Macbeth and his script editors had torn it to shreds. They'd left the apparition of the bloody child – a real infant, wailing piteously and covered in what I hoped was tomato ketchup, was carried on to show that "none of woman born" would harm the king. And they'd left unaltered the child who comes on holding a tree and gives a speech about Birnam Wood and

Dunsinane. But they'd replaced the line of eight kings, supposed to be followed by Banquo's ghost, with a line of eight royal figures wearing masks in the likeness of the cult leader. Talk about self-worship. It went down well with the crowd though.

The noise almost made me take my eye off the stage at the moment when the bogeyman made his entrance. Christ knows who he was meant to be – he had his usual torn face and greasy hair on – but he kneeled before his liege and presented him with an even larger crown. Then he spoke. That shut everyone up instantaneously. His voice was terrifying – breathless and cracked like that of a singer who'd taken too many performance-buggering drugs.

"Accept the crown of Scotland," he was saying, "accept the crown and lead us into a glorious future. Your people are calling." Then the monster turned to the crowd and swept his burning eyes over us, daring us not to shout out our approval. I almost joined in with the rest of them, but I managed to restrain myself. Instead I stared back at the freak and tried to catch his eye – unsuccessfully, which was probably just as well.

"What is it?" Hel Hyslop said, nudging me. "You were looking at that guy this morning too. Do you know him?"

I feigned ignorance. "Of course not. I'm just fascinated. This is the first time I've seen a production of Shakespeare given by the clinically insane."

She stared at me then got back to the action. I began to wonder if it was time to let her in on what I knew about the man in the scarred mask.

The other scene that made my eyes open wide was in the last act. I should have spotted the link earlier, but I'd been distracted by disparate thoughts flashing through

my mind like the NATO smart-but-incompetent bombs
that led to the break-up of the European Union when I
was young. Eventually the names Birnam and Dunsinane
got through to me. Malcolm and Macduff were directing
Macbeth's downfall – not that it would come to fruition
in this version of the play – and soldiers were running
around the stage with branches in their hands. Some of
the bits of vegetation obscured their faces as they moved,
the leaves reddened by fake blood. Suddenly it was
impossible not to think of the two Edinburgh murder
victims and the latest one in Glasgow – they all had
branches in their hands, branches which concealed their
mutilated faces.

What had Macbeth and his cult been up to?

I was still in a daze when the play ended with Macbeth
strutting around the stage with the traitor Malcolm's
head in his hands. I didn't even notice that Haggs had
disappeared from the seat to my left until the inspector
raised her wrist microphone to her lips.

"Move in," she said in a low voice. "As soon as the king
takes his last bow."

His last bow? At this rate we'd be here all night. I
looked around and tried to spot Hyslop's people in the
mass of cheering spectators. It was hopeless. Most of the
audience had taken to standing on their seats. I did the
same.

Macbeth was inclining his head regally rather than
bowing, probably worried that his heavy crown would
drop off. I made out Tam Haggs underneath the stage at
the left. I could also see the bogeyman. He was on the
other side, hands resting on his sword and eyes staring
out into the night above the crowd. Then he turned

slightly and looked straight at me. I felt my heart stop and my armpits go sodden. It was like being eyed up by a hungry Moray eel – one that had fought and won numerous battles with squid and groupers. I had to return the cold stare though, I couldn't break the power of his gaze.

"Go! Go! Go!" Hel said into her mike.

I glanced to my right when I heard her voice and when I looked back at the stage the masked man had done just that – he was definitely and indubitably gone.

"What?" I gasped.

Hel looked at me. "What?" she repeated.

"Oh . . . forget it." I jumped down and started forcing my way through the crowd.

There was a series of gunshots, quickly followed by screaming and a general stampede. That made progress towards the stage almost impossible. When I finally got there, I found Tam Haggs with his boot on a motionless Macbeth, pistol in hand.

"Christ, you haven't killed him, have you?" I asked.

"Course not, you arsehole," he said. "Just a bit of crowd control."

I looked back at the empty seats. "And very good it was, Tam. What happened to the king?"

He dragged his prisoner upright. "Wouldn't stand still so I landed one on him," he said.

"That makes a change. Been practising since you missed me?"

Hel Hyslop pushed through the mass of plainclothes police personnel and captive cult members. "We've got the other ringleaders," she said, inclining her head towards a sour-looking Lady Macbeth and a Banquo who was clutching his midriff.

"I hope you're right," I said, trying to find any sign of the man I most wanted to have a heart-to-heart with.

Unfortunately he'd made a very convincing exit.

It wasn't long before the space in front of the stage filled with people in cod medieval costumes. Police officers quickly relieved them of anything akin to offensive weapons, which included the branches carried by soldiers as well as the witches' skinning knives. Although there were a lot of cult followers, they were outnumbered and outgunned by the plainclothed police so they behaved themselves. A few eyed their captured king and queen and grumbled, but none made any attempt to rescue them. It looked like they were fair-weather faithful.

Hel Hyslop was on the stage with a programme in her hand. "There are twenty-seven names on the cast list," she said to the Cult Squad leader. "How many of them have we got?"

He looked at his own list. "Twenty-four, I reckon. Three missing."

I bit my lip. I had a feeling those three comprised the bogeyman and his two side-kicks — the trio whose footprints we'd found in the archive and at the Edinburgh murder scenes.

"Not bad," Hel said. "We'll probably pick the others up in the sweep you've organised. We're assuming the cult leaders were all in the play, are we?"

The other inspector shook his head. "Not assuming. We *know* they were all acting. Macbeth here always insists his confidants appear in the play." He jabbed his elbow into the king's ribs. "Probably wants to keep them in line."

Macbeth straightened himself up and gave the police officers a superior look. "Everything we believe is contained in the play," he declaimed. "We do not act. We affirm our faith every time we appear on stage."

Close up, the cult leader was less of a heroic figure. His raven hair was obviously dyed and his face was heavily lined – he was older than he wanted his followers to realise. There was definitely something about the thin face that was familiar, but I still couldn't place it. Lady Macbeth was something else. She was even more terrifying when you got near to her. Her cheekbones seemed to be on the point of pushing through the unnaturally pale skin of her face and her eyes were a dull, ghostly green. She was keeping them off us – apparently we were not worthy of her consideration.

"Right," Hyslop said. "Transfer the performers to headquarters. The followers you can keep here under guard for the time being."

The Cult Squad supremo nodded and turned to his second-in-command.

Hel's mobile rang. She answered and listened for a few seconds. "Really?" she said, her lips forming into an unusually broad smile. "That is interesting. I'm on my way."

"We're on our way," I corrected. There was no way I was going to miss something that made her so happy. "What is it?"

She headed to the wings. "Tam's found something that'll do for these bastards," she said over her shoulder.

As I followed, I kept my eyes on the king and queen. Suddenly they were looking extremely nervous.

*   *   *

We went up the hill to the top of the graveyard then headed down into the gloom. On this side there were fewer pitchbrands and the streets beyond the boundary fence were ill lit as well.

"Where are we going?" I asked, then tripped over a broken headstone. "Shit!"

Hyslop pulled me to my feet. Her grip was surprisingly powerful. "You were the one who insisted on coming along." She moved away again quickly.

"Duart was the one who assigned me to you," I riposted.

"I haven't forgotten," she said. "Mind the barbed wire here." She stepped through a gap in the wall. "Don't worry, we're almost there. It's the first road on the left."

I followed her down the street – at least it was an asphalt surface, though there were plenty of holes. This was obviously not one of Glasgow's more prosperous wards. A pair of stone-faced policemen were standing outside a house half-way down the terrace. As we went in, they nodded respectfully towards the inspector and ignored me.

"How many are there?" Hel asked Haggs when he came down the stairs to meet us.

"Seventeen," he said, giving me a dismissive glance.

"How many *what* are there?" I asked blankly.

Tam glanced at his boss then answered. "Teenage meat," he said. "Nine females and—"

"Eight males," I interrupted. "I can count, sergeant. Or have you developed another gender in Glasgow?"

Haggs stared at me. "Not yet," he said threateningly, eyes dropping to my groin.

Hyslop nudged him. "Enough. Let's take a look at them."

So we did. They were split up between the two rooms on the ground floor and their counterparts on the floor above. There were bars on the windows which looked recent and the adolescents in the sparsely furnished sitting- and dining-rooms were very scared. They were dressed in good-quality Glasgow clothes and, apart from their frightened eyes, seemed to be in good health. The fashionable outfits and the teen connection brought Dougal Strachan to my mind.

"That pair of Macbeth wankers was guarding the place," Tam Haggs said, indicating the kitchen in the rear. The men were lying motionless on the floorboards, automatic pistols beyond their reach. "Don't worry, we didn't use maximum force."

Hyslop started talking to her subordinate in a low voice. I took the opportunity to go upstairs. Where I got a surprise.

There were three girls and two boys in the front bedroom. I didn't know three of them from Adam or Eve, but I recognised one female and one male – I'd seen their photographs in Welfare Directorate files back home. They were two of the geniuses who'd been abducted from Lauriston Castle. The lad's name was Michael, as far as I remembered; I couldn't be sure of the girl's. I glanced down the stairs. Hyslop and Haggs were still in a huddle.

The two adolescents were sitting together on the bed wearing flash clothes they weren't used to and apprehensive expressions. I went over and gave them an encouraging smile. It didn't have any effect.

"Listen," I said in a low voice. "I'm from Edinburgh."

Their eyes sprang wide open.

"I know who you are. You were kidnapped from the

facility in Lauriston. You're Michael and you're . . ." I looked at her for help.

"Lesley." The girl brushed the crinkly red hair back from her ashen face. "Who are you?"

"Dalrymple's the name. You can call me Quint. I work for the Council. After a fashion."

Michael stared at me. "After a fashion? What does that mean? And what are you doing in Glasgow?"

"Looking for you, among other things. Look, we haven't got much time. Don't tell anyone else that I know who you are." I glanced round at the other kids in the room. They were more interested in the view from the window than in us. "Who kidnapped you?" I asked, turning back to the kids. "What happened?"

Lesley shivered. "We were out in the grounds." She gave me a terrified look. "Then they came."

"Who came?"

The boy had dropped his gaze. "Men in kind of medieval costumes," he said haltingly.

"Did you see their faces?"

They both shook their heads.

"They were wearing masks," Michael said. "Horrible masks with scars all over them."

"How many were there?"

"Three," Lesley replied. "One big guy with a long cloak and two others – they were smaller – in leather jerkins and sort of breeches."

I nodded, hearing feet on the stairs. "Have you seen them since?"

Michael shrugged. "They put blindfolds on us not long after we were taken."

"We were on a boat," Lesley put in. "Then they brought us here." She registered the alarm in my face as the footsteps reached the landing. "Where's Dougal? He was with us on the boat but we haven't seen him since."

I stepped back. "I'll try to find him," I said, unable to tell them what had happened to their friend. "You'll be all right now. Just do what they tell you."

The door banged open.

"What the fuck are you doing?" Haggs demanded, gazing fiercely at me.

"What you should be doing," I said, brushing past him. "Giving these poor kids a kind word."

That only made him laugh.

I heard a policewoman making arrangements on the phone. The adolescents were going to be put up in a city hostel after their statements had been taken by the Cult Squad. I was trying to work out what the hell was going on. What did the crazed actor and his ghoulish queen want with Edinburgh's next generation of geniuses?

"Right," Hyslop said when I came down the stairs. "Time to interrogate the man who would be king." She stepped outside and commandeered a Llama. "Are you coming?"

I nodded. "What about Haggs?"

"He'll be along shortly," she said. "Since when did you care about his movements?"

The answer was, since I'd found the kidnapped kids. I didn't want him extricating the fact that I knew who they were. I could only hope that they'd keep their mouths shut. They were Edinburgh's brightest but at this moment they also looked like Edinburgh's edgiest.

"Why was Macbeth keeping a house full of lads and

lassies?" I asked as Hel drove round the eastern slope of the necropolis to where she'd left her own vehicle.

She glanced at me. "That's what we're about to squeeze out of him."

"Yeah, but you've got suspicions, haven't you?" I was thinking about Dougal Strachan again – should I tell her his identity?

"Oh yes," she said sibilantly, "I've got suspicions all right."

In a flash it came to me why Macbeth looked familiar. The guy with the American that I'd met at the banquet, the one who'd been staring at me so intently. He had had the same gaunt features. "They wouldn't happen to have any connection with the Rennie Institute, would they?" I asked, remembering the location of Dougal Strachan's body.

She was nodding slowly. "I would say you're heading in the right direction, Quint. Kelvingrove is definitely in the frame."

"East is east but west is best," I said, rubbing my chin. I hadn't had a chance to shave recently and I was beginning to feel like a Haggs replica. Bad news.

The inspector pulled up by her own Llama. "I couldn't agree with you more," she said, jumping down.

"Only joking," I said. "The east of Scotland is much gentler than the west. This place is wild, man. Wild and nasty."

She shook her head at me like she didn't know what I was talking about. That gave me a warm feeling inside.

Macbeth was in the corner office off the squadroom, in the chair Leadbelly had been shackled to. Another chair had been brought in for his lady queen. She was staring at the wall as if it wasn't there, but the king was more agitated. He kept shaking his chains and chewing his lips.

"This is an outrage," he said, his voice hoarse. "I demand to see my lawyer. You have no right—"

"We have every right to detain you." Duart had walked in without any of us noticing.

Hyslop and Haggs stiffened but I stayed slumped against the wall. My lack of sleep had caught up with me big-time.

Macbeth jerked round in his chair. "On what charge?" he demanded. "Mister Duart." He pronounced the title like it was a blasphemy from one of his tame witches.

Glasgow's number one operator twitched his lips. His expression was as inscrutable as ever, but the way his eyelashes quivered made me think he might be excited by what was going on.

"The charge is a matter for the Major Crime Squad," Duart said, glancing at Hyslop. "And the police are entitled to hold you without recourse to legal representation for six hours."

That wasn't long. The City Guard in Edinburgh would have serious difficulty operating under a restriction like that – then again, they were used to keeping suspects without charge and on a few crumbs of mouldy bread and a sip of water for as long as they liked.

Macbeth had turned his regal gaze on me. "Who is this individual?" he asked. "He wears no warrant badge. Why is he here?"

Andrew Duart strode over to the shackled figure in the chair and leaned over till his face was only a couple of inches away from Macbeth's. "This individual is Quintilian Dalrymple, Edinburgh's foremost investigator."

For a moment the king looked surprised, but he quickly regained his composure. "You're evading my question, Mister Duart. Why is he here?"

The first secretary grinned at the prisoner. "He's here to help us nail your arse, Mister Rennie."

I suddenly felt awake again.

"And after we've nailed your arse," Duart continued, "we're going to nail your brother's. Don't imagine your links with the institute are unknown to us."

Now I understood the suspicions Hel Hyslop had alluded to as well. Things were beginning to come together – but I was still more in the dark than an Edinburgh citizen in the suburbs after curfew. Time for a private word with the chief.

I caught up with Duart as he entered the main squad-room, before he rejoined his aides. "Hang on a minute," I said. "You owe me an explanation or two."

He raised a hand to stop his gang in their tracks. "About what, Quint?" he asked softly.

"Don't play games, Andy," I said. My tone discouraged him from objecting to the diminutive. "No one bothered to tell me that Rennie and Macbeth are brothers. Don't you think that would have been a good idea?"

Duart stroked his cheek with perfectly manicured fingers. "Possibly. I did consider it after the boy's body was found near the institute." He let out a sigh. "But, you see, I'm concerned that I have become obsessed by the activities of Professor Rennie. The same probably goes for Inspector Hyslop and her team. I wanted your objective take on the investigation."

I gave him the eye. He stood up to it but that didn't make him any more credible to me. "What about Lead-belly?" I demanded.

PAUL JOHNSTON

"Leadbelly?" he asked, his lips twitching. "You mean the prime suspect you're so fond of?"

I nodded. "The suspect who works at the Rennie, who remembers nothing about the murder he supposedly committed and who supposedly tried to kill himself in police custody."

Duart's expression hardened. "I'm not comfortable with those implications."

"Aren't you?" I opened my eyes wide at him. "You wouldn't be trying to frame an institute employee by any chance, would you? Or doing away with a fall guy who might spill something more than you expected?" I gave him a tight smile. "Just suggestions from an objective observer, you understand."

He clicked his fingers for an aide and took a file from him. "This is the report on the attempted suicide." He handed it to me. "Read it. You'll find that one of Inspector Hyslop's men discovered the prisoner on a routine check only a few minutes after he'd strung himself up. That hardly suggests attempted murder."

I took the file. "Might have been an officer who wasn't in on the scam."

Duart shook his head contemptuously. "Concentrate on the real villains, Quint – the madman in there and his power-hungry brother." The sharp smile he gave me relegated mine to the lower divisions. "That way you might just see Edinburgh's soot-stained buildings again."

I got his drift.

CHAPTER FIFTEEN

I love an all-night interrogation. The way Hyslop and Haggs went after Macbeth and his queen suggested that they did too. We gave the suspects the hard man/ soft man, hard woman/hard man, soft woman/hard men routines – every permutation of method and gender in the book. We offered them deals, we threatened them, Haggs even put the boot into one of the cult followers in front of the leaders. Nothing. No boogie. Not a sausage. The pair of them kept up the imperial act, staring at us with measured arrogance and only deigning to answer monosyllabically – which on most occasions meant the word "no". About the only thing they admitted to was their real names. He was Derek Rennie and she'd been Wendy Windsor in the real world. Given the antics of the former United Kingdom's former royal family, you could see why she'd changed her name as well as her image.

While Haggs was ranting and Hyslop sweet-talking the suspects one more time, I took a look at the Cult Squad files. The Macbeths had started five years back and had steadily built up support. They seemed to have a source of income that defied identification – unlike most of the cults in Glasgow, they never showed much interest in extorting funds from their new members. Their ethos was also different – it was political rather than profit-driven. They really did seem to believe that their destiny was to reunite Scotland's warring states under the aegis of the great and supposedly misunderstood king. It wasn't the most insane political agenda I'd ever come across – not quite.

Towards the end of the session, the king even denied all knowledge of the house behind the necropolis with the seventeen adolescents, claiming that his lieutenants sometimes acted independently.

"You must think we were fucking born yesterday!" Haggs yelled, leaning on Macbeth's shoulders and decorating his face with spittle.

The prisoner looked pointedly at Tam's hands and waited for him to step back before speaking. "Sergeant," he said calmly, "it is a matter of no interest to me when you or any of your colleagues were born." He stared away into space. "Although there may come a time when you wish you'd never come into this world."

"What?" Haggs stepped forward again, his fist drawn back. "Are you threatening me?"

Hel Hyslop put a hand on his shoulder. "All right, Tam," she said in a low voice. "We haven't got much time."

I glanced at the wall clock. It was after five. In an hour the prisoners' lawyer would be knocking on the door. I'd heard that she was a real hotshot. We badly needed a breakthrough. Hyslop wasn't optimistic about holding Macbeth for any longer. I'd already tried to arrange a private chat with the king so I could press the bastard about the Edinburgh kids, but she'd told me what to do with that thought.

I took her to one side again. "Let's show them the photos of the last murder," I said. "I've got an idea I want to try out."

"The teenager?" she said. "We haven't managed to find any link between him and the cult apart from the handbill in his pocket."

"No," I whispered, keeping the identity of the other adolescents to myself. "But he was found near the Rennie. Maybe the cult's tied up with the institute. The guys in charge are brothers, aren't they?"

Hel bit her lip.

"Duart's desperate to nail David Rennie," I reminded her.

"I know that, Quint," she said sharply. "I am as well. I don't like the power base he's built up in Kelvingrove any more than the first secretary does. But we've got to carry out the investigation according to regulations."

I gave her a sceptical look. "According to regulations may mean no progress, inspector. Watch their faces." I took the Strachan file from her desk and slid the murder scene photos out of their envelope.

"Have you ever seen this person before?" I asked Macbeth, thrusting a shot of the dead teenager on the mortuary slab in front of him. Hel took another and held it up to Lady Macbeth.

They were good. They hardly moved an eyelid. At least Shakespeare's hero and heroine had the decency to show some emotion in the presence of violent death. Then again, people old enough to have lived through the drugs wars at the beginning of the century got used to mutilated corpses.

"Who is this unfortunate?" the king asked.

"That's what I'm asking you," I said, keeping my eyes on him.

He looked up from the photo. "I think I read about this

in the *Herald*. The boy was the latest in that series of revolting killings, wasn't he?"

I nodded and tried another tack. "Does this photo suggest anything to you?" I asked, putting another shot in front of him.

Macbeth gazed at it intently then let out a bitter laugh. "Oh, very imaginative, Mister Dalrymple. Very imaginative indeed. But I hardly think you can build a case on that." He turned to his queen. "Look, my dear. Birnam Wood has come to Dunsinane."

I showed her the photo of Dougal Strachan as we'd found him, branch covering his face.

Lady Macbeth's detached expression didn't change. "Is this a joke?" she asked. "Are we supposed to know something about this crime because of a far-fetched connection with our play?"

I shrugged. "You're not supposed to know anything," I said. "Your husband was the one who made the far-fetched connection."

Macbeth sighed, shaking his head. "Don't play dumb, Mister Dalrymple. You thought of it yourself."

"It doesn't matter what I thought," I said, removing the photos and taking another one from the desk. "It's what the crazy bastards behind the killings think that counts." I showed him the photo. "How about the man in this shot? Is he familiar?"

The king looked at Leadbelly, stoned and covered in the blood of his supposed victim, who was lying underneath him. He shook his head. "The mutilation suggests that this is another of those appalling murders. But the man? No, I've never seen him before." His face didn't betray any nervousness. "Who is he? Is he dead? There was nothing about a double killing in the papers."

Hel Hyslop stepped forward and snatched the photo out of my hands. "There was nothing about that in the papers because this man is very much alive and is a prime suspect. Are you sure you don't know him?"

The king shook his head. "Quite sure. We don't mix with murderers. We're responsible citizens."

Haggs dropped his cigarette on the floor beside the chair and stamped on it hard. "If you're responsible citizens, I'm a horse's arse," he said.

Macbeth stared at him. "That's the first intelligent thing you've said all night, sergeant."

Soon afterwards the lawyer turned up. It took the flame-haired harpy no more than half an hour to get the king and queen out on bail. The Cult Squad cobbled together charges of staging the play without proper safety insurance and equipping actors with offensive weapons, but that was about it. The other twenty-two performers were held for further questioning – the brief waived their six-hour rights – but Mr and Mrs Macbeth walked. Magnificent.

Seven in the morning. A tray of coffee and rolls was sent up from the canteen. Davie would have been impressed – the coffee smelled glorious and the bacon was divine. None of that was enough to prevent me wilting.

Hel was sitting ashen-faced at her desk, having just put the phone down. Andrew Duart had ripped the shit out of her for blowing the interrogation. I don't know what he'd expected the king to blurt out, but he was seriously unhappy with the blank we'd drawn.

"Duart's a wanker," Haggs said. "If you'd let me use the electrodes, I'd have—"

289

"Shut up, Tam!" Hyslop shouted. "You know we can't do that with high-profile suspects."

I couldn't resist the temptation to wind them up. "Electrodes, eh? Not even the City Guard in Edinburgh is allowed to use that kind of gear."

Big Tam glared at me. "Watch it, pal. I could easily attach them to your extremities."

Hyslop's phone rang and broke up the sparring. She spoke briefly then put the handset down.

"Good news," she said, looking at me. "Your friend Leadbelly has come round."

"Good news for him," I said. "Maybe not so good for whoever set him up."

They both stared at me.

"You really believe he's innocent?" Hel asked.

"That's what I'm going to ask him again," I said, grabbing my jacket and heading for the door. "You can come too, if you want."

She caught up with me in the squadroom. "All right," she said. "Hang on. I need to sort out Tam's duties."

I watched as she went back and laid down some law or other to her sergeant. He didn't look too pleased.

"Trouble?" I asked when she rejoined me.

"Nothing special," she said, walking past. "Something he forgot to do."

I wondered what that might have been for a couple of seconds then followed her to the lift.

"Where is the reprobate?" I asked as we got into the Llama.

"In the Western Infirmary," Hel Hyslop said.

The name rang a bell. I looked at the road atlas. As I thought, the infirmary was in Kelvingrove, less than half a mile north of the Rennie Institute and the maternity hospital it adjoined. Dougal Strachan's body had been found between the two medical facilities. I turned to her.

"Don't even think about it." Hel's tone was peremptory.

I grinned at her lewdly. "I wasn't."

"Piss off, Quint," she said, pulling away from the kerb. "You know what I mean. We can't get into the Rennie without a warrant."

I looked out at the morning rush. Buses and cars had packed the central streets. The air was thick with exhaust fumes that the motor manufacturers no doubt swore were harmless. I had a flash of Edinburgh's relatively empty streets, but there was no point in getting homesick — the fumes were even worse over there because of poor-quality diesel and ancient exhaust pipes.

"What makes you think I wanted to get into the Baby Factory?" I asked.

"You had that look on your face," Hel replied. "The one that says 'Danger — Smartarse at Work'. You've been wearing it a lot recently. Why don't you come clean?" She gave me what she thought was an encouraging smile. "You know more than you've been letting on, don't you?"

I didn't go for it. What I knew about the Edinburgh murders and the missing kids I was keeping to myself till I saw a way out of Glasgow. "You'd like to get into the Rennie yourself, wouldn't you, inspector?"

She glanced at me then nodded. "Duart's right, I think. Professor Rennie's up to something dirty. There's been too much money pouring into Kelvingrove ward. I'm sure that tosser in the crown is in on it."

"So why don't you get a warrant? Why doesn't the first secretary arrange one?"

She swerved round a corner at more than regulation speed. "Because this is a democracy, you fool. We can't walk in on people without due cause. There are courts, judges, lawyers." She looked at me. "You do know what those are, don't you?"

"Very funny. Okay, Edinburgh doesn't have an independent judiciary. All the same, we nail criminals more successfully than you do."

"Oh aye?" Hyslop sneered. "I haven't seen you catch any since you've been here."

"Just wait," I said under my breath. I looked away. This was getting out of control. I decided to offer terms. "Hel, let's try and act like human beings instead of tearing each other's throat out."

She shrugged noncommittally. "All right." She drove across the motorway and headed towards the university's tall tower.

"So why did you join the Glasgow police?" I asked.

She laughed. "Spare me the fake interest in my life story, Quint."

"It's not fake. I like to find out what keeps investigators going. It's not exactly a job that fills you with joy on a daily basis, is it?" I looked across at her. "I mean, Tam Haggs is different. I know plenty of guard personnel like him. He likes ordering people about and putting the boot in whenever he can."

Hel turned to me angrily. "Lay off Tam. You don't know anything about him. He has his own problems."

I raised my hands in surrender. "Okay, okay, I'm laying off him." I opened my eyes wide at her. "As long as you tell me what makes you tick."

"Jesus," she said, hands tight on the wheel. "I'm not making deals with you, Quint."

"Come on. We're working a case together. What's wrong with a bit of background?"

"Oh . . . all right," she said, her voice softening. "What do you want to know? I was born down the road here, I was brought up in Bearsden—"

"What did your parents do?" I asked.

The interruption put her off. She didn't speak for a few seconds. "My parents? I never knew my parents. They were . . . they were killed in a car crash when I was a baby. I spent most of my childhood in care."

"Ah. Sorry."

She glanced at me. "It's all right. You weren't to know." She stopped at a red light and watched a line of cult followers cross. They were dressed in green robes and were carrying yellow plastic fish, their arms extended. "After school I studied law and criminology at university. The police was a logical career move."

"That's it, is it?" I asked, trying to cajole her into something more revealing.

She looked puzzled. "What more do you want?"

"Do you want a list? Are you married? Have you got kids? What do you do in your spare time? Do you like seafood? What's your favourite kind of music?" I grinned. "For a start."

Her lips twitched. "No. No. Read contemporary women novelists. Yes, especially oysters. Glasgow Granite."

I tried to make sense of that lot. Most of it checked out. "What's Glasgow Granite?"

Hyslop laughed. "God, you Edinburgh folk are so out of it. Granite's a cross between blue grass and urban metal. Great for leaping around to."

I took her word for it. Shortly afterwards we pulled up at the infirmary. Time to do the granite with

293

Leadbelly. I wondered what the old blues addict would make of it.

We were led by a nurse through a hospital that took my breath away. I wished my father had been in Glasgow when he had his heart attack. This place was something out of the twenty-fifth century – high-tech equipment everywhere, comfortable public rooms with small wards clustered round them, architecture and fittings that were pleasing to the eye as well as functional. Sophia's Medical Directorate was in the Stone Age compared with this.

"The patient has his own room," the freckled nurse told us as we approached a door with a policeman standing by it. "He's still recovering. Please stay for no more than five minutes."

I took Hel's arm, feeling her jerk as I touched it. "Since we've been getting on so well, can I ask you a favour?"

She looked at me dubiously. "What is it, Quint?"

"Can I talk to Leadbelly in private?" I watched as her face set back into its usual hard expression. "Give the guy a break," I pleaded. "He's in a foreign city, he's had a near-death experience and you want him to have another one. At least he knows me."

She wasn't impressed but, to my surprise, she went along with it. That's what you get when you ask someone about themselves – however much they try not to, they end up trusting you more than they did before. Not that I did it only to get a few minutes on my own with Leadbelly.

I went into the room. The patient was lying on a high bed surrounded by machines that bleeped and hummed.

"Leadbelly?" I said quietly.

There was a bandage round his neck and various leads and wires ran in and out of him. The skin on his face and arms was clammy despite the air-conditioning. He had his eyes closed.

I tried again. "Leadbelly? It's Quint. I'm on my own."

That did the trick. His crusted eyelids came apart. He nodded his head at the jug of water on the bedside table.

I held a plastic glass to his scabby lips. "There you are, man. Now you can tell me all about it."

"All . . . about . . . what?" He was wheezing like an Edinburgh coal miner.

I leaned closer. "All about what happened in the holding cell." I looked over my shoulder. "We haven't got much time."

Leadbelly blinked a couple of times.

To my surprise I saw that his eyes were damp. I clutched his bony arm. "Come on. Tell me who put the lace round your neck and I'll nail the bastard."

He was staring past me, his eyes bulging. "No . . ." He looked back at me helplessly. "No . . ."

"You can tell me, Lead," I said. "You're safe in here. I'll make sure they don't get to you."

Leadbelly shook his head. "No . . . they . . . they . . . didn't . . ." His voice trailed away.

I shook his arm. "Tell me, Leadbelly. Was it Hyslop's people? Tell me."

"Christ," he gasped. "What . . . what if . . . what if I really did kill her?"

I looked at him. Was that what was bothering him? Did he think that he really did murder the pregnant woman?

Suddenly Leadbelly started jerking his head from side to side. "The bastards . . ." he said, his cracked voice louder. "What they did to those poor fuckers . . ."

"Who are you talking about, Lead?"

He stared up at me. "The poor fuckers," he said, his words almost inaudible. "The poor, tortured fuckers . . ." He closed his eyes.

"Who?" I said, trying to keep the volume down. "Tell me, Leadbelly, for Christ's sake. It's the only way we'll ever get out of Glasgow."

But he wouldn't open his eyes again. By the time the nurse came in, he was sobbing. That got me a disapproving glare.

I walked out with my head in a spin. What the hell had happened to the hard man who used to run with the Howlin' Wolf? And who was tormenting him so badly?

Leadbelly wouldn't talk to Hyslop — no surprise there — so we headed out of the hospital.

"That was a complete waste of time," she said as we hit the car park.

I glanced at her. If she'd been behind Leadbelly's supposed suicide, she'd have been worried that he might have said something incriminating to me. All I could see was irritation that she'd been distracted from the main thread of the investigation.

"What now?" I asked as we got back into the Llama.

"I'm going back to the chambers. You?"

"I'm so knackered that a squad of naked nuns couldn't keep me awake." I saw her look of distaste. I'd been hoping to provoke a response as I still wasn't sure if Hel Hyslop was a fully functioning human being. "Can you drop me at the hotel?"

She nodded. "You're lucky it's on my way. Otherwise you'd be hoofing it."

When we got to the St Vincent she kept the engine running.

"I don't suppose you fancy a second breakfast," I asked as I opened the door.

She gave me a cool look. "I thought you were ready to crash out, nude nuns notwithstanding." She smiled primly. "Anyway, you don't suppose correct," she said, turning to the front. "Too much to do."

I shrugged. "Okay. Can you send me round copies of the interrogation reports as soon as they're completed?"

Hel nodded. "All right. When are you planning on gracing us with your presence again?"

"I'll let you know, inspector," I said with a laugh. "Good night."

I slammed the door and walked away across the sunlit pavement.

I thought I'd got away with it. Wrong. Hel was way ahead of me. A hotel security guy joined me in the lift, followed me down the corridor to my room and locked me in. Bollocks. I'd been thinking about going on an unguided tour of a certain research facility in Kelvingrove. It looked like I'd have to crash out after all. So, after calling reception and telling them not to disturb me, I did.

Not that the sleep I got was particularly restful. I had a lot of visitors from out of town. First there was the old man, lying on a bed in the infirmary back home, his face drained of colour and his mouth slack. Then there was Sophia, the bulge in her midriff pushing out her surgical robe. She was saying something to me but I couldn't hear any words, just the incessant hum of hospital monitors like the ones attached to Leadbelly. Then I saw Hamilton and Katharine and Davie. The guardian was tearing a strip off the others, his finger wagging and his face purple. Again, I couldn't hear what he was saying but this time the background noise was a deafening racket, that of an industrial plant working full out. Katharine was reacting to authority as she always did – with extreme disdain. Davie was being a bit more respectful but he didn't look too impressed either.

Suddenly everything went black. The clatter disappeared and was replaced by a gentle hissing, the breath of a light breeze over a heather-carpeted hillside. Then a face flew out of the darkness. I recognised it immediately. It was Caro, long-lost Caro. The dark hair was loose around her face, not drawn back in a grip as it had been the last time I saw her on the drugs gang raid that led to her death. And her expression was joyous, her moist lips parted and the straight white teeth visible between them. She kept smiling at me, mouthing words which I wished I could hear. But the wind was blowing stronger now, carrying everything she said away. Then she too was gone, back into the void.

I woke up in a sweat, the bedcovers all over the place. It took me a long time to get my breathing back under control. A couple of mouthfuls of malt whisky helped. Christ. Caro. She'd been coming back to me a lot recently. As for the others, I didn't usually dream about them – certainly not Lewis Hamilton. What was going on? Being away from Edinburgh was getting to me in a big way.

It was three in the afternoon. The best way to banish the past was to work. I called the desk and asked if anything had been delivered. There was a package from the Major Crime Squad. I asked for it to be sent up, along with a double order of bacon rolls and coffee. Then I had a bath and got down to the files.

Which weren't particularly revealing. The interrogations of the twenty-two *Macbeth* performers didn't give us anything about the cult's funding or any links with the Rennie Institute. At least I found out the name of the masked man with the cloak. He was called John Breck. Not to his face though – the culties had to address him as Broadsword, or else. The other two missing actors, the ones I assumed were the bogeyman's side-kicks, had been Joseph Graham and Eric Nigg before they metamorphosed into medieval men-at-arms with the monikers MacAlpine and Aidan. No one seemed to know much about any of them – cult members were encouraged to cast off their past existences like snakeskins.

As for the men who'd been guarding the adolescents, they claimed they had no idea what was going on. When Haggs applied what the file described as "firm questioning" – which I took to involve electrical equipment – they only repeated that they were nothing more than sentries and that Broadsword was in charge.

I sat back amidst the debris of crockery and green folders and tried to make sense of what was going on. I was the only person who had the full range of information, stretching from the burglary, kidnappings and murders in Edinburgh to the dead adolescent near the Baby Factory and the suspected involvement of the Macbeth cult in Glasgow. The question was, did I have too much material? Was everything connected? I took a gulp of what was by now very cold coffee and thought about it. Was there a thread, a line that ran through the apparently disparate crimes? Every instinct I had told me there was. One thing my years in the Public Order Directorate taught me was "always keep sight of the beginning". And the beginning of this convoluted case or cases was the break-in at the old Parliament archive. A trio of men who I reckoned were now on the loose in Glasgow had taken a Genetic Engineering Committee file attachment. That had to be the key.

I followed the line from there. The burglars – Broadsword the Bogeyman, MacAlpine and Aidan, I was pretty sure – had connections in Edinburgh with Knox 43, the first victim. But who would have sent them to get the file attachment? Professor Rennie was the obvious answer. Perhaps there was something in that document that he needed. Perhaps he also needed the missing adolescents – their high intelligence might play a part in his research into the human potential referred to in his mission statement. It could be that Knox 43 was killed to keep him quiet, while the physical training instructor was simply in the wrong place at the wrong time. Then I remembered the modus operandi. I could understand why the *Macbeth* trio would have worn their costumes in Edinburgh. There are plenty of Tourism Directorate operatives wandering around every day in festival production get-up, making it as good a disguise as any. But why leave branches over the victims' faces? They may not have been a very obvious link to *Macbeth*, but I reckoned they were a link all the same. Except the eight Glasgow victims before Dougal Strachan had been found without branches over them.

The phone rang.

"You awake, shite?" Haggs asked.

"Evidently, Tam. What do you want?"

"You. I'll be round in ten minutes. Make sure you're ready." The connection was cut.

While I was shaving, I followed the thread of the case through to Glasgow. What was behind the killings here?

I was still sure Leadbelly wasn't a murderer, even though he'd behaved strangely in the hospital in the morning. But he was employed at the Rennie so he was involved in some way. The fact that Macbeth was the professor's brother and the fact that Andrew Duart and Hel Hyslop were suspicious of the institute made me sure that the line ended there. But the Baby Factory was a no-go area. The Baby Factory. What exactly was the significance of the name? I remembered Crummett, the American businessman Rennie had with him at the banquet. Exactly what kind of deal did they have going?

The door was unlocked as I was pulling up my trousers.

"Come on," Big Tam said impatiently.

"You need some beauty sleep," I said, taking in his bloodshot eyes and pale skin. "A couple of hundred years ought to do it."

"Fuck you, Embra wanker," he said, stepping forward with his fist raised.

I walked past him, allowing the sleeve of my leather jacket to slap him lightly on the face. "You're not my type, darling," I said, heading rapidly for the lift.

We worked the prisoners and the files into the evening — and reached the big nowhere. Searches of the cult's numerous premises hadn't turned up anything incriminating either.

"We'll have to let them walk," Hel said around ten p.m.

I shrugged. "Why not? Either they're in the dark about what Macbeth's been up to or the bastard's made them learn their lines perfectly."

She nodded, scribbled on a form and handed it to Haggs. "Get the Cult Squad duty officer to countersign that and let the culties go. Grade 2 surveillance is approved."

He walked off without a word.

"What next?" I asked her.

She stared at me, her face wan. "God knows. I've just about had it." Her expression hardened. "I know you're keeping things from me, Quint."

I tried to look surprised. "What things?"

"Don't fuck about. What did Leadbelly tell you this morning?"

"Nothing," I said, breathing a sigh of relief. Lies were unnecessary. "He was still out of it."

I could see she didn't believe me, but she was too tired to argue. "I'm packing it in for the day. Come on, I'll drive you back to the hotel." She moved to the door.

"Hel?" I asked, flicking back pages in my notebook. "Is it normal practice in Glasgow for murder victims' backgrounds to be ignored?"

She gave me a curious look. "What do you mean?" Her eyes flashed. "Are you criticising our working methods?"

"No," I said appeasingly. "But you've got eight sources of potentially useful information on motive and you haven't investigated more than the last few months of their lives." I glanced round the large squadroom. "You're not short of manpower, are you?"

Hel headed for the lift. "Not particularly. But you said it yourself. We've had eight violent deaths – nine including the adolescent – over a relatively short period. Every time we get into the victims' past histories, another corpse turns up."

I nodded as the doors closed and we moved downwards. Series of murders do put investigating teams under heavy pressure, but something about her answer didn't ring true.

"You've been sleeping all day," Hel said as we reached the ground floor. "What are you going to do now?"

"What choice have I got?" I said ironically. "Your flunkies in the St Vincent will lock me in as soon as I arrive."

She stopped by the Llama and smiled. "I don't think we need to bother with that tonight, Quint. After all, Edinburgh's a long way away and where else are you going to go?" She pressed the electronic lock control. "You wouldn't be crazy enough to case the Rennie, would you? As senior investigating officer, I couldn't possibly condone that." Her tone wasn't exactly discouraging.

Hel Hyslop was a more devious operator than I'd thought. Pity she wasn't coming too.

Two and a half hours later I was in a bush to the west of the institute. I'd walked all the way, having decided that the underground railway the locals call the Clockwork Orange was a bit too obvious. Besides, I was never a fan of the novel of that name – too many difficult words.

I'd been there long enough for my feet and hands to start tingling in the cold. The perimeter fence was twenty yards away and it was the main problem – twelve feet high, the top three strands consisting of vicious-looking razor wire, bright lights every second post and what I reckoned were hyper-sensitive alarm cables wound through the barbed stuff. To top that, there were cameras on the walls of the main building. Fort Knox had nothing on this place. That only added to my suspicions. What was so secret and sensitive to require all this security?

I gave it another five minutes then withdrew to the parkland behind. The undergrowth was thicker there and there were trees to provide cover as well. Any thoughts I had of effecting a clandestine entry to the Rennie had disappeared faster than a Glasgow citizen's fashion allowance. The comforts of my hotel room, not to say its central heating, were becoming an irresistible temptation.

Then I saw him. My stomach clenched for a second before liquefying. Jesus. It was the bogeyman. Or Broadsword, John Breck, whatever the lunatic wanted to call himself. His long hair and scarred face were visible in the lights of the Rennie and his cloak was flapping as he strode straight towards me.

My breath rasped in my throat as he got closer. In his right hand he was holding a branch that was partially bare of leaves. Something metallic glinted beneath it. And in the left hand was the solid mass of a mallet. I looked round, frantically calculating if I could reach the trees before him. No chance. Birnam Wood was on its way to Dunsinane. The mutilated faces of the victims and their third eyes flashed before me. That stiffened my resolve. The bastard. He owed a debt for what he'd done to them.

I swallowed hard, stood my ground and faced the foe.

CHAPTER SIXTEEN

I stood motionless as the branch-wielding figure approached. When he was about five yards away, he stopped and stared at me. I could see his eyes glistening behind the mask. Close up, the scars were even more ragged and the material looked worryingly like real human skin. He dropped the branch — it was from a copper beech — and I saw what was underneath it. A chisel. At this point the fact that I'd been right about the implement used to mutilate the victims didn't make me rejoice.

"Why didn't you run?" The bogeyman's voice was cracked and high-pitched, as it had been when he was on stage. "Do you want to die?"

I kept my eyes on his, even though the urge to bolt was hard to resist — at this range the killer was even more terrifying than the witnesses had described. I clenched my fists, wishing I had something more than them to defend myself with.

Broadsword took a step forward. "Eh, dick? Curiosity getting the better of you?" I could see his lips form into a malevolent smile through the hole in the mask. "You know what curiosity did to the cat." He lifted the mallet and chisel a few inches.

I took a deep breath. "I know what you did to nine

people in Glasgow and another two in Edinburgh."
Provoking psychos is a seriously risky business. You
either get them to give themselves away or you die – or
both eventualities occur in quick succession.

Now he was looking at the instruments of death in
his hands. "Nine people in Glasgow and two in Edinburgh?" he repeated, his voice scratchier. "Eleven
dead." He seemed to lose the plot for a few moments.
Then he raised his eyes to mine again. "Yes, that's
right. We've killed eleven." He took another step towards me. "And you're about to become number
twelve."

I'd been in situations like this before. The only thing to
do is keep your assailant talking. "Look," I said, trying to
stop myself gabbling, "you wear a mask. I don't know
who you are. There's no need to kill me."

The laugh that issued from the hideous face made me
quiver. "Oh, you've got to die all right, Dalrymple. There's
no getting away from that. You know too much."

"How do you know my name?" I asked. "I don't
remember being introduced to you, John Breck."

The mask's fixed features didn't conceal the twist of
his lips. "I don't like being called that." The voice was
low in volume but there was no mistaking its intensity.

"Okay." I smiled, hoping my extreme nervousness
wasn't visible. "How about Broadsword?"

He laughed. It was a hoarse, empty sound. The bogeyman was about as far from having a sense of humour as I
was from becoming an auxiliary again. "Like I say, you
know too much." His gaze suddenly dropped again.
"Christ, we've gone too far," he said in a harsh whisper.
"We shouldn't have killed the boy."

The boy? He must have meant Dougal Strachan. "Why

was he killed?" I asked before I could swallow the question.

Bad move. The bogeyman looked up again. "You're too curious, dick. The others are right. We have to deal with you." He raised the mallet and drew it back.

There wasn't time to think about who the others were, I had to go for broke. "The institute's finished," I said, glancing over my shoulder. "Duart and the executive know all about Rennie's involvement in the murders." That line was the best I could come up with on the spur of the moment.

Broadsword laughed again. "Good," he said, moving forward. "That'll put me in the clear." The mallet was pulled right back now. "This is it, Dalrymple."

Everything slowed down. I'd taken a step away, but what I'd seen when I glanced round at the Rennie was puzzling me even as the lunatic made his move. Or rather, who I'd seen. Surely not.

"Hit the ground, Quint!" yelled a familiar voice.

I was already in the process of doing that. As I dived to the grass, my attacker swung the mallet and lost his balance. He straightened up quickly and took aim at me again. Then, with a dull plop, the haft of a knife appeared in the upper part of his right arm. He let go of the wooden weapon.

"Step back, you in the mask!" came a barked command.

Broadsword didn't hang about. He took several steps to the rear then turned and ran, the cloak spreading out behind him like an octopus discharging its ink. In a few seconds he was through the line of trees and away.

I twisted round on the damp ground and took in the figure that was racing towards me.

"Are you all right, Quint?" he demanded, sliding the last yards on his knees.

"Aye, Davie. Thanks to you." Then I took another, even more surprised look as Katharine stepped swiftly out of the undergrowth.

From Gothic horror to romance in the blink of an eye.

We were in the bushes on the far side of the grass from the institute. There was no sign of the guy who'd been about to deal with me. To be honest, he wasn't uppermost in my mind at that moment.

"What the fuck are you two doing here?" I gasped.

"Good to see you too, Quint," Davie said with a loose grin. He was wearing good-quality jeans and a leather jacket that was almost as cool as mine. "Just as well we made it when we did."

"Bloody right." I was staring at Katharine. She hadn't needed to bother with Glasgow chic as her own wardrobe was already pretty off the wall. She was in a pair of loose black trousers and a fluffy orange jersey that concealed her figure effectively. But she still looked stunning, her eyes bright and her face split by a smile.

"Darling, are you okay?" she asked ironically. "We've been so worried." She squeezed my hand to show she wasn't just taking the piss.

"Apart from having the operational life of my heart reduced by about half, yes, I'm remarkably okay. What about Hector? Is he all right?"

Davie nodded. "I checked before we left. He was fine – improving all the time."

"Great. Thanks, Davie." I looked at them. "How the hell did you two come to be lurking in those particular bushes? Come to that, how did you get into this bloody city?"

They exchanged anxious glances, which immediately made me suspicious.

"Come on, out with it," I said, ducking down as the lights of a passing car shone over us.

"Em . . ." Davie was looking more sheepish than the specimen called Dolly.

"We tailed you," Katharine put in. Her eyes were lowered, concentrating on the leaves she was brushing from her clothes. "There was a butt from a Glasgow cigarette on your landing. Given the other connections the murder victims had with this city, we were pretty sure you'd been brought here. So we hitched a lift on a Fisheries Guard vessel then tramped to the border. We made out that we were refugees from the wicked Council. They let us in like a shot."

If they hadn't kept avoiding my gaze, I might have bought the story. But there had to be more to it. "So that got you to Glasgow. But it's a big enough city, even if you don't include the rest of the territory it controls. How come you ended up in this precise location?"

"Em . . ."

"I wish you'd stop saying that, Davie," I snapped.

The eyes above the heavy beard opened wide. "All right," he said, fumbling in his pocket. "If you must know, we traced you with this."

I peered at the electronic device he was holding out. It took me a while to identify. It was one of the new tracking monitors that the Public Order Directorate had commissioned. The penny dropped.

"You bastards," I said, glaring at them. "You put a bug on me."

"Not me," they said in unison.

"It was Lewis Hamilton," Katharine continued. "He authorised it."

"Why?" I gasped.

Davie was shaking his head. "It was your own fault, Quint. You were forever disappearing when the guardian wanted you. And you often turn your mobile off." He shrugged. "When it came to choosing subjects for the equipment's trials, you were at the top of his list."

"Where is it?" I demanded, patting my clothes. I soon stopped. "This is all Glasgow gear. Where the fuck is it?"

Katharine pointed to my feet. "In the heel of your left boot."

"Did you know about this?" I asked her.

"Of course not," she replied indignantly. "I only found out after you disappeared."

I looked at my footwear. Thank God I decided to continue wearing my steel toe-caps, rather than the loafers I'd been supplied with in the hotel. Pity I hadn't thought of using my boots on Broadsword though.

"We couldn't pick up a signal until we entered Glasgow," Davie said. "Once we were here, we got you after a few hours."

"You might have made contact a bit earlier," I complained.

"We came as soon as we could," Davie said. "Sorry."

I grinned at him. "In the light of subsequent exploits with your auxiliary knife, I'll let you off, guardsman."

"Bastard got away with my blade," he said, scowling. He put his hand inside his jacket. "Just as well I brought another one." The double-edged steel glinted in the light from the street-lamp behind the trees.

Katharine stood up and looked around. "We'd better get moving. What is that place?" she asked, inclining her head towards the Rennie. "It's fortified better than a barracks back home."

"I'll fill you in later," I said, only realising what I'd said when a smile spread across her lips. "I mean, we need to talk."

Davie wasn't impressed. "Let's get back to the car," he said, moving off through the bushes.

"You've got transport?" I said in amazement. "You didn't nick it, did you?" I had a vision of Tam Haggs salivating at the prospect of arresting car thieves from Edinburgh.

Katharine frowned at me. "Certainly not. It belongs to a friend of mine."

I ducked under a low branch. "You have a friend in Glasgow?"

"Several, actually," she said.

"Don't tell me. They used to work with you on the farm." Katharine had spent over four years on a dissident collective outside the Edinburgh border before she came back in 2025.

She nodded. "This particular one was very happy when I turned up this morning." She laughed quietly. "He wasn't quite so pleased when he saw Davie in his off-duty rags – he had him down as an Edinburgh guardsman straight away. I managed to talk him into lending the big man a slightly less conspicuous outfit."

We'd reached the edge of the undergrowth. Davie climbed into a dark blue off-road vehicle that was the Llama's rich relation – obviously the police didn't get top-of-the-range models in this city. Before we ran to join him, I turned to Katharine and touched her hand.

"It's good to see you," I said. "Even if you cut it a bit fine."

"There's gratitude for you." She smiled. "It's good to see you too, Quint. Even if a mallet blow might have knocked some sense into you."

Trust Katharine to hanker after lost opportunities.

It turned out that her friend's flat was in the Merchant City, to the south-east of the City Chambers. As we approached the centre, I lay down on the back seat. The last thing I wanted was Hyslop or one of her goons spotting me. At least I would be within walking distance of the hotel afterwards. The area was full of warehouse conversions and the like, expensive cars and security doors lining the streets. Davie pulled into a parking space that had the Super Llama's registration number painted on the asphalt.

Katharine said her name into a silver panel on the frame and the door clicked open. "Neat, huh?" she said. "Voice recognition. Ewan programmed mine in before we left."

"Ewan?" I said as we stepped into a silent lift.

Davie was examining his fingernails with studied indifference.

"My friend." Katharine pressed the button marked "Penthouse".

"Your friend?"

"Not that kind of friend, Quint," she said, registering my dubious tone. "If it's any business of yours."

Davie coughed.

"Or yours, guardsman," she said fiercely.

Davie grinned.

"Cool it, you two," I said. "We've got things to talk about."

Katharine nodded and stepped out of the lift after it

pinged. She led us to a heavy brass-panelled door, said her name again and walked in.

I followed her. "Jesus Christ. What does this Ewan do? Deal in Charles Rennie Mackintosh artefacts?" The flat was a vast duplex, ceiling-high windows looking out towards the lights of the towerblocks across the Clyde. It was decorated with artworks that were obviously high quality. The furniture and fitments looked handmade as well.

"Good guess," Katharine said, sitting down on a long red leather sofa. "He designs computer games, actually. There's a massive market for them everywhere in the world except Edinburgh."

I glanced around. "So where is he then?"

"Don't worry. We're on our own. He and Peter are at their club."

"Who's Peter?" I asked, unable to control my jealousy any longer.

Davie sat down heavily at the other end of the sofa. "Ewan's boyfriend." He glanced dubiously at his clothes. "These belong to him."

"Don't worry, you won't catch anything from them," Katharine said acidly.

I was glad to see their partnership on the trip to find me hadn't ruined their mutual antipathy. I was also glad that it appeared Ewan was a friend rather than an ex-lover. I went over to the drinks cabinet to celebrate. It was three yards long and almost the same in height – and it must have contained just about every whisky known to man.

"Think we can have a drink?" I asked.

Davie got up. "Now you're talking. Peter said we could help ourselves."

Katharine joined us. "See, Davie? Ewan and Peter are not all bad."

I let them get on with squaring up to each other. I was too interested in a limited-edition dark brown malt from St Kilda. The remote island had been repopulated by a colony of very brave naturist crofters in the early years of the century. Presumably they traded full-frontal photos for barley – I couldn't see much growing on that barren gannet colony.

We settled on and around the sofa with well-charged glasses and I told them what had been going on. That kept them away from each other's throats.

Davie eyed me sceptically when I finished. "Have you been drinking a lot of that stuff since you got here, Quint?" He was nursing about half a pint of Carstairs, Cream of the Lowland Blends so he was hardly talking from a position of superiority. "It all sounds a bit too complicated."

I raised my shoulders. "Take it or leave it, guardsman."

Katharine leaned forward. "You've obviously done enough to wind the wanker with the mask up. Are you sure he was the one who killed the auxiliaries in Edinburgh? What does he call himself? Broadsword?"

"The Mallet of the Scots," Davie observed, stifling a laugh.

"Very bloody funny," I said. "Next time, you try giving him the time of day." I turned to Katharine. "The witnesses in Edinburgh saw someone of his description, the kidnapped adolescents confirmed it and he was going to take me out – what more do you want?"

"Okay," she said, nodding. "So why don't we just leave him to this Major Crime Squad woman you've been getting on so well with . . ." she shot me a sharp glance ". . . and bugger off back to the perfect city."

"It's tempting." I took a slug of St Kilda and felt my throat melt. "But the bastard managed to get into Edinburgh before. He'd probably follow me back home."

Davie was nodding too. "Exactly. We can nail him there."

"Thanks very much," I said. "You want to set me up as a target and ride in at the last minute like Ivanhoe in a polo neck again? No thanks."

I felt Katharine's hand on my arm.

"Cool it, Quint," she said. "Master Davie took a major risk in coming to save your skin."

I nodded, surprised at her sudden defence of the guard commander she loved to hate. "Yeah, sorry," I mumbled. "I appreciate the knife you stuck in the bogeyman."

Davie wasn't meeting my eyes.

"That's not what I mean," Katharine said. "After you went missing, we reviewed the case and proposed a rescue mission to Hamilton. He vetoed it — said there wasn't enough evidence that you'd have been taken here. I didn't care. I do what I like and I was coming whatever. But Davie disobeyed the guardian's direct order. He stands to be demoted."

"Christ." I chewed my lip then punched the big man lightly on the arm. "Thanks, Davie. Don't worry, I'll square things with Lewis when we get back."

He gave a wry laugh. "You? You're about as capable of squaring things with the guardian as I am of sucking his—"

"Spare us your hidden desires, commander," Katharine said. She looked at me seriously. "What are we going to do, Quint? If we're going to head for the border, we'd better go while it's still dark."

I thought about it, but not for long. Dougal Strachan's

ravaged face and Leadbelly's frightened eyes flashed in front of me. "No. You two go if you want. I've got unfinished business."

"I'm not going anywhere," Davie said, shaking his head. "I came to this shithole to take your sorry carcass back home and that's what I'm going to do."

I grinned at him. "Spoken like a madman."

Katharine stood up. "What does that make me?" she asked, walking to the far end of the room.

Davie and I looked at each other.

"Don't bother answering that, guardsman," I warned. "Where are you going, Katharine?"

"Bed," she said. "Are you coming, Quint?"

This time it was me avoiding Davie's eyes as I set off after her.

Ewan and Peter had pretty good taste to go with the riches they'd amassed. Apart from a bed that was big enough for a sultan and a sackful of sultanas, the bedroom was kitted out with chrome and leather furniture and fittings that must have dented their wad severely.

There was a clock in the shape of a computer screen on the wall. Three-thirty a.m. I wondered if my hotel room had been checked. Too late to worry now.

Katharine sat on the mock zebra-skin bedcover and undid her boot-laces. "Won't anyone be wondering where you are?" she asked.

I sat down next to her and started taking off my own footwear. "I imagine the bogeyman would like to know my whereabouts." I picked up my boot and tried to spot where the bug had been inserted.

"How about that female police officer you've been

spending so much time with?" There was only a hint of jealousy in Katharine's voice.

"Hel?" I laughed. "She may be female but she's not exactly open to propositions."

"Just as well," Katharine said, pulling her blouse over her head and looking at me.

I raised my eyes from her black bra. "We haven't got much time," I said. "I'll have to be away by first light and we need to set things up with Davie before I go."

She took hold of my shirt then pulled me close to her. "That'll be plenty of time," she said, her voice low.

Apparently I was no longer in the dog-house I'd been consigned to in Edinburgh. That was a relief. So I kissed her, she kissed me and things began to move ahead rapidly. It was only when she released my tumescent cock from my underwear that I remembered.

"Shit. No condom."

"Don't worry," Katharine said, sliding her hand into her trouser pocket. "I came prepared." She smiled contentedly. "Or rather, I will do."

In fact, we both did.

When I came round, the noise of traffic in the streets below was greater than I expected in the early morning. I looked at my watch. It was after eight.

"Fuck," I groaned, sitting up and swinging my legs out of bed. Hel Hyslop would definitely be after me now.

Katharine rolled towards me. "What was that?" she asked sleepily, a smile forming on her lips.

"No," I replied. "No chance."

A hand glided over my thigh.

"I love a challenge," Katharine said, her voice hoarse and warm.

I could never resist that so I didn't bother trying. Whether it was because I hadn't woken up properly or because my mind had taken up residence in my dick, I completely forgot about protection this time. Until it was far too late.

"What's the matter?" Katharine asked when she saw the look on my face.

I rolled off her. "The small matter of rubberwear."

She nudged me. "Did you really think I'd forgotten?" she asked. "I'm due today. The chances are non-existent, especially at my age."

I looked round at her. "I hope you're right."

"Trust me," she said firmly. "The last thing I want is another Quintilian."

I wasn't sure how to take that.

"Coffee in pot," Davie said laconically as I stumbled into the living area.

In daylight the penthouse was even more amazing. Sunlight poured in through the high windows and the hills to the south glowed dull green. Not even the wealthiest tourists got accommodation like this in the Council's Edinburgh.

"Good morning to you too, commander." I took an ornate mug from the antique dresser and filled it. There was a bunch of bananas in a fruit bowl on the kitchen surface. I grabbed two. That was my breakfast sorted out – in the perfect city we get bananas about as often as we see guardians dancing cheek to cheek. "What's your problem?" I enquired. "Pissed off about sleeping alone?"

"You know what I think about your girlfriend," Davie replied. "The only thing she and I have got in common is a desire to keep you alive." He turned away.

"Very good of you to bother," I said, not feeling too comfortable with his mood.

Shortly afterwards Katharine appeared and we got down to a bit of strategic planning – such as it was.

"So we're staying in Glasgow till you catch the masked wanker, are we?" Davie demanded.

I nodded. "He's got two assistant masked wankers with him, don't forget." I scratched my chin. "I wonder where they were last night."

Davie swallowed a mouthful of banana. "I still don't understand why you won't leave the police to catch them. They're pretty obvious targets in that gear."

"They may be pretty obvious but they aren't the whole story – not as far as the Edinburgh connection goes. I want to get inside the institute and find out how the stolen GEC file attachment fits into the case. They call that place the Baby Factory. I want to know what Rennie's been doing there."

Davie ran his fingers through his beard. "Even if there's a connection with Edinburgh, that file's over twenty years old. Why are you so interested in it?"

I shook my head at him. "This isn't just a pre-Enlightenment affair, big man. The attachment was stolen now – in October 2026, remember?" I didn't intend telling them about the committee Lewis and Sophia were on until I'd made sure that the murders didn't tie up with it. If they did, I intended to find who in Edinburgh was involved.

"There's also the small matter of the kidnapped kids," Katharine put in.

"Exactly," I agreed. "We need to find a way of getting them back home. Hyslop and her people don't know where they come from."

Davie held his hands up in submission. "Okay, okay,

319

you've convinced me. The question is, what do we do next?"

I smiled at him. "Simple. I get inside the Rennie."

Davie was staring at me. "Did you see the security on that place? Razor wire, alarms, cameras . . ."

"Don't worry," I said. "We'll let the experts find a way in for me."

"The experts?" Katharine and Davie said in unison. They'd definitely been practising.

"The Major Crime Squad," I said. "If Hyslop and Haggs can't do it, nobody can. They're keen on nailing Rennie. Their problem is that they're police officers. In this city that means they're democratically accountable. They need a volunteer to do the dirty work." I gave them my best gung-ho grin. "I am that volunteer."

Now they were shaking their heads together. The double act was definitely coming along.

"It's too dangerous," Davie said. "What if the psycho's in there? He'll have got himself a replacement mallet by now."

"Don't worry about him," I said. "I know exactly how to sort him out."

"How?" Katharine demanded. "By standing up to him and letting him take a swing at you like last night?"

I looked at both of them. "I know what I'm doing," I said. There was no way I was going to tell them how I planned on doing it at this stage.

More synchronised head-shaking. Eventually they gave up – dizziness had probably kicked in.

"What are we supposed to do while you and your Weegie friends are setting up this break-in?" Davie asked.

"Tail me," I said. "I'll need all the back-up I can get."

Katharine nodded and produced a mobile from her jacket pocket. "Take this. It seems to work here, amazingly enough. Davie's got one too, so you can keep in touch."

I thought about it. "No, it's too risky. Mine was taken from me. If Hyslop finds another one on me, she'll be on the look-out for other Edinburgh residents."

"So?" Davie's face was set hard. "I'm not bothered about making her acquaintance. I'll take her and her sidekick on any time."

"Cool it, guardsman," I said. "Anyway, what's the big deal? You've got the tracking monitor. As long as I've got my steel toe-caps on, you know where I am. If nothing happens we'll meet back here at midnight, okay?"

They stared at me then nodded reluctantly.

"This is not a plan made in heaven, Quint," Davie said as I got up to go.

I put my arm round Katharine and kissed her on the lips. She pushed me away gently, her brow furrowed.

"Well, what kind of plan do you expect from an atheist?" I asked as I departed.

When I pushed the street-door open, I bumped into a couple of exhausted-looking guys in sweat-stained clothes. Ewan and Peter, no doubt. I hoped Katharine had remembered to change the sheets.

I decided to go straight to the City Chambers. Unfortunately the sentry at the main entrance knew exactly who I was and what to do. Handcuffs were applied before I could blink. I was hauled up to the fourth floor and shoved into the corner office.

Hel Hyslop looked up from her desk. "Quint. Where in God's name have you been?"

"Hell," I said, sitting down in the prisoner's chair. Haggs was leaning against the wall with a cigarette clamped between his lips. He was looking pretty demonic himself.

"Tell me where you've been this minute," she said, her voice low and threatening.

"Wouldn't you like to know?" I said.

Haggs jerked forward, the butt dropping from his lips and bouncing off his green jacket on its way to the floor. "You're fucking right we would," he said. "Wait till I put those shackles on you, scumbag."

"Leave it, Tam," Hyslop said with a shake of her head. "Just tell me where you were last night, Quint."

"I told you," I said. "I've been to hell." As Haggs took another step forward, I hit them with it. "I met Broadsword there."

That stopped the sergeant in his tracks.

Hel looked at me uncomprehendingly. "What happened?"

I told her, editing out the part played by Katharine and Davie.

"How the fuck did you really get away?" Tam demanded when I finished. "I can't see a puny shite like you fighting that monster off for long."

I shrugged. "I told you, I was lucky. A car stopped on the road and caught us in its lights. The bogeyman got stage fright."

I didn't know if they were going to buy that so I hit them with another fabrication. "The interesting thing was that Broadsword headed for the Rennie after he left me."

That got them going all right. They were very interested in linking Professor Rennie to the killings.

"So," I said, looking at them encouragingly, "now you'll be able to get a warrant for the Baby Factory, won't you?"

Suddenly Hyslop and Haggs had lost interest in me. Big Tam stood up straight and brushed the ash from his front.

"I don't think that would be a very good idea, do you, inspector?"

I turned round, recognising the understated voice immediately.

Andrew Duart was wearing a charcoal-grey suit which must have been been cut by a master tailor. The imperious way he was regarding us made it clear who the master was here.

Hyslop gave me a look that said "Keep quiet". Then she gave the first secretary an update of the investigation and a potted version of what had happened to me.

Duart gave me a cold smile. "How exciting, Quint. Though one wonders what you were doing out and about at night on your own." He turned his bloodless lips towards Hel. "Remove the handcuffs from our Edinburgh friend. Of course, this changes nothing. There is no evidence to justify a warrant. All we'd do by applying for one would be to alert the professor's lawyers." He put a limp hand on my shoulder. "Good work, though. You must keep at it. I am determined to cut this cancer out of Kelvingrove." He smiled again, proud of his metaphor. "Find a more – how shall I put it? – a more subtle way of gaining entry to the institute."

I moved to shake his hand off. "One that doesn't incriminate your executive, you mean," I said.

He didn't favour that with a reply or a smile; just turned on his heel and left.

I looked back at Hyslop and Haggs. They weren't at all happy.

"Don't worry," I said as Tam unlocked the cuffs. "I've got an idea about the Rennie."

Hel's face took on a suspicious expression. "What is it?"

"I'll tell you in detail," I said, my eyes focusing on her waist.

She glanced down. "What are you—"

"But it'll cost you one of those," I interrupted, pointing at her belt.

"One of those what?" the inspector asked dubiously.

"One pistol, holding bad guys at bay for the use of," I replied, dropping into Supply Directorate syntax.

Their eyes opened so wide that for a moment I thought a shrub brandishing a mallet had crept up behind me.

CHAPTER SEVENTEEN

We spent the rest of the morning planning the programme for the night. After a venison pie from the canteen at lunchtime, I ran through the murder victims' original files – the thought had struck me that maybe Hyslop had sent over edited highlights to my hotel room. Apparently not. I also wanted to see if we'd missed any link between the Baby Factory and the Macbeth cult. Again, nothing doing – the names of all the performers who'd been arrested were run through the computerised archive and no connections showed. Brilliant. There hadn't been any more sightings of Broadsword or his side-kicks either, despite every police officer in the city having their descriptions. My money was on them lurking in the depths of the Rennie.

I called the infirmary and asked to speak to Leadbelly. The nurse was away for a couple of minutes then came back to the phone.

"Em . . . he doesn't want to talk to you," she said.

I was taken by surprise. "You gave him my name?"

"Yes, Mister Dalrymple. Like I say, he doesn't want to speak to you. Or to anyone else, he gave me to understand."

"Strange. How's he getting on?"

"As well as can be expected. We're still waiting for the

results of the brain scan and there's some damage to his larynx but otherwise, okay so far."

"And there's a guard outside his room?"

"Oh yes." Her tone suggested she could have lived without a cop in her hair.

I thanked her and put the phone down. By his own admission, Leadbelly had no friends in Glasgow. So why was he refusing to talk to someone from his home town? He knew he could trust me. I was sure he was hiding something and I considered going round to squeeze it out of him. Then a wave of exhaustion broke over me. That changed my priorities.

"I need to get some sleep," I said to Hel. "In the next five minutes."

"Where were you all night?" she asked. "I checked with the hotel."

"Taking in the Glasgow nightlife," I replied. "I needed a drink or twelve after Broadsword made contact."

She looked at me doubtfully then got back to her paperwork.

"I can catch a cab to the St Vincent if you and your team are too busy," I offered.

"No chance, pal," Haggs said, pulling on his jacket. "I'm coming with you." He leered at me. "And I'm locking you in personally."

I shrugged. "As long as you're on the other side of the door, I don't care what you do, Tam."

As we headed downstairs it struck me that there had been no further communication from Andrew Duart. Just as well. If he found out what we'd set up for later on, he'd do serious damage to his limited-edition boxer shorts.

*   *   *

I waved a fond goodbye to Haggs in the corridor and heard the key turn in the lock. Before I headed for the bath, I looked down at the street. A dark blue Super Llama was parked near the corner. Just as I was about to accuse Katharine and Davie of major incompetence in carrying out surveillance from such an obvious location, the vehicle pulled out and disappeared. It probably wasn't them – there were more expensive cars in Glasgow than Edinburgh had bicycles.

Before I hit the sheets, I picked up my left boot again. The bug was still bothering me. I thought about it then called room service and asked for a steak. I was more interested in the knife that came with it but I ganneted the meal all the same. Then I used the knife to prise out the tiny device that had been buried deep in the heel. Something told me that keeping it loose in my pocket would increase my options.

Then I fell backwards and slept the sleep of the completely shagged out.

Hyslop and Haggs turned up at half-eleven that night.

"Everything ready?" I asked.

The inspector nodded. "They're all standing by."

I laced up my boots, hoping that the damage to one of the heels wasn't too obvious.

Haggs was standing at the door. "Come on then, dickhead. It's time."

"Aren't you forgetting something?" I turned to Hel and raised my eyebrows.

Her lips were a straight line. "No, I remembered." She put her hand in her pocket. "I hope you don't make me regret this, Quint."

I stared at the minuscule gun she held out to me. "What exactly is that?"

"It's a Vietnamese five-millimetre," Big Tam said, making no attempt to disguise the sneer in his voice. "They call it the Ladykiller in the nightclubs."

I glared at Hel. "You expect that to scare off Broadsword?" I took the weapon and weighed it up. Featherlight was heavy compared with this.

She smiled briefly. "There's nothing wrong with its stopping power. Just make sure you aim at a major organ."

"Great." I didn't tell Davie and Katharine about my plan to lay hands on a gun because for Edinburgh citizens, most auxiliaries included, firearms are the work of the devil. I needn't have worried. If they saw this specimen, they'd burst out laughing. As would the bogeyman and his pals.

"Sorry," Hel said as we headed out. "It's the best I can do. My job would be on the line if you were issued with a police weapon. I found the Ladykiller in the confiscations locker."

"You're not worried I might use it on you?"

She opened her jacket. "Feel this."

"Sometimes you say the nicest things, inspector." I touched her left breast. It was protected by a bulletproof vest.

"Expecting trouble?"

"Oh yes, Quint." Hyslop's expression was sombre. "Trouble's definitely on the menu tonight."

I felt the flimsy gun shift in my pocket. Next to it was the bug. I sincerely hoped Katharine and Davie were still picking up a signal.

The crowds were out in force in the city centre, but I wasn't paying attention to them. I'd begun to get very

apprehensive about what was about to go down. If I'd
been on my own in the Llama with Hyslop I might have
tried to instigate a rethink. The thought of how Haggs
would react to that put me off.

Hel spent most of the trip to Kelvingrove on her mobile
to the other units. Unfortunately they all seemed to be
very much on the ball – appropriate enough in a city that
was football-crazy.

"Okay," the sergeant said as he pulled up in a side-
street near the Rennie, "we're in position." He glanced at
me. "Ready to be heroic, are you?"

"Oh aye, Tam." I grinned at him provocatively. "How
about you?"

Hel terminated a call. "Shut up, you two," she said.
"This operation is complex enough without you behaving like five-year-olds."

I was trying to imagine how much experience she had
of small children when her mobile rang again.

She listened for a few seconds then checked her
watch. "Right," she said, "I'm switching to VHF." She
handed me her phone and picked up the radio mike. "All
units, all units, this is control officer, code 45. Initiating
Operation Aardvark."

Hel was following the movement of her second hand.
"Panzer to roll in X minus ten . . . X minus five, four,
three, two, one. Roll!"

All we needed now was some rock. The vehicle code-
named Panzer was about to provide that as well.

We were parked round a corner so we couldn't see the
petrol tanker as it crashed through the perimeter fence of
the Baby Factory. We heard it all right. The Llama's
windows were open and the roar of the truck's powerful

engine as it revved carried clearly through the still night air. Then came a noise like a sledgehammer going through a plywood panel, followed by the scream of brakes and the single, deadening smash of steel running into a brick wall.

"You're on, Quint," Hyslop said, nudging me and smiling with slightly more warmth than she usually managed. "Don't forget – use my mobile to call us in as soon as you find anything conclusive. Good luck."

I nodded and climbed out.

Haggs leaned across. "No shooting the suspects, okay, Embra shite?"

I gave him the finger and ran down the street at medium pace, wondering what the hell I was doing. The Major Crime Squad sets up a series of major crimes then sits back and lets me do the dirty work. Even Edinburgh guardians wouldn't come up with something that devious.

I looked cautiously round the corner and down the main road. The petrol tanker had done a massive amount of damage to the security fence and its nose was crushed against the Rennie's wall about twenty yards away from the main entrance. The driver had clambered out and was talking animatedly to a couple of the institute's staff. He'd be telling them that he had a full load of petrol and that his safety monitor was flashing "Danger" in capital red letters. In reality the tank had been fully vented and filled with water, but no one was likely to check that out in the near future. If everything went according to plan, the institute would be evacuated and I would have a free run for the next few hours.

I turned to the left. There was a double red flash from a

torch in an area of darkness where the fence curved away. I ran towards the light.

"Okay, everything's ready for you." A guy wearing black clothes and a balaclava shone a narrow beam on the ladder that had been set up against the fence. "We cut the power here the second the wire was taken out," he said. "The cameras are down and one of my team is waiting for you at the window over . . ." he flashed the light once through the fence, illuminating a crouching figure ". . . there. Go, go, go."

I went, went, went. Up the ladder, on to the ground and straight across the grass before I lost my bearing on the special forces operative.

"Here," came a loud whisper as I collided with the wall. It was a woman. "I've forced the window. The alarm didn't engage. You're okay." She pulled the window open.

"Wrong," I muttered. "You're okay. I'm on my own." I caught a glimpse of her eyes as she shone her torch on the window-frame. They looked sympathetic. I was sure that, unlike Hyslop and Haggs, she'd have come along if I'd asked for her help. I resisted the urge. This was definitely a job for me alone.

"Remember the set-up?" she said, handing me a torch. "We'll be waiting in the bushes beyond the fence if you run into trouble. Three flashes if all's clear, two if you've got unwelcome company."

I nodded, hoping that Davie and Katharine would steer clear of that area. If things went as planned I'd be walking nonchalantly out the front door, but it's as well to have a fallback option. I climbed through the window into the room. It was pitch dark so I risked a flash of light. No sign of anyone. I turned the torch on full beam. The place seemed to be a storage depot, the walls lined with shelves which were stacked with boxes and bottles. Hyslop had tried to find a general layout of the building but – surprise, surprise – the archive copy had disappeared, so I was going to have to follow my nose. At least I'd been provided with a smart swipe card that was supposed to open every door in the place. Now was the time to test that out.

I located the security panel and ran the card down it. The door clicked and swung open. I stuck my head out gingerly. A long corridor with plenty of doors leading off it, dim overhead lights glowing – an emergency generator must have kicked in – and no people tramping up and down. I took a deep breath and slipped out on to the cork-tiled floor. There was a chemical smell in the air, a cross between formaldehyde and something worse. That didn't make me feel any happier. In the distance I could hear a piercing, repeated alarm siren but down here it had been completely disabled. I hoped I wasn't about to run into any staff with impaired hearing.

Moving down the passageway, I checked the panels on each door. Most of them weren't interesting – Maintenance Office, Staff Toilet, Boiler Room, that kind of thing. What I was after was the Rennie's archive, but I'd take a look at anything to do with research or that might explain the Baby Factory nickname.

There was a muffled thud further down the corridor and I flattened myself against the wall, feeling in my pocket for the Ladykiller. The prospect of waving that at a potential assailant wasn't helping my heart-rate. I waited, the sweat trickling down my arms. Nothing. I couldn't see very far in the dull light, but it seemed that whoever made the noise had headed in the other direction.

I continued past the door. To the left was a notice saying "Doctors' Rest Room"; there was a window set into the wall by that door and I risked a flash of the torch. Chairs, a couple of beds with the covers thrown back, a table with an electric kettle. The usual chaos left by medics. But what were doctors doing in a research institute? Looking after babies?

I went on. The next door on the right stopped me in my tracks. Red and white striped tape ran all round the upper panel and the sign said "Secure Unit – Entry Only With Authorised Security Personnel In Attendance". That really got me going. Then I read the smaller writing underneath. "Danger – Unstable Subjects – In Case of Security Breach Apply Code A + + +", it proclaimed. Christ, what did that mean? There was only one way to find out.

I took the Ladykiller in my left hand and moved the smart card towards the electronic panel. Then I realised that the door was half an inch ajar. So much for Code alpha triple plus. I pushed gently and the door swung open further. Total darkness. I stepped in, tried to get control of my breathing and switched on my torch.

I didn't see anyone in the restricted beam but I heard a movement, a sudden scurrying like a frightened animal diving for cover. And a low moaning sound that made the hairs on my neck rise. Jesus, what was in the room with me? I moved the torch round and revealed chairs and tables. Then arrested the movement of my arm. There were straps hanging down from the chairs, shackles like those on the prisoner's chair in Hyslop's office. I remembered the security warning and looked back towards the line of light at the door. That was when I was taken out.

I landed on the floor with a thud and tried to disentangle myself from the heavy weight that had landed on me. The torch had flown off to my left and the beam was rolling to and fro. It disclosed a figure in white robes and a flash on the upper part of the body gave a bit more away – large, bald head and a slack, wet mouth. Then the light moved down again and I pushed hard. Forget it. I might as well have been buried beneath a ton of potatoes.

"Get off," I gasped. "I'm not armed." Lying is always a good option when you're up against it.

"Doctor? You one of the doctors?" came a voice that was a curious blend of gentle and threatening.

"No, I'm not one of the fucking doctors." It had occurred to me that this guy might have a major antipathy to the people treating him. "Let me up and I'll tell you who I am."

My attacker thought about it and, after what seemed like an eternity, relaxed his grip on my arms. He pulled away from me and I heard the breath scratching in his throat. Then the torchbeam rolled back over his face and I saw a sight that I'd been fervently hoping I wouldn't encounter again. Like the murder victims there was an eye in the middle of the forehead, but this time it was much worse. This time there was only one eye. And this time its owner was very much alive.

After a few seconds the overhead light came on.

"That's better." A heavily built figure was standing by the door. He didn't seem to be interested that it was open. "Now I can see you." His large round face broke into a smile that was almost benevolent. "And you can see me."

I got to my feet, rubbing my limbs, and tried not to stare at him. The white T-shirt he was wearing bore large red stencilled letters that said "Inmate". That didn't reassure me much. Strangely the soft face did, despite the malformation of its upper part.

"It's all right," he said. "You can look. I'm used to people looking."

It was hard not to. I realised he was young, probably in his early twenties, though the complete lack of hair made it difficult to be sure. The single eye was regarding me unwaveringly, the dark brown iris standing out against the pallid skin around it. I had the feeling that this individual hadn't seen the light of day for a very long time.

"Cyclops," he said with another smile, this one briefer. "That's what they call me."

"Oh aye?" I said, unsure whether he was making conversation or looking for a reaction.

He nodded. "The doctors and the scientists, I mean. My friends in here just call me Big Eye." He smiled again and I convinced myself that he wasn't harbouring violent intentions towards me. "I'm a rarity, you know," he said proudly. "Cyclopian malformation leading to a single median eye is very uncommon."

"Em, yes, you're right there," I said, glancing around the room. It was large and the far end was taken up by half a dozen beds. "Are you on your own in here?" I asked, looking back at the inmate. "What do you want me to call you?"

"You can call me Big Eye," he said. "You're a friend, aren't you?" He shook his head. "There used to be more but now there are only two others. Byron and Selkie. They took them away before you got here." He inclined an ear to the distant alarm. "Is there a fire?" The prospect seemed to excite him.

"No, we're all right." I was thinking about the names.

"Byron. Does he have a club-foot?" Big Eye nodded enthusiastically. "And Selkie – what about him? Or is it a female?"

He shook his head. "Male. There are no women in here, at least not any real ones. Don't you know the old folk tales? A selkie's a man on land and a seal in the water."

I looked at him blankly.

"Selkie's got a condition called phocomelia." Big Eye pronounced the word carefully. "He doesn't have much in the way of arms and legs. His hands and feet are attached to his body like flippers."

I felt my jaw drop. Then I remembered Leadbelly and his references to the "poor, tortured fuckers". He worked in the Rennie – he might have seen these guys.

"Don't worry," Big Eye said. "He doesn't mind. He doesn't know anything different."

I scratched my cheek as I tried to find an inoffensive way to extract information from him. I needn't have bothered.

"We're the results of genetic modification, you know." The young man wasn't embarrassed. If anything, he was pleased. "The scientists here tried all sorts of things with us." He gave me a conspiratorial wink. "I'm a true hermaphrodite, you know. I have an ovary as well as testicles."

I didn't know what to say to that. Fortunately, he didn't seem to be expecting congratulations.

"And they've made me indifferent to pain," he continued. "Look." Before I could stop him he'd closed the door on his little finger. The smile never left his face.

"Jesus," I said under my breath. So this was what went on in the Rennie. But what did the research have to do with the murders? I was bloody sure it was connected, that the third eye mutilation was some kind of link to this poor soul, but I needed harder evidence. I glanced at my watch. We were twenty-five minutes into Operation Aardvark. Time to get a move on.

"I've got to go, Big Eye," I said, moving towards the door and hoping that my smart card would open it.

"I'll come with you," he said cheerfully. "I can show you around."

I stared at him. "Aren't you locked up in here all the time?"

"Oh no," he replied. "They take us to the laboratories and the exercise rooms almost every day." He smiled at me. "I keep myself very fit. I can do two hundred press-ups without stopping. And hit the punchball for ten minutes." He gave a hoarse laugh. "That's why they didn't try to take me on when they came for the others. Here, we can look for them, can't we?"

I nodded slowly. "All right then." He was between me and the door and I didn't fancy taking him on either. I headed over there, offered up a prayer to the god I'd never believed in and ran the card down the panel. There was a click and Sesame opened. It seemed that security code A + + + didn't run to a more complex locking system.

"Where would you like to start?" Big Eye asked, sounding like an unusually user-friendly tourist guide.

"Is there an archive room?" I asked. There was no reaction from him. "You know, somewhere the records are kept? The files?"

He shrugged then stared at his feet. They were bare and the nails were long and horny. "Don't know." His face had darkened. It looked like I'd caught him out. I didn't like the way he'd gone from happy to resentful in two seconds. Change of subject required.

"Never mind. How about the labs? Where are they?"

His expression lightened. "There are a lot of those. I'll take you to the ones I know best." He headed off down the corridor at a quick pace.

I followed more cautiously, looking round corners and through glass panels. There was no sign of anyone. We passed a door marked "Record Room – Security Code A +". I'd revisit that later.

Finally, at the end of a corridor, we came to a heavy door. This time there was no identifying panel and, instead of a card swipe, a digital pad protruded from the wall.

"Oh shit," I said.

"Don't worry," Big Eye said. "I know all the doctors' code numbers. He tapped out four digits.

We were in.

The door slammed behind us and I breathed in the antiseptic air of a seriously high-tech lab. The lights were blazing – presumably this area had its own emergency generator. Instruments and machines stretched away like an Edinburgh computer warehouse in pre-Enlightenment times, before the mob took exception to the rip-off prices and firebombed them. No evidence of fire damage here, nor of lab staff. In the middle of the area was a glass-enclosed section with a high bed in it. With a clench in my gut I saw that there was someone lying on it. Then a figure in a white coat rose from behind a control panel to the right.

"Who's . . ." I left the question incomplete because Big Eye was already on his way over to the man. I followed slowly, my hand on the weapon in my pocket.

"Professor!" Big Eye called. "Here I am."

The scientist was looking at me intently. I recognised

the gaunt features of David Rennie, the ward representative I'd met at the banquet who was founder of the
institute and also Macbeth's brother. Although alarm
had registered on them initially, it rapidly faded. He
didn't look pleased to see his inmate but he offered me a
welcoming smile. That put me off my stride.

"Cyclops," the professor said sharply, "what are you
doing here? Where's your escort?"

Big Eye grinned. "Gone. They left me all on my own
when the alarm bells started."

For a couple of seconds Rennie's expression suggested
that the security personnel were for the high jump over
the Erskine Bridge, but he quickly got a grip. "I'm rather
busy at the moment, Cyclops. Why don't you go back to
your quarters?"

"Too busy to see me?" Big Eye said haltingly. "But I'm
your favourite subject, that's what you always say." His
expression was black again, but his voice was as quer-
ulous as a child's.

The professor eyed him with a hint of anxiety then
pointed to a chair. "Why don't you sit down for a minute?
I have to speak to your new friend."

Big Eye glanced at me and smiled. "Fine." Then he
looked lost. "But I don't know his name."

Rennie laughed. "Didn't he tell you? He's not much of a
friend then. This is Quintilian. You'd better call him
Quint. That's a lot easier, isn't it?"

"Quint," the young man repeated, smiling at me.
"Quint."

I nodded, trying to make out the condition of the figure
beyond the professor. The body was sheathed in a white
robe and the head turned away. The long dark hair and
the slender form suggested it was a girl.

"Yes," the professor said. "Quintilian Dalrymple." He gave me another long look. "I've been expecting a visit from you. I imagine the farce at the front entrance is your doing. Yours and that idiot Duart's, along with the idiots in the Major Crime Squad." He played with some buttons on his console. "What exactly do you hope to find?"

"The evidence that will nail you and close this place down," I said, glancing at Big Eye. He was looking at me in horror. The poor guy obviously regarded the institute as home.

"Don't be ridiculous," David Rennie scoffed. "This facility provides the ward and the city as a whole with an enormous amount of income, primarily from our American friends."

"What exactly is it that you provide for them?" I demanded. "Cloned children?"

Rennie's eyes flicked uneasily over to the inmate. Then he nodded. "Among other things. Since the religious right over there prevailed in the abortion wars there's been a huge market for the genetic engineering services that they banned. We're world leaders in the field."

I wanted to ask him where Big Eye and his wretched friends fitted into the grand scheme, but I had other priorities.

"You needed a file attachment from the old Parliament archive in Edinburgh, didn't you?"

The scientist's eyes were still locked on mine. "I wondered if you knew about the break-in. You're not in Glasgow just to do Duart's bidding, are you? How did you manage to link the file attachment to me?"

I wasn't planning on telling him about Leadbelly or the Edinburgh murders, at least not yet. "And you arranged the kidnap of three hyper-intelligent teenagers from

Edinburgh via your brother's good offices, didn't you?"
After a few moments he nodded. "Why? Had you run out
of specimens?"

Now he was grinning triumphantly. "You're out of
your depth, Dalrymple. You're flailing around like a
drowning man."

Then it hit me. "Jesus, those kids were genetically
engineered too, weren't they?" I scarcely heard his affirmative reply. None of the kidnap victims was older
than seventeen. That meant they'd been produced after
the ban on genetic engineering in Edinburgh. Someone
had been carrying out illegal research under the guardians' noses for years.

"Those adolescents are particularly fine examples,"
Rennie said. "I needed to carry out tests on them to
further my work."

"Who was responsible for producing them in Edinburgh?" I asked breathlessly.

He laughed. "You don't expect me to tell you that, do
you?"

"You're fucking right I do!" I shouted. The figure on
the bed in the observation chamber moved slightly.
"You'll be in the cells before the night is out," I said,
lowering my voice. "You'd be well advised to co-operate
with me."

The professor found that very amusing. "Co-operate
with you?" he repeated. "It's you who'll be begging to co-
operate with me, my friend." He turned back to his
monitors and made a note in a file. "As I said, I've been
expecting a visit from you."

"I suppose Broadsword told you about our meeting
outside here the other night."

He looked up – for a moment I thought he was

surprised – then he went back to concentrating on his console.

"Dougal Strachan was here, wasn't he?" I said. "Why did you have to kill him?"

Rennie stared at me. "I had nothing to do with Dougal Strachan's death. I never even met him."

"Bullshit."

The professor shrugged. "Please yourself. But think about it, Dalrymple. Would I be stupid enough to arrange a murder within walking distance of the institute? And why would I want to dispose of a subject I hadn't even had the chance to use?"

"Maybe some of your minions are out of control."

The professor thought about that. "What are you suggesting? That I employ the person responsible for the mutilations and murders?"

"You or your brother." I stepped nearer him.

"Stay where you are," he ordered.

"All that bollocks about the Macbeth cult and Scottish reunification is just a cover to provide you with subjects for experiment, isn't it?" I looked at Big Eye. "What do you think about being a victim, my friend?" I had the feeling that I needed all the allies I could get. Rennie's confidence was making me wonder where Broadsword and his side-kicks were.

"A victim?" the inmate said, his forehead above the single eye heavily lined. "What do you mean, Quint?"

"A victim to be used as the subject of experiments," I said. "That's what happens to you, isn't it, Big Eye? He keeps you locked up here when you could be living an ordinary life in the outside world."

Rennie laughed harshly. "How many people can you see behaving normally when he's in the room, Dalrym-

ple? He's a freak. We produced him to test the limits of
our procedures." He glanced at the young man. "And to
give us material for future experiments."

"The name Frankenstein springs to mind," I said. "You
can't treat people like that, even if you do produce them,
as you so delicately put it."

The scientist turned his back on me again. "You're in
no position to stop me." He leaned forward and spoke
into a microphone. "Derek? Come to the main lab now."

I had my hand round the Ladykiller but I kept it
concealed for the time being. I wanted to see what
happened next.

"You are impotent, Dalrymple," Rennie said, standing
up and pointing at the bed in the chamber. "Totally
powerless. Take a look."

I stepped forward, registering the arrival of Macbeth
at the far end of the lab. He was in normal clothes for a
change, the tweed jacket making him look worryingly
like an Edinburgh guardian.

"I mean take a look in the observation unit," the
professor said, turning a switch under the mike. "Wake
up, Aurora," he said in a soft voice. "Wake up. There's
someone who wants to see you."

I stared at the scientist then looked to the front.

The occupant of the bed stirred and sat up, rubbing her eyes. She turned towards us and lowered
her hands. Her eyes met mine and I felt the floor
beneath my feet move violently. Earthquake, disloca-
tion, the sensation that my heart was being torn
apart. For a few seconds I even thought I heard
Sonny Boy Williamson singing "She Brought Life
Back to the Dead."

The girl was about eight or nine. The face that the

black hair shrouded was a beautiful one, the lips slightly parted and the eyes brilliant dark pools. It was also a face that had been imprinted permanently on my mind. It was the face of my long-dead lover Caro.

CHAPTER EIGHTEEN

I was staring at the little girl, staring at her like the world, time, the order of things had all lost their meaning. Which they had. I was back on the hillside at Soutra, my eyes on Caro as she prepared for the last operation against the Howlin' Wolf gang. The girl's face, it was Caro's face – younger and softer, but indisputably the features I'd loved and never been able to forget. And it was a living face, not the reddened, contorted horror that I found on the floor in the barn as the rope choked the last breath from Caro's lungs.

Then the child looked at the four men ranged around the observation chamber. Her eyes screwed up in panic and she began to sob desperately. Macbeth was holding a heavy-duty automatic pistol in his right hand. Both he and his brother had empty expressions on their thin faces. I heard a low moan from Big Eye. No doubt he'd been in that chamber often enough himself. I got the impression that he was sympathetic to Aurora's plight. Aurora. For a moment I thought about the beautiful name which meant "dawn" in the original Latin. Who had given her that name? Then I wondered how many of us would see the dawn that was approaching. The Ladykiller was still in my pocket, but I couldn't risk a firefight with Macbeth – he was on the other side of the chamber and Aurora was between us. I took my hand off the weapon and my finger encountered the other small object in there.

"Well, Dalrymple," Rennie said in gloating tones, "what do you think of my latest subject?"

"What have you done, you sick bastard?" I said. I looked past him to the little girl in her awful distress and my heart cracked again. Another moan from Big Eye suggested he was being affected in the same way.

"What I've done," the scientist replied, "is take steps to ensure that you constitute no danger to us." He beckoned to Macbeth. "Come round here, Derek. Dalrymple appears to be seeing sense, but there's no point in taking any chances."

I stepped forward. "Can I . . . can't we do something to put her at ease?" I could hear Aurora's loud sobs through the console speaker.

Rennie laughed. "Are you good with children, Dalrymple?"

I felt Big Eye move up to my side. The sight of him made the girl squeal in terror.

Macbeth arrived with his weapon and pushed the inmate back. "You're frightening her, Cyclops," he said, a tight smile appearing beneath his regal beard. "Get back to your den."

"Lay off him," I said. "You're the one who's scaring her." Aurora's eyes were locked on to his gleaming weapon. I turned to the professor. "For God's sake, what have you done?"

He ignored me and leaned towards the microphone. "Take off your robe and get dressed," he said. "Your clothes are under the bed."

Aurora jumped when his voice came over the speaker

346

in the chamber. She was still crying as she bent down and retrieved her clothes.

"Hurry up, girl!" Rennie added.

She looked out at us blindly and I was crushed by impotence and guilt. But Macbeth had stepped up to me and levelled his gun at my midriff. I stood a better chance of helping Aurora when she was out of the glass-enclosed space. She turned her back to us and slipped out of the robe. I turned away but Rennie and Macbeth watched as she pulled on her clothes. I could hear Big Eye's uneven breathing somewhere to the rear. I looked round and saw tears running down his nose.

"Good," the professor said into the mike. "Now sit down and wait. And stop that whimpering."

"Leave her alone, you fucking bully." I doubled up and dropped to my knees as Macbeth rammed the butt of his gun into my belly. I heard Aurora wail again. Her breath was coming in traumatised gasps.

David Rennie looked amused. "Well done, Derek," he said. "You owed him that. He thinks the cult is just a scam to provide me with human subjects."

Macbeth pulled me up. "Is that right, Dalrymple?" He belted me again but didn't allow me to fall. "That's a big mistake. I'm deadly serious about reuniting Scotland. There are far too many feeble-minded scum like you in the city-states. I have a vision for the nation we once were."

"Believe him, Dalrymple," his brother said. "He's even set up a cult cell in Edinburgh."

I felt Macbeth's grip loosen.

"Quiet, David," he hissed. "He doesn't need to know that."

The professor laughed, the callous sound making me

shiver. "He's not going to bother us any more." He came up to me and took my chin in his long fingers. They were surprisingly strong. He forced my head up till it was level with his. "So I'm going to satisfy his curiosity about the girl." He looked to one side of me. "What are you doing, Cyclops? Sit down on that stool and behave yourself." He used the same tone with the hapless inmate as he had with Aurora.

"How did you do it?" I asked. "How did you bring Caro back to life?"

"Caro? Is that what you called her? Caroline was the name I had from the file. Along with that ridiculous barracks number that your rulers impose on their auxiliaries."

Bell 24. Caro's barracks number was one thing about her that I'd forgotten over the years. Now it came back to me as unexpectedly as the scent of a long-forgotten flower.

"Your name was in that file too," Rennie was saying. "You were down as her closest colleague. Quintilian Dalrymple. I was hardly going to forget that outlandish appellation, was I?"

I peered at him. "Wait a minute. Names and barracks numbers are classified archive material. How did you have access to that?"

He laughed but didn't reply. The conclusion wasn't hard to draw. Although Glasgow had been seen as a pariah state in Edinburgh since the early years of the Enlightenment because of its attachment to democracy, some lowlife or lowlives must have been dealing with it. And since Caro had been dead for eleven years, those dealings were longstanding, as the genetically modified teenagers also proved – only high-ranking auxiliaries would have been able to access classified archive material.

The little girl was still weeping but silently now. I smiled at her. That only seemed to make her more apprehensive.

"My contacts in Edinburgh provided me with certain material," Rennie said. "I won't bore you with the microbiology. Among other things, I needed a steady supply of human eggs. But only from the best specimens available. Your woman was certainly one of those."

My mind was spinning. "But how . . . how were the eggs obtained?"

Following standard gynaecological examinations. Usually the donors were told that they needed a scrape or suchlike." Rennie bent to the microphone. "Be quiet, girl! I won't tell you again."

Aurora swallowed her cries and sat with her head bowed.

"Bastard," I said, straining in Macbeth's grip. That got me another blow in the gut. I heard Big Eye moan in sympathy on his stool.

"An interesting term," the scientist said, wiping sweat from his high forehead. "Is this child technically a bastard, do you think?"

"Who cares?" I said. "She's alive, she's healthy, what does it matter?"

Rennie laughed. "You surprise me, Quintilian. I would have thought the lineage of this specimen would be of particular significance to you." He shook his head. "No? Well, I suppose it's true that she has nothing to do with you genetically. The egg was fertilised by an American sperm donor and implanted in the uterus of a Glaswegian woman, so why should you care?"

"How does she bear such a close resemblance to Caro then?"

The professor looked gratified by the question. "As a result of pioneering work carried out in this very laboratory. As well as enhancing the potential for advanced intelligence, we have developed techniques that guarantee an almost perfect clone of the genetic parents – either mother or father." He smiled. "You can imagine how valuable those products have proved to be in the global marketplace."

"So you made a fortune and ploughed some of it into your brother's insane cult."

This time Macbeth didn't bother to hit me with the gun. Instead he shoved me to the floor and aimed a kick at my groin. Fortunately I managed to get my thigh in the way. It still hurt like hell.

"Apparently Derek doesn't want to talk about that," the scientist said. "Anyway, we were discussing Aurora, weren't we? Lovely name, don't you think?" He glanced round at the girl, who was staring at me with her mouth open. Obviously the poor soul had never seen a street fight.

"It is lovely," I said, getting my breathing under control. "Who gave it to her?"

"Her adoptive parents." Rennie picked up a folder. "Jack and Sheila Garvald. If you're interested, he's a graphic designer and she's a nurse. They've got two natural children, a boy aged twelve and a girl aged eleven. They called them Josh and Ailsa."

I saw Aurora's eyes spring open when she heard her siblings' names. Then her expression became even more distraught. She must have been missing her family terribly – and trying to understand why they'd handed her over to the professor.

"How did you get her here?" I demanded, standing up shakily. "Your usual technique of kidnapping?"

David Rennie shook his head. "Certainly not. The Garvalds were told that Aurora had a problem with her liver which needed special tests. I wanted her as insurance, of course. After I saw you with Duart and remembered your name from Caroline's . . ." he broke off and smiled at me malevolently ". . . sorry, Caro's file, I expected a visit. I was sure the girl's resemblance to your dead lover would stop you in your tracks." He drew his hand across his cheek. "Now that I've got her in the institute, perhaps I'll make use of her in my current research programme." He stared at Aurora like a slaughterman sizing up a calf.

There was a groan from the stool to my left.

"That's enough, Cyclops," David Rennie said. "If you don't keep quiet I'll be forced to use the clamps." He glanced pointedly at a box near the console which sprouted wires. I suddenly thought of Tam Haggs and his electric interrogation equipment.

Big Eye let out another long, disconsolate noise.

"Right, that's it," the scientist said, picking up the box.

Big Eye was panting hard. I thought he'd given in, but I was wrong. With an ungainly leap off the stool, he took Rennie down to the floor with a crash. That sent the electrical instrument flying. It also made Macbeth crouch like a wounded lion.

"Take the girl," the professor gasped at his brother. "You know what to—" Then his voice broke off. There was a flailing of limbs as Big Eye laid into him.

Macbeth had already opened the chamber's glass door and grabbed for Aurora. She shrieked as he approached, then carried out a sidestep that an international rugby player would have been proud of. Before he could lay a hand near her, she was out of the door.

"Close it!" I shouted, realising it only opened from the outside.

She stopped dead and stared at me, then felt Macbeth to her rear. She ran straight to me and nestled in my arms. The thrashing on the floor to my left had stopped. Big Eye was lying over his prey, as motionless as a grave slab.

"Give her to me," Macbeth said from outside the chamber, the heavy automatic pointing straight at Aurora's chest. I was pretty sure the bullets fired by that weapon would go through both of us at that range. Checkmate. I squeezed her arms lightly then slid my right hand down to the pocket of her jeans.

"You have to go with him," I said, making sure my voice was loud enough for the putative king of Scotland to hear. "Don't worry, you'll be okay." Then I pushed her forward gently and bent my head. "I'll be right behind you, darling," I whispered.

She looked round and gave me a smile that broke what was left of my heart. Then she walked slowly forward to Macbeth and let him circle his arm round her chest without a murmur.

He pulled her towards the exit, the gun against her head. As they passed Big Eye and the inert form beneath him, Macbeth bit his lip. The pistol shook in his hand.

Shit, no, I thought, stepping forward. Not Big Eye.

Macbeth caught my movement and that seemed to put him off. He strode away to the door, Aurora caught in his grip, her feet kicking the air feebly.

"If I so much as catch a glimpse of you coming after us, she dies, Dalrymple," the king shouted over his shoulder.

I knew he was serious. I felt as bad as I did when I was cradling Caro's body in the barn on Soutra. Caro. Aurora. I'd failed them both when they needed me most. I sank to my knees and buried my head in my arms.

But not for long.

As soon as I heard the door slam, I scrabbled in my pocket for the mobile I'd been given. "Hel?" I shouted. "Advise all your units to look out for Macbeth. Don't tackle him though, do you understand? He's got a hostage. A child. Call me when he's in sight. Out."

I cut the connection and called Davie's number. After what seemed like an eternity – presumably while the system tried to makes sense of the Edinburgh number – he answered.

"It's me," I said. "Where are you?"

"Got a phone now, have you? We're in a side-street off the Dumbarton Road – about three hundred yards from the Rennie. I have you on the monitor."

"No, you haven't. I've tranferred the bug to someone else."

"You've what?"

"There isn't time to explain. Track the bug at a safe distance. D'you hear? A safe distance. The bug's on a hostage that Macbeth's taken. He'll kill her if he thinks he's being followed."

"Her?" Davie asked.

"The hostage is a little girl." I wanted to tell him who Aurora was but explaining would take too long. "I'll keep in touch with you. Don't call me unless you want the Major Crime Squad up your arse."

"Got you. Out."

I got moving. "Come on, Big Eye," I said as I went towards him. "Are you all right?"

He rolled off the scientist. "I . . . I think I killed him," he said in an unsteady voice. "I didn't mean to."

"Never mind about him," I said, glancing at the sprawled body. The head was at an unnatural angle to the torso. "I've got to follow Macbeth."

"And the wee girl," Big Eye said, suddenly right behind me. "We've got to help her."

I nodded. "Aye. Do your trick with the door, will you?" I could only hope that Macbeth was far enough away by now.

The inmate punched out numbers on the pad. I noticed that one of his thumb nails had been torn away. Otherwise he seemed unscathed. I wasn't sure how much use he'd be on surveillance though.

"Listen," I said, "why don't you go and look for your friends?"

"Byron and Selkie?" Big Eye stopped in the corridor outside the lab and thought about it. "Where can they be?" He slapped his thigh and gave a wide grin. "I know. The basement. The guards take us down there when there are visitors to the institute, visitors the professor doesn't want us to see." He looked at me seriously. "I didn't mean to kill him," he said. "I don't care what he said about me, but he shouldn't have been nasty to the girl. She was so frightened."

I took his arm. "Don't worry," I said. "He deserved everything he got." I knew that Duart and Hel Hyslop wouldn't take the demise of their target so well, but I didn't have it in me to criticise the poor soul.

"I'll see you later then, Quint," he said, smiling at me like a kid on an outing.

"Yup. Be careful, Big Eye." I wasn't too happy about letting him loose on his own – Christ knows what the security guys were armed with – but I didn't have time to go with him. I needed to guess about the exit Macbeth would have headed for. I hadn't heard from Hyslop so the chances were that Macbeth was still in the building. The rear of the facility seemed more likely than the front where all the noise was coming from, so I followed the corridor I'd been up earlier. The lights were still low.

I was about twenty yards from the Record Room when the door slammed open and a large form blundered out. I flattened myself against the wall, thinking it was Macbeth carrying Aurora. Then I looked again as the figure turned away from me. It wasn't the cult leader, it was one of his followers. Broadsword was in his usual garb and he wasn't carrying human cargo – what he had in his hands was a large pile of files. I set off after him carefully, certain that he would be hot on the heels of his lord and master.

Then my luck ran out. Just as the bogeyman reached the end of the passage, the lights were suddenly restored to full power. He looked round and I was caught in the act tiptoeing after him. Jesus Christ. I clutched for the Ladykiller.

Broadsword glanced down the corridor to his right – that must have been the way that Macbeth went – then turned his head back in my direction. The mask with its scars and straggly beard was as horrifying as ever, but the eyes were staring less intently than before. I sensed indecision, which is always an encouraging trait in assailants. Maybe Davie's knife had got to him mentally as well as physically. The only way I was going to be able to get after Aurora was by dealing with this arsehole so I moved closer.

Bad move. Since I last saw him Broadsword had evidently renamed himself Broadgun – he'd pulled a wicked-looking pistol from his belt.

"Dalrymple," he croaked, dropping the files. "We meet again." He extended his arm and aimed the weapon at my chest. "For the last time."

Shots rang out in quick succession, the noise nearly rupturing my ears in the close confines of the passage. I dived to the floor and whipped out the Ladykiller, the safety catch already off. The trigger guard was small and I'd been struggling to fit the stump of my right forefinger into it, but I managed to get off all six shots at Broadsword's bulky form. At least three of them entered his upper abdomen and one hit his right hand. His weapon flew backwards. He stopped in his tracks and peered down at me with what looked like surprise. Either he hadn't expected me to be armed or he was amazed that I'd turned out to be a better shot than he was.

I waited for him to fall. That never happened. He expelled a long gush of air, shook his head a couple of times then turned his back on me and disappeared round the corner. So much for the Ladykiller's stopping power. I clambered to my feet and stumbled after him. By the time I got to the corner there was no sign of him.

At least he'd left his gun behind. And his files. I took possession of all that gear.

"We lost them," Hel said, shaking her head.

"What?" I stared at her incredulously. "Broadsword as well as Macbeth and the hostage?"

She forced herself to meet my eyes and shrugged. "We had to keep our distance . . ."

We were standing in the institute's main entrance, the oil tanker's shattered front end poking through the wall.

"But you had special forces people all over the place."

"And our own people," she said, glancing at Haggs. For once he was looking seriously uncomfortable. "Somehow they slipped through them in the dark. Maybe they had a secret exit and a vehicle in the vicinity."

"So the king and his bodyguard are on the loose in Glasgow with a terrified little girl to bargain with, even if . . ." I broke off and glared at her ". . . and it's a big if — if the Glasgow police manage to locate them."

Haggs stepped aside as a large figure in white barged into him.

"I found them, Quint." Big Eye was looking pleased with himself. "They're okay." He pointed behind him. I made out a guy with a heavy shoe on his left foot and giveaway Byronic hair. Next to him was a crumpled figure in a specially constructed chair. The seal man waved a hand that was only a few inches from his shoulder.

"Well done, my friend," I said. "These officers will make sure you're looked after." I looked at Hyslop and Haggs. They both nodded, less appalled by the state of the inmates than I'd expected. Big Tam was even regarding the one-eyed young man with something that almost looked like compassion.

"What are you planning to do now, Hel?" I asked after Big Eye had moved off.

She was chewing her lip. "Give Duart the bad news, I suppose."

"About Rennie's unfortunate demise?"

She nodded. "The institute's lawyers will have a field day. So will the newspapers. Illegal entry to private property, illegal damage, illegal use of the truck . . ."

"Fuck Duart," I said. "Fuck the lawyers and the newspapers. We've got to find Macbeth before anything happens to Aurora."

Now Hyslop and Haggs were the ones registering surprise.

"Aurora?" Hel said. "Unusual name." She narrowed her eyes at me. "You seem very concerned about the girl, Quint."

"Why shouldn't I be?" I yelled. "She's an innocent victim, she doesn't deserve any of this, she—"

"All right," Hyslop said, taking my arm in a firm grip and leading me away. "What do you want from me?"

I glanced back at Haggs. He had his eyes locked on the files I was still carrying.

I thought for a few moments. "This is what I need. A Llama and the authority to use any means to find the bastards." I wasn't planning on telling her about the means I had in mind – Davie, Katharine and the bug monitor.

Hel was shaking her head, her expression hard. "No chance, Quint. I can't give you carte blanche. You're not even a Glasgow citizen."

"I can catch them," I said desperately. "I can catch them and set Aurora free."

"You're not being straight with me, are you?" she said, her eyes opening wide. "You've got some kind of lead."

I slapped my free hand against my forehead. "Oh for fuck's sake." I moved closer to her. "You're right, Hel. I've got a lead. But I'm not going to let you in on it. Your people didn't even manage to spot them when they escaped."

Hyslop was looking at me intensely. "All right," she said, "here's the deal. I'll give you whatever you want, but you have to share it with me and Tam. Only us, okay? We have to come with you."

I glanced back at Haggs. He was giving a junior policeman several pieces of his mind. I shook my head. "No. I don't trust Tam. He'll want to take the targets on." Then I thought of Aurora and her beautiful face – Caro's face. I'd never be able to look at my own wasted features in the mirror again if I didn't find her. "Okay, here's what we'll do. You and you alone can come with me. I'll tell you what I know and we'll finish this together. Is it a deal?"

She wasn't overjoyed but eventually she nodded. "All right, it's a deal." She turned to Haggs and told him to supervise the search of the Baby Factory. Now they were in and Rennie was dead, Duart was going to want as much back-up evidence as he could get.

"Where are you going, inspector?" Tam asked.

"She's coming with me," I said. "To find out how the experts do it." The bravado in my voice did nothing to mask the feeling of dread that had settled over me like an autumn mist.

Hel turned the Llama out of the Rennie's car park. "Who are you calling?" she asked suspiciously.

I raised my hand to shut her up. "Katharine, it's me. Where are they?" I felt Hyslop's breath on my cheek as she looked at me.

"On the M8 heading north round the city centre."

"What kind of vehicle is it?" I asked.

"Flashy off-road vehicle," she replied. "Bit like the one we're in. Red."

"Okay, keep your distance. How many people are there inside?"

"Not sure. Driver and small child definitely. There may be another person in the back."

"Okay." I glanced at Hel. "You can call me any time now. I'm about to come clean to the inspector." I gave her the mobile number.

"Come clean?" Katharine asked. "What does that mean, exactly?"

"Out." I turned to my chauffeur. "Did you catch that? Head for the—"

"I heard," she said, accelerating away. "Who's Katharine?"

I told her. And about Davie. And about the bug. But I didn't tell her about Aurora's background, or about the kids from Edinburgh. I didn't trust her that much.

The mobile rang. "Quint, it's Katharine. The target's taken the M80. Are you after us?"

I confirmed that we were and signed off, then made sure that Hel had heard the route. To our right the lights of central Glasgow blazed out brighter than the tourist zone in Edinburgh ever does. The place was wealthy, but how would it be affected by the loss of the Baby Factory's profits? I wondered if Andrew Duart and his supposedly independent judiciary would bury the institute. Maybe they'd just replace the management and redirect the funds to the executive's coffers. I didn't much care. All I was interested in was getting Aurora away from the lunatic who'd taken her.

The vehicle's phone rang. I heard the first secretary's smooth tones after I spoke.

"Quint?" he said in surprise. "Where's the inspector?"

"She's driving, Andrew. Shall I put her on?"

"Just a minute. You have some questions to answer, my friend."

"I know. I'm giving Hyslop the full story."

"I'm not sure if she's fit to handle the investigation after the débâcle at the Rennie. What happened to the professor?"

"Look, I don't have time for this. We're in pursuit of the guys behind the murders and they have a hostage."

"Ah. Very well." Duart's tone was business-like now. "What can I do to help?"

"Nothing at the moment. I'll let you know if we need your services. Out." I replaced the phone and realised that Hel was shaking her head.

"What's the matter?"

"You can't talk to Duart like that." She took the slip road and joined the M80, flashing her roof-lights to clear the traffic out of her way. "He'll have my warrant card." She gave a humourless laugh. "Who cares? My career's down the Clyde anyway after tonight."

"Not if we catch Macbeth and Broadsword."

"Maybe." She gave me an inquisitive look. "You still haven't told me everything, have you?"

I looked ahead at the northbound traffic. "Where do you think Macbeth's heading?"

"Answer the fucking question, Quint!" she shouted, swerving round a refuse lorry and making me slam into the door.

I glared at her. "No, I haven't. I will do though – if you concentrate on nailing the dickheads."

She pursed her lips and pressed the accelerator harder. "Where do I think Macbeth's going? You tell me. The last time I came down this road was with you when we came back from your home town."

"You don't think he's heading there, do you? Why would he?"

"How would I know?" she demanded. "You're the one with all the fucking answers."

The phone rang before I could respond to that.

"Inspector Hyslop?" It was a female voice I'd heard before but couldn't place.

"She's busy. Who's this?"

"Nurse Lennox. And you are?"

"Dalrymple. You're the one looking after Leadbelly, aren't you?" I felt a stab of anxiety. "What's up?"

"Em, your friend . . . Leadbelly." She pronounced the name as if it were infectious. "I'm afraid he's dead. He killed himself."

"What? What happened?"

"He wrapped an electric lead round his neck and threw himself off his bed. I think his heart had already been weakened."

I immediately suspected the worst. "Did he have any visitors? Where was the guard?"

"No visitors," the nurse said calmly. "No one went into the room, including the guard. You can take my word for it. I was at my desk down the corridor all evening. I was the one who found him."

Before I rang off I ranted at her, my suspicions about the earlier suicide attempt still alive. Then I remembered Leadbelly's eyes and his air of desperation. Maybe this was one conspiracy theory too far. Maybe the poor bastard really did believe that he'd killed the pregnant woman in a drunken, drug-fuelled haze. Not only that. He obviously knew something about what was going on in the Rennie. I reckoned he knew Big Eye and his friends. It looked like the "poor tortured fuckers" had got to him and made the former hardman feel guilty about what he was involved in for the first time in his life.

I turned to look at Hel Hyslop. Maybe the idea that she and Haggs had framed Leadbelly was also a fantasy, nothing more than a nightmare from the darkest recesses of my imagination. Leadbelly hadn't been able to take it any more and his second suicide attempt had been successful. But the real killer or killers, the ones who'd set him up, were in the vehicle further down the road – and Caro's daughter was with them.

I gave Leadbelly a quick, muted verse from "Must I Be Carried to the Sky" and let the old reprobate slip away.

CHAPTER NINETEEN

"You've gone very quiet," Hel said.

I was looking out over the slopes of the fields to my left, the darkness dotted here and there with the lights from isolated settlements. The city was well behind us now – we were back in wolf country.

"Quint?" she said, her voice rising. "What is it?"

I still couldn't talk to Hel about Aurora. The shock of seeing her face in the lab had been replaced by a numbness that made the idea of explaining who the little girl was impossible to entertain. I was very far from coming to terms with what Rennie had done.

"Can I use that bag in the back?" I asked, deflecting her question.

She glanced round. "If you like," she replied. "The bulletproof jackets Tam and I drew were in it." She shifted in her seat. "Christ, I've still got mine on."

"Don't worry," I said. "I emptied the Ladykiller into Broadsword so you're safe from me." I leaned over and took the nylon hold-all. I stuffed the files the bogeyman had dropped into it, along with his gun. I wasn't sure how many rounds were left in it and I didn't want to get Hyslop on her high horse by telling her about it, so it became another secret. The bastard things scare me shitless, but I was beginning to see that they had their uses.

"What are those files?" Hel asked.

"Don't know yet. They're from the Rennie. I'd check them out now but reading in vehicles always makes me throw up."

"Don't even think about reading them now," she said firmly.

My mobile rang.

"Quint? Davie. The target's turned towards Grange-mouth. We're about a mile behind him." He gave me the locations. "There's no other traffic out here so he'll see someone's after him if we go much closer."

"Keep your distance, whatever you do," I shouted. "There's a hostage, remember."

"I know that," he said, registering surprise at my agitation. "What's eating you, Quint?"

I wasn't going to answer his question. I looked at the map by torchlight. "We're about three miles from you. I tell you what – stop and wait for us. We need to come up with a plan of action. Out."

Before she could ask what I had in mind, the Llama's phone rang again. I grabbed it first and answered.

"Ah Quint, Duart here. What's going on?" There was an uncharacteristic tension in his voice.

I told him where Macbeth had gone and what we were doing.

"There's nothing for him in Grangemouth," the first secretary said. "The place was destroyed during the drugs wars."

"There are still harbour walls and the like though, aren't there?" I said, remembering a report from one of the Public Order Directorate's recce squads a few years back.

"I don't know," Duart said. "What are you getting at?"

I had to give him something in return for what I was about to ask. "Listen, Andrew, I haven't been as open with you as I might have been."

"What a surprise," Hel Hyslop said under her breath.

"You see," I continued, "there are a lot of Edinburgh connections in this case." I reckoned I was better off sharing the information with him as well as with Hel – I wasn't sure how she was going to react.

There were a few seconds of silence. "Go on, Dalrymple." My first name had suddenly gone missing in action.

"There isn't time to explain everything now. What I can tell you is that Rennie had been using genetic material and subjects from Edinburgh for years. In fact, he arranged for the kidnap of three hyper-intelligent teenagers from a special facility in Edinburgh at the same time you people grabbed me." I told him that Dougal Strachan was one of them and gave him the two survivors' names. "I want you to arrange their return home, Andrew."

"And why should I do that?" he asked frostily.

"Because I'm going to tell Hyslop everything else I know. After we've got the girl away from Macbeth and his psycho followers." I could see a dim light on the road ahead. "I'm going to have to cut you off now, Andrew. Do we have a deal?"

"Maybe."

"Definitely," I corrected. "Out."

Hel pulled up beside the dark blue Super Llama, her headlights sweeping over Davie and Katharine.

"So these are your friends," she said, pulling out her gun and checking the safety catch.

I put my hand on her arm. "You won't need that."

We got out. Katharine gave me a quick smile and Davie nodded. I made the introductions and there were a few seconds of mutually suspicious looks. Then Davie angled the portable bug monitor away from the light.

"Bloody hell, they're out on the water," he said. "Heading east."

"Jesus," I said. "Maybe the mad bastards really are heading for the perfect city."

"We'd better get over to the boatyard at the Kincardine Bridge," Hyslop said.

"Why do you think they'd be going to go to Edinburgh, Quint?" Katharine asked.

"He thinks he knows everything," Hel said sarcastically, turning back to the Llama. "Follow me."

She meant the three of us to follow the Llama, but I took her literally and joined her in it. She was punching out a number on her mobile and frowned when she saw me.

"Tam, it's me," she said. "Where are you?" She listened for a while. "Right, see what you can do about that. We're heading for the bridge. Then probably to Quint's home town. Wish me luck." She listened and then glanced across. "Tam says you're to make sure you look after me."

"Sure," I replied. "At least as well as he looked after me in Glasgow. Where is he?"

She started the engine and swung away. "He's still at the Rennie. Duart's insisting that the place be taken apart."

"I hope someone's taking care of Big Eye and his pals," I said as the lights from the other vehicle flashed in our mirrors. "No doubt Glasgow's welfare services are world beaters."

Hel nodded, not favouring my irony with a reply. Then she called the dock at the Kincardine Bridge.

"We're in luck," she said when she finished. "There's a boat alongside. They're fuelling it up now. Edinburgh here we come."

I looked at her. "It's not a certainty that Macbeth's going there. Maybe he's heading for Fife or even further north. I heard he's got cult members all over the place."

"Really? I'm not exactly in a position to judge, Quint," she said bitterly. "You've kept quiet about so much in this investigation."

I shrugged. "I suppose I haven't got over the way we started — with a hypodermic full of dope in my thigh."

She gunned the engine as we hit the bridge approach road, her lights catching the skeletal shapes of cars that had been burned out decades ago. "Don't tell me you haven't enjoyed the trip," she said in a mocking voice. "At least you got a decent jacket out of it."

I ran my hand down the smooth leather. "I suppose the last few days have had their moments," I replied. Then Aurora's phantom face came out of the darkness and stopped my heart again. "Look," I said haltingly, "it'd be better if you didn't come with us. If you're discovered in Edinburgh, the guardians will have you in the castle dungeons before you can draw your pistol."

"I'm sure you'll put in a good word for me," Hel said, slowing down as the boatyard's perimeter fence appeared in the headlight beam. "Save your breath, Quint. I'm coming. End of story."

Not yet, I thought. Not until Aurora was safe.

*   *   *

"You'll need to give me the passengers' names, inspector." The captain of the converted trawler was looking at Hel anxiously. "I can't sail without a manifest."

I was glad to see that bureaucracy was flourishing even in go-ahead Glasgow.

"Yes you can!" she shouted up from the deck. "This is a Major Crime Squad operation and there's no time to lose. Move!"

The skipper nodded reluctantly then waved to his crewmen. The lines were slipped off the bollards and we headed out into the middle of the channel. Astern I made out the shape of another boat in the murk under the bridge. There were no lights on it.

I turned to Davie. "Where are the targets?" I asked, peering over his arm at the bug monitor. I couldn't make head or tail of the green and yellow lines and the red numbers on the miniature screen.

"About two and a half miles downstream." He glanced at me. "Who knows what kind of boat they've got? If it's a fast one, we'll be hard pressed to catch up in this wreck."

I felt a shudder through the whole of my body. It wasn't only because of the clammy chill out on the water. I wondered how Aurora was coping. The poor lass might never have been on a boat before, never mind one crewed by murderous lunatics.

"What about your friend's car?" I asked Katharine.

"Ewan won't mind. The yard manager's going to let him know. I told Ewan and Peter earlier that it was a matter of life or death." She smiled at me encouragingly. "Snap out of it, Quint. We'll nail Macbeth. The wee girl will be fine."

"Come below," Hel said, eyeing Katharine uncertainly. "I'm told there's coffee and sandwiches."

We followed her down to a surprisingly comfortable mess-room where food and drink had been laid out. There was a bottle of good-quality whisky on the table but I steered clear of it. Davie got stuck in – not that a couple of heavy slugs would have any effect on his performance.

A sailor came down the gangway and pointed to the bunks lining the cabin walls. "You can bed down there if you want. We'll all be on watch."

Katharine and Hel stretched out, still regarding each other without much enthusiasm, while Davie and I stayed at the table.

"Are you all right, big man?" I asked. "You're the only one who can read that contraption, so it's no shut-eye for you."

He nodded. "I'll go up to the bridge and keep the skipper on the ball. I'll let you know if anything exciting happens."

"Make sure he keeps his distance."

"Aye," Davie said, screwing his eyes up at me. "You should get some kip, Quint. Or is there something you need to get off your chest?"

I was tempted to share the load with him but I couldn't. He was as close a friend as I had and he'd never let me down. But things were different with Aurora. She came from another time, a time before I knew Davie or Katharine. Keeping quiet about her was the only way I could feel close to her – and, through her, close to Caro. After eleven years I thought I'd finally managed to cope with the death of my first great love, but now I knew that was a delusion.

I sat back after Davie went up. I was stretching and yawning but I didn't think sleep would come. Then, under the table, I spotted the black hold-all I'd brought in from the Llama. I picked it up and opened the zip carefully, trying not to wake the women. Both of them had apparently passed out seconds after their heads hit the grubby pillows. I took the heavy pistol out and checked the clip before slipping it under my belt. There were still three rounds in it.

Then I had a look at the files Broadsword had dropped. There were eight of them; eight names that rang several bells. They belonged to the four men and four women who'd been murdered and mutilated in Glasgow. I felt my jaw go slack. What the hell were files about them doing in the Baby Factory? I flicked back to the covers of the cardboard folders. Each was headed "Rennie Institute", with a second line reading "Director – Professor D. J. Rennie MA, MSc, PhD" – the bent scientist obviously liked seeing his name in print all the time. It was the third line that really caught my eye. It contained the words "Personnel Department".

I spent a long time reading the contents of those files.

I went up to the bridge later on when I heard the revs being cut. I was immediately soaked by the haar which Edinburgh is famous for. The chill sea mist had rolled across the Forth with a promise of winter.

"Where are we?" I asked the captain.

He glanced round from the wheel. "We're shooting the supports of the old rail bridge."

"Where's Macbeth's boat?" I asked Davie as I looked out to my right. This time I could see nothing of *Britannia*.

"About a mile ahead," he replied, eyes locked on the monitor. "Fortunately it seems to be even more of a rust-bucket than this one –"

"Here, watch it," the sailor complained.

"– so we made up some of the distance." Davie turned to me. "Get any sleep? You look a bit less wiped out."

"Looks can be deceptive, my friend." I was feeling exhausted and I was still very nervous about Aurora, but I had also begun to feel the rush that I always get when a case builds towards its climax.

"Fucking haar," the skipper said, eyes on his radar. At least the ramshackle boat was kitted out with reasonable equipment. "The one good thing about it is that it's keeping the headbanging Embra boats in port."

I nodded, looking ruefully at Davie. The Fisheries Guard tended to ram first and ask questions afterwards. We were within the Edinburgh mobile phone system's range now, but I wasn't planning on giving the City Guard any advance warning yet.

The next hour dragged by. They were enlivened only by breakfast, when Katharine and Hel tried to win awards for the most vicious look and the most snide comment. Overnight they seemed to have taken an inordinate dislike to each other. Davie and I went back up top, shaking our heads. I took the black hold-all with me.

Then Davie leaned forward over the bug monitor. "He's changing course," he said after a few more seconds. "Yep, he's on a bearing of 160. He'll hit the shoreline pretty soon."

"How far are we behind him?" I asked.

"Twelve hundred yards," the skipper said after checking his instruments.

"Shit," I said, gripping the chart table. "If he beaches, we'll be stuck out here while he gets clear."

Davie was looking at me. "Not only that. The border guards on the shore might spot them and pin them down."

I felt a razor-sharp blade run through my heart. Jesus. The border guards are one of the few units issued with guns in Edinburgh. I remembered Macbeth's heavy automatic. The idea that Aurora might be caught in an exchange of fire was making my heart pound.

"Give me your mobile, Davie."

Katharine and Hel had just climbed up to the wheelhouse.

"What is it, Quint?" Katharine asked.

I didn't reply. I was too busy trying to raise the public order guardian on his mobile. The old bugger must have been asleep. Eventually he answered.

"Lewis, it's Dalrymple."

"Good God, man, where the bloody—"

"Never mind that. This is an emergency. Tell the border patrols on the shore to the west of Granton to withdraw immediately. There's a landing party on its way in and it's essential you allow them free passage. We're about ten minutes behind them."

"Landing party? Free passage?" the guardian spluttered. "What on earth—"

"Do it, Lewis! Now!" I shouted. "I'll get back to you soon. Out."

"He's almost hit dry land," Davie said, looking up from the monitor. "It's sand there so he's probably going right in to the shore."

Hyslop stepped up to me. "What's going on, Quint? Who were you talking to?"

I looked at her. "Someone you never want to meet. If you think Duart's bad . . ." I let the words trail away and turned to the skipper. "Can you get us ashore a safe distance from the target boat?"

He nodded. "Oh aye. I've landed people often enough around here. The guards are more miss than hit in this midden of a city."

Davie looked like he was about to take the Glaswegian out, but Katharine just laughed. The sight of Hel and Davie in simultaneous high dudgeon had made her day before sunrise.

The tide was on the ebb so we had a long trudge across the sodden sands in the early morning light. The boat disappeared into the mist, which was clearing but still sufficient to soak our hair and clothes. There was no sign of the craft that had delivered our quarry. They were probably smugglers whose extortionate rates would have been no problem for Macbeth. The northern suburbs of Edinburgh gradually took shape in front of us, looking about as welcoming as a town full of hungry ghosts. I had a quick flash of the necropolis in Glasgow and that made me think of Macbeth and his cult. The way my home city was going he'd probably get fifty thousand members on the spot if he staged a performance — not that he could do that without finding a way of keeping it secret from the Council and the guard.

"Where do you think they'll go?" Davie said from my left, sinking up to his laces in the muddy sand. Katharine was beyond him while Hel was sticking close to me on the right.

I shrugged. "That isn't our problem. We can track them on the monitor easily enough. The problem is, how do we get the girl away?"

"Wait a second," Katharine said. "How are they going

to get around the city? Surely they won't have transport."

"Remember the missing Labour Directorate van," I said, glancing at Davie. "Where are they now?"

He held the monitor to his face. "In the middle of Muirhouse. They're moving slowly so they're obviously on foot." He looked closer. "Not any more they're not. They're going faster now, heading towards Ferry Road."

I looked at my watch. "Six-thirty. The workers' buses have started. They may have taken one of them. We need transport ourselves."

"I'm on to it," Davie said, pulling out his mobile and calling the command centre.

We reached the top of the shore and started stamping our feet on the road that runs alongside. It wasn't particularly cold, but the damp had seeped into my boots and buggered up the circulation in my toes. Fortunately my brain seemed to be unaffected.

"Broadsword," I said under my breath.

"What about him?" Hel asked, her face wet from the haar but her eyes as unwavering as ever.

"The last time I saw him he was wearing his mask and medieval costume. He might get away with that in the central tourist zone but not in the citizen areas."

"Wouldn't they just think he was off to work in some performance?" Katharine asked.

"There's a Raeburn Barracks Land-Rover on its way," Davie said. He grimaced. "The public order guardian's heading down here as well."

"Oh shit," I said, turning to Hel. "You're about to be nailed."

"Why?" she demanded, eyes wide open. "I haven't done anything illegal."

"Yes, you have," Davie said, raising his arm as a guard

vehicle came round the corner, lights blazing. "This is a closed city. You need a Council authorisation to cross the borders." He grinned at her. "In my experience, one of those has never been granted to a member of the Glasgow police."

A smile appeared on Katharine's lips again. Time for me to step in and promote some togetherness.

"Don't worry, Hel. Lewis Hamilton is putty in my hands."

Davie and Katharine both laughed as the guard Land-Rover pulled up.

"This time he is," I said, picking up the hold-all. "This time he's going to do everything I say or he'll be spending the night in one of his own dungeons."

That put a stop to their levity.

Hamilton appeared a few minutes later, his Jeep turning on to Pennywell Road as we were about to turn out of it. I would have kept going, but the auxiliary driver stopped obediently when he saw the guardian's agitated hand signals.

Lewis got out and made for us. "Dalrymple?" he said, his face lowering over the windscreen like a bearded full moon. "What the bloody hell's going on?"

I smiled at Hyslop and got out, motioning to the rest of them to stay put. "I'm very pleased to see you too, guardian," I said, taking his arm and leading him down the pavement. A couple of male citizens in blue overalls and donkey jackets stared at us with the contemptuous indifference that's generally applied to guard personnel in the suburbs.

"Well?" the guardian demanded. "Where have you been, man? What's all this about a hostage?"

I told him the basics then wound myself up for the punchline. "I'm taking charge of this operation," I said. "And you're going to do everything I say."

That had the predictable effect of making his cheeks redden and his chest puff out like a seabird's during the mating season. "Have you lost your—"

"You're in very deep shit, Lewis," I said, cutting his question off before it turned into a diatribe. "I know that this city's been doing genetic engineering deals with Glasgow."

That deflated him instantly. The small doubt I'd had that the secret committee he and Sophia were on was not involved with Rennie's activities disappeared. He looked as guilty as a cat with cream-covered whiskers.

I raised my hand. "I don't care about the reasons, Lewis. The Glasgow executive's tearing the research facility over there apart as I speak. It's finished. All that matters is saving a girl who's been taken hostage."

"Have you been in Glasgow?" he asked in disbelief. He looked round at the Land-Rover. "Who's that female? Is she from—"

"I told you, I'm in charge. She's with me. And another thing. There's to be no question of Hume 253 being demoted. Got that? If you argue, I'll tell the Council about the secret set-up you and Sophia are running with the science and energy guardian and Billy Geddes." I stared at him. "Billy is in on it, isn't he?"

Hamilton nodded slowly. "He's been handling the financial side." He looked at me. "We didn't do it for monetary gain. You do believe that, don't you, Dalrymple? The birth-rate's dropped horrifically; we need the benefits of modern science."

I shook my head at him. "I don't care about that now.

You can convince me later. The girl is all that counts now. The fucker who's got her is a madman. He and his followers were behind the murders of the auxiliaries."

That made Hamilton pull himself together. "Very well," he said. "What do you need?"

"Nothing for the time being," I said, turning on my heel. "Go back to the castle and make sure I get everything I ask for the second I ask for it."

"All right," he agreed reluctantly. "And Dalrymple?" he called after me. "It's . . . it's good to have you back."

I almost fainted. I didn't think the old hardnose had it in him. Things must have got really bad since I'd been gone.

We headed up to Queensferry Road and then into the city centre. The targets were on foot again and had left the east end of Princes Street.

"They're moving round the lower slopes of the Calton Hill," Davie said, his eyes on the monitor.

"Get over there," I said to the driver. I could have sent other guard personnel closer, but there was no need. Anyway, I didn't trust the guardian enough to be sure he wouldn't try a full-scale intervention if his people were involved. Then it struck me. "Shit, he's heading for Royal Terrace," I said, glancing at Katharine. "The superannuated scientist."

She nodded. "Doctor Godwin and his extremely strange pet."

Hel was staring at us. "What are you talking about?"

I told her about the animal geneticist who had supposedly been retired. I reckoned that was horseshit – the old bastard was probably still hard at work on a daily basis. The question was, where? A lab conducting illegal experiments could hardly be located in a standard Science and Energy Directorate facility.

The Land-Rover jerked to a halt at the traffic lights at the foot of the Mound. The tourist tat shops on Princes Street were open but deserted at this early hour, citizen workers tramping through the drizzle with their shoulders hunched and the collars of their thin Supply Directorate coats up. The city's visitors would still be in their beds, brains numbed by the booze dispensed in the clubs and genitalia worn out by Tourism Directorate hookers. There wasn't a single child to be seen. My heart seized up for a few seconds as I thought of Aurora being dragged along by Macbeth. I could only hope that she was being smart and doing everything he told her.

"They've stopped," Davie said, bent over the monitor. "Towards the far end of Royal Terrace."

I nodded. "That'll be the retirement home. I have a feeling they won't be there for long." I turned to the driver. "Go down to the Playhouse Leisure Centre and pull up there. We'll wait for them to get on the move again."

He did so. We sat wiping the windows of the vehicle as they clouded up with the steam rising from our still sodden clothes and footwear. After a few minutes Hel, who was in the back, stretched her arms and legs then leaned towards us. I felt Katharine shy away.

"What's in those files, Quint?" she asked, pointing at the bag at my feet. "Can I have a look at them?" There was a slight edge to her voice.

"Nothing interesting," I said nonchalantly. "Who knows what Broadsword wanted with them?"

"Can I have a look at them?" the inspector repeated.

"Movement!" Davie said. "Faster than pedestrians. They've found a vehicle and they're heading eastwards round Royal Terrace."

I grabbed the Land-Rover's mobile and got the retirement home's number from the central switchboard. The effete auxiliary in charge remembered me and tried to pass the time of day. I threatened him with the mines and was told that Dr Godwin had gone off in a taxi with a thin-faced, bearded man. And yes, there was a girl – a very pretty, shy one – with him. But he'd seen no sign of anyone else in the cab.

The target vehicle had swung round on to Regent Terrace and was heading west. I told the driver to go up to the top of Leith Walk and wait for them there. The fact that they were in a taxi showed that Godwin still had high-level clearance – only serving senior auxiliaries and tourists are allowed to use cabs.

"All right, let's move," I said as the taxi went past us and down Princes Street. "And keep your bloody distance!" Guard drivers aren't much use at tailing as there are so few vehicles in Edinburgh. I caught a glimpse of Macbeth's head but no one else was visible. He was obviously making sure that Aurora didn't get a chance to attract attention.

"Where's Broadsword got to?" Davie asked.

"I reckon he's keeping his head down in the taxi," I said.

"Trying not to scare the locals," Katharine said grimly.

"Or he might not have been with Macbeth in the first place," Hel pointed out from behind us. "We're only assuming he joined up with his leader on the way out of Glasgow."

"True enough," I said. "He might also have keeled over from the bullets I pumped into him." I turned to face her. "But I'm not counting on that. I'm pretty sure he's here. He's been before, he knows his way around."

The taxi turned left at the lottery kiosks around the foot of the Mound and ground up the hill. Our driver got himself behind a diesel-spewing bus, which provided plenty of cover.

"Drop back a bit more," I said, still panicking about being spotted, although Godwin would tell Macbeth that guard vehicles are everywhere in Edinburgh. I wasn't taking any chances with Aurora's safety.

The target vehicle disappeared where the road forms a right angle by the Finance Directorate. That edifice brought my former friend Billy Geddes to mind again. Not for the first time I'd found his sticky fingers where they shouldn't have been. I wondered if getting involved with the genetic engineering business had been his idea a long time ago, or whether Sophia or the science and energy guardian had resurrected it more recently. Christ, Billy might have been in on the deal when Caro was still alive.

"Where are they?" I asked Davie, trying to concentrate on the operation in hand.

"They went over the Royal Mile. They're heading south down George IV Bridge."

I told the driver to stop outside the central archive while we let them go on undisturbed. After a few minutes Davie looked up from the monitor. "They've stopped," he said. "At the junction of Lauriston Place and Lady Lawson Street."

"Let's go," I said to the driver, wondering what was

going on. Then I had it. The former college of art buildings were now a warren of partly used office premises
and storage depots. In pre-Enlightenment times they'd
been packed with tutors and students, not all of them
with dodgy haircuts and paint-spattered smocks. The
Council's view of art was severely limited – the odd stern
monument for the city's streets and scenery for the
tourist theatres were about the limit. Despite the Platonic
doctrines which the guardians claim they follow, there
isn't any provision for art teaching in the schools so very
few people study the subject these days. The college
takes up only a small part of the complex.

"I wonder if the college of art is where the mad doctor
has his labs," I said.

Davie looked at me thoughtfully. "Could be. I was in
there a few months ago on a routine security call. It's as
quiet as the grave."

"Nice simile, big man," I said. "Okay, pull up here."

The driver stopped on Lauriston Place, about fifty
yards away from the college.

"I'm going in on my own," I said, jumping down.

Three voices said "What?" at the same time.

I leaned in the Land-Rover's window. "You heard me.
Stake out the outside and wait for my call." I gave them
all the eye. "No one's to come in without the word from
me. I'm serious, all right?"

Katharine, Davie and Hel Hyslop nodded, none of them
with any enthusiasm.

I turned away but Davie called me back.

"Don't you want this?" he asked, holding out the
driver's mobile. "It'll connect to the Edinburgh network
quicker than the Glasgow one you've got."

"Good idea, commander," I said, sticking it into my

pocket. As I did so, my fingers felt Broadsword's automatic.

I hoped for Aurora's sake that I wouldn't have to use it.

CHAPTER TWENTY

There was no one around outside the red stone structure of the main building. A battered sign outside the entrance proclaimed that it was part of the Supply Directorate. I continued on to a rectangular structure from the 1970s. It was notable for the complete absence of windows in the numerous metal frames — obviously a use had been found for them elsewhere. Perhaps a deliberate attempt had been made to give the place a desolate air as well. I reckoned Godwin's lab was in the depths. The fact that this facility was only a few minutes' walk from Sophia's base in the infirmary improved the odds.

I stopped and listened. Not a sound nearby. Further away I could hear the rumble of trucks and buses at Tollcross, but the building in front of me was a mausoleum in brick and discoloured mortar. I made sure Broadsword's heavy pistol was lodged firmly out of sight under my jacket and moved inside carefully. The outer door was missing. A more unlikely way into a lab at the cutting edge of genetic research I couldn't imagine. That's why I was almost sure that I was heading in the right direction. No one covers their tracks like guardians pulling a fast one on their fellow Council members.

The floor was uneven and filthy. That was a big help. I

dropped to my knees and examined the surface – scuffed marks suggesting unsteadiness from the aged scientist, the elaborate prints from the soles of a child's trainers and larger ones from Macbeth's heavy boots. No sign of Broadsword's larger feet, which made me breathe a sigh of relief then wonder where he'd got to.

I followed the tracks to the end of the corridor and lost them in the gloom. I risked a flash from my torch and saw a handrail leading down to the basement. There were more of the same footprints on the worn steps. I paused and tried to work out the safest course of action. Davie hadn't called so the bug was still in the same location, but how could I get closer without being spotted? I wasn't able to come up with an answer to that so I went on cautiously, hoping for a lucky break.

At the bottom of the stairs I got one. Light was shining out from an open door half-way down the passageway. I moved slowly and quietly towards the illuminated section, feeling the breath rasp in my throat and my heart slam in my chest. Christ, what next? How was I going to get Aurora out? When I reached the edge of the lit-up patch of floor, I stopped and tried to get my breathing under control. I cocked an ear and listened into the room beyond. Dead quiet, not even the hum of computers. The reek of chemicals permeated the air. I waited, steeled myself then squatted down and risked a look round the door-frame.

The first things I saw from my low position were desks, drawers and shelves full of files, computer disks and bottles of various sizes. I looked higher and saw an array of computer equipment that was more high-tech than anything I'd ever come across in Edinburgh. This project certainly wasn't short of funding. That made me think of Billy Geddes – he'd obviously been hard at work. I tried to see how big the place was. The aisle between the desks stretched away and I couldn't be sure that there weren't dozens of scientists working away in the nether regions. It was too quiet though. I scurried forward and took cover behind the first desk. Still no sign of anyone. I began to get a bad feeling.

Then I glanced round the desk and saw the body. Shit. I recognised Gavin Godwin's head immediately, the thin grey hair plastered across the scalp with whatever grease he used. He was flat out on his back about five yards away from me, his arms outstretched in the space between the desks. One wrist was bent up against a bottom drawer, the fingers curled round loosely. I listened, then moved closer.

That was when the noise started. The high-pitched growl made the hairs on my neck spring to attention. I looked to the right and saw Godwin's pet rat-catcher in the leg-space of the desk next to the body. Cerberus was standing on the tips of all four paws, showing his heavy, saliva-drenched teeth to me. Jesus. If there was anyone in the vicinity, my cover was well and truly blown. I moved back but the animal didn't give up. If anything the growl became even more manic. In desperation I pulled out the automatic and pointed it at the genetically modified creature. That shut it up.

I stood up slowly and looked around the cavernous laboratory. Plenty of equipment, but no people operating it – the mad doctor must have given them the day off. There was no sign of Macbeth or Aurora either. When I approached Godwin, gun still aimed at Cerberus, I saw something that made me freeze. Carefully positioned on the scientist's pallid forehead, its metallic sheen glowing in the artificial light, was the tracker bug.

I sank to my knees and started cursing under my breath. Then cursed some more at full volume. Then I pulled out the mobile and rang Davie. "Macbeth and the girl have gone," I said. "Get in here." I gave him directions. I could have told him to advise the command centre but I didn't want some glory-hunting auxiliary to have a go – let alone Hamilton to stick his aged oar in.

While I waited for the others, I examined Godwin's body. Cerberus had sat down now, his jaws still drawn back over his yellow fangs but his appetite for a fight or a meal apparently under control. The animal was eyeing my weapon uneasily and I soon saw why. His master had been taken out with a single, large-calibre gunshot to the chest. I thought about that and reckoned that I would have heard a shot – so it looked like Macbeth or whoever killed him had a silencer. Great.

There was a clatter of nailed boots on the stairs and Davie shot through the door. Katharine and Hel followed at a slightly more restrained pace.

"What happened?" Davie demanded, looking at the body and then frowning when he saw Cerberus. "What the hell's that?"

"Name's Cerberus," I said. I pointed to the corpse's forehead. "Macbeth found the bug."

"Oh no," Katharine said.

I nodded slowly, looking around the lab. There was a door at the far end. "That was probably his way out." Then I took in the desk beyond the body. It had been ransacked, the drawers pulled out. The computer and screen on top had been knocked over.

"What went on here?" Hel asked, stepping forward.

I rubbed the stubble on my jaw. "Macbeth brought the scientist here for a reason," I replied. "Looks like he was after something. Godwin probably had something he wanted. Something worth a lot of money on the global market, I'd guess."

Katharine was squatting down by the animal and making soothing noises at it. To my amazement it stopped growling and let her touch the top of its head.

"Good boy," she said.

I turned to Hel. "What do you think? Will Macbeth be on his way back to Glasgow now?"

She shrugged. "You tell me. The Rennie Institute's not exactly a going concern any more. If he's taken a programme or data from here, he could be headed anywhere to sell it."

"What do you want us to do, Quint?" Davie asked. "Shall I put out an all-barracks alert?"

"No way," I said. Aurora's beautiful, terrified features had risen up before me. "We're going to have to sort this one out ourselves." I had a pretty good idea of the next move. "Let's go and see your boss. It's about time I put the squeeze on the public order guardian."

Davie looked at me in horror. The idea of having a go at his superior had always been a difficult one for him to grasp. Time for me to give him the latest in a long series of lessons.

Lewis Hamilton was in his quarters in the castle. I stormed into them ahead of the others, leaving the grey-suited female auxiliary in the outer office with her mouth open wide. I'd considered bringing Cerberus but decided it was better to pack him off to the zoo.

"What is it, Dalrymple?" the guardian demanded from behind the perfectly aligned piles of folders on his desk.

"What it is, Lewis, is the end of the road for you." I heard Davie's sharp intake of breath to my rear.

The guardian's cheeks above his beard were almost as pale as the murdered scientist's. "What do you mean?" he asked hoarsely, peering at Hel and Katharine.

"The fugitive from Glasgow is still loose in Edinburgh. As well as the girl he's taken hostage, he's in possession of an automatic pistol and silencer. He recently used those to kill Doctor Gavin Godwin."

Hamilton's eyes sprang wide open. "What?" he gasped.

"So talk!" I yelled, bringing my fist down hard on his desk. The pencils and rubbers jumped up and scattered across the polished surface. "Tell me everything about your illegal bloody committee. Who else is involved?"

"You already know who else is involved, don't you, Quint?"

I turned round rapidly at the sound of Sophia's voice. She was wearing the usual guardian's tweed jacket and dark trousers, her abdomen swelling out under the white blouse. She glanced disparagingly at Katharine and then subjected Hel Hyslop to prolonged scrutiny.

"She's with me," I said. "And no, I don't know everyone who's involved, Sophia." I took a step towards her. "Lately I've had other things on my mind. But I have found some worrying links with a research institute in Glasgow . . ." I broke off and glared at her ". . . as well as with the murders of the two auxiliaries in Edinburgh."

The medical guardian looked briefly at Hamilton. "I see no reason to divulge details of the committee to outsiders. Especially not outsiders from democratic states." She frowned at Hel. "Do you have to wear that uniform here?"

389

The inspector looked down at her green jacket. "Rather this than the old man's stuff you've got on."

"Women talking about fashion. What a surprise." The sardonic voice from the door made everyone look round again.

"Billy," I said, taking in the wizened, wheelchair-bound figure. "Just the man I wanted to see."

My former friend grunted. "You wanting to see me, Quint? What kind of shitty joke is that? You've been ignoring me for years." He shook his misshapen arms and legs. "Ever since you put me in this contraption, in fact."

"Look, you self-serving little shit," I said, moving over to him. "Your money-grabbing schemes have led to the death of at least four Edinburgh citizens. They've also put an innocent child at risk." I stood watching as my vehement tone made him jerk back. Suddenly it struck me that he might be the weak link in the chain. "You know the Rennies, don't you, Billy? Derek, the one who plays at being Macbeth, is on the run in Edinburgh. Have you got any idea where he is? Tell me or I'll nail you to your chair."

"Quint." I felt Davie's hand on my shoulder. "Give him a chance to talk."

I nodded, taking in the concern on his face. Maybe I'd been a bit hard on Billy. He was looking away from me, his gaze on the floor.

"Tell him," Hamilton said. "Tell him what you know, Geddes. Otherwise he'll tell the Council about the committee."

A worried look appeared on Sophia's face. She moved towards Billy. "Do you have any idea of Rennie's whereabouts?" she demanded. "Has he been in touch with you?"

The wheelchair shuddered as Billy tried to reverse towards the door. I stood behind him to block his way. That made him laugh, but it was a broken, feeble sound about as far from humour as it could go. "Always get your man, don't you, Quint?" he said in a cracked voice.

"You slimeball," I said in a low voice. "You've spoken to him, haven't you? Where is he?"

More empty laughter. "Fuck you. I'm not telling you anything."

I knew how stubborn Billy could be. When he was a trainee auxiliary, he once did thirty days on the border rather than own up to stealing the commander's malt whisky. And a few years back, he concocted a vicious plot to snare me because of what I'd done to him. Breaking him down would tax the most experienced guard interrogator, as the Council's arm-twisters and ball-squeezers are officially known. But I had to find a way to do it – I had to, for Aurora's sake. That was it. Aurora. She was the answer.

"Come on," I said, grabbing the handles of his chair. "We're going for a little trip." I nodded to Davie, Katharine and Hel. "As for you, guardians – stay here and hope that I find out what I need. Otherwise you'll be demoted by tonight."

Sophia had her hand resting on her convex midriff. I felt a pang of guilt for what I was putting her and her unborn child through. Then I thought of Aurora again and pushed Billy out of the room.

We got the citizen formerly known as Heriot 07 out of the Land-Rover in Gilmore Place, leaving his wheelchair in the guard vehicle. Davie carried him up to my flat in a fireman's lift, the rest of us keeping our distance to avoid his passenger's ill-directed kicks.

"Dump him on the sofa, Davie," I said, heading for the bedroom. I stuck my hand into the top drawer of the chest of drawers and found what I wanted. Hel and Katharine were standing as far apart from each other as the confines of the main room allowed. Hel was taking in the decor. It didn't look like she was too impressed.

"So, Billy," I said, sitting down next to him. "You've got a grievance against me."

"Several," he croaked.

I shrugged. "Fair enough. You think I've been a shit to you on several occasions. Well, here's the good news. As far as I'm concerned, this can be the last time we ever see each other."

"Good," Billy muttered, his head away from me. "You fucking smartarse. Why can't you leave me alone?" It wasn't the first time I'd buggered up one of his deals, but that wasn't my problem.

I twisted his head round and stuck the small, framed photo in front of him. "What about her? Have you got a grievance against her?"

There were a few moments of silence. I was aware of the other three gathering around us, craning to see the photo.

"A grievance against Caro?" Billy said, his irritation turning to an unlikely tenderness. "No, of course not. She was . . . she was my friend when we were young." He looked at me in bewilderment. "What's Caro got to do with this, Quint?"

I stared at him, not letting his eyes move away. "The girl who's being held hostage. Her name's Aurora. She's Caro's daughter."

Billy's eyes bulged and I heard Davie, Katharine and Hel Hyslop gasp.

"But how can that be?" Billy asked, his voice faint. "Caro's been dead for over ten years. There was never any talk of her being pregnant. What age is the . . . what age is this Aurora? How do you know she's Caro's?"

"Because she's the perfect image of her," I said. "She's around eight. Think about it, Billy."

The veins on his ravaged face grew dark blue and distended. "Oh my Christ," he gasped. "Oh my bleeding Christ. The bastards took an egg from Caro and stored it." He toppled forward and caught his head in his fleshless hands. "Oh Jesus Christ, Quint. I didn't know, honestly, I didn't know."

"Is this true, Quint?" Katharine asked in a tortured voice.

"You think I've made it up?"

Her face reddened. "No, of course not. But how . . . how could it happen?"

I told them what David Rennie had said. Billy's reaction suggested he'd been dealing with the Glasgow scientist when Caro was still alive; that is, for over ten years.

For all her toughness, even Hel seemed to be finding this aspect of the case hard to take. "You . . . you recognised her when you first saw her?" she asked.

I nodded. "Instantly. There's nothing of me or any other male apparent in her. She's Caro brought back to life."

Hel was biting her lower lip. "I'm so sorry, Quint," she said. "I never imagined taking you to Glasgow would—"

"Grosvenor Crescent," Billy said quietly. "Number eight. Top flat. That's where he is. Not for long though. I don't know where he's planning on going afterwards."

393

I felt a wave of relief dash over me. "Thanks, Billy."

He turned and shrugged, eyes wet. He was once very fond of Caro.

As I headed for the door, the relief turned to cold terror. I still had no idea of how to wrest Aurora away from Macbeth. But I felt myself being drawn to his lair like iron filings to a magnet – or Birnam Wood to Dunsinane.

Grosvenor Crescent faces another elliptical street across a small tree-lined park. From the air the locale must look like an egg. Or an eye. That last idea hit me as we stopped behind the vast blackened walls of what was originally a triple-spired cathedral and is now a venue for the year-round festival. There were hoardings advertising InCirc, the Independent Edinburgh Indoor Circus. It featured exploding clowns, barebottomed bareback riders and complementary cannabis – another victory for the Tourism Directorate.

"How do we do this?" Davie asked. He'd taken over from the driver at the wheel of the Land-Rover; the fewer guard personnel who knew about this operation the better.

I got out and went to the lichen-encrusted corner of one of the ex-cathedral's walls. A heavy drizzle was falling. The crescent curved away into a blur. I'd discovered from the detailed City Guard map that number eight was towards the middle. I heard the others gathering behind me and waved them back.

"You're not going in on your own again, Quint," Katharine said, pre-empting me and attempting to lay down the law.

I swivelled round. "Yes I am. The upper flats only have

one entrance. There's no way we can storm our way in without being spotted." I looked at them sternly. "Which could be fatal for Aurora."

Davie was nodding. "Right enough. They're pretty easy to defend, those flats – I remember that from the drugs wars. One way in and then at least fifty steps up broad staircases with no cover." He caught my eye. "One guy will make as good a target as half a dozen, Quint."

"Too bad," I said, going back to the Land-Rover and pulling out a rain-jacket with a hood. "The drizzle's making for pretty poor visibility. I'll try to get as far as the door without raising suspicion." I shrugged. "After that, I'll play it by ear."

Hel stepped towards me. "Let me come with you, Quint," she said. "I've been trained to handle situations like this."

"And we haven't?" Davie demanded.

I shook my head at Hyslop. "The last time Macbeth saw you was when he was shackled to the interrogation chair in your office, Hel. He's hardly going to hang back if he sees you coming up the stairs, is he?"

Katharine smiled as the inspector stepped back.

"I can handle him," Hel said in a low voice.

"Forget it. I've got a mobile so I can call you in if I need back-up." I also had the automatic but I wasn't going to tell them about that. Davie would relieve me of it before I could blink and I didn't fancy going up against Macbeth with only my diplomatic skills to hand. Then I thought of Aurora. I could only use the weapon in the last resort.

"Go on then, you idiot," Katharine said, her smile vanishing. "And take care, you hear?"

I squeezed her arm. "I will, dearest."

She glared at me and I hit the road before she could

reply. She'd never been keen on terms of endearment, however ironically they were couched. I pulled the hood down as low as I could and zipped up the rain-jacket. Fortunately it had "Labour Directorate" stencilled on the back rather than "City Guard" – Davie's junior colleagues often purloin them because they're more weatherproof than standard guard-issue jackets.

I walked slowly down Grosvenor Crescent, glancing up at the terraced houses. They'd been built in the late eighteenth century and had grand bay windows for their upper-middle-class owners to survey the world from. Under the Enlightenment the houses were mainly turned over to tourist hostels and the like, but the Council kept a few back as private accommodation for foreign businessmen. No doubt that's how Billy knew about number eight – I was guessing he'd arranged the keys for Macbeth. The high walls and the railings at street level gave the place a fortified aspect, which was appropriate enough: the king was in his castle and I was the poor bloody infantry trying to get through his defences – without even a branch from a blood-red tree to protect me.

As I approached the entrance I kept close to the railings, hoping he didn't choose that moment to look down. Then I ran up the half-dozen steps to the heavy black door and took cover under the lintel. Getting in wasn't going to be a problem – a pass-key had been sent down to us by guard vehicle. The question was, had I been spotted? There was only one way to find out.

I slipped the key into the well-worn brass lock and turned it cautiously. Nice and smooth. The bolt moved silently and I put my shoulder against the wood. Fortunately there was no Gothic creaking as the door swung open. I stepped in quickly and pushed the door to, holding the key in the lock to avoid any click. I was in.

The problem was that the entrance hall and stairwell were pitch-dark. These houses were built with a glass cupola in the roof. This one must have been dealt with during the drugs wars and replaced by a solid cover – of poor-quality wooden slats if I knew anything about Housing Directorate practice. I still had the torch in my pocket but I didn't want to risk using it, so I moved slowly towards where I thought the stairs started, my arms extended forwards. That didn't stop me losing my balance when my boot encountered the bottom step. I leaned my shoulder against the wall and started on the climb, counting off the stairs silently as I went.

Twenty-four got me to the first-floor landing. I paused for a moment then slid along the wall. When I reached the door-frame I moved away slightly. Not far enough. Suddenly the door opened. I was engulfed in a flood of light which blinded me for a second. That was long enough for a hand to grab the collar of my rain-jacket and haul me inside. I hit the deck heavily and rolled round.

"Dalrymple." The voice was high-pitched and as harsh as a hanging judge's. "I was expecting you to turn up." Broadsword was standing over me in his usual garb, the mask and ragged hair looming down. He reached under his cloak and came out with a mallet – he must have got a new one – and chisel. There was a bloodstained bandage on his right hand, presumably from a Ladykiller bullet, but it didn't seem to be hampering him much. "This is the end of your road, arsehole."

"Wait, wait!" I gabbled. "I can help you. I can get you safe passage out of Edinburgh. You and your leader."

"My leader?" The bogeyman gave a laugh that made me shiver despite the sweat I was exuding. "My leader? Fuck my leader." He leaned closer and drew the mallet back.

The time for negotiations was over. I whipped my left leg upwards and caught him in the groin with my steel toe-cap. That made him cant over to his right and stick a hand out to break his fall. I slithered out from under him and scrambled over the ornate tiles on the flat's hall floor.

Broadsword coughed and spat. "That was really dumb, Dalrymple. Now you don't get stunned. Now I split your head open without an anaesthetic."

I pulled the automatic out of my belt and raised it at him. He stopped and peered forward as I slipped the safety off.

"That's mine, you fuck. Give it back." He stepped heavily towards me.

I was panting like a bull on the killing line, trying to weigh up Aurora's chances if a shot rang out. Then Broadsword came closer and the debate ended. I pulled the trigger and the heavy weapon jerked back, almost breaking my wrist. The noise made my ears ring. Even though I'd needed to fire in self-defence, I still hated guns.

The bogeyman was sprawled on the floor, his legs wide apart. A low groan came from him, then he rolled on to his side and struggled back to his feet.

"Jesus," I gasped. I'd aimed at the middle of his chest. What did it take to put the guy down? Then I remembered what happened in the Rennie. I'd pumped several shots from the Ladykiller into his chest there and he still walked away. The bastard must have been wearing a bulletproof vest.

398

"Farewell, Quint," he grunted, pulling back the mallet.

"Farewell, John Breck," I said, pointing the pistol at the ragged mask. This time I remembered to squeeze the trigger like I'd learned on the auxiliary training programme.

He flew back again, a red spray exploding from the back of his head. Then he slid across the polished tiles and came to rest against the wall. His legs didn't jerk for long.

I got up and went towards him unsteadily, avoiding the trail of gore on the floor. A mobile phone had fallen from underneath Broadsword's cloak and landed in the crimson pool. I left it where it was. The mask was shattered at its epicentre, a blackened hole glistening where the nose used to be. I took a deep breath and slid my hand round to the back of his shattered head. That turned out to be unnecessary as the impact of the bullet had destroyed the mask's elastic bindings. I wiped my hand on his cloak and pulled the leathery covering away – then looked down on the face of the killer.

What I saw knocked me back on my heels. The entry wound in the middle of the young man's features was horrendous enough, but what was above it made me feel even worse.

Broadsword's eyes were grey, as I'd seen through the slits on the mask. But above the bridge of his nose there was a dark brown and bloodshot third eye.

Before I could do anything else, I threw up on to the tiles.

When I'd finished, I headed out of the first-floor flat at speed, automatic in one hand and torch in the other. There was no need for caution now. I had to get to the top flat before Macbeth did anything to Aurora. Besides, the gunshots were the first anyone in central Edinburgh would have heard for years. The guard would be round any minute unless Davie could stop them. Christ, he'd be heading this way himself.

I reached the upper door and hammered on it frantically. "Macbeth! Rennie! It's Dalrymple. Let me in! You need my help if you want to stay alive." I looked down at my right hand. The pistol was the only weapon I had, but it was hardly going to inspire confidence in the hostage-taker. Reluctantly I slid the safety catch on and dropped the gun down the stairwell. I heard it land on the tiles of the entrance hall with a sharp crack.

"Dalrymple?" Macbeth's shout came from well inside the flat. He wasn't taking any chances by approaching the door. "What's going on? I heard gunfire."

I heard the street-door slam open and heavy boots crash into the ground floor.

"Let me in," I pleaded. "I'm unarmed. The guard's on its way. They'll take you out, Macbeth." I pounded on the door again. "Come on, open up. For the sake of the girl!"

There was a pause during which nailed boots started on the lower stairs.

"Quint?" came a shout from below.

"Stay there, Davie," I screamed. "Don't let anyone up."

"What's going on, Dalrymple?" Macbeth demanded, his voice closer now.

"You heard me," I said. "They're not coming any further. But you've got to let me in."

Another pause. "Now why would I want to do that?" he asked.

I was racking my brains to come up with something to

tempt him. "I'll be your hostage," I said. "The Council will value me much more than a kid from Glasgow."

"She's not just any kid, is she, Dalrymple?" he said, making it clear that he was in complete command.

"Of course she isn't!" I shouted. "That's why I'm here. But you're still better off with a second hostage. One from Edinburgh."

The chain slid off and the door opened slowly.

Macbeth's face drew back from the gap. "Very well," he said. "I accept your offer. But any tricks and the girl dies."

I squeezed into the flat and closed the door after me, applying the chain personally.

Whatever happened, I wasn't leaving Aurora again.

CHAPTER TWENTY-ONE

"Sit over there, Dalrymple." Macbeth pointed to a leather armchair against the far wall of the comfortable sitting-room. His other hand levelled a pistol with a long silencer at my chest.

On the opposite side of the room Aurora was curled up in the corner of a velvet-covered settee. Her head was buried in her arms and her thin frame shuddered with barely repressed sobs. When Macbeth sat down next to her, she shrank even further into the cushions.

"Is she all right?" I asked. "Aurora? Don't worry. Everything will be fine."

The little girl held still for a few moments but didn't look across at me. Then she started shaking again.

"What have you done to her?" I said, jumping to my feet.

There was a dull thud by my knee. A hole had appeared in the surface of the chair.

"I won't tell you again, Dalrymple." The king's voice was steel-edged. "First the girl will get it, then you. Do we understand each other?"

I nodded slowly and sat down.

"If it's any comfort to you," Macbeth said, "I've done nothing to harm her."

I looked across at Aurora, the impulse to console the

terrified child almost impossible to resist. Somehow I managed, telling myself that I had to keep cool and wait for my chance to disable her captor.

"Nothing except kidnap her and drag her around Edinburgh like a rag-doll," I said. A horrible thought suddenly struck me. "Jesus, did she see what you did to Godwin?"

Macbeth shrugged. "I imagine so. She was right next to me when I pulled the trigger."

I felt the blood rush to my head. It was all I could do to stay in the armchair. "You're as bad as your brother," I gasped. "You just don't care, do you?"

He stared at me unwaveringly. "I care about my cause, Dalrymple. That's more than enough for one man to worry about."

"Your cause," I scoffed. "Your deluded, self-centred cult, you mean."

Macbeth's head twitched, but the imperious expression on his face remained. "Believe me, Scotland will be re-united. There's nothing that you or all the other doubters can do to stop the force of history. That's why I disposed of the old scientist. He had a computer disk containing his latest research that my brother told me about. Godwin was so proud of his lab that he agreed to show it to me." He laughed harshly. "Unfortunately for him, he refused to hand the disk over so I had to take it by force. It'll finance my activities for years." He laughed. "It was after I killed him that I saw the lump in the girl's pocket. I suppose you slipped the bug in there in the lab." He looked at me inquisitively. "What happened downstairs, by the way?"

I glanced at Aurora's tremulous form. "Your loyal servant Broadsword has gone to Hecate's kingdom," I said, trying to conceal what I'd done from the child.

A look of what appeared to be complete incomprehension flashed across Macbeth's face. "Broadsword?" His voice registered astonishment. "Broadsword was downstairs?"

"Come off it," I scoffed. "He's been with you all the way from Glasgow."

Macbeth shook his head. "No, he hasn't. The last time I saw him was at the performance in the necropolis, the one Inspector Hyslop and her friends ruined."

"Cut the crap, Rennie. He was with you in the institute last night."

He kept moving his head from side to side. "No he wasn't. I was waiting for him to call me, but he never did. I don't know where he's been or what he's been doing. He was downstairs, you say?" There were deep furrows in his forehead.

I gave him the eye. "Broadsword did kill the auxiliaries here last week, didn't he?"

Macbeth looked even more surprised. "What auxiliaries?" I told him about the two Edinburgh murders. "I don't know anything about that," he said when I finished. "My brother asked me to arrange the kidnap of some teenage geniuses. I left it to Broadsword to work out the practicalities."

"And Broadsword didn't mention the murders when he got back to Glasgow?"

He shook his head again. I almost believed him. There was a way to get confirmation of some of what he'd said. I turned to the little girl. "Aurora?" I said softly. "Aurora?"

She lifted one arm. I could see glistening brown eyes beyond it. "What do you want?" she said in a voice that was stronger than I expected. Her accent wasn't much like Caro's but the sound still took my breath away.

"Aurora," I asked, "was there anyone else with you apart from this man when you came to this house?"

She ran her forearm across her face and looked at me with drier eyes. "No." She glanced at Macbeth contemptuously. "Just this big bully."

I swallowed a smile. Good girl. She seemed to be holding up well enough. Then I thought about Broadsword again. So he wasn't with Macbeth. The way he'd cursed his royal master gave credence to that, as did the lack of footprints his size in the former college of art. What the hell was going on?

"He was another of your brother's products, wasn't he?" I said, remembering Big Eye and linking him with the additional organ in Broadsword's brow.

Macbeth nodded. "An early one. He was a bit of a mess, really." He spoke in an offhand manner, like he was describing a botched recipe. "The extra eye didn't function properly and the fool was so embarrassed by it that he always wore a mask of some kind. He was enormously gratified when I gave him the calfskin one festooned with that revolting beard to wear in the play."

His callous tone washed over me as I tried to work out what Broadsword had been doing in Edinburgh. How did he get here so quickly? I'd seen another boat at the yard by the Kincardine Bridge, but would the man in the mask have had the authority to use it? Perhaps he'd hijacked it – he was certainly capable of putting the shits up the crew. But how had he found his way to the building Macbeth had taken refuge in? Obviously someone had opened their big mouth. Billy Geddes was the first name that sprang to mind. But why would he have put Broadsword on Macbeth's trail? Was he after what Godwin had refused to hand over to the king?

"What's on the disk?" I demanded. "People are dying for it."

Macbeth looked at me then raised his shoulders. "I'm no scientist but from what my brother David told me, Godwin had been working on a method of prolonging human life." He smiled harshly. "By replacing the human heart with a more reliable organ modified from pigs and dogs."

"The old dream of immortality," I said, shaking my head. Then I took in the little girl again. For me she was Caro brought back to life, immortalised – meaning that I had bought into the dream as much as anyone else. But I wasn't going to allow Macbeth any hope of a family future. "It might interest you to know that your brother the professor has gone to the same place as Broadsword. Big Eye did for him while you were running away."

Derek Rennie's face hardly went a shade paler. He sat back loosely. "I wondered why he wasn't answering his phone." He shrugged his shoulders at me. "Oh well. His work will live on."

I stared at him in disbelief. His brother's death meant no more to him than Broadsword's. What kind of man was I dealing with? The frightening potential of genetic engineering was nothing compared with this maniac's twisted soul.

"What next?" I asked. "Are you planning on staying in Edinburgh to kill more old men?"

Macbeth shook his head. "Now I have the disk, I'll go elsewhere to sell it."

"Elsewhere?"

His face darkened. "I'm not sharing my plans with you, Dalrymple."

"Why not? I'll be coming with you, won't I?"

He laughed. "Only as far as the Edinburgh border."

"Let the girl go," I said desperately. "You don't need her now you've got me." For a few seconds I thought he might accept the offer. Then his jaw tightened and he shook his head.

"Two hostages are better than one," he said. "I imagine the people David dealt with here have run for cover. The City Guard's already waiting downstairs."

"They won't bother you," I said. "I'm in charge of this operation."

Macbeth snorted. "You, Dalrymple? You're not in charge of anything. I have your destiny and the girl's in the palm of my hand."

Sitting in the perforated leather chair and watching the familiar way he handled the silenced automatic, I couldn't think of a way to dispute that.

Later in the afternoon Macbeth allowed me to communicate with Davie. The king had finally accepted that without my okay he wouldn't get past the guard. He wanted safe passage for us and for two local members of his cult. I wondered if they were the two companions Broadsword had with him during the archive burglary and when he killed the auxiliaries. The arrangements were finalised. Macbeth wanted a guard vehicle outside at eight o'clock.

"And Davie?" I said urgently before I finished the last call. Rennie brandished the gun at me then turned it back on Aurora. I got the message. "Davie, whatever you do, don't let Hamilton or anyone else in on this — especially not Billy Geddes. If you have to, threaten the guardian with the Council. You've got nothing to lose." I had the feeling they would do anything to get the disk back from Macbeth – I hoped its loss hadn't been broadcast.

"Got you, Quint," Davie said. "We'll be on your tail."

"No, you won't be on my tail," I said clearly, looking at Macbeth. "Any sign of guard personnel and we die." I let the words sink in.

"Aye, okay. Out." Davie was obviously reluctant to hold back. I'd just have to trust him to remember that Aurora was in the firing line.

Macbeth relieved me of my mobile and made several calls from the far corner of the room, shielding his mouth so I couldn't hear what he was saying. While he was doing that, I managed to attract Aurora's attention. I smiled at her and winked in what I hoped wasn't an off-putting way. Finally I got a brief, nervous smile out of her. That made me very happy.

Then I calculated the chances of us surviving the night. Given Macbeth's indifference to normal human values, they were probably about as good as the odds of each Edinburgh citizen winning the compulsory lottery – that is, about 300,000 to one.

"The Land-Rover's here," I said from the window.

Macbeth waved me aside and watched as the driver ran off down the rain-drenched crescent under the low-powered street-lights. Earlier we'd seen Davie and the others come out of the street-door and drive away. The king didn't seem to recognise Hel Hyslop – she had a guard beret jammed over her head.

"Move, girl," Rennie said sharply, pointing the pistol at Aurora.

She stood up and gave him a disdainful look that

almost made me burst out laughing. I frowned in an attempt to get her to be more co-operative.

"You go first, Dalrymple," he said. "Remember, I've got the gun in the girl's back." He grabbed Aurora and held her in front of him.

"Okay, okay," I said, arms open wide. "Nobody's going to try anything." I walked slowly out of the room to the flat door.

"Turn on the stairwell light," Macbeth ordered. "Then go down very carefully with your arms outstretched."

I nodded, breathing deeply and trying to convince myself that Davie would have cleared the area completely. I got down to the first floor without incident and walked past the open door. Fortunately Broadsword's body wasn't visible. Aurora had already seen enough.

In the ground-floor hall I saw no sign of the handgun I'd dropped from above. Davie had probably picked it up. Even if he'd left it, I wouldn't have risked bending down to grab it. I pulled the heavy front door open and stuck my head out slowly. The night air was chill and the drizzle was still coming down. Outside, the guard vehicle sat under a street-lamp, the orange light showing windows with no condensation on them – that suggested there wasn't anybody hiding behind the metal panels.

"You're driving," Macbeth hissed as he pushed me out into the street. "Open the passenger door, then get in and wait for us."

I pulled the near-side door open as instructed and walked slowly round to the driver's side, glancing both ways down the crescent as I went. No sign of anyone. Even people with a reason to be here would have been stopped on Davie's instructions. I got in and felt for the key. It was in the ignition.

Macbeth bustled Aurora into the seat between us and slammed the door.

"Where to, guv?" I asked, smiling at the little girl. She looked at me as if I was crazy.

"Head for Muirhouse," Macbeth said, making sure the vehicle's phone was switched off. "I'll give you more directions later."

I nodded and pulled away, narrowly succeeding in engaging the gears – I was never much good with Land-Rovers. Muirhouse. The run-down citizen suburb where we came ashore. It looked like Macbeth was planning on departing from the same beach he'd arrived on.

I headed down towards the Water of Leith. There's hardly any traffic in this part of the city as the roads are too steep for buses. There weren't any of the normally ubiquitous guard patrols. Davie would have ordered them off.

As we headed down the slope towards the northern sector I nudged Aurora gently. She turned her head towards me slowly, trying not to attract Macbeth's attention. I winked at her again and this time her face was wreathed by a spectacular smile that took my breath away. I remembered Caro smiling like that at special moments.

"Turn left at the roundabout," Rennie ordered. Then he started giving me more complicated directions. After a few minutes of turning back on ourselves – making sure we weren't being followed – he pointed at a narrow driveway. "In there."

I followed the track and the headlights swung over a harled eighteenth-century villa. I hadn't been there before but it had obviously been through a lot during the drugs wars. Some of the most destructive gangs came

from the north of the city and they must have tried out
their rocket launchers and grenades on this house. There
were no windows or frames in the gaping holes of the
façade and the rusted remains of a late-twentieth-
century car were hanging crazily off the entrance steps.
The Housing Directorate had evidently forgotten the villa
existed.

"Good place for a meet," I said to Macbeth, trying to
put him off his guard. Then I caught a glimpse of a red
pick-up at the end of the house. It looked like it had
Labour Directorate markings. Could it be the one Broadsword and his friends had used at the time of the break-
in?

Rennie grabbed the vehicle's torch and got out. "Kill
your lights," he said, pulling Aurora after him roughly.

I bit my lip as I obeyed the command. Then I climbed
down and followed the two of them to the entrance.

Macbeth stood listening and looking for a long time,
then pushed Aurora up the steps and through the space
where the door had been. He flashed the torch five times
then spoke in a low voice.

"All hail Macbeth." He repeated the line three times.
Trust the self-obsessed tosser to choose that as a
recognition code.

A light returned the flashes from the depths of the
house.

"All hail Macbeth," came a female voice, then a male
joined in. Footsteps approached.

"There you are," the king said. "You weren't followed?"

Shaking of heads.

"Well, well. How are you, Bell 18?" I said, recognising
the spectacular features of the Labour Directorate super-

visor we'd interviewed after the first murder. "Don't tell me? You believe in Scottish reunification too?"

She gave me a fierce glare. "Fervently, citizen."

I looked at the man. He was wearing standard citizen-issue clothes and I'd never seen him before. While I was peering at him in the dull light, I moved closer to Aurora surreptitiously.

"The boat is standing by," Macbeth said. "Dalrymple will drive us down to the foreshore and we'll be away within the hour." His tone was clinical. I was sure his plans for Aurora and me didn't extend any further than the beach.

"Let's get moving," Bell 18 said, brushing past me.

I had to go for it. I slammed her into Macbeth and leaned forward to sweep Aurora off her feet. I made a good job of it. Before they could recover, we were out of the door and on to the top step.

Then, in the pitch darkness, I took a heavy blow to the jaw and felt myself fly backwards. I heard shots ring out. Aurora screamed, but I couldn't do anything to help her. I was swallowed up in a vacuum that stifled my cries to her. Then all my systems shut down.

I wasn't out for long. When I came round, alternately spitting blood out and gulping breath down, I made out Macbeth. He was standing in the hallway in the light from a torch – but now he wasn't holding his pistol. He was cowering against the wall, his face finally showing some emotion. It did me a lot of good to see that the emotion concerned was abject terror. I swung my eyes round and spotted a body lying sprawled on the floor near the king. Jesus. I couldn't see how big it was. I staggered to my feet and ascertained it was an adult –

the male cult follower. I couldn't see the female auxiliary and – thank Christ – I couldn't see Aurora.

The person who was terrorising Macbeth could see me though.

"I thought I'd laid you out for good, Quint," came a voice from the shadows. "Stand still, Rennie, you shite."

"Haggs? Is that you, Tam Haggs?" I screwed my eyes up but still failed to distinguish him. I saw a brief red glow and realised that he was smoking a cigarette.

He shone a light on his face briefly. "Aye, it's me all right. Surprised to see me in your perfect city?"

"Where's the girl?" I asked, desperate to know if Aurora was alive but also playing for time. A cascade of jigsaw pieces had begun to fall into place.

"She ran off," Haggs said. "Lucky for her."

I exhaled a sigh of relief that almost tore away the lining of my throat. "What are you doing here, Tam?" I asked, my mind struggling to compute the data it had just been presented with. "How the fuck did you find us?"

"Wouldn't you like to know?" he said with a bitter laugh. He shone the torch into Macbeth's eyes. "And wouldn't *you* like to know why I'm here, thane of fucking Glamis?"

Derek Rennie's eyes were bulging. He looked towards me. "What's going on, Dalrymple? What's a Glasgow policeman doing in Edinburgh?"

I closed my eyes and got a grip. Haggs the smoker. I remembered the Glaswegian cigarette butts near the murder victims. Jesus, they must have been his.

"You didn't just come to Edinburgh to kidnap me, Tam, did you?" I said, leaning against the rickety railing. "You know all about the murders, don't you, you bastard?"

Haggs dropped his butt and crushed it under his boot. "Is that right, smart fuck? So what am I doing back here now? I'm bloody sure you can't tell me that."

I spat out more blood and wiped my mouth with my sleeve. "You came to kill the king, didn't you?"

A guttural laugh was dredged up by the stubbled sergeant. "Not bad," he said, stepping forward into the open doorway. "But why would I want to do that?"

Neither he nor I got the chance to answer the question. There was an ear-cracking report and Haggs rocketed back against the pocked stonework of the wall, then slumped lifeless to the floor.

Lights came on at the far end of the drive and revealed that the top of Tam's head was no longer there. I can't say I shed a tear.

"Quint?" Davie's voice was loud. "It's okay, we've got the girl."

I breathed out another sigh of relief as I stepped over Tam Haggs and collared Rennie. He was looking more like Ethelred the Unready than Macbeth – obviously being up against the business end of an automatic didn't suit him. I pocketed Haggs's weapon in case the king got any ideas and dragged him towards the lights.

As we got closer I made out Davie standing by a guard vehicle with a wide grin on his face and an assault rifle at his shoulder. Katharine was there too, her hand on Aurora's shoulder, and Hel Hyslop was behind them. She had the usual impassive look on her face, eyes narrowed to focus on me in the headlight beam.

Then everything, including my ravaged thought processes, went into slow motion. Haggs never did anything without Hel's approval – the chances of him running a one-man campaign against Macbeth were non-existent. I peered into the glare and spotted the bulge made in the inspector's breast pocket by her mobile phone. That was it. In all the confusion earlier she must have managed to send Broadsword to Grosvenor Crescent and, more recently, tell Tam where we were.

Before I could shout to Davie or duck out of the light, Hel had her police-issue pistol against his head. Now I regretted keeping Hamilton off her back when we arrived in Edinburgh – he'd definitely have confiscated it from her.

"Drop your weapons!" Hel shouted. "Both of you!"

I tossed away the pistol I'd picked up to my rear, then watched as Davie ejected the ammunition clip from the rifle and let it drop to the ground. He was shaking his head dolefully.

"You two, come closer," Hyslop said, waving Macbeth and me forward. She shoved Davie, Katharine and Aurora into the light to join us. Then she raised her weapon and pointed it straight at my face. "I've been wanting to do this for a long time, you interfering bastard."

I caught a glimpse of Aurora's face. Her eyes and mouth were wide open. Caro used to look exactly like that when she was surprised. I lowered my gaze, taking that image with me and losing myself in it.

I barely heard the shot when it came.

CHAPTER TWENTY-TWO

T he blast and then the scream to my left made me jerk my head round.

Macbeth was on his back, blood welling from his right shoulder. I could hear Aurora whimpering. Katharine drew her closer and wrapped both arms round her.

Hel Hyslop had a faint smile on her lips. "That's just the beginning, Rennie," she said bitterly. "Lie there and squirm. I'll come back to you later."

Macbeth was groaning, his hand clamped over his shoulder. From what I could see it wasn't a life-threatening wound, but it sounded like it wasn't the only one he was lined up for. Davie kneeled down next to him and held a handkerchief to the source of the blood.

"Let Aurora and Katharine go, Hel," I said, taking a pace forward. "You don't need them."

"I'll be the judge of that, Quint," she said. Her face was pale and drenched in sweat. Suddenly she had the look of someone who had lost control. But the gun was levelled at me in a steady enough hand.

"You and Haggs were the ones with Broadsword in the Parliament archive and when he killed the auxiliaries here, weren't you?" I said, getting the feeling that she might be wanting to come clean.

She stared at me dully then nodded. "The professor

416

and this bastard so-called king . . ." she glared at Macbeth '. . . they set up the raid with John – or Broadsword, as he called him. They wanted the kids to be kidnapped and the file attachment to be taken from the Parliament archive. That attachment outlined research that was never fully developed – something very much ahead of its time to do with the application of animal genetics to humans. Then Duart ordered your kidnap because of Leadbelly and the Glasgow murders." She raised her shoulders. "We combined the operations. Tam and I had known John for years. Christ," she said with a sob. "They're both dead. You shouldn't have . . ."

Hyslop broke off and tried to get a grip on her breathing. It took her a while. Then she continued, still compelled to tell her story. "Tam and I, we replaced John's usual headbangers and came across in the trawler. John came back with us as well, but you didn't see him. We kept him and the teenagers in the forward hold." She smiled weakly. "In case you're wondering, Tam and John followed us in the other boat that was in the yard last night. I managed to keep in touch with them on my mobile."

I was struggling to make sense of this. "You knew Broadsword for years?"

Hel was looking at Aurora. "Don't worry, little girl," she said in a voice that was unlikely to comfort a hardened guardsman, never mind a traumatised child. "We'll soon be finished here. Then you and I will go on another boat trip."

She turned her gaze on Macbeth and nodded grimly when she saw that he was still writhing. "What?" she said, glancing back at me and finding her place again. "Oh yes, John Breck was a family friend when I was a kid. Then he disappeared when he was about twelve. It destroyed his parents and mine – they were very close." Her voice was hoarse. "That perverted professor had been taking children off the streets for years and using them as subjects in his experiments. Tam's sister went missing too." She shook her head. "We found out about a year ago that she died in the institute."

"So you and Haggs set out to nail the professor," I said.

"Yeah." Hyslop wiped the sweat from her forehead. "But we could never find any hard evidence. He had the best lawyers on his case. Even when Duart's people got suspicious about Rennie's business dealings, nothing came out. And, of course, he made sure he donated plenty to his local ward's coffers – and to the city's central funds."

I stared at her. "The files Broadsword was taking from the institute last night. The eight Glasgow victims were all ex-employees of the Baby Factory."

"We got desperate. We started killing them to put the squeeze on Rennie. But the professor didn't give a shit. So when we were over here, John decided to try out the angle with the branches. We were sure this bastard was in on his brother's activities. We reckoned the Birnam Wood branch in the victims' hands would make them panic when we tried it in Glasgow." She nodded at me. "The files made you wonder, didn't they, Quint? We wanted them so that we could construct a more coherent case against Rennie. And to deflect any suspicion away from us. But we didn't want to make it too obvious until we were ready, so we steered clear of current staff members and kept the full details out of our own files."

Katharine looked up from Aurora. "Are you saying that Glasgow police officers were behind nine, no, eleven murders including the two here?" Her face was a picture of horror.

Hel shrugged. "John – Broadsword – did the actual killing. He was let out of the Rennie a couple of years back to act as Macbeth's enforcer. The bastards never thought he might turn against them. Or that the failed ocular experiments might have damaged more than his forehead."

"But you stood by and let him get on with it," Katharine insisted. "You covered for him."

Hyslop faced up to the accusation. "Yes. I don't regret the killings. People who made their living from the institute deserved anything they got."

"What about the auxiliaries in Edinburgh?" I demanded.

This time a look of anguish flashed across the inspector's features. "Yes, well, John had got a taste for that form of mutilation by then. I tried to stop him—"

"Not very hard," Katharine interrupted. She looked at Aurora then glared at Hyslop. "You're disgusting. You connive in murders and now you're putting a child through a nightmare experience. How can you do it?"

The words seemed to wound Hel. The gun she was pointing at me shook for a few moments.

"Things . . . things got out of hand," she said finally.

"You're bloody right they did!" I yelled. "What about Leadbelly? You tried to frame him, didn't you?"

She wasn't looking proud of herself. "We decided to increase the pressure by incriminating a serving member of the Rennie's security staff."

"Which resulted in the poor bugger committing suicide," I said, shaking my head at her.

She raised her shoulders ineffectually. "What could I do? I put a guard on him."

"Bollocks," I said. "You're responsible for Leadbelly's death as much as you're responsible for all the others." I still felt sorry for the former criminal. Even though he'd been a vicious drugs gang member for years, he tried to go straight after he did his time – and he killed himself in the mistaken belief that he'd murdered a pregnant woman. If Leadbelly hadn't demanded to speak to me, Duart wouldn't have ordered Hel to kidnap me and I'd never have gone to Glasgow. Then an even more horrifying thought struck me. "Dougal Strachan," I said. "You sick fuckers. You took him from the boat and executed him near the Rennie, didn't you?"

The inspector licked her lips and kept her eyes locked on Macbeth. "John did, yes," she said after a long pause. "It seemed the most obvious way of putting even more pressure on the professor." She glanced at me. "And of putting you on his track."

I almost went for her, the teenager's mutilated face flashing repeatedly before me. The only way I managed to restrain myself was to look at Aurora. She was all that mattered now.

Hyslop straightened her back. "The genetic experiments that went on in the Baby Factory were illegal and immoral," she said. "We had to find a way to stop them."

I still had my eyes on Aurora. She was the result of supposedly immoral and definitely illegal science, but I was very glad she was a living human being. "For Christ's sake, Hel, it's not that simple. Even if the professor was responsible for numerous mutilations and deaths, that didn't give you the right to take the law into your own hands." I caught her eye. "It doesn't give you the right to do any more damage to Macbeth, either. No matter what his brother did to John Breck and Tam Haggs's sister."

The king started groaning louder when he heard his name. Hyslop looked past me and turned the automatic on him again. Her aim was unsteady at first but she tightened her grip.

"No!" Macbeth pleaded. "No!"

We were all waiting for the shot. It never came. Hel let out a long, exhausted breath and the barrel of the automatic dropped towards the ground. Then she moved towards me and handed the weapon over.

Davie had the cuffs on her a second after I'd taken hold of it.

The guard personnel who came down to Drylaw House were all close colleagues of Davie. Until I decided how to handle things with Hamilton and Sophia, I didn't want any word getting back to the Council. Paramedics had taken Macbeth off to patch up his shoulder. He was lucky. The bullet had gone straight through and appeared to have done only a limited amount of damage. The bodies in the house – Haggs and the unidentified cult follower – were bagged and carried out.

"What shall we do with Aurora, Quint?" Katharine asked. The little girl still had her arms wrapped tightly around Katharine's midriff. When I kneeled down and smoothed her hair away from her tear-stained face, she managed to give me a brave smile that almost made me break down.

"Take one of the Land-Rovers and go back to your place with her," I said. "I'll join you later."

She nodded. "Come on, darling," she said, unlatching

Aurora's hands gently. "I've got some hot chocolate at home. Would you like that?"

The child nodded shyly. "I'm hungry too," she said in a small voice.

"No problem," Katharine said. "I've even got food."

They were both laughing as they climbed into the vehicle. Katharine beckoned me over.

"You might want to take charge of this," she said in a low voice, handing me the heavy pistol I'd dropped down the stairwell at Grosvenor Crescent.

"You picked that up?" I looked at her. "What were you intending to do with it?"

"Shoot your Glaswegian friend as soon as Aurora was out of the way," she said, giving me a tight smile and pulling the door shut.

I watched her reverse away. I didn't doubt for a second that she'd have done what she said.

Davie had appeared at my side. "The wee lass is beautiful, Quint. Thank God nothing happened to her."

I shook my head. "Plenty has happened to her, my friend. How long do you think it'll take her to get over what she's seen in the last twenty-four hours?"

"Kids are better at that kind of thing than we are," he said, squeezing my arm.

"Are they?" I said uncertainly. I looked away across the driveway. It was criss-crossed by the headlight beams, which were falling on a large copper beech at the far side of the house. The blood tree, I thought, remembering the branches over the dead auxiliaries and in Broadsword's hand as he came towards me outside the Rennie.

"We've got Bell 18 in custody," Davie reported. "She gave herself up a few minutes ago."

"Bell 18?" I said. "She's probably traumatised as well. Get one of your people to look after her."

He nodded. "Was she one of Macbeth's people?"

"Yup. The cult's roots had extended to Edinburgh, believe it or not. The first victim was one of them as well."

"Why did they kill him?" Davie asked.

I shrugged. "Broadsword wasn't exactly full of the milk of human kindness. Neither was Haggs, neither is Hyslop. They needed a victim and he was at hand."

"You got that right," Davie said. "Eventually. By the way, we found a taxi in the bushes too. Haggs must have hijacked it to get down here."

"He was a dab hand at taking things that didn't belong to him."

"What about us?" Davie asked. "What do we do now?"

"I don't know about you, guardsman," I said, heading for the Land-Rover that had Hel Hyslop in the back, "but I'm going to the castle to have a serious talk with your boss."

From the look on Davie's face I could see that he wasn't quite as keen on that as I was. All the same, he came along for the ride.

I called ahead and told Hamilton to get Sophia over to the castle. He sounded surprised by the tone of my voice, but I broke the connection before he could complain.

We headed south towards the city centre on streets that were slippery and deserted. Edinburgh citizens either had their noses in Council-approved books at home or were serving the tourists in the bars and clubs. None of them was dumb enough to walk around on a night like this. In the distance the lights of the central zone shone out through the murk. I turned and saw Hyslop studying the city, her jaw slack. She was avoiding my eyes and I didn't feel much like talking to her.

"What are you going to do, Quint?" Davie asked dubiously. "The Council—"

"Never mind the Council," I interrupted. "The question is how we deal with Hamilton and the other guardians." I spent the rest of the trip considering that.

"Keep me out of this," Davie said when we arrived on the esplanade. He showed no inclination to move from the Land-Rover.

"Oh no you don't," I insisted. "Hamilton threatened you with demotion. We've got to sort him out on that once and for all." I pushed him towards his door. He opened it with a long-suffering look on his face. I let Hel out of the back and led her past the sentries. They didn't ask for clearance – they'd seen me bring stranger specimens than her into the castle in the past.

There was no one in the public order guardian's outer office. I reckoned Hamilton had sent his staff away – he knew there was about to be a showdown. I walked into his sanctum without knocking.

Lewis and Sophia were sitting at the conference table. The lights were turned low, presumably to save their blushes. I could remember several occasions when the law had been laid down to me around that piece of furniture. Not this time.

"Would you mind telling us what's been going on, Dalrymple?" Hamilton demanded with a vain stab at taking command. He peered at Hyslop like she was the plague on two legs, which wasn't a bad assessment. "I heard an unconfirmed report of gunshots in Grosvenor

Crescent." He glared at Davie. "Why wasn't I kept fully informed, commander? A dangerous oversight considering you're already under threat of demotion."

I raised my hand. "Let's get one thing clear from the beginning. You two guardians and your associates are an inch away from being hauled up in front of your peers in the Council — for authorising banned genetic research, conspiracy, illegal foreign trade. . . the list goes on and on."

Neither of them said a word.

"There might be a way to sort this out," I continued, "but my first condition is that Hume 253 here is absolved of all charges relating to his unapproved trip to Glasgow." I gave them both the eye. "I presume you agree."

Sophia nodded without giving the demand any thought. She was sitting back from the table to allow her swollen abdomen more room. Lewis Hamilton's response was less immediate but eventually he signalled his acceptance too.

"Now will you tell us what's been going on this evening?" he asked impatiently.

So I did — everything from Billy Geddes's admission of the safe house's location to Hel Hyslop's surrender of her weapon.

"Has this Glasgow police officer been charged with illegal entry to the city?" Hamilton demanded.

"The point is to avoid charges being brought against anyone in this room, Lewis," I said. "Let's see how you talk yourself out of ten years down the mines before we decide about the inspector." As far as I was concerned, she could take her chances back in Glasgow, capital punishment notwithstanding.

"I thought you said she was involved in numerous murders," Sophia said.

"Is your own conscience clear?" I said bitterly. "Unauthorised research into genetic engineering has been going on in Edinburgh under your directorate's partial supervision. How many people have acted as guinea pigs? How many people were permanently damaged?"

She picked up a glass of water and put it to her lips.

"How many?" I shouted.

"I . . . I don't know," she replied in a low voice. "We only got directly involved in the last year, after the birthrate dropped. Godwin was in charge of the details."

I stared at her in horror. "The details? Jesus Christ, Sophia, we're talking about human beings and human genes." I paused. "Godwin was an animal geneticist originally. Who provided the human genetics expertise?" I was thinking about Aurora. Someone had removed an egg from Caro years ago. "This research has been going on for a long time. Who's been responsible for it?"

Sophia glanced at Hamilton. "Dorothy Taylor," she said. "She was a professor at—"

"I know who she was," I said, remembering the name from the list of Genetic Engineering Committee members in the Parliament archive. "So the file data about her having crossed the border years ago was bullshit."

Lewis Hamilton nodded reluctantly. "I wasn't aware what she was doing," he said. "The request for an amended file entry came from the Medical Directorate in 2009."

I shook my head. Scientists had been playing with genes for over fifteen years and keeping it from the full Council. I wish I could say I was surprised, but nothing about the propensity of people in positions of power to corrupt themselves surprised me any more.

"Why the hell didn't you just change Council policy

about genetic engineering?" I asked. "It's not as if this is a bloody democracy. You wouldn't have needed popular support."

"Impossible," Sophia said dismissively. "Many of our colleagues are passionate about the sanctity of human life."

"Bullshit," I said, matching her tone. "You guardians are used to a culture of secrecy and that's the only way you can live your pathetic lives. You stand by your principles but as soon as things get tough, you sell out as quickly as anyone else."

Hamilton's cheeks were red. "That is grossly unfair, Dalrymple. Our contacts in Glasgow asked for File Attachment 4.1.116. A large amount of foreign currency was offered, but I refused to hand it over. As far as I'm concerned, animal genes should be kept separate from human ones. This was a step too far." He glared at me. "Besides, Edinburgh isn't the only place with a culture of secrecy. This research was kept from the authorities in Glasgow too. So much for democracy."

"You should have taken the money, Lewis," I said. "That way you'd have saved a lot of lives."

Hamilton glanced at Sophia then dropped his gaze. It seemed that he'd taken my point.

"Your contacts in Glasgow?" I asked, going back to what he'd said. "You mean David and Derek Rennie?"

Lewis nodded. "They were originally from Edinburgh, you know. David Rennie worked at Heriot-Watt in pre-Enlightenment times. He knew Gavin Godwin."

That explained Macbeth's accent.

I looked at the guardians balefully. "Listen to me. Here's how it's going to be. Given the declining birth-rate, Edinburgh needs the benefit of genetic engineering.

That much is obvious. If we're lucky, the city might even fill a temporary gap in the international market now that the main Glasgow facility has gone through enforced meltdown." I looked at Hel Hyslop but she kept her head bowed.

"But now everything has to be above board," I said, turning back to the guardians. "Work out a research proposal, use Billy Geddes to plan the finances and put it to the Council for approval. If they ask for an explanation of what's been going on, make one up yourselves. I've got other things on my mind." I sat down opposite Sophia. "And make bloody sure there's an ethics committee, okay?"

She nodded and looked away. I hadn't told her about Aurora and I didn't intend to. She had enough problems of her own concerning reproduction.

"Who's the father, Sophia?" I asked in a low voice. "Or does your child come from a test-tube?"

Her eyes flashed cold fire at me. "Certainly not. I made use of a less technical form of eugenics." For a moment she looked almost wistful and my stomach flipped. No, I wasn't the one. I hadn't been her lover for well over a year, since the time that Katharine returned to Edinburgh.

"The hyper-intelligent teenagers who were kidnapped," Sophia said, her eyes still lowered. "Where are they?"

I felt my jaw drop. "Oh my God, Sophia, it wasn't one of them?"

She smiled weakly.

I glanced at Hyslop and tried to work out a way of telling Sophia what had happened to Dougal Strachan. I couldn't, so I took the coward's way out.

"Which one was it, Sophia?" I asked. "Just tell me."

Her lips twitched a couple of times. "Michael," she said. "Michael MacGregor. Is he all right?"

I swallowed a sigh of relief and nodded. "He'll be back soon."

Sophia raised her shoulders. "Not that it's of importance to me. He's done all I wanted him to do. I don't intend seeing him again."

I bit my lip and managed to hold myself back. Not for the first time I wondered if guardians had their emotions surgically removed before they were appointed.

Davie and I were leaning on the wall of the esplanade, looking out over the lights of the tourist zone. The rain had let up and there was a fullish moon away to the west. We'd just put Hel Hyslop back in the Land-Rover and cuffed her to a stanchion.

"Is she all right?" Davie asked, glancing over his shoulder.

"Who knows?" I replied. "At least she seems to be developing a conscience."

"I suppose she had some justification," he said. "Given what was going on in the Baby Factory."

"She and her friends killed a lot of innocent people, Davie. Including a teenage kid who hadn't even started to live."

"Will they execute her, do you think, Quint?"

"Who knows?" I'd called Duart on Hel's mobile and told him about the end of the case. He was very keen on seeing her and Macbeth again. Hamilton and Sophia were also desperate to see the back of all Glaswegians connected with the case, so an exchange had been arranged – Hel and Derek Rennie for the two surviving

Edinburgh teenagers. I got the feeling that a large law suit to terminate Macbeth and his cult was in the offing over in the west. Hel was another matter. "They'll probably brush a senior police officer's crimes under the carpet."

"So much for democracy," Davie said, shaking his head. "Is the corruption in Glasgow as bad as it was over here in pre-Enlightenment times?"

I thought of giving him a quick rendition of Bobo Jenkins's "Democrat Blues" but thought better of it. "No, I don't think so," I said. Then I remembered the empty looks Lewis and Sophia had given me. "Forget pre-Enlightenment times, pal. Edinburgh under the Council is just as corrupt as it used to be. You might as well face it. Everywhere's corrupt. It's nothing to do with cities or political systems, it's to do with human beings. Not even genetic engineering will change that. It's in our nature to look after number one."

Davie looked like I'd slapped him in the face. "Not all people are like that, Quint. You're far too bloody cynical. It is possible to think of others as well as yourself."

"Is it?" I asked doubtfully. I nudged him in the ribs. "By the way, I'm a sceptic, not a cynic. There is a difference."

"Is that right?" he asked, smiling then looking into my eyes seriously. "What are you going to do about Aurora?"

"Good question, my friend," I replied. "I haven't worked that out yet." I turned to the Land-Rover. "Run me over to the infirmary before you take the inspector to her hotel, will you?"

I'd arranged for Hel to be put up in a small tourist hotel rather than a cell. I owed her something for surrendering, but I couldn't forget that, in addition to everything else she'd done, she'd sanctioned Dougal Strachan's death and – I guessed – slipped the Macbeth handbill into the innocent teenager's pocket when we were at the crime scene.

As far as I was concerned any debt I had with her was now paid in full.

It was when I was walking through the infirmary reception area that a final thought struck me. The missing file attachment at the beginning of the investigation had been given the codenumber "4.1.116". It was a long shot but I'd always been keen on those. I followed the signs to the hospital library and found a copy of Shakespeare's collected works. And there it was. *Macbeth*, Act 4, Scene 1, line 116 – "What, will the line stretch out to th'crack of doom?" David Rennie hadn't been a member of the Genetic Engineering Committee back in 2002, but it looked like someone else on it had a literary bent, not to mention a well-developed sense of irony. Perhaps it was the mysterious Dorothy Taylor.

"You can't go in there, citizen," the nursing auxiliary said firmly. "They're all sleeping."

I put my finger to her lips. "I won't make any noise. I'm just going to look in on my father."

She thought about arguing then stepped back.

I walked into the ward and the sound of twenty people snoring and wheezing enveloped me. In the dim light I could make out Hector's bed. I went up to the head of it and looked down at the old man. His wizened face was at ease, the parchment-like skin less wan than it had been the last time I saw him. His breathing was easy and his eyelashes were twitching as he dreamed. I hoped it was a good one.

I was thinking about Aurora again; and Caro; and whether to tell him about the little girl. She was the last branch – direct or indirect – of the Dalrymple family tree, of our blood tree. I considered the quotation from *Macbeth*. The line, our family line, didn't stretch out to the crack of doom. Everything ended with her. The old man had a right to know that she existed. He was entitled to know that at least Caro's side had been perpetuated.

Then I shook my head. There was nothing of me or my family in Aurora. And no matter how much in love Caro and I were, we'd never married; such a rite was and is impossible for Edinburgh auxiliaries. So what kind of immortality did Aurora confer on those of us who, unlike Caro, had survived the Enlightenment's early years? The only real immortality is in the memories of the living and when they die, it's farewell my lover.

I felt my eyes dampen. After touching the top of Hector's hand, I walked quickly away.

I let myself into Katharine's flat as quietly as I could. Although the electricity supply was still connected, I left the light off. In the glow from the emergency candle that I lit, I saw her curled up on the sofa with a blanket over her. I went through the open door of the bedroom and lifted the light over Aurora. She was sprawled across the bed, one foot protruding from the covers, the gentle whisper of breathing coming from her half-open mouth. I took in Caro's almost perfectly resurrected features again and felt my heart flood with emotions I never thought I'd experience again. It was almost too much. I went back into the main room and put the candle down on the table with a shaking hand. That roused Katharine.

"Quint. Where have you been?"

"Tidying things up." I sat down on the floor and nestled into her. "You smell good." I breathed in her warm, sweet odour and kissed her.

"Mm." She blinked and looked at me. "Are you all right?"

"Yeah. Knackered. Did Aurora give you any trouble?"

"No, she was fine. She was very tired." She looked at me with her eyes wide open. "Quint? I've been thinking about—"

"I've been thinking too," I interrupted.

"Oh yes?" Katharine pulled herself up and leaned on her elbow.

"About Aurora. I'm going to take her back to Glasgow. And I'm not going to tell her anything about Caro. Or about me."

She nodded. "That's what I was going to say. She's been asking for her Mum and Dad, and for her brother and sister. It seems to be a very close family. She belongs in it."

I rested my head against the arm of the sofa and tried unsuccessfully to hide what I was feeling.

"Oh Quint, it's all right," Katharine said, swinging her legs out from the blanket and enveloping the top half of my body in her arms. "I understand how devastating it must be for you. To see . . . to see Caro again after all these years in the little girl's face, it must be so hard . . ."

I was shaking my head, trying to get my breathing under control. "It's not devastating, Katharine," I said eventually. "Or hard." I swallowed a sob. "In a . . . in a weird kind of way it's affirming. I think it's added something to my pitiful waster's life."

She pushed me back tenderly in order to see my face. A few seconds later she leaned forward to kiss me. "That's good," she said. "And by the way, it's not such a pitiful waster's life." She wrapped me in her embrace again.

I stayed there for a long time. Finally I shook myself free.

"Right, that's settled," I said. "Tomorrow I'm going on the exchange with Aurora and Hel Hyslop and Macbeth."

"Wrong," Katharine said. "Tomorrow *we're* going on the exchange."

I shrugged. "Okay. And after that I'm coming back here to sleep for a week."

"Wrong," she said again. "After that *we're* coming back here to sleep for a week."

"Of course," I went on, "after a day or two, I might begin to get bored with sleeping."

Katharine rolled towards me and grabbed my shoulders. "Don't worry, I'll think of something."

It looked like she already had.

PAUL JOHNSTON

BODY POLITIC

Winner of the Crime Writers' Association John Creasey Memorial Dagger for best first crime novel of the year

'Think of Plato's Republic with a body count'
The Sunday Times

'An intricate web . . . Johnston is a Fawkes among plotters'
Observer

'Fascinating and thought-provoking' Val McDermid,
Manchester Evening News

An independent city where television, private cars and popular music are banned, where the citizens are dedicated to the tourists attending the year-round Festival, and where crime is virtually non-existent, Edinburgh in the year 2020 has its drawbacks for blues-haunted private investigator Quintilian Dalrymple.

But the brutal killing of a guardswoman – the first murder in five years – is enough to scare the Council of City Guardians out of complacency. It looks like the Ear, Nose and Throat Man has returned. And they are forced to turn to the man they demoted to uncover a conspiracy of violence and sexual intrigue that reaches into a dark heart of corruption and threatens to dismember the body politic.

HODDER AND STOUGHTON PAPERBACKS

PAUL JOHNSTON

THE BONE YARD

New Year's Eve 2021. The one night of the year when the guards are less vigilant. The perfect time for murder.

Welcome to 21st century Edinburgh. An oppressive, crime-free independent city state, run by the Council of City Guardians. Subversive, blues-haunted private investigator Quintilian Dalrymple and his side-kick Davie are back on the case, trying to solve a series of murders in which music tapes are planted inside the victims. And the solution lies in the Bone Yard. If they can ever figure out what the Bone Yard is . . .

HODDER AND STOUGHTON PAPERBACKS

PAUL JOHNSTON

WATER OF DEATH

'An acclaimed crime series . . . Johnston brings an intelligent perspective to the dark excitement of the thriller'

Nicholas Blincoe, *Observer*

'Both prescient and illuminating'

Ian Rankin, *Daily Telegraph*

'Johnston's vision is shot through with the bleakest of black humour, never losing sight of the humanity of his characters. This series is getting better all the time'

Val McDermid, *Manchester Evening News*

'A thoroughly enjoyable tale'

Sunday Telegraph

Edinburgh, 2025 — an independent, almost crime-free oasis surrounded by anarchic city-states. Except global warming has turned summer into the Big Heat and water, like everything else, is strictly rationed. Citizens live only for the weekly lottery draw while serving the tourists in the year-round festival. When a recent lottery winner goes missing, subversive investigator Quintilian Dalrymple is called in to deal with a minor case of the summertime blues.

Then a body is discovered face down in the Water of Leith — the only clue to the death, a bottle of contraband whisky. Quint thinks he sees the first traces of a ruthless conspiracy to destabilise the city. And the body count, like the temperature, keeps on rising . . .

HODDER AND STOUGHTON PAPERBACKS